NEVERMORE SQUIRRELS

Terrance M. Craft

Nevermore Squirrels

ISBN: 1973750554
ISBN-13: 9781973750550

Dedicated to all
who are different;
who likes the strange
and not the ordinary.

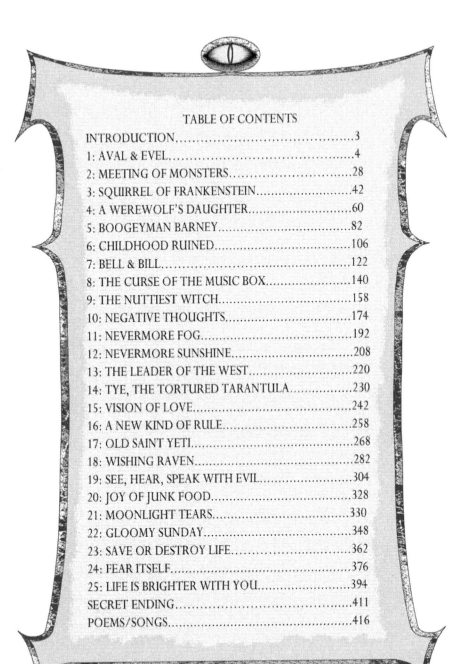

TABLE OF CONTENTS

Introduction

It is always pleasant to take time and enjoy the quiet night life. Whether taking a stroll under street lamps or sleeping under the stars, it seems to be more enjoyable compared to the noises in the daytime. However, most fear hungry and ferocious creatures that lurk in the dark. Have you ever wondered if they're just as tired as us and really detest hunting in the dark? They have to get up for work in the morning or possibly even school.

It would be nice to know that creatures big and small were just like us. Of course, many of us had already seen or possibly read about these worlds where animals took the place of humans; but what if they actually coexisted? Where the only things they feared were fear itself and bloodthirsty monsters.

This story is about that. A tale of monsters rising above the mortals, told by a peculiar creature that took an interest in that world. That creature found it most fascinating and made it its mission to tell what calamities ensued in the world of Nevermore Squirrels.

1
AVAL & EVEL

The redundancy of petty troubles that plague human lives is in every chapter in every story. Whether it's finding tasteless love, fighting meaningless wars, or deciding what to eat for dinner, these stories are reality; they are lifeless and yet so priceless.

I hardly ever showed interest in them. I found myself wondering if there was more to this world than the same old thing. The second I wanted to leave this land that was so frail, I spotted a squirrel holding a hammer and nail. The odd creature wore small clothing and walked upright. It was an interesting yet peculiar sight. I saw him speak and act like a human; he also had an artsy wife and helpful children. That squirrel family was building a marvelous home made of bricks. It was something one could only see in films or comics. The sight of that intelligent family was so sublime. I was amazed that I started to speak in rhyme.

However, some of these creatures were beyond the state of ordinary. I soon discovered that some were gifted with abnormal abilities and cursed attributes, like monsters or even more. The human race was not alone, and I knew that life on Earth would be the same nevermore.

I remember a place in time, not too long ago, where the days of peace soon put the world on the edge of extinction, thanks to two little squirrels. Peculiar, isn't it? Though I promise that this story gets more peculiar than that. So get comfy, turn down the lights, and maybe block out the noise of reality with some music, for I will tell you the tale of Nevermore Squirrels.

It all began in a land that was filled with high mountains, sparkling lakes, and tall trees. This country was so connected with nature that they placed a leaf on their flag. That country was Canada, but within that land lay something more.

In the vast wilderness and behind a range of mountains was a quiet town that was occupied not by humans but by woodland critters. There were little creatures, such as squirrels, beavers, chipmunks, and many others alike, living together as a rather civilized community.

They lived peacefully in their little woodland town, and they always had time to greet one another with a smile. It was all indeed well at the time, yet the name of the town never quite fit the times they wished were normal. They pretended to laugh, and they pretended to smile, just to mask their fears of what might happen in their town called "Nevermore."

The town was fairly decent and calm during the day, but by nightfall, it was anyone's guess if they'd live to see the next morning. The little critters lived in fear of their supreme dark rulers, two particular squirrels that were over two hundred years old, though they did not give the appearance of withered old fossils. They were young, smart, and powerful squirrels whom no one dared to touch. They were a married couple blessed with the curse of vampires, and they were the only ones left in existence. These wicked squirrels were named Aval & Evel.

These two vile creatures stalked their victims in the darkest of shadows and waited for the right opportunity to steal their lives away. However, they did not allow any to live and blossom into vampires. No, they preferred to be the only night stalkers that walked the earth, and they preferred to have all the blood for themselves. So instead, they would rip the bodies apart with marvelous strength and devour everything to the bone.

Aval & Evel were cannibalistic, and they enjoyed torturing their victims, like skinning them alive just for the pleasure of hearing them scream. No critter was shown mercy, and none was truly safe in the dark. The best way to describe the horror was a poem told by an old hedgehog near an old stump deep within the grassy fields.

In times of goodwill and life without grief
lived a town that was named Dew Leaf.
A place where many creatures lived in delight,
where they lived in harmony day and night.
Surely there were bad times in Dew Leaf,
but a better tomorrow came with great belief.

Though like in other towns with secrets so dark
lay a cemetery none should ever embark.
The dark side of Dew Leaf, oh so dreary,
lived two squirrels full of death and misery.

Husband and wife lived among the deceased;
night falls, and these terrible vampires shall wake.
So lock your doors and hide for goodness' sake,
for it's on the blood of innocents they're sure to feast.

Dew Leaf is no more;
it is their land,
forever named Nevermore.

Aval & Evel lived in the town's cemetery, Luminous Acres, appropriately named for its wonderful moonlit spots. The cemetery field was never clean, and the grass slowly decayed from the feel of dread in the air. Mourners would never come during the days of funerals, for they feared the two vampires would make them attend their own.

In the center of the cemetery was their lovely home, which was older than themselves. It was the one oak tree that stood in that gloomy paradise. It had loose black shrouds that covered its bark. At the top of that tree was a giant umbrella covered in solid black sheets that could block out the rain and sun. The home had a red stairway with iron spikes that led to the front door, which was a grave welcoming to visitors. It had a gray mailbox with its lid replaced with the jawbone of a piranha and was covered with the furry skin of a small skunk for the sake of decoration.

Then there was their high balcony, containing the largest and only windows on the tree. The windows were used as doors and an entrance of flight. Aval & Evel would release their long vein-ridden wings from their backs and fly to wherever they pleased.

Then, most peculiar, were two long-haired coconuts shaped like voodoo skulls that hung from the two longest branches. They lit up red from the inside whenever it was time for Aval & Evel to awaken from another slumber. No one knew how the coconuts glowed like that, much like the ground-covering fog that followed the vampires wherever they went. You could guess that it was their evil presence casting its dreadful energy onto the land, and you would be right.

Inside the tree, in the attic where the walls were covered in dreary drapes, lay two conjoined coffins on top of a plushy red platform. The coffins lay quietly still, with the exception of a couple of snores. The bright half-moon then shone in the sky, and the only noise that could be heard was the gentle sounds of wind whistling through the dead grass.

Suddenly, their bedroom-wall clock made loud gong sounds that echoed throughout the house. It was precisely eight o'clock, time for them to awaken. With an upward push on their creaking coffin doors, foggy mist poured out and spread through the floor. The two vampires rose with their arms across their chests, and when the gongs stopped, they let out huge yawns of tiredness.

Aval & Evel, to most, looked oddly identical, with their long silky-black fur, pale-white complexions, and the lazy eyes that made them look tired and uninterested in anything. They had two black dots, shaped like little eyebrows, on their foreheads, and the inside of their mouths, oddly, were colored gray. Like the other inhabitants, they wore clothes, since the civilized nature of animals moved them far beyond the awkward public-nudity scene.

Aval wore a green unbuttoned suit with a black-and-white-striped undershirt. He wore green and pointy cavalry pants that were held together with a skull belt; the pants gave him a sense of authority, though they gave the illusion of large hips since they were a little tight around the midsection. It was uncomfortable at first, but like a human, he learned to endure discomfort. Complete with long black-leather gloves, boots, and a sharp bow tie, the outfit made him Aval.

Evel wore a one-piece heliotrope dress, which is a pinkish-purple color for some, with long streams that went down to her knees. She wore a black-and-white-striped corset around the waist to make her look thinner. It looked confining and out of place, but like a woman, she learned to endure fashion remarks—mostly. It was held together with the same skull belt as Aval wore, only with carved eyelashes. With long black-leather gloves, pants, and a sharp heliotrope bow on the back of her head, that outfit made her Evel.

The two vampires stared at each other, reminding each of the other's presence. They held hands, and they slowly proceeded downstairs to prepare for their marvelous hunt. Their house was a home of treasures, from the living room full of book novels and hunting trophies to the basement of medieval splendor.

The room the vampires enjoyed the most was the kitchen. Even though the two weren't exactly gourmet chefs, they still enjoyed the process of cooking. Whenever they brought home live food, the serving instruments most foul were right at their fingertips—saws, hooks, chains, staple guns, and other tools—to make an exquisite midnight meal. Some would see it as torturing rather than cooking, but certain creatures like these have unique ways of doing things, and they do them well.

That cold night was to be the most famous of all nights, for they had never walked so calmly to suppress their hunger. It was as if they were mentally preparing themselves for the most savage slaughter. They made their way into the kitchen, lighting the candles on walls to brighten the area. They opened a nearby drawer beneath a countertop and reached for deadly, horrifying, bone-chilling, loopy straws.

Hmm, that was certainly new. Then they approached their fancy refrigerator machine that was coated in frost. They opened the door that poured stone-cold air through the floor and reached for two glasses of blood. This nightly routine was a bit unusual—or should I say a bit too normal.

The two closed the fridge door, sipped their drinks with their weird straws, and proceeded to the living room. The main attraction the room provided was a trophy of a stuffed rattlesnake conveniently hung over the sitting area, with its eyes replaced with black buttons.

With a match, Aval lit the small skull candle on the table that lit what little space was necessary to use for their next preparation. They sat in their separate chairs positioned against the wall, where they hardly faced each other, and sipped more blood from their cold glasses.

They then placed the drinks on the table to save for later, without the use of any coasters. I guess that's kind of scary. Aval stretched out his arms with a yawn. He reached for an old newspaper and began to read quietly. Evel yawned as well and grabbed her favorite book, Gone with the Shadows, and began to read silently.

Hmm. All of that wasn't part of their usual agenda. Normally they would burst through the balcony windows, fly into the night air, and feast on the necks of villagers. Yet, they were just lounging. Maybe things would move along if I used a more forceful tone.

Ahem!

The two ghoulish bat spawns from hell rose from the shadows and flew into the cold winds of dusk to feast upon the weak souls of Nevermore! Aval & Evel still sat around and did nothing.

I never realized they were such a lazy bunch, but at that moment, something caused a stir within Aval. With his right hand, he picked up a battle-ax near his chair and began to twirl it around and around. Perhaps he wanted to test his close-combat skills. He twirled it faster and faster, until he let go and launched the sharp ax at me. Wait! Wha—?

Swish! Clank!

Luckily for me, with my amazing reflexes, I avoided the vicious ax attack. That squirrel should have known better than to try and kill me. I am the narrator!

"Well, your narrating is cheesing me off," Aval said as he went back to his paper. "So would you be quiet? I'm trying to read the obituaries here." Aval was always the laid-back, no-nonsense kind of squirrel.

"Be mindful, Aval. No sense in killing someone trying to do his job," Evel said as she tried to bring some peace. She was always the pleasant squirrel girl. Yet, at times, she could be ill-tempered. Suddenly, she looked at me and said, "But I will strangle you if you call me a girl again. I am a lady, so get it right!"

As I gazed upon Aval & Evel and their tired eyes full of annoyance, the question had to be asked: What kind of vampires were they? They sat around, read boring literature, and drank substitute liquid from a fridge instead of getting fresh blood from the living.

"These are from the living," Aval said to me. "More specifically from blood donors."

After hearing such words, I had to speak out. "Why, Aval & Evel? Why are you doing all this nonsense?"

Evel explained, "When it comes to substance, mortals tend to be a bit limited. Sure, we can terrorize them one by one in an unceasing bloodlust, but when all is said and done, only the sounds of lonely crickets remain—although crickets aren't very aggressive compared to the villagers. These villagers used to have the unmitigated gall to break into our home and attempt to kill us. We grew tired of those annoying attacks on a regular basis, so we made an agreement with them. We and all the other monsters would not kill a single soul again. In return, they reward us with nourishment and leave us alone. We are at peace now. Plus, Aval and I are currently practicing vegetarianism to better fit in with our fellow mortals. Great, isn't it?"

Aval scoffed. "Great? No. Stupid? Definitely, as well as this peace. We used to physically feed on our enemies, because that's who we are. This is a travesty in the eyes of monsters everywhere—an absolute spit in the face and an ax to the gullet."

"I'm surprised you didn't say 'a kick to the balls.' Unfortunately, I have yet to see yours," Evel zinged.

"Oh, that's awfully funny coming from a featherweight whose eyes are bigger than everything else on her body," Aval zinged right back. "I tell you, one of these days I'm going to have myself a nice succulent boar, while you'll take the place of this snake on the wall."

Evel rolled her eyes and said, "Don't be too sure, Sergeant Buzz Kill. If you yearn for boars, I'll make sure you'll have a thousand happy beasts that would gladly trample your sedated hide in the dirt. And forget about putting me on this wall; it desires your body, not mine."

Aval finally looked at her and said, "You're right, a wall can do so much better."

Well, as you can already tell, these are two vampires no one thought would turn to a life of stale boredom and bitterness. I remembered them as cannibalistic and bloodthirsty creatures, once feared and revered by all, casually going about their ways while still honoring the vampire name. Suddenly, they have changed.

I confess to the horrid truth, and I can't hide it any longer. The legendary vampires, Aval & Evel, have degenerated into ordinary commoners! They lost their interest in bloodsucking and converted to blood sipping. To make matters worse, their marriage became dull and predictable to where they felt the need to kill each other whenever they got bored. The only one who longed for the good old days of being vicious and free was Aval. But with the peace among mortals, their rank of authority became laughable. Both, in fact, became laughingstocks. Girl Scouts would even walk through the front door and try to sell them cookies. Sugar-free cookies! How dreadfully dishonored Aval & Evel had become.

Not just them, but other monsters around the world as well. Modern society hacked away at the monsters of horror by making them look like one big joke. These days, monsters from the unknown who thrive on fear are outshone by masked slashers that thrive on killing teenagers. Back then, those were called "misunderstood souls." Now it's just overprivileged yuppies whose only motivation comes from lack of sex. I guess crime of passion is the new kind of horror.

The monster era that I liked so dearly was dead. Even Aval & Evel couldn't bring back the fear. The probability of those vampires changing back immediately was practically zero, but not for me. For I promise in the tales to come, the monster name that was long forgotten will be renowned again, and I'll start with these two vampire squirrels.

After the slight altercation with…well, me, Aval & Evel continued their ritual of quiet peace and mild contentment. They read whatever suited their interest without speaking one syllable to each other, like a studious married couple with no desire to kiss. But just then, Evel had a strange feeling in her muscles, a feeling to get up and move.

She laid the book down on the small table and walked to the balcony windows to observe the moonlight. There wasn't a cloud in the sky, and the stars shone so nicely. It would've been a shame to miss out on such fine weather; perhaps going outside for a little stroll would make a nice change.

Suddenly, a strange sensation struck Evel's head, causing her gears to turn in a gradual motion. A smile came to her face, and if there were a flashy lightbulb hovering above her head, you would have known that she had an idea. She walked back to the table and held the skull candle under her face. She stood in front of Aval with the look of an excited child and eagerly waited to be noticed.

Aval looked up from his newspaper to the suspicious squirrel, and he said with a sigh, "Please tell me you don't have an idea."

"Oh, but I do," Evel said. "I see your eyes, and you see mine. What do they say? Quiet cries and silent pleas to kill this marriage. It has become dull and stale, like leftover bread forgotten in the desert. Our lives are but a mysterious pentacle of petulance and decay in the room of twilight obscurity. It's a great way to improve my poetic vocabulary, but it's becoming so unbearable that even I don't know what I'm saying anymore. But I say, nay! There is a chance to save that stale bread! All we need is a way to rekindle our spark."

Evel wanted to save their relationship badly, but she did not know how. It was then I suggested that they should have a date night at a fancy restaurant in Nevermore. It was called Chez Snobby, a fancy establishment located on a mountainside on the upper-east side. It was where all the rich squirrels go—not really to eat but simply to brag about their success to others.

It was a perfect place for Aval & Evel to go to rekindle that spark and maybe meet new faces. Evel simply lit up with joy, but Aval didn't like the idea of going to Chez Snobby. From what he read in the newspapers, it was a terrible place where they discriminated against the poor and other creatures that weren't squirrels. As for the food, it was only good to those who had a form of flavor sickness.

Evel didn't care. She wanted to go. Aval had to remind her that they did not have enough berries to enter. Getting into the restaurant cost 137 berries for a couple. Luckily for them, Evel just so happened to find a bag of berries that, mysteriously, landed near her feet. It was from a generous soul whose name rhymed with vibrator. Awfully nice of that vibrator to help her out in her time of need.

So why berries, you might ask? Because of Canada's unnatural number of berries overrunning the plantations, they became a major source of food that later grew to currency for the woodland creatures. It was very efficient, and it was a good way to end hunger. With the bag of berries in hand, it was time for them to put on their best faces and their best green and purple attire and venture out while the night was still young.

Letting go of the newspaper, Aval folded his arms and said, "The night is young, but it wishes to be left alone. I'm not going, Evel."

"Oh, come on, you green sourpuss!" she said. "Think of this as a chance to save our marriage while meeting some new blood. The only real cost would be time, and we certainly have plenty of that." The mention of new blood caught Aval's attention, though as stubborn as he was, he stood his ground—or stewed in his chair, as it were.

"Look, I am the man of this tree," he claimed. "When I say I'm not going, I shall not be moved. There is no force on Earth that can remove me from this chair." It was hard to get Aval out of that chair, but Evel knew exactly what to do.

A few moments later at Chez Snobby, guests began to pile through the doors of the restaurant. From far and near they traveled, not on foot, but on fancy birds that graciously flew them to the mountainside, for a fee of course. One by one they were greeted by the manager outside the doors, welcoming all the fine squirrels who entered his place of business.

Mr. Soyer was his name, and what a very shrewd squirrel he was. He was dressed like a penguin in his black-and-white tux, but his fur was completely covered in white. With a high posture and carefully combed white mustache, he had the authority to let the best-suited creatures enter his establishment.

Surely that squirrel didn't completely discriminate against nonsquirrels. I thought a special individual like myself would've been allowed inside without a hassle. I was proved wrong, for Mr. Soyer didn't see me as a squirrel; he saw me as an unknown creature without a fluffy tail. The only explanation I offered for what I was, was simple. I was a creature that was allowed anywhere I wished to go: a narrator. Mr. Soyer said I was crazy and told me to shove off. I stuck out my tongue, and he stuck out his middle finger.

We could've gone back and forth, but it was best to move the story along. I perched myself on a far tree, looking at that squirrel from afar. He was alone and unprotected, like a pointy-nosed kitten left on the side of the road. It soon became quiet, as he felt a sudden cold chill in the air. He looked around and noticed the road was being consumed with fog.

Colder it became, and denser the fog as he tried to ponder how the weather changed so quickly. He grew a bit scared, so he thought it was time to go back inside the building. Then without warning, a demonic shadow flew down from the sky and scared the living daylights out of him.

It landed in front of him, and on further inspection, it was merely Evel with her illustrious black wings opened wide. In her hands, she carried Aval in his chair, who was not at all pleased to be outside.

Mr. Soyer was relieved to see those peaceful vampires, because for a second they gave him quite a scare. Evel had to apologize. She was always in the habit of "dropping in." Those two shared a few chuckles at the corny joke.

Evel then retracted her wings and immediately requested a table for two. She tossed him the bag of berries, and he carefully tested the weight with his hands. With the powers of careful management, he felt the amount was all in place, so he opened the doors and led them in. Evel carried Aval inside, like a king being carried off or a big baby being hauled off. Aval felt emasculated, but he didn't have the strength to fly away from the restaurant. All he could do was pout and curse under his breath.

Inside, it was an exceptionally clean paradise. Wall-to-wall white marble and clean peach-scented floors showed clear reflections of all who observed. Towels and plates were neatly stacked in separate groups, and even tables and chairs were aligned to a specific and straight degree. Bright candles were placed on walls every forty inches from the floor and separated by thirty inches from one another, while an odd number of three chandeliers were dusted every two hours.

As for menus and the matter of food, those were the most absurd. The request for a menu itself cost thirty berries for those who wished to eat. It was no wonder how Chez Snobby was doing so financially well; they sucked the pockets of their guests dry. The rich guests didn't mind though. They were always so busy chatting away about their daily schedules and plans that they didn't care where their berries went.

All might have seemed well at the time, but in Aval & Evel's eyes, it was not. When they were escorted through the restaurant, a special table was made just for them. In the center of the dining room was a restricted zone surrounded by velvet ropes with a sign: SPOOK SECTION.

They were then seated, and they felt a little uncomfortable sitting in a weird, not to mention undignified, space. Aval looked around the spacious room at those who smiled and enjoyed their time, ignoring the vampires' existence. Aval & Evel were unjustly separated from the others, and no one seemed to care. It was like reliving their school years all over again.

An hour had already passed since the two ordered their food, and yet no food was delivered. While they waited, Evel tried to make conversation with squirrels who passed by their table, but she was ignored still. Aval & Evel became more annoyed and bored than ever before. Aval began to tap his finger on the table out of frustration as his blood began to boil to a blaze.

Just then, a couple with their child walked by the table with their firm noses held high. They ignored the two vampires, sure, but Aval stared at them with a strange gaze. He could sense their blood pulsing through their veins with each step they took and every heartbeat that pumped from the inside of their chests. His dead eyes began to widen with hunger, and his finger began to tap faster. Many years he managed to control his hunger, but there were times when even the strongest men could break. Evel saw his hungry eyes and began to worry. She did her best to keep his mind astray with conversation.

She said to him, "Stay with me, Aval, and forget about these snobs. We can still have a fine evening by having nice conversations with each other. OK? OK. So do you remember that town called Gizlberg? You know, the town where it rained every day to the point that the landscape was covered with scattered lakes? Where a mysterious murder happened every blah-blah, blah-blah-blah-blah, blah-blah-blah?"

Aval wasn't listening to a word. He couldn't turn away from all the pulsing activity that filled the room. The bloody veins of mortal squirrels, pumping and beating. So tempting it was just to bite one neck and suck the precious life dry.

His senses became wider, and his hunger grew to intense levels. Soon, he heard little voices in his head that told him to give in to his urges and be a true vampire. They wanted him to break, but he kept fighting back and staying strong. Yet the hunger was too much to ignore.

He couldn't take it; he was about to break. It was about to turn into a massive massacre until the sound of plates hitting the table snapped him out of it. The waiter finally arrived with their food, and what a relief it was. Aval kept his cool, and he sat straight like there was nothing wrong at all.

"Sorry for the delay," said the waiter as he laid their plates and drinks on the table. "The head chef was on a break, the servers came down with a slight cold, and the rest were out chasing some chipmunks in the back alley."

Aval looked at the waiter. He observed him closely and could sense his blood flowing at an alarming rate. If what he said was true, then why act such a way that made his heart race? Was he attempting to lie to them, or was he scared of them? Aval could tell it was both.

All that really mattered was that their food made it to the table. The waiter left the two to enjoy their meal, but it wasn't at all what they expected. Both dishes contained several strands of glistening leaves on each side of a tofu patty, and acorn bits were sprinkled all over the food.

It was exactly what a simple vegetarian meal looked like, and the very sight of it made them cringe. As for the refreshments, juices from raw meat were extracted and then poured into their glasses. There was no time for skepticism; their bellies were rumbling, and it was time to eat. Aval took a small piece of his patty with his fork and tasted what seemed like uncertainty. With no taste or good flavor infesting his mouth, he quickly spat it out.

"Blech!" he said in disgust. "Is this tofu even considered food? It tastes like Styrofoam."

Evel shrugged and said, "Fancy cuisine can taste different at first, but it's just a matter of getting used to it."

"You know we can't eat like this," Aval said. "We need real meat covered in blood. It's the only thing we can actually taste without blowing chunks."

Evel refused to listen. She wanted to eat healthy to destroy her cannibalistic side. She took a bite out of her patty. She chewed and chewed the strange meat, mushing it around her mouth, slowly trying to process it.

She finally swallowed it and said breathlessly, "Ugh, delicious…blecchhh!"

She threw up on the side of the floor; even she didn't find it edible. When the regurgitated mess was made, a busboy dashed over and quickly cleaned it up with a mop and detergent and went away in the blink of an eye. An awkward pause fell, as Evel began to feel thirsty.

Maybe the drinks were better. Evel took a sip from her glass and sighed pleasantly, saying it had a funny aftertaste. Then in a split second, she threw up on the other side of the floor. The busboy returned and cleaned up more of her mess and left in a flash. They couldn't believe it—that high-class restaurant even had bad blood.

As I looked through the clean windows of the building, I could tell that their date night was a total disaster. It was the perfect opportunity for me to bring back their viciousness and get a little revenge on Mr. Soyer. I signaled a kid squirrel in the room to come to me. I instructed him to start a joke that everyone would surely love, and so it began.

A few minutes later, Aval saw a most peculiar thing across the room. He saw a child with two straws stuck in his upper mouth that posed as fangs. He also raised his black jacket wide open to make it look like a cape. The rumbustious child was acting like a vampire and was mocking the two has-been monsters in the middle of the room.

The child shouted in a stereotypical Dracula voice, "Hey, everyone, gaze upon me! I am Count Veggula, and I vant to suck your minerals and proteins!"

His family laughed, the guests laughed, and all the servers laughed. The whole restaurant chuckled up a storm as they pointed at the shameless mockery. Aval & Evel, those poor vampires, were being laughed at in public, and they couldn't do a thing about it.

Aval looked at Evel in concern, but all she could do was smirk nervously and try to eat another piece of tofu. The embarrassment, the humiliation—it was too much to bear. The anger-repressed Aval clenched his fists on the table, still hearing the sounds of arrogant mortals, still hearing the silent whispers in his troubled head. More and more he had to endure, until a piece of his brain that held his tolerance together snapped.

Aval stood from his chair in anger and smashed the table in two with his bare hands as he yelled, "Enough!"

That loud outburst made the restaurant turn silent. All eyes were on him. Even Evel was shocked to see her husband act in such a way.

"Uh, honey," she said in a nervous tone, "eyes are staring."

"Good! Let them!" Aval yelled. "I'm sick of all of this! We are eating this veggie crap while they laugh at us! Like they have forgotten that we are the higher beings they should fear!"

The squirrels around them started to become nervous and frightened, something they hadn't felt in a while. Inch by inch they stepped near the front exit, which only made Aval the more upset. Escaping would do them no good, for I should mention that one of the key powers the vampires possessed was shadow control. It gave them the ability to interact with anything at any distance by using their own shadows.

Aval extended his own to knock over a huge statue, blocking the front door. He then knocked over others to block the windows and then more in other directions until all squirrels were completely trapped.

There was still the matter of other squirrels in the kitchen that could easily get away through the back exit. It did them no good either, because in front of the back door appeared Aval in a cloud of black dust. Another power the vampires possessed was the ability to vanish anywhere in a shroud of darkness, meaning no one could outrun them or escape them.

Aval grabbed every squirrel in the kitchen and tossed them in the dining room. He made sure that no one would leave that restaurant alive. Man, woman, or child. Evel went over the confined ropes and told Aval to stop.

"Aval, stop this right now!" Evel shouted as she held him by the arms. "We have changed beyond this! Don't mind him, everyone; he's just a little insane in the membrane."

Aval then shook his wife by the shoulders and said, "We can't change who we are. We are vampires! We are cursed creatures of the night! We need real blood and real meat, because we can't taste anything that isn't blood ridden! We must feed on these mortals to survive."

"Aval, I won't let you do this. What about the peace?"

"Screw this peace; they don't deserve it!"

He tried to talk some sense into her so they could go back to the natural order of things, where monsters weren't treated so disrespectfully and weren't total laughingstocks. He shoved her away and walked around the room, looking at all the scared squirrels.

"Look at them, Evel. How can we continue with this?" he asked her. "How can we possibly live in their perfect little world when they still show us no ounce of trust or respect? I say no more! We vampires aren't made to endure all of this. We weren't made to be vegans, we weren't made to be peaceful, and we were never, ever, ever made to be involved in some bizarre love triangle with a teenage basket case and some werewolf wannabe!"

He then threw a nearby romance novel across the room at a random fangirl holding an apple, which caused a series of gasps to spread throughout the room. Aval leaped toward the girl and grabbed her in a vicious manner. He looked into her eyes and revealed his sharp hungry fangs.

Aval finished his rant with the words of all vampires. "We were made to feed!"

He sank his teeth deep within the squirrel's neck! Screams of panic roared throughout the room while he ripped her limbs apart in a rage of gore. Blood aplenty covered the scene; there was so much that Aval wanted to sip some off the floor.

For the first time in many years, Aval felt liberated and free. He wouldn't stop there; he launched himself at more squirrels to continue his bloody rampage. Evel stood in shock, knowing that the peace was broken, and they couldn't be forgiven.

Mr. Soyer rushed to Evel with a terrified expression. He begged her to make her husband stop. His business would be ruined. She raised her eyebrow and slowly looked at the snob with a scorn. His business was more important to him than his doomed customers. It made her sicker than ever before. She then thought of a quick cure to settle her aching stomach: real blood. She threw away her manners and drove her fangs right into his neck.

Mr. Soyer yelled in extreme pain, right before Evel cracked his neck wide open to sample more of the rushing blood. Once finished, she threw the corpse to the floor and then realized what she had done. Bloodstains were on her dress and even more on her face. Such gruesomeness made her feel alive.

It was a sensational rush that could only be cured with more savagery. Like Aval, she launched herself at more squirrels to satisfy the hunger. They wanted more, so much more! They soon turned Chez Snobby into an all-you-can-eat buffet!

Sucking blood, ripping flesh, devouring meat—for minutes they were at it until the whole restaurant was reduced to a pool of blood and scattered limbs. No survivors were left in sight, just two full and satisfied vampires having a lovely after-dinner dance. The dark couple held hands and smiled without the urge to murder each other.

It filled me with much nostalgia, for those were the old vampire squirrels I knew. They were finally back, but that wasn't the end of it. Aval aimed to strike fear back into hearts far and wide and resurrect the monster era. It certainly spelled doom for the mortals, as one could still hear the same poem being recited by the same old hedgehog.

Husband and wife living among the deceased;
night falls, and these terrible vampires shall wake.
So lock your doors and hide for goodness' sake,
for it's on the blood of innocents they're sure to feast.

Dew Leaf is no more;
it is their land,
forever named,
Nevermore.

2
MEETING OF MONSTERS

On a dark Saturday night, on a full moon, howling wolves were heard near the coasts of Canada. They were calling across a shore, calling for a monster who had traveled to a faraway island called Lesion Island. It was a quiet and isolated piece of land, where anyone could escape civilization and bask in their own loneliness. Sad? I know, but it seemed like the perfect place for a monster.

The wolves' cries were unheard, and their monster couldn't answer their call, for it was late for a special occasion on that island. That wolflike creature was heading toward a bright campfire in the woods, and he did not find humans there; he found his fellow monsters.

It was the Meeting of Monsters. With a title like that, one would think that a group of demonic fiends would come together and plot against the mortals or take part in dark rituals. Sadly, none of them were interested in those activities anymore. Instead, they gathered to share their pains and woes every Saturday night. It was a type of group therapy, but without the therapy, since none were therapists. It was a pity group for comfort and escape, which was even sadder.

Around the campfire sat five quiet monsters. The first one who spoke was a new member, a child in torn black clothes. He was a little green-and-black furred squirrel stitched together with many different body parts from dead pets. He was a little Frankenstein monster named Vincety.

The child had the feet of a bunny, the arms of a meerkat, a bulbous red nose of a mouse, and a shaved tail of a wood rat with a big piece of fur taped at the end of it. What was most peculiar was the long stitch that ran down his face to his neck. It was as if his head was split in two and then was later stapled back together. To make it stranger, his mouth only appeared on the left side of his face, and he could only talk on that side. He was remarkably functioning as a walking corpse, yet he was a saddened abomination with nowhere to venture in the world.

"I don't know where to go. I don't know how to live this life," Vincety said. "I don't even know why I look like this, but I remember being created by a twisted human child named Paulie. I remember him showing me off to the other humans like a trophy. Next thing I knew, he tossed me on the side of the road like a bag of unwanted puppies. I was on my own ever since. I managed to teach myself to speak clearly and act normally, but I can never change how I look. No matter where I go or what I do, people only see me as a freak."

The squirrel's tale was truly tragic, but not enough to move the rest of the group. They had bigger problems than the ones he faced.

Next to the child sat a huge, hairy, slobbering werewolf named Barbosa. He was a red squirrel who was bitten by a werewolf some odd decades ago. During that time, he had himself a loving family. He had a kind wife and a special daughter who was unfortunate enough to carry his curse. The mother did not know they were werewolves, and Barbosa didn't want to tell her. She was his sunshine who shaped him into a better person, and if she found out he was a monster, it would've torn them apart. She soon found that out the hard way, once a full moon transformed her family into monsters right before her eyes.

The father and daughter devoured the mother and were left to see each other for what they had become. They couldn't live with such guilt, and they wanted to be cured. Methods used to cure themselves were beyond a sensible reach, and they were soon imprisoned for their uncontrollable behavior. In prison, professional doctors couldn't stop their transformation, but they did manage to restrain their hunger through advanced psychological therapy.

It worked, and the two squirrels were released back into society, completely reformed. The only thing they could do then was to live a sad life of a working father with a menial job of moving rocks and a high-school daughter who was a teenaged outcast.

"Cast by family? I ate my family," Barbosa said. "It was so easy at first, to enjoy this curse. I loved it. I ate the fattest creature I could easily fit in my mouth. They all tasted the same, like plump, juicy grapes. Until I realized they were my friends and family. The joy just disappeared; now I want to be cured completely. I could never find the original werewolf that did this to me, which means the only cure from this form is death. I will not allow death to be the cure for our pain. Me and my kid gotta live every day and strive every day. So, yeah, that's the story of me."

Next to him stood a humongous tarantula in a dirty purple suit and top hat. He was named Tye. He was a fierce mutant spider with an orange-and-black hair tone, and he was as tall as a grown horse. He was part of an experiment in an Alaskan laboratory that went horribly wrong. He had broken free from his prison and wreaked havoc in various underground caverns. He lay hidden within the shadows, and when small creatures or humans entered his lair, he would drag them into the darkness to feast on their bodies as his appetite for larger creatures grew.

Then one terrible day, he was captured by strange men in white coats and was dragged off to an unknown location. There, they tweaked his mind and reconstructed his body in unimaginable ways. They replaced his legs and feet with human arms and hands, just for the sole purpose of making homemade shoes. That was when he got his name, because he was good at "tying" shoes. Those men were obviously sick on so many levels.

What was also surprising was that their science was so ahead of its time they were able to make Tye talk. Yet they only taught him how to speak with a British accent, because they thought it'd be funny. Those men were terribly sick.

He did not know why they chose him or why they destroyed his life as a tarantula for corporate labor, but the first chance he got, Tye escaped from that horrible place. He was forever scarred and confused since then. All he knew how to do and would ever do was craft shoes. He even crafted shoes out of twigs at the meeting and carelessly threw them into the fire to keep it burning.

"Horrific times call for horrific punishment," Tye said. "I spent hours alone locked away in a windowless warehouse. My daily pay was powdered food packs and being showered with a hose. I couldn't kip, speak, or even sneeze until a lorry was fully loaded with shoes made by my mitts, these bloody human mitts. Before all this, I was a regular tarantula with food on the brain. Now me 'ead knows nothin' but flip-flops, boots, high heels, sandals, baby shoes, house shoes, and the poor bloke who can't afford 'cheese' shoes! What I couldn't understand is why they had to equip me with a suit and hat attire. I suppose it was a way to make me look civilized. I feel foolish wearin' it, but I also feel unnaturally starkers without it."

Next to him was a plump, brown-and-black-furred chipmunk that happened to be a witch. Her name was Nutilda. She wore black-and-green-striped jammies under a torn black-and-red dress. She also wore swirly black elf shoes and a red ninety-nine-cent pendant necklace with the price tag still left on. She was a bit on the crazy side. It was noticeable by her small left eye and a family of roaches that lived in her messy hair. She looked pretty relaxed about the roaches.

"These sad stories make children whimper, but I will make mine a whole lot simpler!" Nutilda said with a rhyme. She always enjoyed talking in rhymes. "I dress like a queen, and I laugh like a hag. I have a flying broom that carries my shopping bags. I hardly tell problems or woes to pass the time. I'm as jolly as a Roger who is still in her prime!"

Nutilda was easily the most irritating among the group. In truth, she was only masking her real pain. That was her problem; she hid from the fact that she was lonely and hated and had spells that always seem to backfire. She was a failed witch who could not even find a proper pointy hat to fit her big head.

She was jobless and hopeless, and every day she became fatter and uglier. It came to the point where even her flying broom preferred to be ridden by women other than her. Nutilda often wished for a single soul to visit her in her lonely tower in the snowy mountains. None would visit the witch, nor would they consider it, because she was an unappealing creature with roaches in her hair.

The last sitting monster was covered in seaweed and moss. It was the legendary swamp creature that was not at all furry; he was a scaly human fish breed. That creature never had a name, so the woodland critters just called him "Weegee," because of how the scales on his chest resembled Ws. The name sort of came to mind.

Weegee made his living terrorizing lake swimmers, but he always met his demise in the worst possible manner. However, he managed to come back to life regardless of his death, because of his body's ability to regenerate. He was certainly hard to keep down, but he eventually became tired of it all. He was tired of chasing teenagers and being killed time and time again. He wanted change.

There were many difficult choices he had to face during the phase of turning his life around. Eventually those led him spending the rest of his days hanging out with the animals that sat before him. He did not bother to tell his woes; his position and standing had no need for words. He was just another sad creature that wanted company.

It was indeed a pitiful circle of shame, but reminiscing over the monster era always seemed to bring a smile to their faces. Mortals used to shriek at the sounds of their very names, yet in reality, they hunted down most monsters and executed them for their crimes.

That era was gone, and the few survivors were moping around a diminishing campfire. If only there was a mighty force of inspiration that could bring back the spirits of those broken-down has-beens. One thing or maybe two to show them that not all hope was lost. Who else other than the great Aval & Evel?

On top of the hill stood those menacing vampires. The bright moon casting their shadows upon the group, while their mysterious fog spread all through the area. They walked down that foggy hill hand in hand, as the monsters soon laid eyes on them. The group stood in shock, for it has been years since they had last seen the vampire couple.

Once the vampires casually made their way to the circle, there were hardly any smiles shown. Believe it or not, their fellow monsters didn't like them at all. Was it envy over their powers or deep-rooted hate for them in general? Perhaps it was both. Whenever Aval & Evel came around, they would tease the monsters and poke fun at them to get a couple of chuckles. Not only that, but the vampires only visited them if they had a sinister plot in mind. The monsters really couldn't stand being mocked and pushed around by scrawny creatures with pale complexions. They wanted nothing to do with those vampires, but maybe that night would be different.

Aval politely said his usual greeting, "You shiftless wastes of skin and bones. Must you always pick an island to wallow in self-pity?"

That comment did not sit well with the others. The enraged Barbosa growled at the little vampires and said, "Shiftless wastes? I'll rip out your bones and use them as toothpicks, you lifeless pukes!"

The savage squirrel's threat was clear, yet his size and tongue did not faze the two for one second.

Evel said to him, "Take it easy there, Barby. We're not here to cause trouble or start hasty fights. We're in a good mood, something we monsters hardly feel in our dark lives."

Tye blinked his many eyes and told those squirrels, "Yer moods are rather scattered on the rails of anger and boredom. Whether straightforward or discombobulated, they constantly swing off only to end up on the same rails again."

"Oh really?" Aval said to Tye. "The only moods you're fond of are depression and the urge to do one thing that six-year-olds can do in their sleep, making knockoff shoes."

Tye then turned away in shame. The group hardly showed good feelings toward those squirrels, but there was one who was truly glad to see those two for the first time. One who adored them and looked up to them as mighty heroes among all monsters. That young squirrel, Vincety, was silent with joy. He stood there in awe and was simply amazed to be in the presence of the great legends. That little squirrel heard stories of those dark creatures and how they were a force of evil that built their whole region around fear and control. He wanted to be just like them and someday have his own land to frighten and torment. It was apparent that Vincety had the moral direction of a broken clock.

Vincety couldn't contain himself any longer. He screamed and happily rushed over to the vampires, but his right leg suddenly fell apart from the sprint. The limb was detached, but no blood was visible, only grayish clumps of meat. He fell face first in the dirt but landed close to their feet. He nervously gazed up at the two and was honored to see that their eyes stared down at him. Making eye contact and forming a wondrous connection brought a huge smile to his face.

"Oh, Aval! Oh, Evel! It is an honor to meet you!" Vincety said with joy. "I'm Lincety—wait, sorry, I mean I'm Vincety. I heard stories, but oh! I can't believe it's actually you! The king and queen of Nevermore, the bringers of death and gloom, Aval & Evel! Oh boy, oh boy, what an honor this is! What a privilege this is!"

The two vampires had no idea they had a fan, and they certainly did not know what to do with one. Aval & Evel did not care for admirers they couldn't devour, so they walked around the squirrel, avoiding further eye contact. Vincety still lay there on the ground, awed by their every movement. The vampires told everyone that the reason for their visit was to offer an understanding of a crucial situation. It was a situation that concerned the reputation of monsters.

The world no longer feared them, and the vampires thought it was time for monsters to rise up and spread their heinous fear across the land. There would no longer be fear of pathetic slashers in masks, only creations of mad science, visitors from smoldering lakes, diseased and incurable creatures, and conjurers of black magic. How lovely it would be for Aval & Evel to lead a marvelous revolution. It would certainly bring all sorts of calamity to the world, but the monsters did not want any part of it.

Barbosa sat back down and said to the vampires, "Forget it. I have a daughter to raise, and the rest of us are trying to find a better living. Besides, every mortal on this stinking planet knows how to kill us. I'd rather live in shame than have a silver bullet go through my heart. Face facts, it's better just to get with the times."

"Truth in words he speak, staying in the past is ever so bleak," rhymed Nutilda. "Creating spells and crafting potions is such a chore; why go through all the trouble when I can buy doses at a drugstore?"

"Because it's not our way!" Aval silenced them with a yell. "Look at yourselves, so pathetic. Huddled together like sad cows waiting to be slaughtered. Like it or not, we might be the last living monsters. We have extraordinary gifts, and I will not let such power go to waste. These mortals must learn that we are the superior beings they should fear."

Tye then scratched his head out of confusion. He had to ask the vampires, "Am I goin' yampy, or weren't you the ones who wanted peace among monsters and mortals?"

"Screw the peace," Aval said.

Evel agreed with him and said, "Last night, we broke our chains and devoured dozens of rodents at a restaurant. It felt sooo right. It's high time the mortals remembered that we are the superior beings—their place is on their knees, licking our boots. Believe me, it's how nature intended it to be."

With that said, Tye turned to Weegee and whispered in his ear, saying that he knew they were off the rails. The swamp creature did not speak. Even when Aval & Evel asked him to join them, he said nothing.

That creature had not said a word all night, but silence allows the brain to think clearly. His red eyes gazed out to the distance, and he thought about a world similar to Aval & Evel's. However, the origin of his existence always seemed to cloud his mind. He never discovered what he truly was or where he came from. All he could remember was living in a lake, alone. Finding the truth was too long a journey to travel. All he could do was watch the world change into a cesspool of problems.

Everyone looked at Weegee and noticed that he hadn't blinked for a while. They wondered if he was still alive, but all he was doing was thinking.

Weegee finally blinked. He stared at the two vampires with his bloodred eyes and asked them, "If you vampires wish to go against the mortals, what's there to stop them from burning you in your sleep?"

That, the two did not know. It was one of the reasons they came seeking support in the first place. Aval & Evel, although powerful, were not able to protect themselves in the daytime, especially when everyone knew where they lived. The group saw that they hadn't thought out their plan clearly. With that said, Weegee thanked the group for another nice evening. Then he walked off into the woods, disappearing into the darkness.

The vampires suddenly felt discouraged; it was a feeling even stranger than the discomfort of hunger. They did not give in, for it would be a cold day in hell when squirrels let a fish tell them any different. There had to be a way of protection, but how? Vincety then crawled toward the vampires and volunteered to protect them. He had no problem with sunlight or pain for that matter. He would have been a great bodyguard, but there were two problems: he was too small and too fragile. Even if he could take pain, he was but a child. A cat could even swallow him whole.

They turned him down, but the boy pleaded for them to reconsider. It would've given meaning to his life to serve a greater force for an even greater cause. His loyalty was appreciated, but it was not enough to move the vampires' cold hearts.

"Kid, tone down the needy fanboy act," Aval said as he hurt what little feelings the boy had left. "Now, help from a child is a nice start, but I'm sure the rest of you can do the same. We are still doing this. On the next Meeting of Monsters, we want to hear some ideas and a change of attitudes from each and every one of you."

"What?" Nutilda said in a rage. "What delusional thing gives tired old squirrels like you any position to tell us what to do?"

Aval put on an angry look, and Evel let out a snicker. The monsters had obviously forgotten how unforgiving the vampires' methods were, so Evel spoke of the consequences. If they refused or failed to deliver, the vampires would simply rip out the witch's chubby innards, tear off the tarantula's arms, and stuff it all down the werewolf's decapitated neckhole. After that, they would roast his corpse and serve it to his daughter on Sunday morning.

Her crude description of punishment was enough to silence the witch, and at the same time, stir bitter fear into the rest. Aval & Evel had a name to reclaim, and they planned to start in one week, with or without the other monsters.

3
SQUIRREL OF FRANKENSTEIN

What is a Frankenstein monster? If a grown person ever asks you such a question, then it's probably safe to call them a caveman. But really, most people confuse Frankenstein with the legendary green monster. The monster itself was a creature made out of different body parts and brought back from the dead by a deranged scientist famously named Dr. Frankenstein. For what real purpose, you may ask. Well, he wanted to prove that man could cheat death and pose as gods by creating life. He succeeded, but he only created a creature with an abnormal mind.

The undead monstrosity may have been dumb, but it had the strength to destroy an entire village with very little effort. It could throw boulders like pebbles and break through walls like paper. The power was inhuman, but could one tiny squirrel live up to the standards of a Frankenstein monster?

Vincety wandered through the sheltered woods of Canada and asked himself the exact same question. However, he knew deep in his tiny heart that he was a creature of destruction. He was very confident in himself and ignored any trace of self-doubt. He would not fail Aval & Evel. He would help them reclaim the glory of monsters everywhere. He first had to improve his physical appearance and become as strong as a real wrecking machine.

On a bright Sunday morning, he found himself near a shallow river that was full of rocks. He rushed toward the nearest set of rocks and sought to use them as weights. Most of them were tiny, but he soon found one that was about his size. He aimed to test his might by lifting that rock over his head. After a few stretches, he grabbed the rock by its sides and attempted to lift it from the ground. He grunted, and his whole body began to shake.

He managed to lift it over his toes, but then he started to wobble and lose his grip. He desperately tried to maintain himself, but the stitches that held his shoulders together suddenly fell apart as the rock slammed him to the ground. His furry bunny feet were trapped underneath the rock.

Vincety did not cry; he simply sighed in frustration. He knew then it was going to be a long workout. He stretched over to one of his loose arms and reattached it with his mouth and tongue; he had a lot of practice doing that. Once the arm was in place, it became a functional limb once again. He then saw the other arm on his right, and he was about to grab it.

Suddenly, a bird swooped down and snatched his arm and carried it to a high tree branch. Vincety was absolutely peeved. He looked up at the tree to see that mysterious thief. He saw that it was a raven in a red suit and a yellow pearl necklace. She had a playful smile and a pair of soulless yellow eyes. The raven held the squirrel's arm with her wing and waved it in the breeze with a chuckle, which made him really annoyed.

"Give that back!" he said.

The raven chuckled some more and said, "No, this is an arm I've been searching for. It serves well as a back scratcher and nothing more."

That peculiar raven then sparked something in Vincety's brain. He realized that she was no regular raven at all. She was an infamous bird that everyone and their grandmother heard stories about. She was a mystical lady with an unforgettable yet unoriginal name, Raven, the wishing raven. She was a powerful being that could grant wishes to anyone that needed them the most. If one needed a house, she would raise her wings to the heavens and conjure a home faster than you can say, "Holy Hula-Hoops hovering over a hot hotel in Hollywood!"

But like most things, there was a catch. She was a twisted and cruel raven composed of all things malevolent. She would grant their wishes for free but would not warn them of the real price. The house she conjured from thin air would ooze various diseases while the victims slept in their beds. By the next morning, the family would sleep silently, forevermore. It's a horrific example of being careful for what you wish for, especially to a raven evermore.

"My, my little squirrel, you seem to be stuck," Raven said with a smile. "These arms of yours are in poor attachment, and your body does not seem to be any better. Maybe a 'wish' would solve this predicament?"

"No, thanks," said Vincety. "Everyone and their grandmother know better than to wish upon a raven. I don't need a wish to get free; I just need my arms. So can you please give me my arm back?"

"With a kind and gentle word like 'please'? Ha-ha! You're funny. What's a kid like you doing outside this early anyway? Shouldn't you be asleep in your bed?"

"I'll sleep when I'm dead. I'm out here training to be stronger. Aval & Evel are starting a monster revolution, and I owe it to them to be the best Frankenstein monster I can be."

The raven scoffed at such delusion. She flew down and landed on top of the rock. She pointed his arm in his face and said they were all living in a fantasy. No good ever came from that. She said those vampires did not have the means to achieve anything, other than being sad and pathetic. As for Vincety, the raven didn't see him as a fearsome monster, but a small rag doll that could never grow and would remain inept, forevermore.

Vincety snatched the arm from the raven and said that fantasy would come true. The vampires would rule the land, and he would be the strongest monster there ever was. The raven chuckled once more and then flew off into the skies, leaving the foolish squirrel with his dreams. The raven's insults did not get to the squirrel, and she failed to crush his spirit, for he was more determined than ever. Vincety reattached the other arm and used them both to claw out his feet, thus freeing him. The bunny feet were a little crushed, but it was nothing a few snaps couldn't fix. With various sounds of bones snapping back into place, the feet became active once again.

Later that morning, he traveled to a nearby town and rummaged through a number of trash cans to find any useful junk. He found loose wires and loads of used duct tape. He used them to help hold his limbs together. He covered his hands and feet with old bandages to cushion the force of blows. Lastly, he found a yellow scrunchie and used it as a sweatband. With all the accessories in his possession, he started his training.

He began with upper-body strength. To perfect that quality, he had to push his tireless body to the limit. He underwent a series of workout techniques, such as 354 push-ups and 276 sit-ups. Those were mere warm-ups; to be more effective, he had to do an even thousand. There were no breaks of any sort, only the burning sensation of fire in his body and the feel of his spine coming loose every once in a while.

He then trained himself to be a better fighter. To perfect that, he followed the technique of boxers by punching everything in sight. Punching trees, trash bags, frozen meat, and cars, and even shadowboxing proved its worth. However, when he punched physical objects, he had a tough time reorganizing the bones in his hands afterward.

Next, he had to work on his agility. He did that by leaping from tree to tree and sprinting up and down hills, back and forth. He never stopped; he wanted to truly increase his movements to be an uncatchable squirrel. However, when his legs fell apart from running too much, he didn't mind crawling to his goals with his bare hands.

Through all the hardships and all the backbreaking trials, Vincety felt like a super squirrel! He felt so good about himself that he ran up the many stairs that led to a museum building, and he did not lose a single leg. He made it to the top of the stairs, and as he looked at the town below, where the sun began to set over the horizon, he raised his fists to the golden sky and yelled like a true champion.

Later that night, the pumped-up squirrel walked through the woods with his sights set on one last goal. He had to put his skills to the test against his most mighty adversary, the rock. The same rock that tore his arms off and broke his feet. All of his training would finally pay off. All he had to do was lift it above his head and throw it to the ground like garbage.

Vincety grabbed both sides without hesitation and proceeded to lift it. With that load firmly in his grasp, he felt the power he worked so hard to achieve course through his body. He managed to lift it up to his knees. He was going to do it. He was finally going to lift the rock! No longer would he be small and weak; he was on his way of being a force of nature!

Until the wires and duct tape on his shoulders came loose. His arms fell apart; the rock landed on Vincety's legs and slammed him to the ground. The little squirrel was stuck and was unable to get out.

"What happened?" Vincety asked himself. "How is this possible? I worked myself to the bone and I still can't do it!"

He thought long and hard about why he failed. Then it came to him. He was an undead corpse; therefore, he could not gain any strength. His muscles could never improve and he would remain the same, like the raven said before. He didn't want to accept the awful truth.

Vincety struggled to reach his arms, but they were too far from his reach. He squirmed and squirmed until he no longer had the will to move. He lay back on the grass and looked at the glittering stars in the dark-blue sky. The pleasant scene offered him no comfort or a bit of calmness; it just made him sad. The stars above could shine, but he could not. The thought of it made the little squirrel cry. He accepted the fact that he wasn't a Frankenstein monster; he was just a rag doll.

Dreams crushed and hope lost,
finding purpose comes with a cost.
The dead will always feel pain,
as their family mourn in the rain.

Feelings for the undead are so bitter;
none have sympathy for bags of litter.
These creations were built so odd,
by others who wanted to play as God.

These creations of mad science can't help but cry;
their lives are pointless and they wonder why.
They are forced to live and never grow;
their simple lives are but misery and woe.

Somehow someday,
others will say,
we all end up that way.

For hours Vincety lay in that spot. He felt so sore about his failure that he simply wanted to rot away. He thought about how his life came to be and how he let Aval & Evel down. He also wondered if there was more to being a monster than just having fearsome might and a frightening appearance. He did not know; he was lost and confused in his own mind.

"Why am I like this?" Vincety asked the sky. "Why was I created? What is my purpose here?"

A hollow voice filled the air and called Vincety's name. The squirrel had no idea where it came from, until a bright hole opened in the sky and showed an illusion of a human child. It was a portly boy with red hair and a green shirt. The image of the boy became clear, and Vincety realized it was his human creator, Paulie. Was Vincety's mind playing an awful trick? Did he completely lose his marbles? Either way, the vision of Paulie spoke to the squirrel.

"Quit your blubbering, you stupid squirrel," said Paulie. "You were created to be my ticket out of middle school and into a university."

"What?" questioned Vincety.

Paulie continued, "I did not go through the trouble of digging up a pet cemetery just to create some house squirrel. I was a big-time *Frankenstein* movie fan, and I wanted to see if it was really possible for the deceased to be reanimated. I succeeded! All I needed were dead animal parts and a big jolt of lightning to create you, Vincety. Once my science teacher saw you, he didn't bother to give me an A plus; he gave me a recommendation to the highest learning institute in Canada, University of Toronto!"

"I knew it," said Vincety. "I was nothing but a tool you used to cut your way through life!"

"That you were, but after all was said and done, I set you free into the wild. Isn't that what you animals want? Freedom?"

"You threw me in a ditch like garbage. I am not garbage. I am a living, breathing thing, dammit! And when I get out of here, I'll make you pay for what you did to me!"

"Oooh, I'm soo scared. If you can't lift a rock, you'll stand no chance crossing a field of butterflies. You're just a fragile, dead little squirrel, and that's all you will ever be, forevermore."

Those were his last words before he vanished from the squirrel's eyes. Was it all really real? It didn't matter to the squirrel once blinding rage began to cloud his senses. He threw a fit and pounded on the rock with his head, desperately trying to free himself. He wiggled his legs and eventually freed one of them, and then he used it to push his body away from the rock. He pushed and heaved, until he parted the other leg from the pelvis. He then crawled back and forth to reattach his arms.

It took some time, but he was able to sew the arms back in place. Then there was the matter of retrieving the leg from the rock. He stood on his one leg with precise balance. He ground his dirty teeth with hatred toward the rock. The furious squirrel leaped forward and bashed it! He did it over and over, moving the rock inch by inch, until he was able to retrieve his other leg.

He stitched it back up and walked away from the heinous object and into the night. Dark thoughts began to course through his mind, and he figured out that strength wasn't the real answer. Training his body like a fool wasn't going to cut it; he needed to do something bigger, and his cursed existence was the answer. He needed to become his own creator and call down vengeance by bringing an army back from the dead.

Vincety went back to town and snuck into a closed library to feed his mind with knowledge. There he studied books upon books of anatomy, bioengineering, and other works of neuromuscular processes. He needed to know everything, because bringing the dead to life was more complicated than what he'd seen in movies. It was so much more than just stitches and lightning.

Vincety also wanted to know what made the mind function and how to have full control over it and the body. It was going to be a tough process to understand, but much like his workout training, he did not give up. He left no page unturned, nor did he leave a word undeciphered. He was going to understand the mad process no matter what.

Hours of reading letters, turning into numbers and periodic understandings that turned into unfamiliar scribes, it was all fascinating to him. Books soon covered the floors, and he somehow ended up wearing geeky glasses and a white shirt with a pocket protector full of pens. By morning, at the cost of turning into a glorified science nerd, he understood everything!

It was all a matter of reviving dead nerve cells through concentrated physics and controlling the brain with specific levels of restraining mechanisms. To put it simply, he needed to process the right amount of electricity to wake up the nerves and power a small microchip attached to the head that would give the brain commands. I was really proud of that young squirrel, for he was more dedicated and educated than Paulie ever was in his short life.

Later that day, Vincety found an abandoned factory deep in the woods, which he could use as his base of operations. What luck! He was then hard at work gathering the tools needed to complete his plan. He took science equipment from labs and appliances from hardware stores, mainly by hauling them off in hot-wired forklifts and storing them in his hot-wired getaway van.

That sneaky squirrel was stealing everything that wasn't glued down. He had a mission to complete, and he did not care about the law, only time. Within days, everything was operational and at his fingertips, but there was still the matter of finding fresh corpses. The bodies needed to have most body parts intact and were already built for combat.

During his travels, he came across a store where the windows were filled with bright TV sets with various channels. One particular channel soon covered all the screens, and the volume was turned to a very high setting. It was big news that informed the locals that a recent terrorist attack was stopped by an army of honorable Canadian soldiers. Unfortunately, a large number of them did not survive. They had plans for a ceremony to honor the soldiers, while their coffins were safely stored inside a military hangar. The hangar was several miles away from Vincety's reach, and it gave him an idea—a horrible, fiendish idea.

A storm broke out that night. Spotlights from the military hangar grew dim, and the guards outside were beginning to drowse away. The rain poured fearlessly, and lightning constantly spread through the skies. It was the perfect storm. There, Vincety stood on top of the hangar, where he set up a tall lightning rod attached to metal strings. The strings were attached to forty-seven bodies inside as well as control chips that were lodged in their heads. Everything was set, and all Vincety had to do was wait for that bolt of lightning.

"Please work," Vincety said. "I need you soldiers to awaken to serve your country once more."

Many days had passed, and many events around the world progressed. On a particular Saturday night, when the moon was only half-full, the Meeting of Monsters arrived again. The monsters were gathered on Lesion Island around the same campfire. With the exception of Barbosa, who showed up in his normal squirrel form and wore his usual white tank top, gray sweat pants, and black slippers. He clearly didn't care for fashion.

There was then a surprise appearance by the wishing raven that had just arrived on the scene. She made herself comfy on a high tree branch to observe the little group of rejects, and she was prepared to mock their wishful ambitions. The monsters knew her all too well during the years and welcomed her with irritated moans. They found her more terrible than Aval & Evel combined.

She was an annoyance that constantly bombarded them with the suggestion of wishes. The only wish they wanted was to see that devilish bird vanish from existence. The raven rejected that wish every time. Regardless of the unwanted company, the monsters began to discuss their plans on how to strike fear back into the hearts of mortals.

Nutilda suggested, "What if I create a nasty stew to put in everyone's room? I'll poison them all to their tragic doom!"

"No," said Evel, "we're not trying to kill them all, especially with a hot meal. Come now, we have to think of our nourishment here."

Barbosa then said, "I could probably cause a global ice age, with computers and stuff."

Aval moaned and said to him, "Are you really that stupid?"

The raven then spoke to them. "Hey, here's a great idea! Why not 'wish' for the mortals to be scared of you? That would make things easier, wouldn't you agree?"

Evel folded her arms and said to the raven, "Nope, not gonna happen. Everyone and their grandmother know better than to wish upon a raven. Correct me if I'm wrong, but wasn't it you who created the black plague in Europe?"

"Jeez," the raven whined. "I grant one rat an alluring perfume that, oddly enough, had a contagious side effect, and I'm branded for life. You really need to let go of the past."

Tye had an excellent plan. "I could make uncomfortable shoes that would give everyone blisters! At the same time, I'll make 'em so itchy that they'll have no choice but to scrape away the skin! Their plates of meat would be so damaged that no one would be able to stop us! Why, when anyone even sees a shoe, they would scream in bloody terror! A horrifyingly heinous plan if I do say so myself."

"No, no, no, NO!" roared Aval. "Are you all this dumb? Do any of you have anything that could work or make sense?"

"Not really," Weegee said as he gazed at the fire. "Yelling at us won't help either. Listen to me, Aval & Evel, if you go down this path, it would mean a quicker death for us all."

After that, Evel looked around in a confused manner and asked Aval, "Did you hear that? I could've sworn I heard the sounds of a noncontributing bum."

"Don't act this way," said Weegee. "You know I'm right."

"There it is again!" She said with a gasp. "This is getting eerie."

It was clear that no one had anything significant to contribute to the cause or give a hand in protection. Aval looked at the sad bunch in disgust, and he felt no need to keep them alive. Just before he did anything, out of the dark came the green squirrel, Vincety, with a stern face. He stepped toward the group and sat near the fire and said nothing.

The group noticed his presence and welcomed him. "Who are you?"

Vincety was not the most memorable or respectable among the group, so he humored them by saying, "I'm Bob the Undead Pizza God...I'm Vincety, you fools! I was here last week!"

"Oooh!" said the group, knowing that he did look a tad familiar.

Vincety ignored the forgetful bunch. He then asked the vampires to give him another chance. He swore he would do everything he could to protect them. Aval & Evel still rejected the offer, and Raven just laughed. She knew they would never rely on a tyke like him to be anything other than a rag-doll joke. Vincety had enough of her insults. It was enough to push him over the edge again.

He looked up at the bird with death in his eyes. He raised his right hand in the air, and he snapped his fingers. It echoed through the woods. Nothing happened. Everyone wondered why he snapped his fingers as if he'd ordered an instant command to someone. Suddenly the strange sounds of metal clicks were heard. And then...

Rat-tat-ata-tat-atatat-atatat-atatat-atatat-atatat-ata!

Rapid gunfire appeared all around, and bullets flew toward the raven's tree. It happened so fast! It was so startling that everyone took cover behind logs and boulders.

Rat-tat-ata-tat-atatat-atatat-atatat-atatat-atatat-ata!
Boooooom!

The thunderous impact from a rocket launcher blew the tree to bits, reducing it to nothing but burning ash. No trace of the raven was found, only a cloud of smoke and floating streams of fire sparks. Vincety stared at the group; he observed them cowering in fear. All except for Weegee. He sat perfectly still the whole time like a statue. He died so many times that he did not care for surprises anymore.

As the monsters rose from their hiding places, they witnessed an army of human soldiers creeping in from the darkness. Those soldiers had pale-green skin and groaned like zombies with every step they took. They had soulless yellow eyes, they wore torn uniforms with the letter F painted red on their vests, and they were equipped with the latest military arms for efficient carnage.

They were Vincety's creations, forty-seven Frankenstein soldiers. He'd actually done it. He brought the dead back to life, and they were under his control. The soldiers soon stopped, while Vincety continued to stare at the group like a cold heartless being. He wanted to hear their mockery; he wanted to hear how he would never become a frightening monster. But indeed he had.

"Some say that I'm useless, but look at what I've done. I have Canada's finest at my command!" Vincety said with confidence. "Some say this world sees us as jokes. Raven said I was a joke, but where's the laughter now? Huh? Aval & Evel are right; if there was a better time to bring back the fear, now is that time. We must be smarter and better than the monsters from the past. Only then can we truly take our place as being the superior beings on the face of this planet!"

Vincety walked toward the shocked vampires and knelt down before them. He bowed his head and stuck out his right hand in loyalty.

"Aval & Evel, will you let me and my army be at your command until the day when your rule is absolute? But for this one request, that the University of Toronto Land be our first target. Then I could make more soldiers from the bodies, to protect you and destroy all. What do you say?"

The vampires looked at each other and weighed their options, but it only took a few seconds for both to come to the immediate response, "You got a deal!"

And so, it happened. Days later on a cold chaotic night, the University of Toronto was overrun by Vincety's soldiers. No one saw it coming. They thought they were friendly Canadian soldiers in Halloween costumes. It wasn't Halloween at all, and before they could figure it out, it was too late. Shots were fired, rockets flew through the air, and screams echoed beyond the explosions. It became a wasteland of dead bodies and flames.

It was taken over before any law-enforcement personnel were able to stop them, due to them being the first to go. Bodies were collected, stowed in trucks, and sent away to Vincety's base. Only one human was kept alive—Paulie, the one who truly mattered.

Inside a dark science lab, Aval, Evel, Vincety, and his soldiers strapped the frightened boy to a chair and wrapped him in exposed high-voltage wires. They made it look like an electrical execution, which would be a fitting end for him. Paulie cried and pleaded for them to let him go, but Vincety wanted revenge so badly that he didn't want to hear his voice anymore.

Vincety ordered a soldier to plug the wire into an electrical outlet, and Paulie lit up like a Christmas tree. The surging currents ran through his body, causing agonizing pain of unimaginable torture. It made Aval & Evel clap with joy.

After twenty seconds, Vincety ordered the soldier to unplug the wire, and it was over. Paulie was roasted to a crisp. He was lifeless, but his muscles still twitched. Feeling unsatisfied, Vincety wanted the wire plugged back in to see if he would come back to life. He ordered the same command again and again and again until he could hear his screams. Aval & Evel began to see the young squirrel become a raving maniac. It was hard for them to enjoy the torture then.

Vincety finally made it stop, and all that remained was a pile of black ash being swept away by the wind. It should have been satisfying for him, but oddly, he did not feel a thing; nerves aside. It was a short-lived victory that soon became a feeling of emptiness. He wanted to be glad and happy that the monstrous child had died, but in the end, was he any better?

He became conflicted, so the vampires came over to ease his mind. They told him that revenge was never about what to feel in the end; it was the journey that made it all worthwhile. On the bright side of things, the vampires became proud enough to call Vincety an honorary monster. Such an honor made him smile. A little.

After the vampires left the room, Vincety looked at the ashes spread across the floor. He still thought about whether he was any better than Paulie. He already knew the answer to that. What he did to achieve his goal not only made him worse than Paulie but also made him worse than the vampires themselves.

4

A WEREWOLF'S DAUGHTER

"Is it crazy to beg for an electric chair?" the squirrel asked the mouse. "Is it weird that I actually want to be locked away because of what I am? Is that even a thing?"

"You're not in prison anymore, Elise. You've paid your debt to society," said the mouse. "If it weren't for Aval & Evel's peace, the doctors wouldn't have considered treating you or your father. Remember?"

"Aval & Evel can't be trusted," said Elise. "No monster can."

"So you're not grateful for their decision?" asked the mouse.

Elise answered, "As long as I'm alive, I'm never grateful."

Deep within a burrow that was surrounded by a tall plain of grass lay an orange squirrel in a doctor's chaise longue. This squirrel was named Elise. She wore a green jacket with torn sleeves and a white undershirt. She wore baggy green pants and had a pale-red shirt tied around her waist as if it was a belt. She also had black gloves, shoes, and a beanie that showed the face of a dead cartoon cat, where a smile was drawn over its taped mouth. It symbolized that curiosity killed the cat. She didn't enjoy dressing like a regular lady.

Beneath her tough exterior, she was actually a troubled girl with the curse of a werewolf. Elise was Barbosa's teenage daughter, and she hated the day she was ever born a monster. Her life was greatly dreadful; she never found a reason to smile, and she possessed suicidal thoughts that wanted her to end the suffering. Her father cared enough to stop her attempts on a daily basis, and he reminded her that their curse would be lifted one day. Elise never did believe in such fairy tales.

The psychological therapy cured her savage hunger, but there was something more troubling that she didn't want her father to know about. On one particular night, she woke from her bed and saw that her room was covered in bloody footprints and scattered bones. Her bedsheets were shredded; her palms were covered in blood, and she found tiny pieces of meat in her mouth. The poor squirrel transformed into a ferocious werewolf whenever she slept.

She visited her mouse therapist, Dr. Derk, to warn him that the treatments did not contain her savage nature but made it worse. It became so troubling that she had to force herself to stay awake. She stayed awake for so long that the dark circles around her eyes were becoming permanent.

Dr. Derk wondered why the treatment worked on Barbosa, but not on her. It may have been genetics that made her less stable, but he wasn't that kind of doctor. He believed that there was something on her mind that caused her to sleepwalk or, in this case, sleep-slaughter.

Dr. Derk asked Elise, "Did you ever find yourself having irrational thoughts whenever you went to bed? If so, how did those thoughts make you feel?"

Elise stared blankly at the ceiling and answered, "I'm a cursed werewolf. Do I really need to explain my feelings? I kill everything in sight with no control; it's horrible. I don't know how monsters live like this."

"I see," Dr. Derk said as he wrote some notes in his book. "Now tell me, is the monster inside you the repressed tension you feel every day? Once it gets out, do you feel liberated without a care in the world?"

"Yes, more than you can imagine," Elise said in a sarcastic tone. "The feeling of your body reconstructing itself, not knowing what you're doing or what is happening, only to wake up naked with a belly full of bones and brains...oh yeah, it's a happy kind of trip. My mind does become clear of worries, but I don't want this; the guilt is too much to take. All the people I've eaten...my mother...I can't even eat anymore. The thought of everything I eat going through my body and ending up in a dirty toilet...I cannot stand that horrible thought. I just want this to go away!"

"Calm down, Elise. We all wish for our inner demons to expel, but like it or not, they are a part of you like yin is to yang. If you went back to the treatment procedures, maybe this condition would subside."

"Are you serious? I have an abnormal curse. Numbing me with drugs and psycho treatments won't keep me from killing your entire family in my sleep!"

Elise shouted and glared at the mouse, though he did not flinch from her outburst. He did not fear his troubled patients, for they would hurt themselves before they would lay a paw on him. Elise calmed herself down and took a deep breath. She confessed that the only thing she thought about every night was how much better the world would be if she were never born.

Dr. Derk then gave her a solution: if she ever wanted to free herself from a troubling condition, she must first free herself from guilt. That was the only cure he could give. Personally, he was about as helpful as a bad fortune cookie. Elise soon left the mouse's home, admitting to herself that it was a complete waste of time. There was no cure for her at all. All she could do then was search for a place to ease her mind.

She couldn't go home, she couldn't stand the sight of the man who brought her into the world, and she couldn't stay at a friend's house because she didn't have any friends. So where could she go?

There was only one place where she could have one shred of peace, though it was not a first choice for some. She went to her mother's grave that lied under an apple tree. It was always her ideal spot for relaxation and communication. How, you may ask. She would sit next to the tombstone and imagine that her mother was right by her side and talk.

They had marvelous conversations together. Elise would tell her about her terrible times at school and sometimes reminisce over made-up adventures they had together. Before too long, she would come to realize that she was merely talking to a piece of stone the whole time. It was a pitiful and tear-jerking sight to behold, but it showed that she really missed her mother.

That day she left the doctor's office was the one time she sat quietly near the tree and stared out into the sunset. She just wanted some peace and quiet. However, it may not have been a good decision with her strange condition and all.

The beauty of the orange sky and the majestic clouds made her grow bored and tired. Her eyelids weighed down on her, and she grew a bit weaker. She breathed harder to resist, but the soothing notion to fall into a deep sleep felt so nice. She closed her eyes, and she was entering dreamland.

Once she started growling through her teeth, her father came just in time to wake her up. Barbosa shook her by the shoulders, and she came back to reality. Elise opened her eyes and suddenly panicked. She was worried that she might have killed during her nap, but all was fine. Elise wondered why her father was there in the first place.

Barbosa wanted to discuss a matter with her. It was late, and he saw that she wasn't home, so he figured she was at her mother's grave. He told her that everything would be all right; they wouldn't have to be scared anymore. The time of change had arrived. He told her that Aval & Evel had finally broken their chains and were putting fear back into the hearts of mortals.

Each monster had to find his or her own part to contribute. He figured that two werewolves, such as themselves, would make the woods their hunting grounds. They could go hunting and spread their curse to whomever survived.

It sounded perfect, but Elise calmly objected. "Have you lost your freakin' mind? We went along with this peace for a better future, and now you want to throw it all away? Why?"

"Elise, we have no choice," Barbosa said. "We have to go along with their game, because when it comes to business, Aval & Evel mean business."

Barbosa tried to make her understand. He held her by the arms and assured her that it was the perfect opportunity to forget about the past and do what they were meant to do: be monsters. She pulled away from him and felt disgusted by the whole situation. She was too ashamed to do anything with him. Barbosa felt hurt and couldn't figure out how to convince her, so he told her why he agreed in the first place.

"Elise, you know I want nothing to do with those vampires," he said. "I didn't like the idea either, but if I refused, they would've killed me, maybe you too."

"Then let them," she said. "Their plan will fail anyways."

"Elise, why are you like this? Why don't you have faith in anything?"

"We are just squirrels, Dad, squirrels with a curse that is not worth living with."

Her father could never communicate on her level, but he did all he could to make her happy. The therapy, the decent food he put on the table, and the chance for her to learn in school again. He even got her into Sunday school, which only lasted ten minutes before she was banned.

The one time he wanted to do something together and put their powers to use, she would rather die. Why couldn't she see the things as he did? Because she knew in her heart what was best—a peaceful and glorious afterlife.

She left her father in silence and did not look back, not saying where she was going or when she would ever come home. No tears or yells came from either one, but one thing was for sure, Barbosa had no daughter.

A son for a mother,
a daughter for a father,
but for monsters of old,
very few stories are ever told.

Rare it can be,
to have a child of their own.
So uncommon do we see,
copies of a monster's blood and bone.

A monster to raise children,
teaching them to hunt, kill, and sing.
But children have no intentions to follow their fathers,
for nothing is more arrogant than an offspring.

Night fell, and hours passed by as the winds began to turn colder than usual. So cold that even the heftiest of furry creatures would snooze near a bonfire, while eating some hot noodle soup. It was hard for anything to keep warm, even while traveling through the treacherous forest named Beverly Pines. Elise had no destination in mind or goal to achieve; she just wanted to get away and stay awake. The cold kept her arms shivering and legs quivering, and a fire and some soup did sound nice.

She came across a family of gophers near a campfire, enjoying the cold winds. They liked to be around a campfire any old time. Whether it was rain, sleet, or snow, the family would sing "Kumbaya" even then. They were a happy, semiperfect family in Elise's eyes. A family that would sing in Mother Nature's face through thick and thin.

She wished she had a family like that, but she had no time for families; she had to move on. Before she could walk away, the gopher family already spotted her. They saw the shivering lost girl, and they became very generous. They invited her to their circle, they made her some soup, and they provided a blanket too. They even offered her to spend the night in their burrow, but Elise refused. She did not want to be around them when she slept, for she had a problem she could not speak of in front of them.

The father gopher just laughed. "Oh nonsense! What are ya, a loud snorer? We heard worse from them bulldozers drivin' 'round. Come, stay for one night. You can use my daughter's old room."

Elise didn't want to be rude to refuse the kind gopher's offer, but she also didn't want to scare her new friends away. She agreed to sleep in their burrow, under the condition that they locked their doors, which was fine, and no questions were asked.

That night she slept soundly in that small bed. She tried to think happy thoughts in order to dream happier dreams so that she wouldn't transform. She dreamed of being in a sunny meadow of pink flowers and songbirds. She smiled ever so happily to finally enter a world of joy and serenity.

There she frolicked through the lovely field, where she discovered a huge fountain of pixies playing old country songs with kazoos and banjos. How very bizarre for a girl like her to dream of something so bizarre.

Speaking of bizarre, you're probably wondering how I, the narrator, could enter one's dream and tell what could not be seen to the otherwise conscious. It's quite puzzling to explain, unless everything here was part of my own dream. Think for a moment of me describing another's dream, telling you this is a dream of my own. It's as if we're on a psychological journey deep within my own state of unconsciousness.

Nah, I'm just messing with you, kind reader. I'm a special kind of thing who is blessed with the ability to appear anywhere at any point in time at will, because I'm a narrator! I live to tell amazing tales that happen in other's lives, worlds, and even dreams. I just felt like it was my purpose for being alive in this universe. So, with that out of the way, let us get back to Elise's serene dream. Cool? OK then.

That happy squirrel gazed in awe at the colors and musical sounds that filled the air with joy. In the middle of the beautiful fountain was the gopher family. They were square dancing and kicking the waters away in slow motion.

Then there came a sudden pillow fight by the kids, and everyone joined in. Elise swung a soft pillow at everyone, and she was very much winning the pillow fight, almost too much. Her swings became quicker as her pillow became heavier. The water, as well as the pixies, turned from pretty pink to blood red. Even the music started to change. There were sounds of glass shattering, dirt crumbling, and nail scratching. The laughter slowly faded into soft screams that grew louder and louder. Until a very loud scream woke her up.

Elise had transformed into a werewolf, and she stood on the demolished grounds of where the gopher home once lay. That beast saw the carnage surrounded her, and she felt much worried. The home was destroyed, and the poor gopher family lay scattered across the area, lifeless and headless. Elise was terribly frightened! She fled from the scene and into the cold night, feeling oh so sorry for the gopher family.

The next day, that squirrel awoke from a quick nap and discovered that she was back in normal form, naked and covered in dirt. The transformation always ruined her clothes, but the only thing that always survived was her stretchy beanie hat. She covered her nakedness with some leaves, and she continued to travel through the forest, right after she cleaned herself of blood and dirt by bathing in a river. She was still shaken by the horrible scene from yesterday, and she promised herself to never do such a thing again.

Later that evening, Elise came across a family of chipmunk lumberjacks who were cutting down trees with axes. After tearing down a towering tree, one of the chipmunks spotted her and, without hesitation, rushed toward her with an ax. She became frightened. They might have heard of her murderous acts and wanted justice for her crimes!

Elise was mistaken. That particular chipmunk merely offered her a buttery biscuit he had in his pocket. He thought the pretty yet mangy squirrel was hungry. She didn't accept it. She was in no mood for fluffy and buttery treats.

The rest of the boy's family began to surround the naked squirrel, offering her things such as fruit and pastry goodies and clothes. Elise refused the offers and told them to go away. She wanted to be alone. Just then, thunder boomed in the sky, and rain started to fall on their heads. Elise then had to seek shelter, alone.

The mother noticed her lonely intentions and said, "Are you crazy, little lady? You'll catch your death out here in the rain. Come and spend the night in our cozy home."

What was with the kindness of others lately? Everyone treated Elise with gracious hospitality, as if she were a royal princess. Perhaps Beverly Pines was full of nice folks that treated everyone neighborly.

Elise, once again, accepted an invitation to stay in a house. That time it was under the condition that she stays awake until the rain stopped. Then she would leave, which was fine, and no questions were asked.

The chipmunk family took her into their home and gave her some warm clothes right after she took a hot bath. As agreed, the family kept her awake by giving her coffee and by playing loud and obnoxious yodeling radio stations. Staying awake through terrible music was an annoyance to endure, yet a helpful one.

It was then midnight, and the chipmunks were quietly in their rooms, unlike Elise, who stared blankly at the rain through a window. It continued to pour down on the land. Every minute the radio played another yodeling song, and she would bang her head against the window. The rain just wouldn't stop.

She then heard the sounds of footsteps creeping up behind her. She turned her head and saw that it was the chipmunk lad she had met before. He happened to have a soft spot for the squirrel. Since they were alone, he thought it was the perfect time to woo her with stories. His stories were his accomplishments in sports and the art of wood sculpting. He turned down the radio, approached her, and started chatting away. He didn't even give her a chance to speak.

He babbled on and on until he put his arm around her and offered her warmth. She became too bored and too tired to notice anything. The coffee was wearing off, and her eyelids began to shut. She believed that resting her eyes for one second wouldn't do any harm.

She closed her eyes, and what felt like a second was more than she expected. She felt peaceful, content, and hungry. Her eyes opened shortly after, and she found herself standing in the middle of the shallow river in her werewolf form. Twigs and rocks flowed through her wet feet, and in her hand she held a severed spine, while she held a meaty rib cage in the other. She'd done it again. She had murdered another kind family.

She didn't want to believe it, but the river of blood and bones proved otherwise. Alongside the river stood witnesses to the horror. The little critters were scared of the savage monster and screamed for help. Elise had to get away before she had the urge to silence them all. She leaped out of the water like a frog and jumped through the trees like a monkey, fleeing once again into the night.

The next day, Elise woke up as a regular squirrel and did the same routine. She cleaned herself of dirt and blood and found more leaves to cover her body. Even after bathing in another river, she still smelled like a stinky murderer. The poor squirrel was also becoming ill, for large bones and chunks of unchewed meat were stuck in her small belly.

It felt like knives were scraping her insides. She had to rest by a rock and figure out how to get the bones out before they could cause more damage later. She stuck her dirty hands in her mouth and tried make herself puke out the bones. Suddenly she heard a loud honking noise.

Out from the bushes came a little wagon full of circus clowns! The wagon stopped beside her, and out came a group of smiling, colorful clowns that were mainly hedgehogs and squirrels. The creatures saw the squirrel looking so sad, so they decided to cheer her up with flashy antics. They fooled around with horns and sprayed one another with soda to make her smile.

Elise was in no mood to smile. She told them to go away and leave her alone. Just as the clowns became sad, the circus manager came out of the wagon, wearing a zany red outfit and a tall top hat. That flashy squirrel ordered the clowns to stop while he talked to the girl.

"What's wrong, little lady?" he asked her. "Life's got ya down? Terrified of clowns? Well, we have other attractions to offer at Willy's Crazy Circus! My name's Mr. Willy, by the way. Let us take you down to the show so you can be dazzled by our stupendous performers!"

Elise just couldn't be left alone. If she didn't come clean, they would just drag her off, and the cycle of death would continue. With a sigh and grunt, she made them look at her mangy fur and bulging belly. She told them she was a werewolf with a transformation disorder, and it would be their funerals if they took her along.

The clowns were spooked to be in the presence of a monster. They screeched and ran around and bumped into one another. Some of them became so frustrated that they threw pies and poked at one another's eyes. While they were acting like idiots, Willy became intrigued. Strangely intrigued.

He wondered if she was really a monster or a crazed lunatic. Either way, she made his clowns twice as funny. He wasn't going to leave her alone. He intended to take her to his circus, to lift her spirits or market her misfortune, whichever came first.

Mr. Willy assured her that everything would be all right. Then he took out a frying pan from his jacket and knocked her unconscious. The blow to the head knocked her out cold, and they dragged her off to their destination.

Later that evening, she started to come back around, but all she saw was total darkness. She heard the sounds of chains rattling and children laughing as well as howls and even more annoying clown horns. It quickly escalated to nightmarish screams. It was hard to describe what was happening, but all she felt at that moment was anger. In the middle of it all, she could hear the soft sounds of her mother calling her name, telling her to stop and to open her eyes.

Elise was amazed to hear her voice once again. She wanted to talk to her, but the voice only told her to stop and open her eyes and nothing more. Elise opened her eyes slowly and saw many blinding lights around her. She looked around and saw that she was in a big tent that used to be filled with joy. However, because of her, it was only a bloody scene of faceless corpses and severed clown heads.

Feelings began to come back to her, and she felt devastating sorrow and emotional pain. The werewolf fell to her knees and cried for the innocent families she had just killed. While she cried, small claps were heard from the empty stands. There were two squirrels that enjoyed the monster's performance and cheered for an encore. Who else would be so dark and so ghoulish than the two vampires, Aval & Evel?

Elise stood on her hind legs and eyed the two creeps. She wanted to rip them apart, but instead, she ran toward the exit to avoid confrontation. As soon as she dashed, Evel flew off and landed on the monster's big head and asked her where she was going. Elise shook her off and became really enraged. She turned her massive hand into a fist and launched a punch toward Evel. Before it hit the vampire's face, Aval appeared from a black cloud of dust and caught the fist with his bare hand. It was like stopping a charging bull in its tracks.

Elise's werewolf form had the remarkable strength to stop a speeding car head-on, but it wasn't enough to move those two squirrels. With that much strength, Aval & Evel could simply stop a speeding truck. Well, possibly, if they wanted to. I haven't known Aval & Evel to do jackass stunts. Either way, it was a fight Elise could not win. Aval calmly pushed her fist away and told her to relax, but now she was determined to destroy them.

With a mighty roar, she launched a swift kick at the vampires. They did not stand for that; they vanished right before her sharp toenails even touched their fur. Elise only kicked a cloud of dust, and the force was so strong that she flung herself in midair.

Before she hit the ground, Aval reappeared and punched her straight into a wooden pillar! She hit the object hard and fell face first on the ground, where Evel awaited to restrain her with her mystic shadow control. Elise's arms and legs were stuck to the ground. She couldn't break the hold no matter how much she struggled. The powers of a werewolf were incredible, but compared to a vampire, there were certain limits.

"Let me go, you freaks!" Elise yelled.

Evel looked at Aval with a smirk. "Well, isn't that the hunchback calling the priest grotesque? Can you believe her? We're the freaks. Just let me get out my little mirror to compare—oh wait, no reflection..."

"Evel, please focus," Aval said as he walked toward the creature. "I'm interested to know how this werewolf transformed without a full moon in the sky." He observed the beast closely. Looking at the similar structure and the funny-looking hat, he immediately recognized her as Barbosa's daughter.

It has been years since either of them had seen Elise. The whole speculation and altercation could've been avoided if she had just talked instead of growled. Elise had nothing to say to them; they were the ones who broke their own peace, but she was no better.

She openly confessed to her night slaughters. She couldn't control her transformation, no matter what she did, and she couldn't take it anymore. Elise told the vampires to kill her. She wanted to die for her crimes.

Aval & Evel were surprised. They didn't see anything wrong with her condition; it was more of a thing to be desired. The power to terrorize the living in her sleep was beautiful. She could wake up refreshed with a clear mind and a full belly, but it wasn't beautiful to Elise at all. The poor folks of Beverly Pines were the victims of her misfortune.

The two vampires were more surprised. They admired her ignorance, for she didn't know the truth behind that certain forest. Evel released her from the clutches of her shadow, and the vampires planted their hands on Elise's huge shoulders.

Evel sighed. "Ah youth. How I miss those simple, NAÏVE days."

Elise became confused and said, "Didn't you hear me? I killed those innocent people. I'm a monster!"

"True that—you are," said Aval. "But they're not innocent. These vermin that infest these woods have a bad reputation that was never dealt with. They act nice to strangers, especially the younger ones. They offer them food and invite them to stay, but for what possible reason? Because they're just so darn kind? Listen to my words, little girl, they were going to violate your innocent body and bury you in their backyard."

"No, that can't be true," she said.

"Open your pupilless eyes, girl," Evel said as she slapped her shoulder. "You don't let strangers into your home, so why would they invite you? It's how they get their kicks. These mortals are the real monsters. They have a choice. We don't. This transformation disorder of yours was like a defense, a way to keep them at bay. Why are you so ashamed of your gifts?"

"Because I killed my mother!" Elise yelled at the two. "I have to live with that for the rest of my life!"

"Well, what a sad life you live in," Aval said as he paced the ground. "We killed our loved ones too. We got over it, because the hunger was something we couldn't control. Like black widows eating their mates, it's not a decision; it's just nature, freaky nature."

Between Dr. Derk, Barbosa, and the vampires, Elise did not know who to listen to anymore. Their views of right and wrong eluded her in so many ways, but she thought about everything that was said at that point. Seeing that she was lost in thought, the vampires decided to leave her alone to think.

Elise did not want them to leave just yet. She asked the vampires if they knew a solution to her sleeping problem and how to rid herself as a werewolf. The two answered most profoundly. They did not know, and they did not care. They accepted her as she was. If they could, couldn't she?

The two wished the best for her and flew away into the night. Elise sat in that empty tent and pondered and pondered about what they had said. Just then, she was struck with an idea. All that time she hated herself and wished to die, but what if she loved herself and embraced her powers?

It sounded crazy, cheesy, and a bit lame, but it was a shot she was willing to take. She closed her eyes and hugged herself, quietly being thankful for her gift. She thanked it for protecting her and making her young life more interesting. She stayed that way and repeated those words over and over until she felt like she actually meant it. She said it one last time, but that time it was from the bottom of her heart.

She opened her eyes and saw a miracle. She was back to her normal squirrel self. Her condition was cured, and all she had to do was love herself! She was overjoyed but slightly embarrassed by the sight of being naked again. Elise went to fetch some clothes quickly, for she had found a real mission to complete. She had to find some way to repay Aval & Evel for their generous advice. She hoped that her mother understood what she had to do.

A couple of days later, Elise returned to Dr. Derk and sat in that same chaise longue. That time, she sat upright and held a bowl of warm tomato soup with a smile. She told him about her week, about how she traveled blindly through a forest and how she almost got violated and murdered. She would've killed the whole population if it weren't for Aval & Evel's inspiring words of wisdom, about how she needed to love herself and such. Dr. Derk was glad to see that she was all well, but he was a bit disturbed by hearing the story.

Elise moved the bowl around in her hands and said, "It feels so nice to sleep without the worry of waking up with blood on these hands. Well, I still become a monster on a full moon, but I have more control over my hunger. Speaking of hunger, would you like some soup? I made it myself."

As strange as it was, Dr. Derk took the bowl for a quick sip and found it quite tasty. It made him feel so warm and refreshed.

"This is mighty kind of you," he said as he drank some more. "I must say, it hits the spot just right."

"I'm glad you like it, Doctor," she said. "I've been handing them out to the folks around here for free; it was rather chilly today."

"This is most generous of you, but why go through the trouble if it's not profitable?"

Elise stood from the couch and stretched her arms, knowing he would eventually bring up the talk of profit. Greed is a disease, and she wanted to cleanse it with acceptance and freedom. Everyone had to do so if the world could ever prosper.

She had a funny view of philosophy, and it practically confused the doctor when she said it. She stood there, silent, waiting to hear a comment come from his mouth. He had no idea what was going on. Then he caught her eyes gazing at his empty bowl of soup. The doctor looked at the bowl and then at her smirky face. He realized that it was a trick! He coughed and panicked at the thought of being poisoned.

"Don't worry, there is no poison," Elise said to the mouse. "Just some tomato juice, garlic, some curry leaves, and tiny bits of my werewolf fur…that's right, little strands of my DNA are flowing through you, and by the next full moon, you and all the others will experience my curse."

"Ughh, but why?" He coughed. "I helped you and your father!"

Elise then grabbed a golden trophy off his bookshelf and said, "I know. We feel in control. I don't have mental problems anymore, which means we don't need you anymore!"

Whack!

She knocked the mouse unconscious with his own trophy. Elise then left his burrow with a smile on her face. She was successful at spreading her disease, and all she had left to do that day was return to her father.

On the dirty porch of her messy log house, Barbosa sat taking a nap in his rocking chair. When Elise woke him up, she noticed the displeased look in his eyes. She knew he was still angry at her, but she told him to listen. Barbosa needed to understand that her life wasn't easy. It was filled with grief and guilt, and she needed some time to cope with. She needed to get away, and she needed to find herself.

Barbosa understood that a long time ago, ever since he figured out she liked to sneak out of her room every weekend. He wanted to know the reason she bothered to come back that time. Well, her solution for everything was running from her problems, but not anymore. She had no other home to go to, and she wanted to be his little monster again.

She easily convinced him by telling him the same story of her travels and affecting the creatures with the werewolf curse. Barbosa was shocking and amazed. He couldn't believe that she actually did something that benefited their lives. At that moment, he couldn't have been happier to call her his daughter. The two squirrels hugged for a moment—for what seemed like an eternity—and went back into their little home. They knew that everything was going to be OK. Forget the past and live in the now, as some would say.

Another Saturday night arrived, and on Lesion Island sat the lonely Weegee. He wondered why he was the only one at the monster meeting. He sat quietly near the campfire, hoping a single soul would show up, when along came a bird from the trees. Weegee saw that it was Raven, the wishing raven. Everyone thought she was dead, but she was very much alive and well.

She pestered the swamp creature and asked him if he was going to join the monster regime. Everybody else was doing it, enjoying it in fact, but that quiet swamp creature still decided to stay out of it. He knew the others would come back to their senses and return to the island, eventually.

The raven smirked, and she said to the creature, "They are already doomed and rotten to the core. Soon life on this planet will continue nevermore."

5

BOOGEYMAN BARNEY

The monsters have come back from the darkness and were already spreading their dreadful fear. All the critters from across the land were terrified to even leave their homes. Day or night, there was no telling what creatures of terrible horrors lay just around the corner.

Parents found it impossible to make their children sleep. Telling them not to be frightened and promising them that everything would be all right hardly worked at all. The children knew there were monsters out there. Instead of playing outside as they used to do, they spent the days cowering under their sheets. They were afraid that a bloodthirsty beast would get them and take their lives away.

On one of those cold and sleepless nights in Nevermore, a family of squirrels worried about their troubled teenaged son. His name was Rick; he wasn't able to sleep after hearing about monsters wreaking havoc upon the land. With each passing night, he feared that it might be his last. It was hard to believe, for Rick had the appearance of a hard-core-metal lover. Yes, even tough squirrels like him quivered in terror in times such as that.

His parents didn't know what to do with their complex child. Just then the mother thought of something that could work. It was a bit unorthodox, but it may have been the solution for his troubles. She told Rick to go to his happy place; he needed to go back to his wonderland.

As long as she could remember, Rick used to close his eyes and escape reality by going to that special land, inside his creative little mind. He had happy little imaginary friends that would play with him and a colorful little world where everything tasted like cotton candy. Seeing him play in an imaginary world was certainly strange from a regular person's perspective, but he was happy, and that's all that ever mattered to kids.

Alas, he'd grown into a full-fledged teenager with a certain love for metal music and all things hard-core. His innocence was gone. He threw away his bright-colored clothes and wore only torn dark ones. He pierced his ears, dyed his fur from gray to red, and grew a spiked Mohawk too. He did it to be cool, and he did it to impress the girls.

Despite his appearance, he couldn't really fit in anywhere. He was just a troublemaking poseur who grew to care for nothing but his own life. Some would guess he would find some interest in the recent disturbance, but deep inside, he was scared like the rest of the critters.

He couldn't return to his wonderland. He knew it was never real. Though in times where life was scary all around, it never did hurt to take one's mind off it. Rick finally decided to go back, so he concentrated hard and hoped to return to that special place he once knew.

He tried to imagine, but soon he fell sound asleep. His parents heard him snore, and they were glad to hear those peaceful sounds. At that moment, Rick was drifting away into dreamland. It was dark at first, as all dreams started. He found himself floating in a dark void that soon turned to a flash of bright white. The brightness blinded him for only a second, and then his vision became clear. He was descending to a land that was not full of joy and wonder, but instead, nothing. All he could see for miles was a clean white land of nothingness. The only thing that stood as a significant object was a black tree with one swing hanging from a branch.

As soon as he landed softly on his feet, Rick walked toward the strange tree to investigate. Once he got close, he noticed that the swing was occupied by a slender man in a dirty black-and-gray suit. He was twice the size of Rick, and the body resembled no type of woodland creature he knew but close to that of a human. The man swung away, humming a little tune that the boy remembered from his childhood. The man stopped humming and swinging when he sensed a curious creature watching his every move.

Rick walked to the side to see who and what was on the swing. The face he saw was rather disturbing. The strange man had the palest of white skin, and his eyes were stained with black paint. His eyes looked painfully tired and dreadfully veiny. Below his stitched neck was a body covered in dark gray rashes. It was as if he were diseased and it was too late to save the previous head.

The man was completely monochrome. He showed not one ounce of color, even on his torn and stitched clothing. Everywhere from his messy black-and-gray hair and his torn tie that showed a creepy smiley face to his spiked black belt that featured a fiendish upside-down face and even to his open-toed shoes that resembled sad demons with stripped socks for tongues.

He had no eyebrows or ears at all, but he did have a pointy nose like a mosquito. He had a mouth that contained the tongue of a snake and the teeth of a shark. He had a long striped tail that resembled the curl of a chameleon's tail.

His key feature was his menacing grin, which stretched to the outside of his face, and he always seemed to be smiling. The right side of his face had a long stitch that ran from his mouth to his open scalp, which was punctured with nails. Nails were not only in his head but also in his back, tail, and abdomen; they acted like buttons on his suit. He felt they were as painless as natural hair. This creature clearly did not look kind natured; he resembled something that escaped from a twisted Halloween cartoon in the 1930s.

That creature slowly turned his head to the squirrel while maintaining his strange grin. He said to him in an eerie tone, "Salutations, Rick. Welcome back to Wonderland."

The boy was shocked. The stranger knew his name. How did he know? Who was he really? The man revealed himself to be Rick's old imaginary friend, Barney.

He was his first friend he ever had in his life. They played sports in the front yard and played checkers on tables, and they even shared a daily meal of pancakes together. Those were their favorite type of food. Rick and Barney were inseparable and were the best of friends, but the creature he saw did not look like Barney at all.

Rick remembered him as a clean, chubby, silly man, full of color. He didn't know what he was looking at now, other than a creepy stranger whom parents warn children to stay away from. The creature told Rick once again that he was Barney. He just changed, as Rick did.

He then stood from the swing and offered to push his old buddy on it. Rick hesitated for a moment, but he couldn't see the harm in it; it was a dream after all. He sat down; he adjusted his tail, and Barney began to push him softly in the air, like the good old days. A few seconds later, Rick asked the slender fellow where his wonderland had gone.

Barney pushed him a bit higher and answered, "You're looking at it. It's not as glamorous as it was before, but time had passed, and now it's just an empty space."

"But this makes no sense," said Rick. "It couldn't have changed this fast. The last time I was here wasn't even that long ago."

"He-he, you don't know time, Ricky," Barney chuckled as he pushed him even higher. "It's been ten years since your last visit. In here, it was literally a thousand years…as long as I've been imprisoned in the back of your mind with your 'other' playmates. Listening to them giggle fifty times a minute and watching them practice musical numbers every hour on the hour. It was all delightful at first. I had no choice but to endure. My, how you've grown into a fine young man. What's your secret for that rough fur? Dirt? Sand? A lawn mower?"

"Barney, quit messing around and tell me what happened already."

Barney stopped the swing immediately, giving Rick a chance to leave his seat and face him. The creepy friend still smiled. Never did he show a frown. He started to rub his dirty hands, for he felt uncomfortable telling Rick what was going on in his own mind, though he proceeded anyway.

The cause was simple. In the early years of innocence, at the younger stages of life, children used their minds to create a wide variety of imaginations, such as wild ideas, fantasy worlds, and even imaginary friends. It was a time when nothing could change it, but many years later, as they become more accustomed to the harsh world, it all disappears.

For the sake of fitting in with society, they succumb to peer pressure, interests so dark, and corrupt thoughts ever so foul. They leave their childhood behind while their imaginations, as well as their dreams, become lost and twisted into the very things they become. It's called growing up.

In the process, Rick forgot all about Barney. He filled his head with impure thoughts, and his imaginary world became distorted and corrupted from the inside. It became nothing more than a wasteland of sadness, regret, pain, hatred, lust, and the insufferable sounds of metal music echoing through the land.

Just talking about his thousand-year torture made Barney twitch. It made his eyes bleed with black blood. His head began to shake uncontrollably, and the black liquid began to gush. That was when his head exploded into goo!

Rick jumped back in shock and desperately tried to clean Barney's blood from his face. He had no idea Barney was that upset. Barney's headless body did not fall to the ground; it remained perfectly still. Then it moved; it stuck its left hand into the squishy neckhole, and it pulled out the exact same head. Barney smiled and apologized for the sickening display. He couldn't help it. He was the result of Rick's horrible mind, after all. Barney stepped over the swing with a peculiar look and started to walk toward the nervous squirrel. Rick saw the strange look in his eye, as if he was about to harm him.

Rick stepped away from the creature and said, "Barney, I just wanted to move onto other things. I didn't mean to cause you pain."

"Pain? He-he, you don't know about pain either." Barney chuckled as he continued to creep toward the boy. "You slit your wrists and bite your tail, but that's not pain; that's just self-pity. You know when you fantasize about making love to females, and I can't do a thing but watch? That's going beyond pain, Ricky, that's just torture. This mind of yours tortured me all these years, but now that you're here, I'd say it's time for some good old-fashioned...revenge."

Barney's eyes sank back into his skull, and the empty sockets bled black goo to his shoes. He reached deep into the oozing holes and slowly pulled out two sharp and crooked knives. He stepped toward the boy with the wicked knives, laughing while he did. Rick began to quiver right before he wet his pants.

It was certain he was doomed, but he remembered that it was all a dream. He could do whatever he wanted. So before Barney was able to strike the boy, Rick closed his eyes and imagined the monster's fate. He opened his eyes, looked up, and from the sky came a ray of hot red energy. It touched down on Barney like a bright spotlight, and it disintegrated the evil creature from the face of existence. The ray of judgment had ceased, and all that was left was a burned circle that stained the white ground. Rick's imaginary friend was no more.

Rick woke from the nightmare, and he was back in his room. The experience left him breathless and covered in sweat, yet he was glad that it was over. From there, he decided to forget about his old happy place and create a new one for him to escape to. Something he could really get into, like a musical world filled with cold beer and hot women.

Just as he started to imagine, he heard a sudden bump. A loud bump that came from under his bed. The scared squirrel shook with fright; he leaned his head to the side of the bed and looked under to see, but there was nothing. Just lint and his usual mess of old books.

That weird dream must have made him more paranoid than ever. He lifted himself up and looked around the room to catch anything out of the ordinary, other than his grotesque posters and plastic medieval weapons. It was all the same, but then he felt a chilling breeze that blew behind his neck.

His window was open, revealing a bright full moon. In front of the window was a man covered in a silhouette shadow, and he was the size of a grown squirrel. Within that shadow showed two white glowing eyes and a bright grin that was stretched ever so wide. There was no doubt about it. Barney had returned.

"Salutations," Barney said as he shut the window with his tail.

Rick screamed and fell out of bed and onto the floor, pulling down the sheets. In a rush, he ran toward his door to escape, but the door wouldn't open or budge. He was trapped. He looked back and saw Barney still smiling in the light.

"Now, now, Ricky," he said, "don't be rambunctious. You don't want to wake your folks, do you? People need their beauty sleep, but I guess we can't relate."

"This has to be a dream," Rick said with his back against the door. "I killed you. You're supposed to be dead!"

"And yet I'm still standing," Barney said as he walked around the bed, watching the squirrel cringe in terror with every step he took. "Call it weird, but I was counting on you killing me. All I really wanted was an escape. So, when you destroyed me, it gave me a chance to manifest myself in your world as a physical being. I'm as real as you see me, and I'm here to stay."

Rick had to get rid of him fast. He reached for the nearest object he could find, which was a plastic iron mace. He threw it at the monster in hopes of plunging it into his skull, but Barney caught it just in time.

He laughed at the squirrel for throwing toys at him. Grasping it in his hands and expanding his mouth like a rubber band, Barney swallowed the weapon whole. He belched and said that it tasted just like blood. Then all of a sudden, long iron spikes sprang from his body in a spontaneous reaction.

They stuck out for a moment while they made his body bleed, until they were instantly retracted back into his body. His wounds were healed, yet his suit was full of holes. Barney could not be killed, for he was already dead inside and out. He welcomed violence and always had a good chuckle out of it. Rick broke down, dropped to his knees, and begged for the creature to spare him.

Barney shook his head in disappointment. "Tsk, tsk, all these hard-core goodies in your room, and you're still a coward at heart. You shouldn't be afraid, Ricky. Now that I'm free, we can relive the good old days by playing our favorite games...all night long."

Barney was serious, and he'd already made plans for a grand night of mischievous fun. He reminisced over the game of base-bomb, and he wanted to catch up on hide-and-go-slaughter. He also wanted to invite Rick's luscious English teacher for some musical Judas chairs. He knew she wouldn't mind at all, but first, he wanted to play a little jump rope.

Barney stuck his hands deep into his own belly and dug out a bloody rope of entrails! It all poured down to the floor, and he sorted them out to form a suitable rope. Barney whistled along as he played jump rope with his own organs. It freaked out the squirrel; he couldn't take watching such playful gore.

Once Barney offered to help Rick make his own jump rope, there was no doubt that Barney still wanted to kill him. With a scream, Rick ran toward the window and jumped through the glass! He fell and landed in the wet grass. Then that scared boy ran off into the cold woods and never looked back.

Barney walked to the broken window and watched him run. He just stood there smiling in a very calm manner. He knew where to find Rick, and he wouldn't escape his grasp. He was a part of Rick; he was his best friend and his worst nightmare. Like a genuine boogeyman who loved to hunt naughty children and make them suffer.

Deep within the woods, Rick ran so much that he had to catch his breath. He had to hide, but he didn't know where. His best bet was to climb to the tallest tree and conceal himself within the leaves. He found a big and sturdy one with lots of leaves to hide under, and he climbed up that tree as fast as he could. Rick silently lay in the center of the tree and looked around with caution, hoping nothing sinister would come his way. There was no sign of movement anywhere, only leaves swaying in the wind.

He felt safe as he gave out a relieving sigh; he decided to use that spot to hide out through the night. The young squirrel lay on his back and closed his eyes to rest. Then he felt a tingly feeling in his nose, a feeling that caused him to sneeze softly. His sinuses were getting to him.

After the sneeze, a distant and eerie voice called out to him, "Bless you!"

Rick thanked the voice, but then he gasped as his sinuses suddenly cleared up. The voice sounded all too familiar. Before he could do anything else, an unknown object flew from the shadows below and smashed into the tree with great force, causing it to break and fall. Rick fell down along with the huge tree and hit the ground so hard that it echoed throughout the area.

Dust dispersed, twigs and limbs shattered across the scene, and Rick suffered some damage in his left leg. He picked himself up and limped a few inches, but he fell down on his shoulder. He cried a little, but he didn't plan on staying there for long, so he decided to crawl. To his surprise, he found a spiked metal ball on the ground near him. A little thought came to him that it might have made the tree fall. Rick looked at the path ahead and saw a shadowy figure, where only its bright smile could be shone.

It was indeed Barney again. He was tossing a spiked ball up and down in his hand, menacingly. He thought about how Rick attacked him with a mace earlier, so Barney assumed the boy would be more comfortable if he played a sport similar to dodgeball: dodgemace.

The playful creature threw the spiked ball in the air and kicked it with his durable foot. He sent it flying toward Rick at incredible speed, and the squirrel was quick enough to roll to the side, neatly dodging the deadly ball. There was no time for crawling, so Rick picked himself up and limped away from the danger.

As he limped away, Barney conjured more balls from his stretchy sleeves like a magician and continued to kick and destroy everything near the squirrel. One by one, trees fell, and balls of death kept flying near him. The assault wouldn't stop. Barney wouldn't stop. He called out playful words Rick used to say to him as a kid. His voice was so clear and so close that if Rick didn't know any better, he could have sworn he was inside his head.

The boy kept running, but he constantly called the creature an illusion, a false image in his head that was the result of paranoia! Suddenly, Rick lost his balance, and he tripped himself into a muddy ditch. The squirrel was too tired and weak to go on. He closed his eyes and whimpered for Barney to leave him alone and let him be.

Barney had the squirrel right where he wanted him, but the creature was nowhere to be found. No sounds of creeping footsteps or voices in his head, just a breezy cold wind. Rick looked around and saw that Barney was really gone.

Was he going mad, or was Barney merely toying with him? Rick didn't know what to think anymore. All he wanted to do was get out of the woods and find help. He climbed out of the ditch and slowly walked along the trail, watching ever so closely for that grinning monster.

After not too long, he came to a steep hill in the woods, an awfully familiar hill. There he saw a flickering blue light at the top. Closer and closer he went toward the strange light; on closer inspection, it was merely an old bug zapper hanging from the porch of an old log trailer. The trailer sparked a memory in his head. His uncle, Hooper, resided there along with his other family. What a relief it was.

Rick ran toward the trailer and began to bang on the screen door, as he called his uncle's name. He continued to bang on the door until he saw someone approaching from the darkness. There came Uncle Hooper in his blue overalls and his scraggly-looking beard.

The old squirrel opened door and said, "Huy, yur depit pina pint pizza bwoy, ish benna dur?"

Rick had just remembered that his uncle spoke in pure country gibberish. It had been years since either of them had seen the other, so Hooper couldn't tell who that stranger was at his door. Rick had no time to make him remember. Rick shoved his way in, closed the door, and locked it tight. In the trailer, it was too dark to see anything. All he could see was furniture covered in plastic sheets and discarded pizza boxes left on the floor. He wondered where his cousins and aunt were, but his angry uncle seemed to be the main concern at the moment.

Rick quickly explained, "Uncle Hooper, I'm your nephew, Rick. I'm really cold, and I need a place to stay."

"Rick? Hita benn disha bin?" asked Uncle Hooper. "Doh der della bem persh, ten to twelve midnightah. Bewoy, git yo reddah tin ono bed sack."

"So what if it's late? I need a place to stay!" Rick still understood some of his language.

"Gedder bedder popo der?"

"No, I'm not running from the cops. It's, I don't know, some monster that's trying to kill me."

"Nonsters? Oh gawdam feggit night boos Aval & Evel!"

"It's not them! There's something else out there, something worse, and I don't know if it's real or not. I just need to hide here for a while."

Hooper took in his words and observed his nephew's muddy body. It came to him that the boy might have been crazy. He didn't know what to do or how to help him, but he didn't want him to stay in his house any longer. Rick didn't want to go out again, not that night, and the trailer was the only safe place he knew. So he pushed his uncle out of the way to find somewhere to hide.

Hooper yelled at him to get out of his house, but he was easily ignored. Rick ran to the left side of the trailer and went into an open room. He stepped through the door without hesitation, but instead of planting his feet on a wooden surface, he fell down a hole longer than the trailer itself. It wasn't steel or manufactured. It was dug by hand.

Rick slid down and found himself in a room he never knew existed. It was a room that had decayed metal tables, dirty marble floors, and torn steel walls. It was full of hooks, chains, saws, chainsaws, bloody body bags, jars of rotten organs, and a tub full of mutilated corpses. It was a butcher chamber that had so much meat and so many bones hanging from the walls like trophies. Rick shivered with absolute fear.

On a table next to him lay a rotten head of an old squirrel that was left for the flies to scavenge. It was the head of Uncle Hooper's wife! The sick sight made Rick throw up on the floor. He gagged in disgust. Then he heard a dinging sound in the room. To his right came Uncle Hooper out of a secret elevator. He stepped out with his hands on his overall straps and showed a look of disappointment. He didn't want anyone to know about his secret, not even his own family.

Hooper stood there and said, "Oh nevew, I frit 'n bit, ket in debber dew jim jam."

"Why, Uncle? Why?" Rick yelled. "Why the hell would you do this?"

Hooper stroked his beard and answered, "Yirr dimma judge me bwoy, ti is wuut finsy yur equla swa."

"No, I don't like any of this! You killed my aunt. You killed your own wife!"

"Mmm, heddet reddit gas gim loprim das 'n dat, bedded bertis def derby jergger jip."

"You butchered your own family for berries?"

"Well higgoit git furler feals, banjo 'n sus. Nata dim dretty dit dert, lager batter meat bag, Rick."

Hooper pushed a red button on a nearby wall, and it opened a huge meat grinder in the middle of the room. Hooper grabbed a long chain, and he slowly came after the boy. Rick ran, but there was no escape for the poor boy. Even the long hole he slid down from was too slippery to climb. He didn't have the stomach to fight his crazy uncle or the courage to reason with him. He was just a kid, wishing that he was back in his bed.

With little time he had left, he huddled himself into a corner, closed his teary eyes, and hoped his death would be a painless one. The crazed uncle inched closer to the scared squirrel with that rusty chain in his hands until something made him stop. Rick opened his eyes to discover that fiendish creature, Barney, was standing in front of his uncle.

When he saw him, he imagined the worst; even Hooper was shocked by the sight of an actual monster. It was a toss-up whom Barney would get first, though he faced neither Hooper nor Rick. He just stared out into space with his usual smile.

He was waiting for a response from the two, and Hooper was the first one to question who and what he was. No answer was spoken, just a slight shove to the uncle's chest. That one push sent Hooper falling into the bloody grinder below.

Bits of blood and bones scattered throughout the room, and the gears of the machine still turned. Hooper was gone, but the boy didn't know if he should thank Barney or be even more terrified. Barney turned to him with blood splattered across his face, grinning with cruel intentions.

"Barney, please don't kill me!" begged Rick. "I know I was wrong. I'll never ignore you again!"

Barney chuckled. "Ricky, it's much too late for that. A thousand years too late. You'd rather settle for cannibals who kill for money. You have no one else, you have no friends, just you and your slowly dying parents. It's best that I save you the trouble and put you out of your lonely misery."

"Barney! You're the only one I could ever call a friend!" Rick stopped Barney in his tracks. "You were the only friend I had. I missed playing with you and eating pancakes with you. I just became this punk to fit in with the other punks. Now I got this bad rep, and I have no one to hang out with anymore. I was wrong for leaving my peaceful world and replacing it with death metal. I missed you, Barney; I want to go back to those innocent days when we were friends. Please be my friend again."

Rick's words, his change of heart, and the mention of pancakes made Barney cry black tears of joy. He was truly touched that his old friend realized his mistake and wanted to go back to the way things were. He walked over to the boy, helped him up from the floor, and gave him a soft and gentle hug.

"That's the old Rick I used to know," Barney said with a grand smile. "Now, let's get out of here. I know you have school in the morning, and we can start off the day with some hot pancakes."

"What? You don't want to play anymore?" asked Rick. "Isn't that what you wanted?"

"No," he said. "You misunderstood my definition of 'play.' At any rate, it's over, and we must get you back home. School should be nicer than this butcher room, I assume. Oh, don't you have a test in biology soon?"

"Well, actually, we're studying…that thing, in that orange tube across the room." Rick then pointed at an obscure object on the other side of the grinder.

Barney turned and tried to see what it was. Was it a liver or a stomach? It was hard to tell, so Barney wanted to take a closer look. Rick, on the other hand, had other plans. He found it apparent that the slender fiend had no place in his life. Not then, not ever. He waited until Barney was completely distracted, and then underneath his breath, Rick said his good-bye to his old childhood friend.

He kicked Barney from behind and watched him fall down into the meat grinder. Rick covered his face from the mutilated chunks of black goo that flew from the metal spikes. The monster that plagued his night and the insane uncle who butchered his family were both gone. His nightmares were no more. He'd survived. He fell back on the floor in relief, feeling glad to be alive. He could go home.

It was a long journey out of that house of sins and through the woods of chaotic wrecks, but he eventually found his way back to Nevermore. When he arrived, he noticed that the morning sun rose rather early. Children were out playing in the fields before school. What's more, the sun shone wondrously through the leaves of his treelike home.

He felt refreshed to see a shred of blissful and heavenly surroundings. He swore he would give up his punk style and go back to being a normal boy. He stood on his doorstep, feeling ever so thankful to be home as he rubbed the door with his hands. He turned the knob and walked in.

He snuck through the door and went upstairs to take a shower to wash away everything, from the dirt and blood to his red fur, and soon enough he became gray again. He later combed his fur to an appropriate curly style and removed his piercings to become a completely new Rick. He changed his clothes from black rags to a brown shirt, blue khakis, and dark-brown shoes.

He felt so right; he couldn't help but put on a smile and start the new day. Strangely, he didn't feel tired at all. He was as chipper as a songbird. He made his way downstairs and saw his loving parents in the kitchen. His dad was reading the weekly paper while his mom was cooking a hearty breakfast.

Rick made his way into the room, and his parents were happy to see their son as chipper as ever. Rick sat at the table near his dad, and his mom placed a plate of steaming hot, buttery pancakes in front of him. She happily drowned the dish with lots of gooey maple syrup and powdered sugar.

Rick grabbed his fork and knife and dug right into the sweet morning goodness. The first bite was grand, and many more followed. He couldn't believe how good it tasted and how good he felt deep inside.

With a marvelous burst of happiness, he shouted, "These pancakes are delicious! These pancakes are amazing! These pancakes are delicious! Pancakes...pancakes...*yum!*"

He and his family were happy—too happy, unnaturally happy. Something was wrong, terribly wrong. Rick couldn't see the reality around him. In his deluded mind, he was enjoying breakfast with his family, but in reality, he was strapped and locked in a softly padded room, deep within a mental facility. Outside of his room was a concerned squirrel doctor and a police bird; they couldn't believe a boy that young could lose his mind so suddenly.

"Amazing," said the doctor. "He keeps rambling on and on about pancakes, and he never lets down a smile. A very strange case we have here. How did this happen?"

The officer answered, "Well, it all started when we got a call from his parents. They witnessed him in his bedroom freaking out for no reason. We thought it was nothing serious, but they said he broke through his window and went off hollering and screaming through the woods. We decided to track him down. We got a tip from some moose family. They said the boy took a nap on their antlers. Then he yelled at them, saying that they weren't real, that they were all in his head! Classic loon, but here's where it got serious. We spotted him at his uncle's place, only to find him thrashing his kinfolk around. Suddenly he kicks his dear old aunt, in a wheelchair mind you, down a hill. She had a slight back injury, nothing real bad, but I served her justice when I beat that boy senseless. We couldn't put him in jail though, because he responded to nothing but pancakes. That's why I brought him here to you. I felt like I bashed his head too hard."

"After hearing such a story, I highly doubt you were the cause of this condition," said the doctor. "Tsk, tsk, kids today. When they're not destroying property, they're destroying themselves. Thank you, Officer. I'm sure we have many tests to go through before we can cleanse this one."

Rick smiled on, but he soon started to cry and laugh at the same time. He was obviously in pain deep inside. Rick was blocked from reality and had to forever live in a world of lies, for his heaven was a shrouded version of an inescapable hell. That same isolated torture was the true measure of Barney's revenge.

The next day, a troubled hedgehog girl sat on a swing set in an abandoned playground. She was shunned by society, because she'd fallen in with a bad crowd. She sat on that swing, minding her own business, hardly swinging at all. Suddenly she felt like she wasn't alone anymore. On the swing to her right appeared a slender man in a dirty suit.

He turned to her with his sharklike grin and politely said, "Salutations…"

From there, the boogeyman was born and was set free to the world. Call it unlikely if you wish, but it was true. That manifested entity was free from Rick's mind, and he began haunting naughty children just to brighten his smile.

This new boogeyman was a psychological manifestation of what could be described as pure fear. He had the ability to appear in creatures' minds and scare them out of their wits, but he could not physically harm them. What he could do was haunt their psyches and trick them to make them believe everything around them was real. He played with them and trapped them in an inescapable world, or he simply killed them cleanly to create a mindless drone. Either method he chose enabled him to replace their inner beings with insane versions of their former selves.

In the end, the mind was damaged beyond repair. His victims suffer inside and out, just like Rick. Barney's method of torture was a little complicated compared to the usual scare-and-slash monster, but that's what made him so special. Fear and madness were his greatest weapons.

A vague memory or a haunting ghost?
He is a friend born from a nightmare.
Imaginary and never seen by most,
he is a shadow that lives to scare.

Like innocence in a child's mind,
it grows ever darker and less kind.
He is there when no one's around;
he creeps near you without a sound.

Boogeyman Barney is his name;
he thrives to drive children insane.
He detaches all truth from reality
and offers a life within insanity.

What would you do in a final stand,
if you should ever face this boogeyman?

6

CHILDHOOD RUINED

The number six—what a strange number that number six was and how it haunted the vampire Aval to this day. Wherever he went, he always saw the number six. From old report cards to the book chapters he read in a day, to the number of pants and boots he had in his six-layered closet.

There would be six berries left in a bag and six cups available in the kitchen cabinet. Patterns on the window curtains symbolized various sixes; strings of fur left on his shower wall curled into sixes, and even the curl of his tail resembled the number six.

Six, six, six.

It felt like some sort of omen every time he came face-to-face with that number. He couldn't figure out why such a number kept showing itself to him. Then on a certain night, content in his living room chair for hours on end, he suddenly felt the need to get up and move. Tired and bored, he decided to rummage through his pants pockets for his pocket watch.

There, he felt a small object in the right side, but it wasn't a watch. He took it out and discovered that it was a tiny piece of paper, with the number six written on it, plain as day. That tiny piece of paper began to stir panic into his heart. Aval tossed the cursed paper away and flew out the balcony window, letting the travel of flight be his means of easing his troubled mind.

Once all was silent, Evel came from the kitchen corner, giggling and smirking. She hinted the number six many times that night just to drive Aval batty. She found it funny, but her joy did not last, because she realized that she was laughing alone. Lonesomeness made her feel depressed among all things.

She walked toward the open balcony and looked at the dreary yet lovely cemetery. The view became questionable since the yard was covered with Frankenstein soldiers. A squadron of them were guarding the vampires' home with guns, flamethrowers, and rocket launchers with a great amount of patience. Their yellow eyes were carefully on watch for intruders, but their brains were still in a fuzz, for their grunting was their only way of communicating. She couldn't really have nice conversations with military zombies.

Evel folded her arms on the rail and let out a low sigh, longing for someone to cherish the moments and someday use her same tricks on others. She was not thinking of friends or long-dead relatives but something much closer—a child.

She always regretted never bearing children of her own. The reason was that she and Aval were vampires. Being the cold corpses that they were, their specific organs couldn't properly function to create a child of their own. Even if by some miracle they had, it could never age or grow. Ergo, having a child was a wishful dream.

It was very sad, very tragic. Evel always thought that having a child would give them true happiness. If Barbosa could raise one, then surely Evel could as well. She knew she was parent material, and she knew she could be the greatest mother squirrel in the world! She then knew what she had to do: she had to find a child of her own.

Later that night, a little after anyone's bedtime, Evel patrolled the quiet homes of Nevermore. She saw many children who were sound asleep in their cozy beds. So cute they were and so very tiny, it was like looking through the windows of pet shops. Evel was looking for the prefect child to raise and care for, maybe two or even three or possibly four.

She soon came across a house that had a little black-and-white squirrel snuggled tight in a red race-car bed. It was a little boy whose room was covered with many cartoon posters and tiny little toys lying on the floor. Evel sensed wondrous energy coming from that child. The boy looked so pure and innocent; he was perfect for her to mold and shape into a vile little vampire.

A while later, the boy began to toss and turn under his sheets. He felt an unfamiliar discomfort. He woke in an instant and saw that he was lying in a red padded coffin the whole time. He was scared, and he wanted to get out of it. He pushed open the coffin door, and his fear grew even more when he discovered that the room was not his at all. He was in a windowless room covered in strange drapery hung from the walls. It was the bedroom of the vampire squirrels.

Evel sprang next to the child and spontaneously greeted him by saying, "Good evening, sleepy poo!"

The boy screamed at the top of his lungs, "Ahhh! A vampire! Mom! Dad! Help!"

"No, no, no! Don't be frightened!" Evel said. "I'm not going to hurt you, so there's no need to wake the dead. Oh, listen to me, I sound like a cliché."

"I-I want my mommy and daddy!" He started to cry. Evel came over to wipe his tears with a purple handkerchief, and she did her best to calm him down.

"It's all right, little one. Monsters are not bad. We are not all that way; people just exaggerate. They say we're too scary, too frightening. Even your parents couldn't take the sight of me. Why, when I kindly offered them a freshly baked pie, they fled the town and abandoned you in that little room of yours."

"Th-they left me? You're lying! You want to drink my blood!"

"Trust me, if I did, I would've done it already. I am a kind vampire. I love children like you, and I will care for you in your time of abandonment. I'll raise you to be an extraordinary gentleman. You'll learn fine values from my experience, and soon you'll be the crown jewel of this little tree nest. I even brought you some breakfast to start off the night."

Evel presented him a tray of cereal and orange juice, to show kindness to the child. She eagerly waited for him to take the tray and eat, but out of sheer fear, the boy knocked the tray on her face.

Evel was covered in a wet mess, and she did not find it funny at all. It was indeed off to a rocky start, but she knew the boy would come around to liking his new mother, one way or another. Before she changed to drier clothes, she tied that boy to a chair and sealed his mouth with duct tape. She was not going to torture the boy for misbehaving; he just had to get used to a new environment.

Evel entertained him and catered to his every need: mandatory feeding, music records for kids, and the occasional waste disposal. What more could a child ask for? She was off to a great start on the first night, yet dawn began to rise, and she figured the child needed some sleep. What better way to put a young mind to rest than with some good old bedtime stories.

Evel flew downstairs to her dusty bookshelf and took out all the classics. She always wanted to read a child to sleep. The boy, still tied and muzzled to the chair, had just enough strength to scratch his way through some of the rope. It would not help though, because when Evel came back upstairs, she informed him that if he were to escape, she would cut off the very things that made it possible. Evel wanted him to stay and behave and to understand that the ones who really care do acts most wicked to strengthen them for the real world. Tough but fair she was.

But the world was full of bad creatures that would harm others for no real reason. Such as the first book she presented to him. It was called *Little Red Riding Hood*. A tale of a young girl in a red hood, traveling across the land to give her dear sweet grandmother a basket of goodies while avoiding a big bad wolf. It seemed nice enough to read.

Evel grabbed a little chair and sat next to the boy and began to read it out loud. While she read, she felt the need to expose the dark side of the story. She told the tale of an innocent girl in shady attire, who was sent to deliver food to her starving grandmother, who was hopelessly abandoned in the far reaches of a wicked forest. Her home was surrounded by lurkers that preyed on the old woman every passing night.

Kindly thinking about her grandmother, the little hooded girl decided to visit her and bring her food when no one else would, carelessly forgetting about the dangers that lay ahead. Through her travels in the woods of noir, she was being watched by a sneaky wolf with the intentions of a sadistic stalker. That terrible creature had malicious thoughts as soon as he first laid eyes on that girl and her basket of goodies. He would've done whatever it took to eat both.

His ways were not so simple, as far as being twisted goes. That big bad wolf went so far as dressing up as the girl's grandmother and silently waited in her bed just to fool the girl. When the little girl came inside her grandmother's home, she could not tell the difference. The big eyes her grandmother had, the big nose her grandmother possessed, and the sharp teeth stored in her slobbering mouth still left the girl in a wonder. She was terribly naïve, for hindsight was not her best quality.

Before the wolf could fool the girl one last time, which would surely end in blood, a crazed huntsman with an ax busted through the window and chopped off the wolf's head! Who was he? Why did he help the girl? Evel explained that he had a vendetta with the wolf and did not care for the girl at all.

When all was said and done, the little girl had to know what happened to her dear sweet grandmother. She noticed a wrinkled hand hanging out of the wolf's gushing neck. The girl realized that her task to deliver food and see an old loved one again was all for naught. The moral of the story was to always be cautious, because the world was a cruel and dark place for anyone to travel alone and live alone in.

Once Evel finished, she could see that the child was not asleep but rather in a state of shock. She knew how to fix that. She went to a nicer book that taught a nicer lesson.

Goldilocks and the Three Bears was the next book. A tale of a wandering girl with blond hair that was as golden as the sun, stumbling across a house that was owned by a family of bears. The girl just had to go inside the house and snoop around for whatever reason, probably out of boredom. Goldilocks was just as dumb as Little Miss Red but a bit more troublesome.

She looked around and found that the house was completely deserted. She then caught a whiff of an enticing aroma that made her tummy growl with hunger. She entered the kitchen, and to her surprise, there were three sets of porridges sitting on the table, ready to be devoured.

Evel had to wonder why a family would not only leave their home unlocked but also leave untouched food on the table. Well, the truth was that the three bears left to take a walk while their meal cooled off. It seemed awfully silly, since they could've cooled the hot food with their own breath. I guess for the sake of a story, it's best not to ask questions and just go with it.

Anyway, Evel continued to tell how the girl immediately made herself at home. She ate the three bowls and found that one was too scorching, the next was too chilly, and the last was just right. Then she sat in their different-size chairs and slept in their different-style beds that were too huge, too doughy, and of course just right. It would have been interesting to know how their bathroom might have looked.

Evel thought out loud. "The first toilet was too hairy, the second toilet was too bubbly, and the third toilet was just too pissy."

The bears soon returned to see that their home was completely trashed. Their food was eaten or scattered across the table and floor. All furnishings were tampered with and felt overused. The family soon caught the girl sleeping in the baby bear's bed. The girl woke up with a shock and jumped out the window and ran away.

Evel saw it as unrealistic, and she felt the need to twist the ending a bit. She ended the story with a grisly encounter between the defenseless intruder and the hungry beasts. In the end, the bears' bellies were whole, and the girl got what she deserved. The moral of the story was to never trespass in someone's home, or else bad things will happen.

Evel looked up. The boy was still awake, but this time he looked a tad disturbed. So ditching the books in hand, she decided to tell a short story she knew by heart.

"Five Little Monkeys Jumping on the Bed" was the name. It was a simple tale of hyperactive monkeys jumping around on, well, a bed. One would fall on the floor and bump his head, and the mom would tell them no more jumping on the bed. The rhyme would just repeat from there as the next monkey did the same. Evel felt the need to spice it up. She told that when a monkey fell from the bed, he would bump his head on an explosive land mine. Yep, land mine, because she figured boys liked explosions.

Five little monkeys jumping on the bed,
one fell off and kaboomed his head.
Mama yelled a warning to quiet their whines,
no more monkeys jumping near land mines.

The moral of the story was to always listen to parents and that ignorance leads to a blissful death. The little boy shook his head in disapproval, and Evel concluded that there was no pleasing him. He wouldn't fall asleep or approve of her stories. He just sat there in tears, murmuring about how much he wanted her to stop and let him go.

Getting him to come around wasn't going to be easy, but she was willing to put in the effort. Before Evel went to bed herself, she got out a small rag and dampened it with liquid from a bottle of chloroform. She held it to the child's nose and made him smell it, instantly causing him to fall into a very deep sleep. Evel left him alone, and she prepared to rest in her coffin. She could hardly sleep at all. She constantly thought about tomorrow's schedule and the joyous years to come. It was certainly going to be exciting.

For nearly three nights straight, Evel continued to parent the child. Never letting him out of her sight, never releasing him from the chair until he was well behaved. During that time, she taught him a new variety of vocabulary by introducing him to deep poetry. She taught him life's most harsh lessons to toughen him up, and she filled his head with her own philosophies that made him question life itself. She told him how everything was just a mere lie, how very few people could be trusted, and how every day was but another day closer to the grave.

The child was convinced that he was living in a terrible world, where the truth was harsher than the lies that were made by the ones he trusted. It was a world where true peace could only be found by resting six feet underground. It was even a world where the establishment transforms people into materialistic drones by using the elements of conformity. Evel was very wise in her views of the world. The boy knew then it was better to know that reality than to live a naïve life.

He started to believe that Evel was doing him a favor, and his innocent face turned to the emotionless style of Aval's. She was pleased to see that the child was finally coming around. Evel even made the boy fall asleep by reading to him a malicious and bloody version of her favorite hook, line, and murder story, *Charlie and the Chocolate Factory*.

On the fourth night, Evel and the child, whom she decided to name "Ivil," observed the thunderous storm clouds from the open balcony. Very little rain came down, and the wind hardly blew at all. Evel decided to share a bit of poetry she recently wrote. She held her hands to the clouds and did some twirls to express her very heart and soul.

I stare out my window to see nothing.
A whisper in the wind and a parade of sand
but never the sounds of a classical band.

I become dreary and ever longing to commute.
I show my blissful and graceful marks as a dame,
though none will talk to a vampire of any name.

Hark!

Change is knocking at my skull as I cry;
I'm subjected to society's rules like a pet!
Chains for norms and shackles for fools!
Why so cruel not to accept?
And why so ignorant to deny?

A steady applause came from the boy, admiring her elegance of
pain. He said it displayed a rather mystical yet charitable feel to her plea
for any sort of company. His vocabulary did improve from the usual
kiddie talk, like "You big poopy head!" or "Waa-waa, woolly
munchkin!" He quickly grew away from that.

The poor boy talked blandly, which matched his new
appearance. He was well dressed in a neat dark-brown suit and black bow
tie. His fur was finely groomed, and of course, he had two dotted
eyebrows on his forehead. How he behaved and how quickly he adapted
to the dark ways made Evel proud to call him her son.

She did it. The child was completely broken. All she had to do then was turn him into a vampire. However, she waited. She wanted Aval to participate in the transformation. Evel wondered where her husband was; it had not crossed her mind until then. She was too preoccupied with Ivil to even notice he was gone.

Then out from the skies, down flew Aval in a major and unprecedented coincidence. He swooped down and landed in the middle of the balcony. He was filled with unbridled emotions from the long journey. Something caught his eye. He saw a neatly dressed boy standing next to his wife. He had little go on, so Evel explained who he was.

"This young gentleman here just so happens to be a very special addition to this family," she said. "I am proud to introduce our heir, our little candlelight of our lives, our son, Ivil! Ivil, say hi to your new daddy, Aval."

"Hi," Ivil said in a low tone.

He and Aval looked at each other with the same dead eyes, and they hardly said a sentence to each other. Already they were like father and son. Evel couldn't help but feel giddy. They were finally going to be a happy unholy family! Aval, however, did not feel the same way. In fact, he decided to change the subject and bring up the reason he was gone.

He went in search of a fortune-teller, a gypsy specialist of a professional degree. He needed to know why the number six haunted him for so long. Through the mystic powers of the gypsy's cards, it was not the number that was haunting him, but rather a trickster of the female persuasion. One who was dressed in purple and was as skinny as a bean pole.

What sheer coincidence that Evel fit the description. Aval was being played by his own wife, and it put him in a violent mood. With that, he wanted Evel to follow him into the dungeon so he could shove six unpleasant items up her bean hole. He could've been joking, but he was dead serious. He actually made a list of things he wanted to shove inside her, from the small and unpleasant to the big and unbearable.

Evel told him not to be so rash in front of the child. She knew about his fear of the number six, and she was only having some fun with him, that's all. It was time for them to forgive and forget and get to know their new son. Aval told her to stop, because he had a lot of questions that needed answers, mainly about how she got the child. Did she find him wandering alone in the woods? No. Did she adopt him? Not even that.

He then said to her, "Evel, please tell me you did not kidnap this child."

"Nooo..." Evel said as she turned her eyes away. "I...rescued him from an unfit environment."

"You kidnapped him from his family," he said. "I can see it in your eyes. The least you could've done was make sure he had no family left at all."

"What? How dare you say such things! Why, I would sooner give a nun a wedgie than even think about doing something so criminally insane. You should be ashamed of yourself, sir!" Evel strongly stood by her word, but then she whispered in Aval's ear, "Look, when they let me into their home, I ripped out their voice boxes. Otherwise their screams would've woken him."

Evel did not want Ivil to hear the awful truth, so she said only lies. She then said out loud, "And that's why they ran away from my pie! His parents left him alone and helpless in that room full of cheap dolls, posters of nonexistent idols, and a bed shaped like some automobile. He would've been beaten up in school on a daily basis! I would not allow that to happen. I wanted him to have a better life than that. Now let's bite his neck together to officially make him our son."

Aval then said to the crazy lady, "We should be the only vampires roaming this earth, not including some kid I just met. We don't need a son. We don't need kids at all. In fact, Ivil, you're not the first child we've had in our home. Remember when we adopted a boy and a girl two years ago, Evel? Tell me, where are they now?"

"Do not go down that path," Evel warned Aval. "I don't want to relive those events. This is a chance to start anew, to raise this one right. You may not want children, but I do. It can make us happy."

"I'm only going to say this once: we are unfit parents, especially you," Aval said as he poked her chest. "Your idea of caring for someone is holding them against their will. Your idea of understanding inner feelings involves an autopsy table. You can never be a parent—know it and accept it."

"No, I am the perfect parent, because I have the one thing that you'll never possess: compassion!" Evel said as she poked his chest. "Your idea of caring for something is preserving meat limbs in a freezer. Your idea of understanding a soul involves a Ouija board. You are no parent. I am! So grin and bear it, buddy!"

The arguing and bickering continued, more than they could ever stand. If one thought about it for a second, it was the decision of the child that mattered. Ivil could stay, or he could leave, if it were an option, considering he was outnumbered by vampires. The worst part was that they wanted to take his mortal life either way. He came to a decision, and he made up his mind as he took a sharp knife from his coat.

Ivil caught their attention and yelled at them, "None of you are fit for anything! This unfeeling man in green would harm his own wife, because he could not take a simple joke. This twisted lady in purple would steal a child, because she could not stand being alone. You two are loathsome and miserable monsters that are better off dead. If this is what the world is coming to, being forced to live with people like you, then what's the point of standing here? I'm dead...Evel taught me nothing but how to become dead. I hope your search for happiness comes to a dead end!"

Ivil took the knife and slit his own throat. He fell down in front of the two, gagging in a puddle of his own blood, and quickly passed away. After it was over, Evel did nothing but fall to her knees and cry.

All she wanted was a child to raise, someone to care for in her days. She couldn't even have that kind of wealth, knowing that her parenting could cause a boy to kill himself.

Evel cried her eyes out over the corpse and mourned for the loss of her bundle of joy. Aval was tempted to drink the spilled blood, but seeing how Evel was so attached to the boy, he didn't bother sampling it. He couldn't stand to see her cry, so he knelt next to Evel and did his best to comfort her. He could never feel the same way as she felt toward Ivil. If he did, he might have considered calling him his son too.

It was surprising to see either of them show an ounce of feeling. Any other killer would look at it as a slight little accident and then move on with their lives, but these little squirrels cried. Deep down in their dark hearts, maybe they could care.

Although their rise as monsters was successful, a question arose. What made Aval & Evel truly happy that didn't involve being so evil? It was a mystery not even a gypsy could solve.

7

BELL & BILL

Switching gears to a more pleasant area would make a nice change. It would be a break from all the grittiness, and it would be a chance to see other little creatures that weren't so terrible.

On the edge of the land that touched the eastern sea was a small harbor town called Emplois. It was a hardworking town made up of good critter folk that had their own shops and fish markets. Yes, even woodland critters enjoyed the occasional fish and profit gain.

There were large beavers that built houses and also offered themselves as transportation, such as being bus beavers or school beavers. The squirrels and chipmunks worked on crops and shops and cooked plenty of food for the hungry workers. The gulls picked up stray trash from the sea, the pelicans taught daily fly-fishing lessons, and the little rabbits delivered everyone's mail.

It was certainly a very busy town, so busy that the maximum sleep they could afford was two hours; then they had to go to their second job. Only the children had the luxury of relaxing during weekends, unless they were put to work. They despised work completely, though there were two particular teens that didn't mind working at all.

On a bright cloudless morning on a busy dock of rafters and fishermen, two teenaged squirrels arrived on a small boat full of fresh fish and lots of spirit. They were a pair of blond-furred squirrels that were nice and well mannered and always began a day with a smile. They were twin brother and sister, Bell & Bill, the friendliest of squirrels.

The two worked hard all their lives, though they did not have much. Being rich and finding mates never crossed their minds—no way. They were too busy with schoolwork and too busy helping their grandfather catch fish on the sea. Some would think Bell & Bill were goody-two-shoes bookworms, and well, some would be right.

Both of them wore matching blue overalls, white undershirts, and brown boots and gloves around town. In school, they wore matching blue uniforms, even though their school did not have a uniform policy. They dressed the same, but their personalities were different.

Bell was considered brave and a perfectionist. She wanted everything to be clean and precise. Like if the head of a fish wasn't properly cut, she would throw the whole thing away and start on the next one. Bill was considered skittish and resourceful. He never wasted anything he could've used for later or at least sold for berries. Like scraping the scales from a fish for decoration pieces—that is, if he didn't pass out from the sight of blood first.

The same routine of school and work molded them into crafty workaholics, but they learned to live with it—especially venturing out to sea with their Grandpa Popcorn. He preferred to be called "Captain Popcorn" because he dressed like a pirate and acted like one. Popcorn wasn't very in tune with reality.

He believed there were still treasures in those waters, and he aimed to find some and make his family rich. Sadly, most sunken treasures had already been discovered. There was hardly anything left. Popcorn didn't believe in such negative talk; all he had on his mind was gold, treasure, and booty. The old captain's mind was slowly deteriorating, so his grandchildren were instructed by their parents to make sure he was on a clear path every weekend. His job was catching fish and delivering them, nothing more and nothing less.

A loading beaver then came along with wooden baskets hanging from his sides, in which the fish were to be loaded and carried to the markets. Bell & Bill carried some nets of small fish and began to toss them in. They weren't handling them very carefully, and it made their grandpa very angry.

"Argh!" said Captain Popcorn. "Careful with the goods, me hearties! If one wee batch of that catch even hits the ground, I'll make ye walk da plank!"

"We're trying, Grandpa," Bell said as she struggled to get one into the beaver's baskets. "It'd be easier if you'd, I don't know, help us!"

"Bell, you know his muscles aren't what they used to be," Bill said as he struggled to lift a batch off the dock. "Unnhh! Gosh this is heavy…"

Watching his weak grandson made the captain very irritated and frustrated. Popcorn left his sailboat to assist with the fish. He grabbed the heavy batch, threw it into a basket, and went back to get some more. He didn't even strain himself.

"Unbelievable," Popcorn said out loud. "Back in me younger days, kids yur age lifted bags of clutter, loads of gunpowder, and sacks full of steel balls by usin' the tip of their very fingers. But then they grew up to become lazy land-lovin' lubbers called fathers. Pah! The generations is sinkin' like a ship built out of swiss cheese. Shirtless barbarians in loincloths, carryin' chains and whips—those were real men! Even clever fish bait wearin' tights snuck into kingly castles and grabbed themselves a handful of sweet family jewels. Those were true pioneers!"

As the old captain rambled on, Bell and the beaver showed a look of concern.

"I'm really worried about him," said the beaver.

"Yeah," Bell said, "I'm worried about him too. But he is my brother; he can't help being the way he is." She defended Bill.

"No, I mean your grandfather," the beaver explained. "His mind is going by the day, and he might do something rash around you two, like harm you. Your parents should put him in a nursing home."

"Those places are awful," she stated. "He's happy living his life on the sea. All we have to do is support him and pray that fortune shines down on us. We could use those riches to build our own fish factory and pay people to work for us. You know, so we can catch up on our studies."

The beaver didn't bother to comment. He figured all three of those squirrels had problems. Before the baskets were filled, Bell & Bill had to do a quick inspection to make sure all sides were balanced just right. Bell checked the left side, and it was perfect. Bill checked the right, and it was just as fine, but something odd poked out the side of the basket that caught his eye.

It was a strange fish skeleton that held something in its rib cage. Within it was a cube that was covered in seaweed. It looked very suspicious. It would've been wise to discard it from the basket and toss it into the ocean where it belonged, but his curiosity was over the point of interest. Bill took out the skeleton and tucked it in his overalls. He thought he might get some berries selling it. Then he took a closer look at the seaweed-covered item. He brushed off the seaweed, and he found a blue music box.

It was rusted and decayed for what looked like centuries. It had bronze metal tips at the bottom, and at the top was a painted yellow symbol with an ancient design. Bill looked at its worn-out handle, and he was tempted to see if it still worked. He placed his hand on the handle, and he gradually started to wind it up. He started to feel slight warmth in his hand. It might have been the gloves, so he continued. Nothing happened yet, no music of any sort, just more heat. Just then, the burning sensation turned into a feel of blazing lava that burned through his glove!

The pain caused Bill to scream and drop the box to the floor. Everyone heard his scream and rushed over to see what was wrong. Bill said it was the handle from that music box; it burned his hand. Bell, Popcorn, and the beaver thought it was just a joke, because there was no way a music box could burn anything.

With hardly a chuckle, the beaver went on his way, and Popcorn decided to let his grandchildren go for the evening. With Bell alone with Bill, she had to ask why he had to make up a weird story like that, but he wasn't fooling around.

Desperate to convince her, he showed her the melted glove and the black mark that was imprinted on his hand. Bell saw it and still believed it was some kind of joke. She was the type who would think everything had a logical explanation to it. She hardly cared for wild stories, which was why she didn't like reading fiction.

It was ridiculous to think something as innocent as a music box would burn someone, but she decided to see for herself. She picked up the box and turned the handle as quickly as she could. To her surprise, nothing happened. No music or burns; it just made them both feel ridiculous. Bell concluded that Bill made it up to leave work early.

Bill, sadly, was the type no one took seriously. Whether he saw a ghost at night or visitors from outer space, no one ever believed him. No matter how many times he tried to prove his case, some thought he needed some rest, meaning that he was crazy. Even Bill thought he needed some sleep, but there was still more to do that morning. They had to help prepare a charity event down the street, study for a spelling competition, and get started on a science project that wasn't due until next week. But since they had their newfound treasures, they decided to go and sell them at an antique shop. They figured a clean skeleton and a broken music box would sell well.

As they walked through the town, Bill couldn't shake the feeling of a bad presence hidden within the strange box. Bell had to slap him on the shoulder. She told him to put away his fears and focus on their upcoming spelling bee. Spelling would certainly get her brother's mind off things, so she tested him by making him spell miscellaneous. Bill didn't bother to say a letter, for he still felt his hand burning.

The two squirrels eventually arrived at the antique shop that was named Snippet 'n' Stick It. It was a smelly and dusty old shop that sold a variety of welded and glued collectables. What made it so welcoming was that it was owned by their uncle, Piblo, who taught them the fine value of finding and selling things that weren't glued down. As they walked in, they caught their squirrelly uncle in a heated argument with an angry chipmunk customer.

"This is nowhere near a bat!" said the chipmunk. "This is a wooden plank on a stick!"

Piblo folded his arms and told the chipmunk, "It's not a plank. It's a cricket bat. Your son wanted a bat, and this is technically a bat, so I sold him a bat. He can still play baseball with it."

"No, he cannot!" said the chipmunk. "It'll be like playing basketball with a football. It makes no lick of sense!"

"Well, consider this," said Piblo. "It will also be like playing pankration with a bayonet strapped to your instep."

"What?"

"Ah-ha! You're confused, which means you win the big fat prize of no refund."

The chipmunk was persistent in trying to get his refund back, but no luck. Just when Piblo was about to whack him over the head with the cricket bat, he noticed Bell & Bill walking into his place of business. He welcomed his nephews with open arms and offered them a chance to settle the situation of the cricket-bat matter, since the two were famous for settling disputes with reasoning.

Looking at the facts, the two squirrels explained that the customers are always right and should be entitled to a refund if they weren't satisfied. The statement seemed fair, so the chipmunk expected his refund. Piblo groaned, but he had to listen to the kids for the sake of the store, so he asked to see the customer's receipt.

The customer soon discovered that he did not have the receipt, which really meant he was spit out of luck. With that said, Piblo thanked Bell & Bill for settling the argument and asked if they had any items for him.

They placed the items on the counter, a clean fish skeleton and an old music box. Piblo observed the skeleton, and unfortunately, it wasn't worth a dime. The whole skeleton faction was not all the rage in town. He bought and sold anything that had a significant value, not something that could be found at a dump. He carelessly tossed the skeleton into the nearest trash can. Bill was shocked at such wastefulness. It could've been used as a necklace or a bracelet, but it was already tainted by the stench-infested trash.

Piblo then looked at the music box. Its rust, markings, and the contents of its design suggested it was made by the ancients. He was more fascinated with that, and he wondered if it still worked. He turned the handle round and around, but nothing happened. It was obviously drowned out and busted by time. He figured it was worth ten berries, tops.

Bill still had a weird feeling about that box, so he said, "I don't know if we should give this thing away. This box has some bad mojo on it."

"Bad mojo? Like a curse?" Piblo laughed. "Boy, there is no such thing as a cursed music box. Cursed masks, however, those make sense."

The customer then jumped into the conversation and said, "Don't be too sure. If you think about it, any simple object can be cursed. This one time, I bought a funny-looking toaster for my friend's birthday party. Next thing I know, her whole family ended up on the side of milk cartons."

Piblo grunted and asked the customer why he was still in his store. Apparently he became interested in the music box as well. Bill thought to further his case. He exposed his burned palm for all to see, and he tried to convince them that there was something wrong with that box. He was the only one who touched it first and got burned. Maybe, just maybe, Bill was the box's chosen one for something dark and sinister. As ridiculous as it sounded, nothing could prepare them for what happened next.

The box's handle suddenly turned on its own, and it played an eerie tune that made their spines shiver.

~Ting-tin-tin-li-tin-li-duu-ti-tin li...~

After exactly ten seconds of playing, the handle stopped, and the song ceased. At the same time, the wind outside rushed powerfully through the streets, and the bright sun was blocked by a sea of black clouds. The sudden weather change made the day seem like night. The citizens outside stood motionless and wondered if there was a storm coming.

Darkness covered the town of Emplois and strangely nowhere else. Bill knew it: the box was cursed, and he had unleashed the evil within it! Bell didn't believe her paranoid brother. There was an explanation for the box playing on its own; it was obviously broken. As for the weather, it just could have been a passing storm. She asked if Piblo agreed with her.

There was no response. Their uncle was nowhere to be found. It was too dark inside the store to see a thing. All that helped them see was the cold dark light of the storm peering through the windows. The chipmunk offered to shed some light with a match he had in his left pocket. One scratch of the match and the three could see a tad more than before. Around the store was nothing but emptiness, but they heard a sound of munching and crunching.

A drop of meat and the splatter of liquid came from above. The three looked up and, to their surprise, saw Piblo hanging from the ceiling with a giant hook impaled through his chest. The terrible munching was from the possessed, floating fish skeleton gnawing at his dead body. With a gasp and a scream from the three, the fish looked down at them with its glowing yellow eyes and let out a huge roar. It flew down swiftly and launched itself at the chipmunk to feast on more flesh. It slammed him to the floor and began to eat his furry body. The lit match was thrown in the panic and landed on a nearby curtain, where it immediately lit up in flames. Bell had to do something, so she grabbed the cricket bat from the counter and bashed the fish into a wall, shattering it into pieces.

No longer did it move, and neither did the poor chipmunk. It was too late to save him. The fire quickly engulfed the room, and they had to get out fast. Bell grabbed Bill, and they ran toward the exit as fast as they could. They reached the door, but it wouldn't open. It was mysteriously locked tight, trapping them inside.

The fire grew faster, destroying everything in seconds, and it began to inch closer to the scared squirrels. They had no choice but to break through the glass windows. With her bat, Bell shattered a window, and both squirrels jumped out into the street, barely escaping the fire. Everything in the store was gone; their only true relief was that the box was gone as well. There was no denying it. The box was indeed cursed.

The townsfolk gathered to see the disaster, and they were filled with fright and sorrow. A police bird showed up from the dark sky. He observed the scene and looked at the two squirrels standing near the fire. Witnesses say they were the ones fleeing the building when it lit up in flames. After hearing that, the cop had to ask the teenagers a few questions.

The bird patted his baton on his wing and asked the squirrels, "So, you two mind telling me what happened here?"

Bill told the cop, "There was this old music box we found, but it was actually cursed. It played on its own and made a fish skeleton come to life. It killed our uncle and a customer, and it burned down the whole store!"

Bell face-palmed herself, because not even a cop would believe such a tale. He then eyed Bill's burned palm, which aroused his suspicions even more. He started to think that Bell & Bill started the fire and made up a story to make them seem innocent. It all made sense in his feathered head. The cop then tweaked his beak, put away his baton, and lowered his hand to his gun. Bell knew they were in deep trouble. She had to do something fast.

"Sir, I know what you're thinking," Bell said, "but we are not responsible for this. It was a cursed box. You have to believe us."

The cop started to grow furious. "Does it look like I was just hatched yesterday? Was this 'cursed' box filled with some illegal narcotics? Huh? Stuff that causes you to hallucinate something like a floating skeleton?"

"Wait," Bill said, "how did you know it floated?"

"Bill!" That dumb response made Bell shout in his ear, for the cop knew for certain they were guilty.

He reached for his gun, but he didn't point it at them. He tossed the gun to Bell, and the girl caught it with her hands. The squirrels were confused why he threw them the gun. What he said next made everything clear.

The cop cried out, "Everyone get down! She's got a gun!" It stirred the crowd into a panic. Once it escalated, he grabbed his baton and quickly whacked Bell & Bill unconscious.

Whop! Bop!

Twenty minutes later, the two squirrels woke in a fuzzy haze inside a police station. They were handcuffed in chairs near the front entrance, with no clue of what had happened or what distant voices were heard. It was hard to hear with their senses slowly coming to. Their vision was flickering like a bleak lightbulb, on and off again. They could see a small candle that lit the room, due to the loss of electricity. They saw and heard that bird cop speaking of their wrongdoings to another bird behind the front desk.

He said that the two stoned squirrels murdered their uncle, Piblo, and a chipmunk, named Augustus. Then they burned down the antique store to cover up their tracks. If that wasn't enough, they made an attempt to shoot the officer with his own gun. The desk bird became rather enraged.

The desk bird yelled at the squirrels, "You sick little monsters! You two are going to be locked away for a looong time...just as soon as we finish the paperwork on this."

"Paperwork? Huey, just let me lock them up already!" The officer demanded.

Huey told the officer, "We've been over this, Gary. We can't just throw crooks in jail all willy-nilly; there's paper that needs filing. Now go check on Gus in the back. He's been on the can for an hour, and we can't get that door open."

Gary let out a huge huff and flew his way to the back. He wished for the good old days where he could lock up hooligans and then throw away the key, literally. All was quiet, and after realizing what had happened, Bill started to breathe at an alarming rate. He knew their reputation was ruined. Never had they entered a police station in their lives, and he couldn't imagine what the inmates might do to them or their butts.

Bill started to cry. "It's over; we're done. Our lives have gone down the tube! We can never go back to school. We can never show our faces in public again. Our parents are going to disown us, or worse, kill us before anyone around here gets the chance!"

"Will you shut up?" Bell said as she headbutted him on the side of his head.

"Ow! Why are you always hitting me?" he asked as he moved around in his uncomfy chair.

Bell explained to him, "It's because I'm sick of you! We could've gone on with our weekend, but nooo! Play with a toy you found in a skeleton, what could possibly go wrong? You always have to find ways to mess things up."

"Well, excuse me, Ms. Busybody," said Bill as he still wiggled in his chair. "We wouldn't be in this mess if you'd just listened to me. Like this morning, I said just for once could we rest on a Sunday, but no! Let's fish; let's do charity work. It's not like we have lives or anything!"

Bell didn't want to hear him talk about having a life or blaming her, so she claimed it was all his fault. Out of anger, she bumped his chair to make him fall to the floor. The push wasn't enough to make him fall though, but something did hit the floor. An object fell from Bill's seat, and what they saw filled their eyes with fear—it was the music box.

Huey was surprised to discover the foreign object. He thought the two squirrels were trying to pull a fast one on him. He jumped over the counter and asked how they had smuggled in the box.

The two truthfully had no idea; it appeared in Bill's seat out of nowhere. Huey came to the assumption that the two snuck in a bomb through Bill's butt! The two were sicker in the head than he had thought, but they weren't. It was the cursed box they tried to tell Gary about. The more they talked about it, the more Huey knew it was a bomb.

It's funny how the protectors of society always assume the worst about everything and everybody. Just when things couldn't get any worse, a couple of unlikely visitors rushed through the doors. It was Bell & Bill's parents.

The father said to them, "Bell, Bill, what's this I hear about you two burning down my brother's store?"

Then the mother said to them, "You two used to be so good. Where did we go so wrong?"

The parents were more ashamed than ever. It got worse when the officer explained that not only did they commit murder, arson, drug abuse, and theft of an officer's gun, but now they smuggled a bomb into a police station. The parents were ungodly embarrassed to even call them their children, for they could only call them true gangsters. Bell thought she was living in a crazy nightmare. Suddenly in the middle of the argument, the box played its creepy tune once again.

~Ting-tin-tin-li-tin-li-duu-ti-tin li...~

All listened to the eerie song, and just like last time, it stopped after ten seconds. Bell & Bill were afraid because they knew something was going to happen. They begged to be set free from the handcuffs so they could flee, but of course, they weren't allowed the freedom. All they could do was sit and wait for what the box had in store.

Distant screams then came from the back of the station, as if someone was in peril. Huey flew to the back without hesitation. The danger had started. More screams were heard, and they grew louder every passing second. Cries of officers and prisoners, loud yells of pain and torture, terrified the squirrel family. Metal clanging, gun firing, and flesh ripping made it sound like a huge slaughter.

It suddenly stopped, and footsteps crept toward the room as the storm outside grew ever so fiercely. From the hallway came the sickened, bloated robin, Gus. He lost his feathers, he bled all over with his guts spilled out, his wings were reduced to loose flesh and sharp bones, and he possessed the same yellow eyes as the fish skeleton had. After a short twitching stare at the frightened family, the ghoulish bird let out a screeching scream that broke the glass doors, inviting the stormy wind to ravage the station.

The gush of wind blew them toward the walls with unrelenting force, as the bird continued to scream. It got worse when the still ground began to rumble and shake like an earthquake. The screams, the wind, the pain—they wouldn't stop for anything. The squirrels were certainly doomed in the chaos, until someone unsuspecting fired a gun.

Bang!

Officer Gary shot the robin in the head! The screams stopped, and the wind faded into a calm breeze. With a thud, the robin fainted with a dying hiss, and its yellow eyes faded away. Bell & Bill were surprised to see a guy like Gary saving them.

Gary limped into the room, badly injured, but he still managed to live. He did not want any thanks; all he wanted was to apologize to the two squirrels. He said Gus was possessed and killed everyone in the station. What else could've caused it but that box? The best way he could make it up to them was to let them go.

Gary came over with the keys and gladly released them from the cuffs. Once freed, their parents held them in their arms tight and apologized as well. It was a touching family moment, but it didn't last long.

Gary looked through the broken doors, but he couldn't see the town. All he saw were dark gray clouds that headed upward at a fast speed. It was as if the station was falling from the sky. The bird knew it was true when he suddenly saw the vast ocean below.

Sploosh!

It plummeted right into the Atlantic Ocean, devastating the entire building with a thunderous splashdown. It sent everyone sliding to the back of the station as the building began to submerge. Water was rushing fast, and half the station began to flood. Their only chance of survival was to get to the front entrance. Gary began to flap his wings, but when he built up enough strength to fly, the possessed Gus came back to life!

He used his sharp skeletal wings to impale Gary in the back and toss him aside like trash. Thinking fast, Bell spotted the cricket bat she had from the shop, floating next to a mass of junk. She swam across the water, grabbed it, and swung it at the robin, but he caught the weapon with his beak. There was a struggle of power between the two as the water began to rise.

The mother and father suddenly jumped forward and bashed the bird away from Bell. They fought it off and gave their children enough time to escape. Bell held the bat close and quickly climbed up to the entrance with Bill. Outside the station was nothing but a foggy ocean with no sign of land for miles. They looked down and saw their parents climbing toward them. Just before the parents were able to reach their children, Gus leaped from the water and dragged them down into the depths below.

"Nooo!" cried the children as they dived down to save them from their fate.

They were desperate and determined, but the water was too deep and too dark to see where they were. Bell looked around and found nothing but red mists and floating debris that rose to the surface. They were running out of air, running out of time, and there was no trace of their parents anywhere. They were gone.

Bell wailed out bubbles for them to come back. She swam deeper in hopes of finding them, but Bill had to drag her back to the surface so she wouldn't drown. By the time they reached the surface, the station had already sunk into the ocean, along with dozens of lost lives.

Bell & Bill couldn't believe it; it all happened so fast. Their day started off so well with smiles and sunshine, and next thing they knew, they were crying their little hearts out in a sea of sorrow.

8

THE
CURSE OF
THE MUSIC BOX

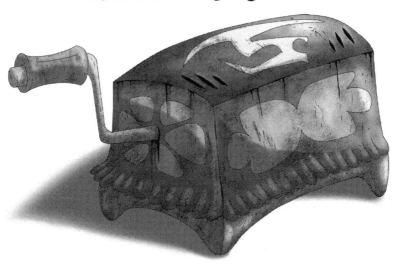

An hour had passed, and Bell & Bill were still adrift in the open sea, floating away on a piece of lumber. The only things they had were the clothes on their backs and the cricket bat Bell refused to part with. She had grown too attached to it. It was their only means of defending themselves, after all.

The skies were still filled with dark clouds, but then an incoming fog started to surround them, making it impossible to see anything. Those squirrels were indeed saddened by the horrible events that led them to the sea. They were hungry and tired and, worst of all, they weren't speaking to each other. Bell didn't want to talk to her brother, and Bill couldn't say anything that would make his sister forgive him. The music box he found destroyed their lives, and they couldn't do a thing about it, except pray that the sea led them to a shore.

Twenty minutes of silence passed, and they soon saw an incoming boat heading through the fog—what a familiar boat it was. It was the fishing boat of their grandpa, Captain Popcorn. The old squirrel immediately spotted his grandchildren and brought them aboard in haste.

Once Bell & Bill were rescued, they hugged their grandpa tightly and gratefully. They were glad to see their old fishing grandfather again. Popcorn didn't know what was going on or why they were hugging him so much. He broke the hug and wiped his clothes dry from their wet bodies.

He said to his grandchildren, "What's with all the squeezin' and huggin' and whatnot? How many times have I told ye that real pirates don't hug? Any wussy fish bait caught doing that would've been keelhauled from their very trousers!"

Bell & Bill were about to explain, but they suddenly saw a shady-looking squirrel in a black coat sitting on the side of the deck. That squirrel sat still and said nothing at all. Popcorn said to never mind that stranger; he picked him up not too long ago from a log out at sea. He had quite a morning, and all he wanted to do was go home. Popcorn was kind enough to give him a ride back, since the weather was too iffy for him to swab the deck.

With that out of the way, Popcorn wanted to know what Bell & Bill were doing in the middle of the sea. They chose their words carefully and did their best to tell a believable story about the cursed music box. They made it short, and they left out some intense details unless they were necessary. After hearing such a tale, not even Captain Popcorn believed in such things.

"There ain't any such thing as a cursed music box," said Popcorn. "Now dolls, those make sense."

"But, Grandpa, it's true," Bill said. "It burned my hand, it caused a massive storm, it made a skeleton to come to life and—"

"Oh, quit yur nonsense, boy!" Popcorn interrupted Bill and began to stroll around the deck in a lecturing manner. "Lowdown bilge rats tell tall tales. You need to be a white lie savvy swashbuckler. Back in me days, boys didn't get their wee hands scorched by a wee girly box. They got their hands scorched by firing heavy cannon loads onto the poop decks of scurvy sea dogs! Even in the face of danger, none flinched, they never blinked at certain damnation. They took their finely polished swords and stuck 'em right up their—"

"Grandpa! Mom, Dad, and Uncle Piblo are dead!" Bell yelled as she stopped his rambling. "They're gone. Piblo was eaten by a skeleton, and our parents drowned in that station. Our family is gone..."

Popcorn stood still. He started to question his family's death, but Bell & Bill would never lie about such a thing. They would never lie to him like that. The terrible news devastated their grandpa; he couldn't even talk in pirate anymore; he spoke plain English for the first time in years. Without his family, his true inspiration, there was no point in carrying on anything. He needed to sit down and have some time to himself.

As Popcorn slowly walked up the stairs to the pilothouse, Bill had to apologize and admit his careless action of touching the box in the first place. Popcorn sighed and told him to stop apologizing; there was no way anyone could've known it was cursed. With that, he went to the room and remained ever silent.

Bell & Bill felt the same pain as he did. After Popcorn left, the two squirrels began to sit down on the deck, away from the shady squirrel. Bell chose a nice spot in a corner, but when Bill came close to her, she told him to sit somewhere else. She wanted to be alone as well, but what's more, she didn't want to be near him.

Bill didn't want her to be that way. Like Popcorn said, there was no way he could've known it was cursed; otherwise, he would've thrown it into the water. If he understood, why not Bell? I guess that knowing he was responsible for his parents' death would make even his sister hate him. Bell told him one last time to go away and to leave her alone, and so he did. Bell & Bill sat apart, and they did not seem like brother and sister anymore.

It was all so quiet. Nothing was heard but the sounds of the ocean. No one talked; they just basked in the gloomy atmosphere until the shady squirrel spoke.

"The music box," said the squirrel. The two siblings turned to the old prisoner and wondered what drove him to speak. Once he got their attention, he asked the teenagers, "The music box—what did it look like?"

Bell & Bill did not want to answer; they feared that even talking about the box would bring it back. The silence annoyed the shady squirrel, so he asked again in a forceful tone, "The box, what did it look like?"

Bill quietly answered, "Blue, with bronze tips on the bottom."

The shady squirrel then asked a different question. "This box, did it have a weird yellow symbol, on the front?"

Bell started to stare at him. She wondered why he was asking so many questions about a thing that was long discarded. Oddly enough, he felt that it was not discarded at all. In fact, the shady squirrel felt the box was close, very close. To prove that feeling, he pulled an object out from his coat, and in his hand, the music box stood.

Bell & Bill jumped up in surprise. Was the box following them wherever they went or was the shady squirrel the cause of their misfortune? The strange squirrel shook his head and said that he found it an hour ago while he was at sea.

He knew the box well, and he told them they would never escape it. The shady squirrel then tossed the box into the ocean and told Bill to rub his ears. It was an odd request, but the boy did it anyway. He moved his hands through his ears and knocked over what occupied the back of his left ear, the music box. It was indeed following him. No matter where he went or how much he tried to lose it, the box returned. Bell had the idea of destroying it. She picked up her bat and attempted to smash the box with brute force.

She kept striking the box in rage, yet not a dent was made. Bill, on the other hand, picked a sledgehammer as a proper tool for smashing. With a powerful slam to the box, all that was made was a mere dinging sound and the shatter of wood from the broken hammer. They could not destroy it.

"Face it, kids," said the shady squirrel, "this box isn't going away." The squirrel went over and picked up the box. He brushed it off and looked at it in fascination.

Bill had to ask. "Who are you? How do you know about this box?"

The shady squirrel dramatically turned away and stared into the fog that surrounded the boat and infested the sea, for he knew exactly what waited in those waters. He never did say his name, but he did offer a little backstory. He told them the box was an old treasure that belonged to an ancient pharaoh in Egypt.

King Kalazar was his name, a magical and powerful crocodile that ruled the Egyptian lakes many eons ago. He was as tall as a two-story house, but he was not feared. Oh no. He was a gracious king and the nicest croc you would ever meet. He made peace with many countries, and he cured diseases with the many spells he had mastered through the years. He had a loving wife, two precious children, and a kingdom that worshiped the ground he walked on.

Then one day, his wife and children were missing from the palace, so Kalazar sent every servant at his disposal to bring them back. On the third day of the search, his family was discovered on the outskirts of the kingdom, half-eaten, with flies feeding on their rotten bodies. He lost the joys of his life. He never knew who ate them or what he did to deserve such a loss. He was never the same after that horrible day. The king who treated everyone with love and kindness was no more. He then treated everyone as his enemy.

Kalazar caused death, he caused misery, and he deprived his people of precious water and kept everything to himself. In the end, everyone turned on him. They banded together to kill the king and take over his palace. He did not fight, and he did not flee. He wanted to be set free from life, but not without exacting revenge. Before his grisly death, he stored his remaining powers in the music box. A gift that once helped his children sleep at night became a concealment of evil that would spread his pain to future generations.

The curse was whoever shall touch the handle shall share the same pain such as his and shall be killed by the king himself.

Bill then looked at his burned palm that sealed his fate. He was terrified but curious. If he was marked for death, how come he managed to live so long?

Well, the curse wasn't meant to kill everyone who first laid their hands on the handle—not right away. The curse was meant to attack your heart. It wanted you to feel the same pain that Kalazar felt when he lost his family. One by one your family and friends would die in front of your eyes, and in the end, you would wish you had taken their places.

The music box of a broken king.
Attacking one's heart is its deal.
From what others made Kalazar feel,
now into a song the box will sing.

Three songs it will play,
the ones you love get taken away.
The pain of loss showers and pours;
death isn't funny when it happens to yours.

Let the box play its fourth song,

for the end is never wrong.

You'll be happy death is cruel that way,

when it steals your sorry life away.

Two songs were already played, and Bill's sister and grandpa were the only ones left. Bill couldn't believe it; his family was truly dying because of him. The shady squirrel had to agree, but he said that there were others who were truly responsible for their misery. The box was long forgotten in the sea, until someone decided to bring back the fear of monsters.

He blamed Aval & Evel. Their very presence and mission to bring terror to the land caused all sorts of horrors to come back to life. Bell started to think about it and figured that his theory was probably right.

As for the curse, the shady squirrel said there was a way to stop it, but it was not an easy one. He said that in order for the curse to stop once more, the cursed one had to live, nevermore.

The solution seemed a bit extreme. Bill wasn't the sort to sacrifice himself, but he wouldn't allow his family to perish. It was either him or them. Before he could think anymore, the handle on the music box turned and played its sickly song.

~Ting-tin-tin-li-tin-li-duu-ti-tin li...~

They were frozen with fear, except for the shady squirrel. He dropped the box and dived right into the ocean. He fled from the horrors the box was about to unleash.

As the squirrel swam through the growing fog, Bell shouted at him, "Coward!"

Lightning suddenly brightened the sky, and a loud thunderclap shook their ears. They grabbed whatever they could to defend themselves with. Bell held her bat close, and Bill quivered with a broken stick. The two cried out for Popcorn, but there was no response. They ran to the pilothouse in search for him, yet he was nowhere to be found.

There was no sign of where Popcorn went, and they silently prayed that he was safe. It was certain the two were all alone in the middle of the ocean. Bell had no choice but to drive the boat out of the fog. She went for the boat's controls and tried to make sense of it all.

They'd spent many years on that boat, but they never actually knew how to sail it. Popcorn warned them to never touch the controls. Only the captain could do that. Unfortunately for her, something crept up to remind her of that rule. She turned around to see her grandfather, slobbering and twitching with bright yellow eyes. Their poor squirrel was possessed.

Popcorn grabbed Bell by the tail and threw her back outside. Once her back hit the deck floor, that crazed squirrel jumped outside and ran toward her with extreme hatred and speed, knocking Bill out of his way.

When the time was right, she struck Popcorn in the head with the bat. He didn't fall to the ground; he merely stood for a moment with his head to the side. He turned to her, and she swung for another hit, but he caught it with his right hand with a smile. He tossed the bat at Bill, and it struck him in the head as he fell.

The crazed squirrel grabbed Bell by the neck, and he began to choke the life out of her. She kicked and punched him with all her might, but the more she struggled, the harder he made the hold.

Bill came out of nowhere and whacked Popcorn with the cricket bat, but it was not enough. The body didn't move an inch. He tried hitting his back, his head, and even his groin. Popcorn just continued to choke the girl, and her body began to weaken as he pinned her to the floor. He applied more pressure to the neck, constricting her veins, turning her face purple, making blood flow to her eyes.

She begged Bill to do something, fast. Bill then eyed a harpoon that was tied near the rails of the boat. He had no choice; he had to end his grandfather to save his sister, but then he thought about the curse. It would only end if he took his own life. He had to either wound his grandpa or end the curse once and for all. He didn't want to make such a decision, but then a little voice inside his heart told him to be a man and save his family. Bill made up his mind as he ran toward the rails. Bell looked over and saw Bill tying the harpoon's rope around his own neck. It even caught the attention of the possessed Popcorn.

He climbed over the edge of the boat and yelled, "Is this what you want, Kalazar? Then you got it!"

Bill closed his eyes and flung himself off the boat and into the water, drowning himself.

"Bill!" Bell cried.

She pounded and pounded on Popcorn to let her go, but he didn't. He waited until the rope was completely stretched out. Once it did, he released her from the hold, for he knew it was too late to save him.

Bell ran to the rails and grabbed the rope, desperately trying to bring Bill back up. She pulled and pulled with all her might. She did want Bill to die, but she just couldn't let him go like that. She soon brought the body up to the rails. Thud to the floor he went. She quickly untied the rope from his neck and checked for any signs of life. What she saw were lifeless eyes and a pale-blue face. Bell's brother had drowned.

In an instant, the yellow eyes from Grandpa Popcorn faded away, and he was free from the spell. He wobbled back and forth with a fierce headache. He had no idea what had happened or what was going on. All he could see was Bell crying over the loss of her brother. She said that he sacrificed himself to end the curse, but she didn't want him to die, no matter how much he messed things up. She still loved her brother, and she couldn't go on without him. If only she had taken his advice and stayed home on that Sunday, but now he was gone.

Popcorn, however, didn't accept the fact that he was gone. He wouldn't let a family member die on his watch, especially on his boat. He went over to the boy and gave him CPR to make him breathe again. He breathed air into his lungs and pumped the boy's chest repeatedly. He attempted several times to bring him back to life, but nothing happened. He didn't give up. He breathed and pressed, breathed and pressed, until Bill's eyes widened and water spewed from his mouth. He was saved!

"Bill! You're alive!" Bell cried as she hugged him. "Bill, don't ever do that again!"

Bill breathed slowly and asked her, "Is it over?"

Grandpa Popcorn proudly gave him a pop on the shoulder and confirmed it to be true.

"Argh! It be over, me boy!" Popcorn said as he talked like a pirate again. "Ye done the family name proud! Ye became a real man! For real men do what is right, no matter how rough these savage waters turn. They can never hold us down!"

They stood Bill up on his feet and immediately had a good laugh. They were pleased that the nightmare was over, but the strange weather never did clear. The fog didn't disperse, nor did the dark clouds or the thunder or anything. Without the curse, they expected a fresh ray of sunshine to appear. Maybe the curse still remained, but Popcorn chuckled at such nonsense.

"Nah, the weather's just stuck, 'tis all," he said. "I'm sure we'll get some sun real soon. Don't forget, this be no fairy tale where there's sunshine and rainbows at the end. We must sail through it all first. Have faith, kiddies, beyond this dark weather lies a new start! A new adventure with me to guide ye, good ol' Grandpa Pop—"

Craa-paaahhh!

A massive lightning strike came down from the skies and obliterated their grandpa, right before their very eyes. It left nothing but a pile of ashes. There were no words to describe how Bell & Bill felt at that moment. The heartbroken squirrels fell to their knees and cried tears of sorrow. The curse would not stop until Bill was completely dead, and it took his grandpa's life as an example. Bill was finally broken. He possessed the same pain as King Kalazar, and he knew what was coming next. Across the deck, the cursed music box played its deadly tune.

~Ting-tin-tin-li-tin-li-duu-ti-tin li…~

The storm grew fiercer than ever before. The rain finally fell down from the skies, and the wind swept away the ashes of the fallen squirrel. The wind's roar, lightning, and thunderclaps were all signs of the final stage of the curse. Waves rose, then dropped, and then rose higher near the boat. Just as the waves could nearly tip it over, it suddenly stopped. On the right side of the boat slowly emerged a giant mummified crocodile.

The large skeletal monster was covered with torn bandages; it wore a torn purple hood and had the brightest of yellow eyes. It raised its head to the judgmental skies and let out a huge roar for the two scared squirrels. The croc was none other than King Kalazar himself, coming for Bill's soul.

Although frightened by the monstrous mummy, Bill had to accept his fate. He walked away from his sister and went toward the mummy. He held down his head in a slump and said with a tear, "Just finish it…just get it over with."

The mummy drew his long bony arm and picked up the boy by the tail. He held him high in the sky, and then he opened his long mouth to devour his body and soul. Bill teared up and said his final farewell to his sister, but she wasn't going to let him go. Bell picked up a rock and threw it at the monster.

"Let him go!" she yelled at the mummy. "He does not deserve this, you despicable croc!"

Kalazar stopped and looked at the girl. A wicked growl came from the monster as he laid his other hand on the boat, slightly leaning it down to the side. Bill warned her to stop; she was part of Kalazar's unfinished work. Bell did not care. She looked that monster dead in the eyes and made a final stand.

"Kalazar! You miserable old lizard! You're not a king. You're nothing but an unforgivable hell-raiser! All the lives you've taken away had nothing to do with the loss of your family! Killing will never bring your family back!"

She stared at the mummy silently and waited for his next move. Kalazar lowered his head and opened his jaw to her, in an attempt to speak.

He spoke in a ghoulish voice. "All killed my family; all must pay and feel my pain."

"No, we don't," she said. "Did a simple antique dealer or a carefree fisherman have to pay? What about nice and caring squirrels like our parents? What about a priest, a pacifist, the blind, the physically disabled, or any other poor soul who died by your curse? If you believe that every living being has to be tortured, then you are torturing yourself! You will never rest, and you will never know peace! So you can growl all you want, but you know I'm right!"

Kalazar was, surprisingly, amazed. He was never confronted by a creature that spoke brave words or gave a harsh lecture that wasn't even heard of in ancient times. Everything felt so questionable to him, like seeking lifelong vengeance and tearing families apart through a music box. The mummy looked at each of the two squirrels, and then he looked down at Bell to ask a question.

"Answer me this," said Kalazar. "Would you take the place of this doomed boy?"

"Of course, I would," she answered with a tear. "He's all I've got left."

The mummy pulled away from the boat and tried to think. Reaping many souls through the years made Kalazar forget what emotions felt like. He forgot how it felt to care and not seek vengeance and to look at oneself and realize that he was no better than the murderers.

Before Bell could figure out what he was doing, the mummy moved his hand toward her. She closed her eyes and hoped for a quick and painless death. The hand, strangely, passed over her. She opened her eyes and discovered that he picked up the music box instead.

With the box in his hand, he lowered Bill next to her and gently released him. Kalazar raised his hand and swept away the horrible weather and the roaring winds. All he allowed was the sun and a clear sky, to make the scene more appropriate. Both were shocked and greatly confused. To put it simply, Kalazar's soul finally had a change of heart, all thanks to Bell.

All the victims he took away perished in cowardliness. Out of all of them, Bell was the only one who stood up to him for her own sibling. It reminded him of how brave his children were, standing up to an abomination like him.

Bell made him realize the error of his ways, and for that, he lifted her brother's curse. He crushed the box into dust with his bare hands and thus removed the mark from Bill's palm. The curse was gone forever, but it was hard for the squirrels to celebrate without their loved ones by their side. The mummy couldn't undo the damage, but he thanked them for saving future generations from the curse.

His yellow eyes began to fade away in the wind along with the dust from the music box. Kalazar said his final farewell and sank back down to the ocean below, where he could finally rest in peace.

It was over. Bell & Bill were finally safe but at a heavy cost. They held each other tight and mourned for their family. They could rest eternally, knowing that their children stopped an ancient curse. With that, it was time to move on and head back to the land.

Within an hour, the two figured out how to work the boat and navigate with a map and compass. Their destination was anywhere but home. They could never go back home. Their reputation was tarnished, and they couldn't prove their innocence with an unbelievable story. It was better to sail somewhere else and start a new life. As they sailed the sea, they started speaking to each other again.

"This is all my fault," Bill said as he worked the wheel. "I should have thrown that box into the water with that fish."

Bell looked away from the map. She wanted to smack him for apologizing so much, but she didn't want to hit him anymore. She sighed and convinced him that it wasn't his fault; anyone could have made the same mistake. If he didn't mess with the box in the first place, the curse would still exist, and more lives would've been lost. It was like a horrible blessing in disguise. Let bygones be bygones and move on, I say.

However, Bell did want to blame someone for their misfortunes. She thought of two certain squirrels that could easily be blamed for all the horrors unleashed upon their land.

"Aval & Evel," Bell stated. "Those two vampires are the ones responsible for all of this."

"Aval & Evel?" Bill questioned. "You're seriously blaming them? Bell, please don't end up like Kalazar by blaming others."

"Bill, that weird shady squirrel guy was right," she said. "When those vampires broke their peace, all these monsters came out of the woodwork. First Frankensteins, then werewolves, and now a mummy. You see what I'm getting at here?"

Bill pondered for not too long and realized she actually made some sense. Their very presence and nature caused all types of horrors to come alive, just like the shady squirrel said. If someone didn't stop them, life as they knew would be doomed for sure.

Bell raised her fist and said, "We can stop them! We can end this by putting those vampires down for good."

"You mean kill them?"

"Well, duh," Bell answered. "We can't let these monsters stomp on our lives any longer. We'll gather tools and use them to bring those tyrants down once and for all. It will inspire the whole world to stand up to monsters and put them where they belong—inside history books and romance novels. We'll do it together, as brother and sister. Are you with me?"

Bill had to think long and hard before answering. He still had his doubts. The thought of being saviors of the world had crossed his mind a couple of times before, but challenging powerful vampires? That was certainly out of the question. But then he looked at Bell. She wanted him to join her, to actually become heroes and clear their names. Besides, they certainly had nothing better to do. They'd already laid one monster to rest, so they might as well take down the rest.

With a confident smile, he answered, "Yeah, for peace."

They boldly slapped each other's palms and set off on their journey to rid the world of monsters. Watch out, Aval & Evel, the good guys are coming for you.

9
THE NUTTIEST WITCH

Nutilda brought some butter, some apples soaked in gin.

Mix it all up in a pot until aroma can

ascend into her nostrils, and sneeze right in the stew.

Makes an excellent preservative for sticky-icky

brew in several toenails, ripped strictly from a bear.

A little dab of bunny blood would give the scent some

snare right in a mirror, then collect the broken glass.

Scrape the skin off dirty bitter rats that said to kiss their

as a matter of fact, pour a bowl of spinach dip.

No need to add some salty chips; they make the bubbles

rip out all the cotton, from a kitchen oven mitt.

Pour a batch of smelly, nasty, yucky, chunky oily sh—

it's turning purple; onions make it green;

a pair of dirty underwear that makes a Mormon scream.

Oh good gracious! She forgot the leech and snail!

She'll make it up by adding a little dainty doggy

tell it's almost ready, a potion filled with doom.

Just add a little nitro to give the kick an extra boom!

In the coldest region of the Canadian Alps came a thunderous burst of energy from a witchy tower. It was a massive explosion, which destroyed the very fragile structure. Burned bricks and charred bits showered down upon the mountainside, and within the snow lay a certain chipmunk in a tattered black robe.

It was Nutilda, who'd blown up yet another fortress of hers. It always happened after she created nasty spells and potions of unimaginable propositions. Only that time she was just making some homemade beer.

Her more serious concoctions were supposed to enable her to breathe fire like a dragon and crumble cities with a single yell or worse, a deadly fart. Yet she failed miserably time after time. She could never get them just right. Whenever she tried one out, she most likely got herself blown up.

It was a wonder how that witch managed to survive her own experiments. The very ambition to succeed might have been the only thing that kept her going, and she would not stop until she perfected her talents. So when Nevermore was on the rise, she was more motivated than ever! The destruction of her home and her most precious possessions wasn't going to keep her down. She stood up from the snow, dusted herself off, and called her flying broom to retrieve her. She whistled and clapped her hands as loud as she could, as if it were a dog. The broom didn't come, and it was nowhere to be seen.

Nutilda then yelled out the broom's name, "Norton!"

In the blink of an eye, the broom soared down from the sky, and it finally came to the witch, but it was the strangest sight she ever saw. Her broom was carrying a loud boom box that was playing terrible rap music. It was also wearing several gold chains around itself. Not only that, but on its back sat two female squirrels in trashy outfits and colorful makeup. Apparently, her broom led a better life than she did.

Nutilda said to her broom, "Norton, you two-timing piece of trash! Lose those tramps, or I'll give you such a thrash!"

One of the squirrels felt insulted and said to the nasty witch, "We're divas compared to a troll like you. And don't talk smack about Norty here. He's like our cutie-wootie boyfriend."

"Boyfriend?" Nutilda said in surprise. "Are you some kind of loon? That's my broom, you obnoxious buffoon!"

Ignoring the comment, the other squirrel asked the witch, "Well, if you're not using him, could he take us to the club?"

The nerve of those squirrels. After calling Nutilda a troll, they wanted to take her only means of transportation to a dance club. Nutilda had enough. She rolled up her sleeves and swayed her arms in a hypnotic motion. She chanted spellbinding words and lit her hands with bright-red energy, and she cast a spell on the squirrels. A thunderous clap of light slammed their bodies and made them shake uncontrollably.

Did her spell turn them into frogs, did it turn their bodies inside out, or did she blast them into another dimension? Unfortunately, it was none of the sort. The spell was a rather odd one. The spell tripled the squirrels' chest sizes, to the point where their tops began to rip and tear.

With such astonishing results, though awkward, to say the least, the two squirrels graciously thanked the witch and decided to go to the club right away. Norton flew off with the squirrels into the evening sky and left Nutilda alone in the snow.

Nutilda had no idea she had that kind of power. Looking at her portly figure, she wanted to try it on herself. She chanted the same words and emitted the same red energy. Once she cast the spell, it only tripled the size of her warty feet. Nutilda did not fuss or scream; she just became mighty depressed by the amount of unfairness.

With nowhere to go and without a lair, she traveled the lonely land with her big feet and the roaches in her hair.

She walked through the dense snow so distant from any warmth. How easy it would've been to turn into a frozen statue, get run over by snowmobiles, and have her broken pieces used as ice cubes for a thirsty polar bear. The very idea made her thirsty. Eventually she made it through the Alps and ended up in the grassy plains of Alaska, where she discovered that her feet were shrunken by the shivering snow. She was very relieved that the bulbous feet diminished, but then she realized something: she had no idea why she walked to Alaska in the first place.

She was clearly lost in thought. She wondered why she never succeeded as a decent witch, at such a young age of seventy-three. She learned everything there was to know about witchery. From ancient books to mystic scripts, she could never get one thing right. Her older sisters, however, were taught by human sorceresses, and they were the furriest of wicked witches.

Pesky Pitillda mastered the art of enchantment and sorcery. She cursed Spain with the growth of man-eating Venus flytraps that lasted five straight years.

Hazy Hermilda achieved the way of earthly magic. She terrorized the European lands with tree giants and golem trolls.

Yucky Yutilda learnt necromancy at the age of seven. She raised skeletons from the grave and made them dance to old-timey show tunes, just for fun.

But their reign of terror was stopped, and the products of their evil were put to an end, by the witch hunts. On a cold February night, all of the witches were shackled together on stacks of lumber and burned alive, and the witches were no more. Nutilda was the last of her kind.

If she continued to practice her craft, would she really want the same fate as her sisters? Of course, she would. She considered it an honor to be put to death for something remarkable she did to the world. But would the new modern world cringe at the sight of a witch, much less a stubby chipmunk? Nutilda could only hope and express herself in song.

Nevermore is on the rise;
vampires lead to my surprise.
Everyone's doing well and going strong,
while I do everything completely wrong…

Tired of doubt,

I'll try one out!

I'll cast a dangerous spell so subtle

it'll turn this tree into a yellow puddle!

Twinkle binkle, sorry tree,

watch me turn you into pee!

No wait!

I turned it into chocolate cake...

It was a peculiar sight to see; she actually turned a tree into a delicious miniature cake. Just then, a motherly chipmunk came on the scene and discovered the delicious-looking cake on the ground. She had the hardest time trying to find one for her son's birthday party; timing like that was ever so perfect. She took the cake and thanked the nice witch by giving her a bag full of fresh berries.

Nutilda did not want them at all. She threw the bag on the ground, and she stomped on the fruit. Before she could tell the mother off, she had already left, leaving the witch with her crushed berries.

I'm a witch, I think,

but my magic simply stink...

So I'll try out yet another one!

Hexing a human is always fun!

There's a man jogging up a hill so free.

Maybe I'll turn him into the smallest flea!

Hexus reckless, stupid man,

being a bug will shorten your life span!

Oh snap!

I sprouted angel wings on his back...

The man took a gander and was truly amazed by his newfound wings. He was just thinking of how he could help the human race and its endless sea of crime. With the ability to fly, he was able to be the superhero everyone wished for! He laughed heroically and thanked the kind witch by giving her a bag of shiny gold nuggets.

Nutilda did not want them either. She threw the bag on the ground, and she tried to kick it, but the weight of the nuggets broke her big toe. Before she could curse the man, he had already flown away, leaving the witch with her bruised toe.

I'm a witch, I think,

but my magic simply stink...

My rut is turning into a ditch;

being this way makes me twitch.

I can't get my way without acting like a bitch...

There's nothing more I can do.

My days as a witch are through!

Boo-hoo!

Just as the witch started to cry, a little squirrel girl came near the sad witch. The girl listened to her sad song the whole time behind a set of bushes.

She had to come out and ask her, "Um, what's a bitch?"

Nutilda saw the curious girl. She wanted to turn her into a frog, but she knew she would end up turning the girl into a royal princess. So instead, she answered her question. "It's another name for a female dog you see. But why people take offense to that is a mystery to me."

"Yeah, me too," said the girl. She wanted to know why she wanted to be a bad witch.

Nutilda answered, "A bad witch is what I am, yet I lack thunderous wham. Forests for the trees and Nevermore for the evil drought, but a failure like me belongs without."

"Without what?"

"Something symbolic to the meaning or something other. Why ask all these questions? I'm not your mother! I'm a witch that's vile as snot and rotten as poo; doesn't that even scare you?"

The girl simply chuckled. She liked the way the witch rhymed. The girl's innocence was so rare. She told the witch that she didn't have to be evil; she was fine being a nice witch. She gave gifts to two people, and in return, they rewarded her with riches—what was not to like?

Nutilda thought about the mistakes and how they were actually good mistakes. Her spells only caused good fortune for anyone other than herself. Maybe that was her destiny, to become a good witch.

Nutilda could see it. Her spells would bring peace to the world and end all of its problems. She would be adored, admired, and appreciated by everyone. She would no longer be lonely and friendless again. Nutilda would no longer be a monster but a savior!

But before she could hop around like a kid in a candy store, she had to test her theory first. The witch offered to grant a spell to the girl, and it could be anything she wanted. It was a nice treat for the child. There were so many things the girl had in mind, but there was one that she found most fascinating. She wanted her fluffy tail to be turned into a shiny rainbow.

It was odd yet no trouble for the witch. She stretched her arms, cracked her fingers, and slapped her own face to get pumped up. Nutilda was finally going to get a real feel of accomplishment. The girl stood still and closed her eyes as the witch waved her arms to generate the mystical energy into a flashy blue color.

Nutilda chanted her spell, "~Bristle brittle, soy to sew! Turn this tail into a shiny rainbow~!"

A cloud of blue surrounded the little girl. It engulfed her with immense energy, and she felt the tingling sensation of change. Once the smoke cleared, she did feel different, but the movement of her tail was quite odd. She opened her eyes; she turned around and saw that it was not a rainbow. It was instead a slimy, pulsating eel that was twice her size!

Before she could scream, the eel expanded its jaw and sunk its sharp teeth into the girl! It munched all the way down to her feet, and it began to eat itself. It bit and sucked its tail, and it bled from the pain until its stomach couldn't take anymore. It curled into a ball and fell deathly sick as it blew chunks all over itself. The eel had died, along with the poor girl.

The witch stood silent and realized what she had done. She killed that precious little girl who showed her kindness and not one shred of spitefulness. All she wanted was a rainbow for a tail, not an eel.

Nutilda cried over the loss. She cried and cried, and then she started to whimper, which soon turned into a chuckle. She suddenly started to laugh hysterically through the tears. She went nuts, bonkers; she rolled around on the ground with a smile. It was awfully strange that she would laugh at the tragedy she created, like she was glad that it happened.

She'd figured out why her spells were always so terrible. Trying to create good spells actually made bad spells, which meant that creating bad spells made good spells. Nutilda figured out her own flaw, and she expressed it by continuing her song.

I then met a sweet girl,
who was as pretty as a pearl.
She showed me the light, and it was swell,
so I granted the sweet girl one free spell.

She wanted a rainbow tail only she could feel,
but instead she was eaten alive by a slimy eel…
Farewell, my friend,
indeed a sorry end.

You have shown me the right way.
I have found what I was doing wrong:
my magic works like opposite day!

Like a backward game of truth or dare!
Like a turtle outrunning a lazy hare!
Like a river flowing through the air!
Like an atheist sinner saying a prayer!

It all makes sense!

(It makes no sense.)

It's perfect sense!

(It's perfect nonsense.)

I see it now.

I'll try one nooowww!

Hocus-pocus, willow wake,

fill this land with delicious cake!

Through her arms came smoldering red clouds that covered the fields around for miles. It was strong, too strong for a witch to transform a field to whatever it turned. She didn't care beyond that point; she hoped that something horrific would happen, no matter what the cost. A big bang and a boom was all that was heard. The witch then found herself in a field full of fiery carnage. She had turned the land into a lava wasteland. The intense heat, the devastation, the whole scene was a lot to take in. Even stranger, casting such a spell did not tire her out a bit.

She never knew what kind of power she possessed. She had the power to destroy an entire country, and she couldn't have been happier! She skipped around the lava and landed so delicately from rock to rock. She then had to cast a different spell for good measure, to really test her opposite theory.

She swayed her arms and said, "Krittle cradle, inky blot. Take me to a hellish spot!"

In a puff of green clouds, she vanished out of sight and appeared in a most humble location. She was in a world of soft clouds and a tender atmosphere of pleasantness. It was a rich and peaceful realm, untouched by mortal man. It was full of joyful light and tranquility, that it could only be a pure example of heaven.

Her spell brought her to the holy gates of eternal peace! Nutilda saw the feathers of angels fall through the sky and glitters of yellow sprites that swayed all around the endless space of clouds. All of it was all too different for her taste.

"Well," she said with her eyes wide, "my opposite theory is certainly right. I need to get out of here. I can't stand all this light. Though I should save this nifty spell for later, if I should ever become an angel slayer! He-he-he!"

Nutilda vanished from heaven and landed back in Canada in the middle of the night. She then knew what she had to do to please those vampire squirrels: she had to cause some witchy devastation.

Aaahh...
A simply gorgeous night,
yet it's not completely filled with fright.
Now is my chance to do this right!

Hello world!
Nutilda is no longer a tasteless hack.
I tell ya, it's good coming from heaven and back!
My naughty little spells have gotten well,
so gaze and gawk as I raise some hell!

I cast this moose with healthy legs;
now they're boneless if not dismayed!
I cast this bird family with hearts of gold;
now their hearts are frozen solid cold!

I cast these chipmunks with the size of dogs;
now their bodies are the size of frogs!

These trees over here could be much cleaner;
now they come alive looking so much meaner!

This is the happiest I've ever been.
I will never feel so down again!
So run and hide, my little pretties,
I have the power to crumble cities!

Until then,
my deepest wish
is to turn my body into an ugly fish.
Furrow turrow, shapeless bowl,
give me the body of a fat, ugly troll!

A bright cloud of pink covered her stump of a body. Nutilda was secretly worried that the spell wouldn't work on her. She was worried that it would change her body into a grotesque creature of ugliness. The smoke cleared, and to her surprise, she transformed into a taller, slender, beautiful chipmunk.

She was gifted with long legs, an hourglass figure, and silkier fur. Even her dress had changed. She wore an open outfit with black buckles that held it together at the waist, along with a cute red bow on the back. The dress had long green streams that had real rubies attached to them, not some ninety-nine-cent junk. She even had a little witch hat that covered her right ear.

As for pants and a covered robe, she had nothing but a streamy black skirt that showed her black and green stockings as well as her panties. It was the body she had always dreamed of having for her own. Absolutely no warts, crooked teeth, or misshapen eyes. Even the pesky roaches were expelled from her perfectly shaped hair. She was perfect.

Full of joy and full of delight, she cast a spell that gave her flight. She took to the skies and soared ever farther above the land. There were many landscapes and many city lights she saw from afar. It was so beautiful that she forgot she ever had a broom to fly with.

Nighttime in Canada was nice, but she felt it was in need of improvement. She flew around the land, twirling her arms about, and sang a misty spell. It was a spell that made clouds follow her flight that soon formed into hazy darker ones. She was forming a shroud that stretched from the skies to the ground. Soon the witch created a dome of dark clouds that blocked any light from touching the surface. No luminous moon or blinding sun could be seen from within. Not even the simple connection of satellites that made radios and TVs come alive.

It was a land of pure darkness. It was simply beautiful in her eyes, and it would no doubt make Aval & Evel praise the witch for her magnificent powers. The thought of that image made her laugh like an insane Valkyrie, soaring through the black skies of her own wickedness. Nutilda truly became the nuttiest witch of them all.

I'm a witch, I think,
my magic no longer stink.
So I'll close this song
with a sexy wink.

10
NEGATIVE THOUGHTS

On quiet nights when it's neither cold or warm, when bright stars and a full moon lit the cloudless sky, some would say it's perfect picnic weather. On a lone hilltop sat two young squirrels that were indeed having a nice picnic on the low-cut grass. They had wholesome wheat bread, fresh-squeezed lemonade, and some fruit and veggies for dessert.

It was indeed a lovely date, aside from the drab food. They had no meat, and they didn't even have sweets to satisfy their sweet tooth. They had no candle, either. Personally, to me, there's nothing more pleasant than sharing chocolate cake and a bottle of bourbon under the stars; I'm very romantic that way. The two squirrels, however, were a bit more shy than romantic that evening.

The nervous squirrel girl said to the boy, "Johnny, I'm not sure if I'm ready for this. I mean, it's not even clean. The icky germs, the yucky bacteria—just thinking about that stuff makes me nauseated."

The sensitive squirrel boy then said to her, "Well, jeez, Gloria, it's only a kiss. This is our third date after all, and I want it to be special if it's still OK with you."

Unfortunately, she did not want to touch lips; she preferred to hold hands, and that's exactly what they did. They closed their eyes and enjoyed the touch. Johnny smiled and knew that they were right for each other.

After a while, Gloria's hand left his palm, and he felt a sudden coldness. It was not the emotional coldness one felt when someone left them; the air began to feel like a freezer. Johnny opened his eyes and saw that the ground was engulfed in fog. Gloria was nowhere to be seen.

Johnny wondered what had happened to her. He stood and called her name, which echoed through the field, but there was no answer. He felt so alone and scared.

Then a voice came from behind. "Hey, keep it down! We're trying to have a romantic picnic over here!"

It was a voice he was most unfamiliar with. He quickly turned around and witnessed a disgusting sight none should ever see. It was the fierce vampires, Aval & Evel, sinking their teeth into Gloria's dead body. The gore, the sounds of feeding, and the polite sharing of the girl's limbs was enough to make the boy throw up.

It was an ideal date for the two vampires, and it was a shame they didn't have any candles or violins to create an enticing atmosphere. Evel turned to the frightened squirrel and politely asked if there were any spare napkins they could borrow. A raw meal such as that tended to get messy. Johnny didn't say a word.

Aval stared at the boy, as if he were dessert in fancy clothes. Aval licked his bloodstained lips in a provocative manner, and in a menacing voice, he told the boy to run. Johnny moved his scared eyes left to right, deciding what to do. He could avenge Gloria or run away like a scared little kitten. His decision was the logical choice: he ran for his life and screamed in terror!

He dashed his way into town. He went from corner to corner, street to street, pushing anything that got in his way. When he made it home, he closed the door and locked it tight. He barricaded it with furniture and boxes, right after he nailed it shut with wooden planks. He even armed himself with garlic and a trusty frying pan.

He didn't know that vampires would never enter a home uninvited. It was not because of a mystic spell that prevented them from entering domiciles; it was merely a common courtesy kind of thing. Aval & Evel were ruthless, but at least they were polite about it.

Regardless, Johnny was prepared for anything, but he didn't count on a different kind of intruder. An intruder that needed no invitation to break through the back door. Behind Johnny stood a beastly and hungry werewolf! The ferocious monster knocked the boy into the kitchen; he released the grip of the pan as his head hit the cabinets.

Shortly after, loud screams were heard from that home, followed by more outside. Werewolves were howling through the streets and ravaging the homes of the little critters. They couldn't be stopped, and the poor townsfolk were defenseless to do a thing. It was a massacre, but it did not stop Aval & Evel from taking a stroll through the park. They casually walked hand in hand through the lovely wet grass and were still covered in blood from their previous meal.

Evel swung Aval's arm about and said to him, "I've never felt so relaxed to be outside. The dreary cold air, the howling music, the ear-piercing screams of torture, and a moonlit dinner. You really know how to treat a lady, Aval."

"I'm glad you are having a terrific time, my dear," Aval said in a relaxing tone. "This way of living is simply perfect...almost too perfect. With all these riches and all this freedom surrounding us, I feel like there's something wrong."

Aval suddenly stopped walking and started thinking. Evel noticed this and said, "Are you worried about the werewolves eating everything? We still have loads of other creatures to feed on, lively or corpsy."

"It's not that," Aval said as he scratched his head. "Something has plagued my mind of late. I feel like there's something missing. Something an evening like this wouldn't be complete without."

Evel thought about it for a moment, and she started to giggle, for she knew what he was talking about. She began to snuggle up against Aval, rubbing his chest in a peculiar way.

She said to him with a seductive smile, "Well, this is an excellent moment to seek pleasure. So should we go home or get wild right here?"

"Blech! I'm not talking about nooky time, Evel!" Aval pulled away from her in disgust, making her feel hurt and unwanted.

He hadn't been too close with Evel lately; all he could think about was the spread of terror. He kept thinking about how it was going so well and how it could be improved. Evel became concerned about him; she was afraid he was developing deep and questionable thoughts, as he usually did.

With a hollow sigh, she leaned close and started kissing Aval on the lips. The kiss smeared the bloodstains on their mouths, and a good bit of it was washed away by the slobber. When Evel finished, Aval showed no reaction. He was still deep in his thoughts.

Evel immediately told him to come back to her, to stop thinking and enjoy the night. He wouldn't, though; he hardly found a means to enjoy it. He couldn't stop thinking and pondering about the one element that had yet to show its hideous face on the joyous reign.

A line of dark clouds soared through the sky at incredible speed. The clouds turned the bright night into pitch black, where only streetlamps provided some light. It was not just that one town, but all around Canada the spread of darkness grew and blocked everything from the outside world. It even blocked the moon's energy, and it caused the werewolves to revert to their normal forms.

Maybe that's what Aval was thinking about, something unexpected that would dampen the perfect evening. Evel always warned him to stop having negative thoughts. The vampires looked at each other, having mixed feelings about the whole situation, and wondered what could have caused it. All they could do then was to call for an immediate monster meeting.

The meeting was held at the vampires' humble tree, rather than at the far reaches of the continent. Their chilly home was filled with lit candles, while their newly found protection of Frankenstein soldiers still stood and guarded the tree. The soldiers watched all around with their guns and their night-vision specs, which emitted a red shine. They were so strict on protection that even the slightest movement of an insect would cause them to shoot on sight.

Bang!

A soldier shot a measly ant, while Aval & Evel were becoming awfully annoyed by their guests messing up their tidy living room. From mangy creatures with fleas, scratching themselves, to the speed-reading Vincety flinging books all over the floor, to the curtain-eating tarantula that was Tye.

Vincety had to confess that the books on their shelves were rather out of date. He suggested some interesting digests that would bring them up to speed on the marvelous world of science. Tye stated that the curtains disagreed with his stomach and were impossible to make into shoes. He asked if they would consider some new decor. The former werewolves complained that their sink did not hold enough of their ever-rushing urine. There was not much to be said about that, but advice about having more towels in the kitchen was suggested.

I, however, did not bring myself to tell them about my little trip to their bathroom. It was an embarrassing fault of my own, so I took out a sticky note and wrote, "Get a plumber, now!" Then I placed it on the bathroom door, which was more than discreet.

The two vampires sat in their chairs and watched their home fall apart with much discomfort. It was a vivid reminder of how much they hated guests. Once the idea of waiting for them to tire themselves out had passed, Aval got out a small chalkboard and slowly scraped it with a rusty hook. It made an awful screeching sound, like hundreds of tiny crows crying for death in one's ear, with microphones. The guests held their hands to their ears in pain and begged for the torture to stop. Aval then ceased the noise as everyone became quiet and still.

"There," Aval said as he discarded the tools and then walked to the center of the room. "Much better. Now that I have everyone's attention, we may start this little meeting. We are short a witch and a sea monster, however; nevertheless, we must proceed. Now, this darkness is indeed a delightful change of weather, but not so much for our werewolf party. Without the moon's luminous light, they cannot transform into meat-craving hunters. I suspect that this spread of darkness is the cause of an unknown force, and I want to know who did it."

Of course, no one knew who or what made the skies turn so dark, until they heard a certain laugh from the outside. The balcony windows blew open, letting in a rush of wind that ravaged the room. The wind died down, and a slender figure flew its way in with a cheeky laugh and a flashy display of green sprites. It was none other than the beautiful witch, Nutilda.

She landed in the center of the room and showed off her new look to the guys. She posed, she smiled, she winked; it made all the men howl and drool like hounds. The women, however, growled and envied her appearance, especially Evel. She saw that the stranger was showing off near Aval, and it made her a tad angry. Surprisingly, nobody knew it was Nutilda. They thought she was some random supermodel that flew in through the windows. It came as no surprise to her, and when she claimed to be the formerly ugly witch named Nutilda, everyone slapped themselves silly!

"That's right!" Nutilda said. "I've improved in many ways, as I can tell by your awestruck gaze. And to make this shock bigger than it is already, I put this blanket over Canada! He-he-he!"

Nutilda smiled ever so wide and waited for praise and applause, but instead she was bombarded with curses. All around the room were complaints about the moon and how the dark was too dark. The dome was nothing but an eyesore that would only draw attention from the outside world. Nutilda felt like she was surrounded by babies.

She told the creatures to live without the moon; anyone could feast inside a dark room. If the rest of the planet discovered the dome, so what? Getting through it would be a difficult cut.

Nutilda mentioned that she added a mysterious spell that would prevent anything from entering or exiting the land. What spell was that? She did not know or care, since she was unaffected by it. All she knew was that the dome was protecting their evil playground. She turned to Aval & Evel and hoped they saw it as an ideal setting for a monster kingdom. Aval held his finger to his chin, for he was consumed in deep thought yet again. Evel, however, sarcastically clapped at the nutty witch.

"Bravo, Nutilda," said Evel, "you truly became a great and powerful witch. Total darkness and concealment is a great environment for our kingdom…but there is just one problem with that: How the hell are we supposed to get out?"

"Get out? What are you talking about?" Nutilda asked.

"We can't stay here forever," Evel explained. "There are other places we must spread fear to, and we can't do that if we're stuck in this dome. Reverse this spell, or I'll personally make your face ugly again."

Nutilda sensed Evel's anger. She had no choice but to reverse her spell. But her ego took ahold of her. Nutilda spent too much time and effort creating a land of darkness. She wasn't going to let a squawky thing like Evel shut down her own masterpiece.

So without fear, Nutilda told a lie. "There is no reversing cure, clearly certain I'm sure. I can, however, expand more darkness over the planet, so there's no need to insight a rage or lament."

"You don't get it, do you?" Evel said as she faced that witch. "You've cursed the land with a blinding eyesore, you deprived our hunters of their abilities, and you think that expanding this justifies the problem? You're a hag that's supposed to turn creatures into frogs and make soup out of children. You are being nothing more than an idiot!"

Nutilda was called a lot of foul things, but being called an idiot was not a thing she took as a compliment. Before the two women could start a brawl, Aval spoke out and said that Nutilda wasn't an idiot. He said that she was free to do as she pleased, and the dome could very well be the start to a beautiful nation.

His opinion turned heads. Aval thought the dome was a good contribution to the cause. Life without light would certainly cause fear to spread. He thanked Nutilda and told her to do some more work inside Canada, and the witch laughed and chuckled with joy. She thanked the thoughtful squirrel, and then she vanished from sight, leaving small strands of dead fur on the carpet. Seeing the dead fur made Aval think a bit more.

With that in his mind, Aval instructed Vincety to continue his studies and fix his soldiers' targeting system. He didn't want any more intruders busting through his windows. Then he told the powerless to make do with the darkness. Then he told Tye to make himself useful any way he could, besides making shoes. The monsters were given their orders and were sent out of the house, ending the meeting. The monsters parted ways across the field of tombstones until it was just Aval & Evel to do as they pleased in their home. The first thing they had in mind was to have a little drink. The whole ordeal made them deathly parched.

They made their way into the kitchen, but their meal wasn't in the refrigerator that night, for their nourishment was strapped and buckled down on the kitchen table. It was a lady squirrel the vampires tortured for talking trash about a certain movie the other night. Duct tape covered her mouth, and her legs were removed and stored in the freezer as frozen treats. What made the torture more unbearable was that her torso was spread open with iron hooks and jagged staples. It must have been a special movie for Aval & Evel to go that far.

Tears flowed down the squirrel's face, and she desperately pleaded to be set free. Her murmuring words were unheard as Aval reached for a loopy straw from a drawer. He drove the straw right into her heart and began to sample the sweet juices. It caused the victim to scream a lot and then a little less until she slowly blacked out. Evel came along and shoved him away from the straw; she wanted to take some for herself. She slurped at a fast pace, and it made her to feel a bit mellow.

"That's right, relax," Aval said as he stuck another straw into the heart.

"Don't tell me what to do," Evel said after she put her dainty thumb over the straw. "I'm not in the mood, and it also doesn't help that this narrator is bugging me out of my mind!"

Well, being the narrator that I am, I could hardly apologize for having a particular interest in their lives. Evel was clearly misdirecting her anger. She was just mad at Aval for making their decisions and that he agreed with Nutilda, a witch Evel found to be a hussy. If I didn't know any better, I'd say she was jealous. I could tell by that throbbing vein on her forehead, that glare in those murderous eyes, and the growls that sounded like a tiger.

I could tell she was jealous. Were there other creatures catching his eye? Was that the reason Aval hardly paid attention to her? I was hoping that he would answer, for I felt Evel had thoughts about what to do with that meat cleaver stuck in the table.

Aval finally said, "Evel, don't be jealous. Females like her do nothing for me."

He was quite right. Looking at drop-dead gorgeous females did practically nothing for him, and some might think it was because he was loyal to Evel. That could be answered either way. As far as I could remember, Aval was never entrapped in the spells of any female, because he considered them to be crazy whiners and fickle princesses. During the early years of seeking certain pleasure, he participated with both genders to find his liking. In the end, he felt it was right to stay with the opposite sex.

Evel did the same in her journey, but she felt very questionable emotions back then. Even though she considered males to be lazy back-scratchers and selfish dogs, she preferred those gullible lugs over prima donnas.

These squirrels were very open-minded back in the day, in a weird sort of way. Just then I saw Aval glaring at me, and I sensed that he also had thoughts about that particular cleaver. So I decided to stop talking about their past romances and let them have their space.

"Good narrator," said Aval. "Now, Evel, I just agreed with that witch for the purpose of a test. Nutilda's overconfidence might be her undoing, and this dome will soon die along with her. Let these monsters play, I say. Let them destroy themselves, for only the strong will have the privilege to stand with us. All we have to do is sit back and watch."

After Evel sipped some more blood, she said to him, "You are so manipulative. You'd let our followers lose themselves right when I thought we were their humble leaders. I would call it evil, but the whole thing is just stupid."

"It's not stupid," he said. "It's a brilliant test of stupidity. I want to see how far we monsters have risen from the dark ages and into the modern century, survival-wise. We've already proved ourselves mighty, and now it's time for the others to sink or swim. So please relax, my dear. Maybe we can head back to that park and do…whatever it is you wish."

"No, no. I grow tired of you this night, Aval. I cannot help but feel you pay more attention to your thoughts and plans than anything else. Right now the only thing that could ease my troubling tension is my trusty blender."

She took the blender from the counter and stomped upstairs to the bedroom. Aval asked her why she needed such a device. Evel told him to just think about it as she slammed and locked the door. It took Aval a good while to figure it out, right when the prisoner's heart was sucked dry like an empty soda.

Having their way or not, happiness never lasted for Aval & Evel; it only created more problems. I guess that's the price of becoming little evil vampires. Sure, they liked being that way, but they weren't always like that. There was a different time where they didn't have evil intentions toward anything. They didn't think about murdering each other or anyone at all; they simply wanted to get another shot at life after becoming vampires.

Those fond memories came back to Aval when he observed the dead squirrel on his table. He examined her pale face and gently stroked her fur. It reminded him of the time he and Evel were attending their first day of school in Dew Leaf, eighty-odd years ago. The opportunity to learn would've proved a significant change from their boring routines, and it would've been a chance to make new friends.

On a bright sunny morning in Dew Leaf, a group of teenagers— two squirrels, a hedgehog, and a tiny skunk—waited on the side of a dirt road for the bus-beaver to pick them up. Yes, even back then, riding beavers were comfortable and convenient. The group chatted away, admitting to one another how they were nervous about the first day of high school and that they were afraid others would treat them as freshmen. Though it was the least of their worries, when they spotted two vampires walking toward them.

The vampires approached the group, hand in hand, carrying old-fashioned backpacks, blood-filled glasses with straws, and a fancy umbrella to shield them from the sun. The vampires stopped next to the teenagers and waited for the bus-beaver as well. There was an awkward silence until the vampires turned to the teenagers. Their faces were a lot different. Their eyes didn't look tired, and the smiles on their faces did not go away.

It was a wonder what they would say to them, but Aval set the tone. "Hey there, fellow learners! Some morning, huh? The wind is fair, the sky is clear, and the sun is just inches away from burning us. What a way to start off a school year, am I right?"

The teens said nothing to the vampires. They were too scared to even make eye contact.

Evel knew they had to introduce themselves first. So she said in a friendly tone, "Hello, my name is Evel, and this is my sweet husband, Aval. You probably have guessed that we're vampires, but don't be frightened by our looks. We haven't used a mirror in ages, and I can't tell a lipstick from a Chap Stick."

How absolutely terrifying. Aval & Evel were friendly vampires! It could've been a trick or an act, but being friendly was what they were doing. They told jokes, they were quirky, and they were indeed playful at times on good days. They even chanced the sun in hopes of making friends. How horrifyingly unlike vampires; it made the very hair turn gray.

They weren't perfect all their lives, though. They had bad days, sad days, and days when they got even with a little blood on their hands. They were good-natured overall, and they wanted a fair shot at life, but it all went downhill when Aval & Evel asked the teens for their names. The skunk girl was the first to speak, and she had a different attitude toward them.

"We don't want you bloodsuckers here," she said. "You turned our town into this pit you call Nevermore. I oughta take that umbrella and watch you turn to ash."

"Oh, you don't want to do that," said Evel, "because we might die, and that would be very rude. You don't see me threatening to knock that spider off your shoulder, do you?"

"Spider?" The skunk turned her body about to find that creepy-crawly bug. To her surprise, there wasn't a thing on her. Evel fooled her just to get a quick laugh.

"Ha! Made you look," Evel said as she giggled.

The skunk girl growled and said, "You two are just asking for it now."

Then Aval said with a smirk, "Asking for what? Cake?"

The skunk shook her head and said, "I'm not talking about cake. I'm talking about a punch."

"Fruit punch?"

"No, pain!"

"Propane? Why would I need gas?"

"Not propane! I'm talking about fu—"

"Whoa, lady, keep it PG over here."

Aval & Evel were very playful back then. Instead of going around killing others, they found joy in messing around with them. The skunk couldn't take it anymore. She was throwing a fit, so one of her friends asked the vampires, "Why are you doing this?"

Evel answered, "We're playing with you, like all friends do. We want to be your bosom buddies."

It was a simple statement, but not easy enough to go along with. One of the nervous squirrels told them that their parents wouldn't like them making friends with monsters. Aval & Evel asked him why, when they hadn't done anything.

Then out of fear, the squirrel boy cried out, "Don't kill me!"

"We're not going to kill anyone," Aval said, "especially children."

It was hard for them to be convinced, so the skunk walked up to the vampires and challenged their words. She held her arm close to their mouths, explaining how even for a skunk, vampires couldn't resist the taste of fresh blood.

She continued to stay and expose her wrist, but she watched their eyes closely. The vampires wanted to look away, but the tingling urge kept their eyes glued to her wrist. She noticed that Aval began to shake his glass in a slight twitching manner. Then she looked at Evel and watched her gulp nervously and wipe her lips quickly with her tongue. It was like putting candy in the face of a fat child or drugs in the face of a junkie. It was a struggle to resist.

The skunk had the proof nonetheless. She proved that they were putting on an act. She knew they were going to eat them, but Aval & Evel claimed that she tempted them. It did not matter; the teenagers did not want any monsters near their school. The skunk knocked the umbrella out of their hands, and she watched the sun burn every inch of their bodies.

The two sizzled from the harmful rays, and smoke came out of their very skin. They screamed, they dropped everything, and they rolled around on the grass like they were consumed in blazing hellfire! They needed shade, protective shade. Aval & Evel quickly crawled behind a nearby tree and shielded themselves from the sun, holding each other and shaking uncontrollably. The sad part was that the others showed no sympathy.

When the bus-beaver approached, the teenagers climbed aboard and acted like nothing had happened. No one else saw the shaded vampires, just an umbrella and empty glasses lying on the grass. The teens proceeded to school, and the frightened vampires were left alone to suffer.

Time after time they were rejected by society, and over the years Aval & Evel developed a certain hate toward mortals. It was one of the many horrible memories Aval had to revisit, just to remind himself of how cruel the world is. He believed no one deserved their kind side; he would rather skin them alive. So there was no question as to where that strange skunk fur on their mailbox came from.

Perhaps Evel was right. Maybe he had to stop having such negative thoughts.

11

NEVERMORE FOG

The dome of complete darkness loomed over Canada for two straight days. Without the warmth of the sun, the land was turning cold as winter. The streets were filled with destructive chaos and bright fires and loud dubstep music, which made it all seem worse.

No one could leave, and no one could enter—or should I say pass through. The barrier of dark clouds was just a cover; the real mystery lay within its foggy walls. It was a mass of dense fog that felt like little sprinkles of water, and it was soothing enough to lure in the most curious souls. The fog spelled doom for anyone who came close to it, yet no one really knew what it was. They never came back to tell.

It was a dangerous land, a destructive and mysterious void. Thanks to Nutilda, there was nothing a single soul could do to liberate the land from the witch's spell, but when a lone fishing boat hit the shore, some could sense a little strand of hope. From the boat came the two squirrels, Bell & Bill, who had just arrived on that quiet morning when the sun slowly peeked above the sea. The squirrels observed the massive structure of fog, and it was one of the most peculiar weather settings they had ever seen.

Bell had a feeling the vampires were to blame for the gloomy dome, and she was more determined than ever to stop them, even if it meant heading into that shroud of mystery. Bill objected to venturing into the dome. He knew there was something off about it. It gave him the chills, the creeps, and the heebie-jeebies.

But Bell told him there was nothing to fear; they had flashlights to help them see and a compass to help lead the way. The worst that could've happened in the fog was running into trees, falling into frozen lakes, or getting run over by a vehicle. Not to mention the possibility of running into monsters that fed on flesh and bones. But with Bell's trusty cricket bat, there was no chance they'd lay one paw on them.

She was sure confident in their survival, even if she wasn't the best at motivational speeches. Bill sighed, knowing there was no other way around it. He decided to throw his cares away and go on an adventure. He lived an OK life as a virgin, after all.

After the squirrels weighed anchor, they grabbed their blue hoodies and snagged all the supplies they could carry in their backpacks for the long journey ahead. They began to walk on the shore, slowly disappearing into the fog with every step they took. Farther in they went, and they saw nothing but pure gray fog and black trees that looked sickly.

The fog was so dense that the sun wasn't able to shed its light on the dreary and mysterious land. Leaves fell like rain, and their structures were limp, like dead flowers looking down at the earth. Everything appeared to be dying; even the grass and flowers were unnaturally withering away.

Bell & Bill's eyes began to tear up, not because of the dreary scene but the misty weather. Rubbing them seemed to help, but not much. As they continued to rub their irritated eyes, they felt painful headaches that lasted only a few seconds, but the weird part was that they felt it at the same time. Ignoring the headache, Bell had the suspicion that they might've been lost and were going in the wrong direction.

"We need to head directly west," Bill said as he took out the map. He never knew Bell was so bad at navigating. "With that compass, it should have been a breeze for you. It's no trouble for the smart and unruffled."

"What?" Bell said with an arched brow. She never heard Bill say unruffled before. "Look, all we need to do is find a sign or something. Otherwise we won't be able to pin...to pin...mghh, to know where we are. I see no signal things." Bell began to feel light-headed as well as Bill.

"Mghh...signs are all around us," he said with a tired expression. "Yet they are just as lost as we are, I believe."

Bell & Bill were acting stranger than usual, but it was probably because of hunger. Bill said they should take a break and eat some peanut butter and jelly sandwiches. It was their favorite meal, and it hit the spot every time. Bell shook her head and refused to take a break, especially in an area of nothingness. She then looked at her compass, but somehow she had a difficult time understanding it. She couldn't figure out why it always pointed north, whichever way they went. She banged the confusing device on her head and told it to work, but nothing happened.

When she demanded to see Bill's map, she discovered a scared look on his face. Bell looked over to see what the matter was. She saw that the map's ink was washing off the paper. The moisture in the air somehow destroyed the map, and the two squirrels were hopelessly lost in the fog!

Bill sat down and composed himself, trying to figure out what to do next, and Bell paced the ground back and forth, constantly telling him they shouldn't panic, freak out, or lose their wits. Bell did not hear a peep from Bill. He just sat there near a pile of dead leaves, with his head deep in his arms. He appeared to be sad.

Bell knew she had to comfort her poor brother. She sat next to him and told him not to worry. They could always find a town and get another map. Hearing that only made him sadder, since they hadn't seen a soul for miles.

They did not even hear the lively sounds of bugs buzzing or birds chirping. It was like everything had died and withered away. Bill lifted his head and felt that it was hopeless to go any farther, which brought about another pep talk from Bell.

"It's only hopeless when you think it is," she said as she grabbed his shoulder. "Don't let this fog get to you. It's just stupid fog that melts ink. Makes it go *blooshhh* like that clear art stuff, you know? It's only fog in a freaky forest. We have stuff to do and stuff left…not to do. You know what I mean?"

Bill then lowered his eyelids halfway and finally lifted his head from his arms. Bell saw that he suddenly formed dark circles around his eyes, like he hadn't slept in days. It worried her.

Bill stared off into the distance and said, "Yes, we must move on. Yet this fog has an ominous and radiant feel to it. It reminds me of my sorrows as well as the sweet ones. I remember the pure essence of serenity when I first walked through a foggy night. The rays of the full moon bounced off every cloud and gave them light, yet the objects around me were covered in sheer darkness. It was like an unknown heaven waiting to be explored or the coldest feat of limbo that left me lost forever."

His poetic insight was an interesting change. Bell, however, did not like the way he spoke at all, but the way she spoke was no better. It was as if she tried to form comprehensible sentences, but her brain couldn't find the words. Perhaps being hungry made Bell & Bill act extremely strangely.

Bell took off her backpack and quickly pulled out some sandwiches she'd carefully wrapped in plastic. They sat there on the ground and started to eat, in hopes of regaining their senses. The sandwiches definitely made them feel better. They enjoyed their meal until they heard some leaves riffling behind them.

Before they could even turn around, a creature jumped out with its arms wide open and shouted, "PB&J? Make mine with extra jelly and hold the jam."

Out of the leaves came not a monster but a happy black-and-brown chipmunk in a gray suit and teal tie. He'd slept in that pile of leaves for some time, until the smell of sandwiches woke him up with delight. He certainly scared the pants off Bell, especially when she saw his eyes. His eyes were his most outstanding feature, which were as big as balloons, and the mismatched pupils moving like googly eyes on a toy. It was unsettling at first, but Bell was relieved to know that he wasn't a psychopath. He was just a hungry chipmunk with a happy-go-lucky attitude and a horrible birth defect. Bill showed no expression or interest in the chipmunk. He wasn't scared either; he was too busy eating his sandwich.

The chipmunk was lost in the fog too, and he was thrilled to see some lively faces in such a miserable place, especially when they had snacks. Bell was kind enough to give him one of her sandwiches. He snatched it and scarfed it down. The chipmunk released a belch of satisfaction and thanked them both, right before he introduced himself.

His name was Roger Hazelnut, a famous comedian in search of a local theater. Bell & Bill never heard of him, which insulted him. He was adored throughout Canada, idolized in America, and praised in New Zealand. The squirrels were awfully confused by the random travel to New Zealand.

"Hey, why not New Zealand?" asked Roger. "Weather's nice, everybody's friendly, and the best part was that my wife booked the tickets that summer. Yeah, she booked mine for New Zealand while she took Hawaii! Ha-ha-ha!"

"You seem cheery," Bill said in a bland tone. "Why so happy in this place so dreary?"

"Well, my doctor says I have this thing called 'angel-man syndrome.' But what did he know? I once saw a guy walk in his office with a knife stuck in his head; the doc just gave him some painkillers and a lollipop!" Roger laughed. "Now how I got here, that's another story. Let me tell ya. I asked this guy for directions to the local theater. He told me to go straight for three miles, then turn left at a lake, right at a fork in the road, cross a riverbank, and head down a road called Saint Gizer Street. So I walked three miles straight, turned left at a lake, right at a fork in the road, crossed a riverbank, and went down Saint Gizer Street. And wouldn't ya know it, I ran into Waldo!"

Roger stood there and waited for the two squirrels to laugh. Sadly, they barely smirked, because they didn't get the comic reference.

"But it didn't stop there," Roger continued. "I thought, 'Hey, maybe Waldo knows where the theater is.' Long story short: I ended up here in limbo! Moral of the story: never get directions from a guy wearing stripes."

Roger still waited for the sounds of laughter, but then he saw that the squirrels began to walk off, enjoying their sandwiches without him. Roger desperately rushed after them. He didn't want to be left alone. He needed travel buddies, and what's more, someone to tell jokes to.

Bell & Bill didn't mind him tagging along, but they had no interest in jokes at the moment. They informed Roger that they were on a mission to reach Nevermore and bring down the rule of Aval & Evel. Any directions would've been helpful, but for some reason, Roger only told jokes.

"Nevermore? Jeez, what a town," he said. "What a town Nevermore is. Let me tell ya, that place is nothing but death and tombstones. Why, every time I stop to take a leak, I hit somebody's grave."

He couldn't help at all. He was stuck in his own world of humor. For ten straight minutes, they walked in the fog, and the barrage of jokes began to weigh down on them.

"Boy, what a town Nevermore is. Let me tell ya, if I had a dollar for every day someone didn't die, I'd be beggin' for change."

Twenty minutes had passed, and the death jokes were really starting to annoy Bell & Bill.

"I mean the only time someone doesn't die is when they're brought back from the dead! Which is kinda ironic, since they're the ones who really do the killing. Hey, I can get used to this dark humor stuff."

They couldn't take anymore. They stopped in the middle of an abandoned road, and Bill had to say something to the chatty comedian.

"Hazelnut, cease these jokes!" Bill pleaded as he fell to his knees. "My ears are begging for peace! It's like your worst quality, telling nothing but terrible jokes."

Roger gasped and said, "Terrible? Oh boy. Not to be throwing stones, but look at you two. I'm trying to lighten the mood, and you act like a couple of sticks in the mud. Imagine, a boy as dull as a dead stump and a gal as dim as a broken lightbulb. I tell ya, you're one unpaid intern away from jumping off a cliff!"

"What? I'm not...whatever you said, just now..." Bell said as she rubbed her head. "You, as for you, there's a little line between funny and...uhh, what's a word for not funny?"

Bill moaned with his face to the road and said, "Annoying, grave, tragic...much like life itself. Entertainment is just a blindfold, a mask, a temporary show for those who wish to escape from reality or face it with much misery..."

Roger noticed the two were acting really weird, but not as weird as the other kids he met during his travel. Those poor children were completely insane. They gave off creepy smiles, they tried to kill each other, and the only thing they ever talked about was pancakes. All they thought about was eating pancakes, hating pancakes, marrying pancakes. Roger couldn't decide if he was in a nuthouse or at IHOP.

The talk of pancakes then stirred something odd in Bell's mind. It was an embarrassing, life-threatening situation she never knew existed. A large amount of anxiety coursed through her body as she discovered something awful—she did not know what pancakes were. It was not the benign ignorance of food but the sudden loss of knowledge. Her eyes widened with deep concern, for there was no denying that something was terribly wrong.

She noticed that her brother acted unnaturally depressed. Even after eating he hardly wanted to move from the ground. As for Roger, he had an obsession for telling jokes for no reason at all. As for herself, the very knowledge was slowly being sucked out of her brain. Bell was becoming dumber, Roger was turning insufferable, and Bill was going emo!

Bell screamed and shouted. She became hysterical and ran off into the forest like a madwoman. It was hard for her to navigate, for she felt her motor control was declining as well. She bumped into trees and tripped over twigs; she even circled a rock multiple times. She eventually slid down to what seemed like a ditch, which quickly turned into a cliff.

Bell fell and hit rugged rocks all the way down to an ashy surface. The fall was not fatal, but the land she entered was worse than any injury. She saw what looked like an apocalyptic crash site, where burned cars and shattered airplanes covered the landscape.

Fire lit the fog in bright orange, and human bodies were scorched and scattered like bacon bits. It was a horrific scene and a cruel answer to where all life went. It all came to that area to crash and burn, like the final destination for the foolish and the reckless.

Suddenly, a blurred figure came into Bell's hazy view. It approached her and said mystical words that she didn't understand at all. Then a flash of light was shone in her face, and in a split second, she fell into a deep slumber.

An hour of total darkness passed, and Bell began to open her eyes. Blurs and colorful spots cluttered her vision, and she felt metal bars behind her head. She found herself in a locked cage dangling like a prisoner from the ceiling.

She was in a filthy shack that had a boiling cauldron in the middle of the room, a gigantic furnace that filled the air with intense heat and, curiously, some stale candy scattered on the floor. She could've pieced all the clues together and figured out who had captured her, but she didn't know what the objects were.

What she did recognize was her gloomy brother lying in a separate cage next to her. His eyes were open, yet he was motionless. She stretched her arm through the iron bars to knock the cage and check if he was still alive. His cage was a bit too far from her reach. Her IQ dropped so much that it was hard just to speak to him. She then began to wonder what she was doing, as she soon started to forget who he was.

Suddenly, a loud kick opened the door, and through it entered a lady with a bag full of potatoes and onions. It was Nutilda, who had just finished gathering the ingredients needed to prepare breakfast.

"Woo! This fog is thicker than a fat man's fart," she said. "I had one heck of a time finding a shopping mart!"

Nutilda slammed the door shut and threw the veggies on a wooden table. Once there, she took a sharp knife and began to carelessly chop them into pieces, making a bigger mess than necessary. It had been ages since she prepared actual food, after all, especially when she was in a chipper mood.

Bell looked at the witch and said to her, "P-please...whelp...gee..."

The witch turned to the drooling squirrel and said, "Did you say 'whelp gee'? What on earth could that possibly be? Whelp gee...oh, you mean 'help me.' That, my dear, I cannot do. I'm in the middle of making some kiddie stew. I never tried it before, but my sisters loved it. They say it's as tasty as jelly on a crumpet."

"Whelp...bek...bbllrrr...fghhsh..." Bell's mind had finally turned to mush.

The witch could see that the two squirrels she imprisoned had no doubt fallen victim to the fog. She explained why they were acting so strangely but in the form of a short poem.

Can you feel the void of this place?
Can you feel the bits of water on your face?

My fog is as wondrous as a star's gleam
and more inviting than boiling hot steam.
Huge and mysterious,
welcoming and curious.

It does more than lie around like residue;
it dampens the feelings held inside of you.

This fog is a gas in a playful way.

Searching your mind for equality,

begging to share your worst quality,

it wants to be friends, and it wants you to stay.

"To put it in a simpler word, my fog brings out personalities most absurd," Nutilda plainly rhymed. "It renders you useless to perform a simple task like navigating or opening a flask. Critters and humans crash and burn in a fiery ring, but I am fortunate enough to not feel a thing! This fog is my home, and you shall forever suffer this nasty syndrome! Well, that is until I eat you; that much I can say or do."

The witch went back to her vegetables, slicing and tossing them into the boiling cauldron while adding a few lizard tails and eggshells for flavor. She even sang another song as the tortured squirrels drifted away into a numb drowse of hopelessness. Once the pot was primed and ready, it was time to add the main ingredients.

Nutilda swung a ring of keys around her finger and skipped toward the squirrels. Bell took a look into the witch's menacing eyes, and with the little sense she had left, she felt that all hope was certainly lost. Noticing this, Nutilda decided to pick her brother first, to make her suffer a bit more. The witch stuck the key into his lock, and right before she could turn it, an unexpected guest entered the house.

"Hey! Guess who's comin' to dinner!" The comedic chipmunk, Roger, kicked open the door and startled the witch. "When I smell somethin' cookin', I come a-runnin', unless it's loaded with beans. Let me tell ya, I ate some chili beans at my cousin Ruth's house, and woo! I had gas so strong, they gave my pants a Viking funeral!"

It was an unpleasant surprise, thanks to the witch's mistake to leave the door unlocked. Who would have suspected someone like him to barge in uninvited? Roger said hi to the two squirrels, but Bill sat motionless, and Bell drooled with her head rolling side to side. Regardless, he joked about them being caged like birds.

Then he saw Nutilda, and his heart started to skip. She was the most beautiful thing he ever saw in his life. The sight of her beauty and her irresistible body made him drool like a dog. After wiping the drool from his mouth, he pulled out a rose from his suit and offered himself to the witch. The very idea disgusted her, and she wanted him to pay for intruding.

She cracked her fingers and prepared to cast a spell upon his face. "Fibbidi fobbidi fibble, make his mouth even more invisible!"

She cast the spell, and to Roger's surprise, his mouth was completely erased from his face! He rolled around on the floor in despair while the witch laughed at his misery. Then she suddenly heard a voice. It was a sad voice similar to Roger's, though it did not come from him. Nutilda looked beside her and discovered that her cauldron had grown a big yapping mouth. How surprising!

"Oh great, now suddenly I'm a pothead!" said the pot, pouring its juices onto the witch's feet. "What a dirty stab at my character! Why? Because I look different? That's the story of my life: no sympathy, I get no sympathy at all... One time I put up flyers around town to promote my next gig—with my face on 'em, mind you. Then, would you believe it, the cops threw me in jail for indecent exposure!"

Nutilda was shocked to see that her magic had a different effect. She cast a different spell on the pot, and it made the mouth vanish. She was relieved to get rid of his voice. Then a few seconds later, the same voice came back, only that time it came from the furnace. It slammed its metal door wide open and began to speak in a clanky fiery tone.

"Jeez, no sympathy, I get no sympathy at all!" yelled the furnace, scaring the witch with its flames. "One time I went to a priest to confess my sins; the guy fell asleep on me!"

Nutilda became frightened, but she had no choice but to cast the same spell again and again until his voice could no longer be heard. After a few more spells, there was nothing but silence and inside murmurs that came from the poor mouthless comedian on the floor. She let out a relieved sigh, but the voice came back still. That time, the voice came from the last place she'd expected it to appear: her butt.

"No sympathy, no sympathy whatsoever!" It flapped out the words, oddly, in clear sentences. "When I was seven, I put a tooth under my pillow; the tooth fairy gave me an IOU! Imagine that!"

It wouldn't stop talking; the mouth wouldn't go away. Her very magic was worse than ever before. Could it be? Could it be that the fog affected her so her worst quality was her magic? It was true—the witch had doomed herself all along. The shocking realization of how foolish she had become drove her mad.

"This can't be happening! I shouldn't be affected. I created the fog! Shut up!" Nutilda screamed at the voice. "Shut up! You're driving me crazy! So crazy that I can't even rhyme! Aahhh!"

She screamed and tore out the hair from her head, begging for the torture to stop. She turned to the open furnace and wanted to jump right in, but the act was too much even to think of. A witch would never die in such a cowardly way, for she feared her sisters would laugh at her in the afterlife. That's what she saw in the flames: a mirage of her own sisters pointing and laughing at the witch losing her mind. Nutilda turned away, scared and ashamed for witnessing such an awful illusion.

Just then, she bumped into the unfeeling squirrel—Bill himself. While she was busy trying to get rid of the comedian's voice, which Bill observed with displeasure, he had the idea to unlock the gate with the key inside and do what was right in his eyes. He wanted to end her suffering. The torment of losing her way and her sanity was not a life one should ever live through.

Bill gazed at Nutilda with his cold dead eyes and softly spoke to her. "It's OK to laugh. The reaper always laughs in the end."

Bill pushed the witch into the blazing inferno and locked the door behind! Nutilda felt the incredible pain of fire burning every inch of her body. She screamed like a tortured banshee and squirmed like a trapped worm. She cried for Bill to open the door, but he ignored her pleas.

He watched her burn with no feeling whatsoever, other than the satisfaction of helping a soul escape to the afterlife. The product of the fog, the result of her own creation of madness, stood there and watched her burn, burn, and burn. There was nothing left but silence.

12

NEVERMORE SUNSHINE

Nutilda was consumed by flames, thanks to the soulless boy, Bill. After she was no more, he felt a sudden burst in his head. It was a spontaneous cooling and soothing sensation, but it made him feel sad and bad for what he did. The numbness and uncaring nature was gone from his body.

He felt scared, and he wanted to get his sister out of that old shack before anything else could happen. He grabbed the keys, opened her cage door, and dragged her out slowly. The dead weight of her body was too much for him to hold, and he fell to the floor along with her. Both of those squirrels fell pretty hard, but at that moment, Bell experienced the same cooling sensation in her head. She didn't feel sad or bad; she just felt a little mad.

As she regained her senses, she said to her brother, "Bill, why didn't you wake me up before dragging me out?"

"I'm sorry," Bill apologized as he wiped her drool from his chest, "but we need to get out of here. I mean, I just killed the witch. I'm a murderer!"

"You killed the witch? Yeah, right," she said. "You couldn't kill a tick before it made its way up your...wait. A tick is a buggy parasite. I know that." Bell suddenly began to think. "Hmm, pancake...it's a flat treat used to complete a nutritious breakfast. I know that too! I know what pancakes are!"

Her knowledge came back to her in a miraculous state. She was so filled with joy that she skipped around the room. She never felt so happy being a smart squirrel. The skipping ceased once she saw Roger Hazelnut lying facedown on the floor. The two squirrels went over and helped him stand up. Once he stood on his feet, they noticed that his mouth was reattached to his face, but he was rather quiet with it. What was more interesting was that he wasn't bombarding them with terrible jokes. Everyone seemed to be back to normal. Or were they?

Bell had to test it. She asked Bill what were his feelings about the foggy weather. Did it ever sooth him in a heavenly way? He did not give an answer in a poetic way; he plainly said that fog was nothing but a mist of evil that scared the heck out of him. Her brother, to her happy surprise, was back to being a timid squirrel instead of an emo squirrel.

Then she tested Roger by saying, "Banana." It was a random word she used to see if he would make a joke out of it.

Roger looked at her with a confused expression and said, "Banana? Why did you say banana?"

She waited a couple of seconds, and he did not say one funny line. Roger's constant joking chatter was gone. He could talk normally with his mouth again! He laughed for joy! If their minds were cleared, then the fog might have cleared from the land.

They walked outside and saw that the shroud of fog and dark clouds, had vanished. There was only the morning sun lighting up the clear blue sky. The dark dome over Canada was no more, and people all over the nation savored the sweet sunshine. The little critters in the nearby town even gathered outside and cheered through the streets. Their minds were cleansed, and their land was saved.

It seemed that without Nutilda's life force, all the spells she cast over the land had vanished along with her. The molten land that covered Alaska disappeared without a trace of magma and brought back its usual green life. Then, somewhere in a big city, a heroic man with angel wings no longer had the ability to fly. He fell from the sky and landed on a couple of cops who were chasing a bank robber on foot. Surely the robber would've given the money to charity.

The country was indeed free from the witch's spells, and a proper praise was in order for some heroes. Roger wanted to bring the kids to the cheery town and show the creatures their saviors, Bell & Bill. Roger was too modest. If it wasn't for his distraction, the witch wouldn't had driven herself mad, and Bill wouldn't have had the chance to push her into the furnace.

Why didn't Roger want the fame? Well, he didn't want praise for being a distraction. His goal in life was to make others laugh, and that was the sort of appreciation he lived for. Roger knew Bell & Bill wanted to save Canada from monsters, and they surely had to be known somewhere. Besides, it was his way of thanking them for the tasty PB&J sandwich. His kindness nearly brought tears to their eyes.

Once he brought them to the crowd and told them of their good deeds, the townsfolk surrounded them with loud cheers and applause. They wanted to know all about those two squirrels and how they managed to kill the witch. Bell & Bill stood there, too shy to say a thing. There were just so many creatures staring at them and asking them questions. Even when they were at school, they weren't used to that kind of attention. But they shouldn't have been frightened; it wasn't like they were threatening them with torches and pitchforks.

With that comforting idea in Bell's head, she finally spoke to the crowd. "We're not very good at public speaking. We're not even used to getting this much attention, but I will say that the witch met an agonizing demise inside a furnace. Though it couldn't have been done without my brother here."

The crowd clapped their furry palms for the squirrels.

Bell continued by saying, "The witch was only the beginning. There are more monsters out there that need to be destroyed, like Aval & Evel! Those vampires will not stop until we're all dead, and we must stop them before it happens."

The crowd gasped at such words, for no one would dare challenge those vampires.

"None of you should worry," she said, "because me and my brother are here to put an end to their reign of terror. With those vampires slain by our hands, you should never fear monsters again. This will be a brave new world, and we'll be your new heroes and you can call us—"

"Bell & Bill?"

On that quiet night, those words echoed through the dark home of Aval & Evel. That same night Vincety came to them and told them about those two blond squirrels. He told them how they single-handedly killed Nutilda and that they were on a mission to destroy all monsters. He was saddened by the fact that the last witch on Earth was gone, but Aval & Evel weren't.

A powerful witch being defeated by two ordinary squirrels brought great shame to the monster name. Now those same squirrels were challenging the vampires? It really got Aval & Evel steamed. What really steamed their beans was that Vincety traveled all the way to their home to warn them, instead of taking care of the heroes in the first place.

Vincety lowered his head and realized his mistake. He was dreadfully sorry for not acting sooner, and he promised to hunt down those squirrels with unforgiving fury. It would've certainly made up for his incompetence, but it did not quite sit well with Aval. That vampire made his way toward the kid with a mean look in his eyes. Without warning, Aval ripped Vincety's arms clean off his body. Vincety shrieked.

Aval threw the arms to the floor and told him to never say "sorry" again. There was hardly ever a need for that word, because very few people knew what it meant. He taught the boy that being sorry was like being a fragile pup. Being sorry meant standing helplessly still while taking all sorts of punishment without the will to do a thing about it.

Vincety did not have to be sorry. He had to be better. Vincety was conflicted, but he understood his words. He had to improve and handle things without even thinking about apologizing. Watching that scene made Evel feel sorry for the two.

Aval then ordered the kid to get his arms and go out and tell his army to track down those blond squirrels and kill them. It was a challenging but simple task, so Vincety accepted. Right when that torn boy knelt to the floor to reach his arms, one word changed the mood.

Evel said, "Vince," and the boy turned to her in surprise. No one had ever abbreviated his name before. She walked over, picked up his severed arms, and reattached them with duct tape. It was strangely kind of her. With all parts in place and after dusting off his dirty clothes, she gave the child a better piece of advice.

"Vince, we always wanted a child," she said. "One so obedient, one much like us. Yet the things we say and do, well, there's a reason why we let everyone roam free. Just do your best and try not to get killed."

She patted him on the head and sent him off to do his little task. On his way out, his face lit up with joy. He couldn't believe his heroes abbreviated his name and actually touched him. He was so happy that he forgot about his current mission, although he was pretty sure it had something to do with making more soldiers.

Meanwhile, in vampires' house, domestic trouble began to rear its ugly head once again. Evel sat in her chair and stared into space with her elbow on the table and her head on her fist. Ignoring her troubling mood, Aval searched the hollow eyes of the trophy snake upon the wall. It was as if he was checking unmentionable treasures inside. The secret stash he searched for seemed to be in place; then he left it alone.

After that, he retightened the buttons on the snake's eyes and sat in his chair, in silence. Both squirrels were silent and weren't doing anything at all. They were stuck in their thoughts. No muscle was moved, except for their twitching tails. It was obvious they were in a mood, which meant they weren't going to speak or move anytime soon. So, to break the silence, I threw a book at Aval's greasy head.

Bop!

"Eghh! Son of a bi—"

"Now, now, Aval," I said to him. "You threw an ax at me earlier. Hitting you with a book seems more than fair, I say."

"Trust me, no one would care if you were gone," Aval said with a growl. "Could you at least make yourself useful and tell me what's wrong with my wife? She's been in a sullen mood for too long."

Evel said, "Really, me? You were in a mood ever since puberty, Aval."

Well, I must confess that I was never a marriage counselor, nor was I the kind to seek advice from. I decided to ask Aval a question: When was the last time he saw Evel happy or himself for that matter that didn't involve feasting or killing or kidnapping? If a man could make his wife happy, then he would be happy. Well, maybe more glad than happy or perhaps more tolerable at a certain cost.

The way I saw it, Evel was displeased that Aval made all of their decisions and motives. Maybe he should talk with her and find some common ground. With that said, Aval got out of his chair and made his way toward Evel.

He looked down at his troubled wife and said, "Look, I know there's been some death, and I know you don't like me being the absolute decider of things, but I got everything under control. So don't worry that pretty head of yours."

Evel stood from her chair. "This pretty head has a brain. It has thoughts, it has plans, and it's very boggled that you haven't noticed what's going on. Aval & Evel...Bell & Bill...good and evil. Is any of this sinking in? Those possible mirror images of ourselves are coming here to kill us! If they can outsmart Nutilda, they could do the same with these mindless soldiers grunting around our yard. This is like a predictable story of good triumphing over evil!"

"...boggle?" Aval said in confusion.

"Yes, boggle," said Evel with a sigh. "It means being surprised that even a lima bean could beat my husband at an IQ test."

"Well, it sure is a better word than 'baffle,'" he said. "You know, being confused as to how my wife is so skinny that starving people in Africa are sending her food. But I agree that this twin situation is rather strange. Rest assured that I won't make this journey as predictable as you may think. Our evil is strong, and it will triumph over this good."

"I am troubled, Aval. I am troubled that Vince and the others will die, and then we'll be all alone."

"If they're strong, they won't die, and we will never be alone."

"Never say never, Aval. I fear this story may end with us being gutted by those do-gooders and monsterkind will be no more. I don't want that future. I absolutely don't."

Evel started to cry; she was unable to hold back the feeling of dying by such a terrible fate. The way her tears washed away her mascara and how it all ran down her cheeks made Aval feel so selfish. He couldn't stand seeing her that way.

Aval went over and held Evel close, comforting her any way he could. He leaned toward her face and asked her what could they possibly do to make it all less predictable? He wanted to hear her ideas, and he would support her all the way.

Evel was ever so glad to hear those words. She pulled away and turned toward the balcony window. She needed time to gather her thoughts, though it only took five seconds for an idea to form. She breathed deep and turned to Aval with a dry and mischievous look, like she never shed a tear at all.

Evel had plans, big plans, ones that did not involve staying home while waiting to be confronted by heroes. Spreading the fear of monsters was over, and it was time for the next big step. She wanted to spread Nevermore's true beautiful essence throughout the land. Where the outright defiance of heroes would end with their heads on dinner plates with a side of mashed potatoes. The first act she had in mind was baking cookies. Yes, delicious chocolate-chip cookies for her favorite human in Canada, the prime minister.

Miraculously, on the other side of the continent, Bell & Bill were being treated with cookies by a family of squirrels, though homemade oatmeal treats took the place of chocolate chips. The taste of it was new, for the two teenagers never tried a single cookie in their whole lives. It's a shame a sentence like that should exist.

Bell & Bill chomped down on their first oatmeal cookies, and their taste buds exploded with all sorts of sweetness and goodness. The family of squirrels were certainly grateful that their saviors liked their cooking, and they were willing to give them anything they could offer.

Giving them free food was a good start, but they really wanted weapons. All they had was a cricket bat, and it wasn't enough. The squirrel family said that nothing was enough to kill Aval & Evel. Garlic, crosses, and even bullets couldn't compare to being snapped in half by their shadows.

They heard tales about vengeful hunters and silent assassins who tried to slay them. All those brave creatures died a merciless death. Some tried to kill the vampires in their coffins, in the middle of the day, but even they died before they could lay a paw on them.

Aval & Evel were fast enough to catch an arrow from a crossbow, strong enough to render a gorilla helpless, and capable of taking down a whole army within minutes. They did not show mercy; they would not hesitate to kill or use one's family as leverage. What made the vampires more frightening was that they gained power every time they sucked the blood from their victims.

Their strength would be theirs, and if they were to suck the planet dry, they would reach the status of gods. So being vampires meant more than just drinking blood. It was about gaining power. They were evil vessels that no one should ever face, even for two young teenagers. The stories made Bill quiver, but Bell wasn't so fazed. It was their mission to face them and kill them. They just needed a strong advantage.

It was obvious that Bell was dead set on fighting the vampires, so the mother squirrel told them to head up north to a place called Churchill Falls. Up there was a group of well-organized and merciless wolves that could create any weapon that was desired—from swords to chainsaws, from grenades to nukes.

Their weapon skills were so boundless that they could craft a weapon to kill an immortal with just one cut. There was nothing too big or too small they wouldn't make or sell, no questions asked.

Surely the cost would be high, but for such a righteous cause, the wolves would've done it for free. Bell & Bill would then have the means to defeat Aval & Evel, and then the world would never fear monsters again. Until then, they had to ask the family for more cookies.

After much baking and much consuming, it was time for bed. The squirrel family let them stay for the night on their soft living-room sofa. It had two pillows and one long blanket for both to share. That night, while the family slept soundly in their rooms, the peace gave Bell & Bill some time to think.

Bell gazed up at the wooden ceiling and said to herself, "Roger should've been praised, not me."

"You said that many times before," Bill said as he tried to find some legroom. "He wanted us to feel like heroes. He gave us the credit because we wanted to slay vampires and he wanted to stay a comedian…oh God, no wonder he didn't take the credit. We're the ones who are going to die!"

"Don't say that; we can do this," Bell said. "In a few days, we'll have the most powerful weapons in our hands, and the only ones who will die will be the monsters. Why do you always worry about things?"

"Because I'm just afraid. I'm scared that we might die, especially when we're up against monsters that can destroy a whole army. Why do you always have to be so confident about everything?"

"I don't know. I guess I'm just looking for a reason to go on. I won't lie to you; I'm afraid and sad at the same time. I mean, our family is gone, and our lives took a turn for the worse."

"But we still have each other."

"For how long, though? You killed a monster while I drooled in a cage. Who knows what will happen next time."

"Look, let's make a deal. The next monster we see, you can do all the fighting, and I'll do all the watching. Deal?"

"Bill, you're such a coward."

She swung her pillow at his legs and smiled for a second. Then she looked back at the ceiling, still feeling a bit sad about everything. She couldn't hold a smile for one second, so Bill threw his pillow at her face to mess with her. With a slight sneeze, she threw her pillow at his face. Then sure enough, they had themselves a little pillow fight to lighten their spirits. It showed that no matter how hard life got, some could always find a bit of sunshine.

Meanwhile, on the other side of town, a traditional theater made its own laughter throughout the night. There stood Roger Hazelnut on a bright stage, surrounded by happy woodland creatures, doing what he did best.

Roger said to the crowd, "You know, the best way to make it through life is not by changing your looks but by accepting your looks, which works fine for me because I always get new material, let me tell ya. There was this guy, this really stupid guy, who came up to me and said, 'Hey! Have you seen yourself in the mirror lately? You look like a troll.' So I took a step back, looked at his dirty mug, and said, 'Yeah, now you can ask your momma who your daddy was!'"

Spread a little sunshine evermore.

13

LEADER OF THE WEST

The next morning, Bell & Bill began their journey to the north in search of the legendary wolves. As they left the town, the little critters waved at the traveling heroes and smiled nervously. They were worried that the young squirrels wouldn't survive the journey and they might never see them again. Whether they made it or not, they would always remember Bell & Bill as their heroes.

For now, we must cut to the human side of things. Ever since the dome of darkness appeared, it became the world's number one topic every hour on the hour. People talked about Canada in all languages, and news stations worldwide were booming about Canada. The prime minister of that land, Monsieur Marin, was then forced to address the nation on the weird disturbance. However, being the politician that he was, he couldn't help but lie to ease their minds. There were no straight answers, just guesses and conspiracies that pointed to Russia. In truth, Marin did not know what was going on either.

After a long day of dodging questions, he retreated to his cozy mansion and took some pills to ease his throbbing headache. Then his telephone rang. He answered it, and it was the one person who demanded a straight answer. It was his main boss, with whom he had no choice but to be honest 24-7.

On the line was the leader of the country that had the most variety of races, species, and terrains than any other land. It was, however, a strange country built on the belief that all were free and equal and protected by their god. Ironically, the people felt controlled and divided, and they often questioned their god for letting so much evil in the world. There was a man in that country who turned that side of the world into a controlled sector of law and order, and it was the president of the United States of America.

The president called for a secret meeting. He wanted Marin and the other leaders to meet in an underground bunker beneath Washington, DC, so that no wondering ear could listen. Sure, it was a bit strange to have them all gathered underground, but in times of supernatural crisis, it never hurts to talk in the shadows.

The bunker was dim and covered in hard mesh walls that blocked any signal from entering and exiting the room. All that the room had was a round table with five steel chairs, a flickering lightbulb that swung back and forth from the ceiling, and a small bowl full of salted pretzels.

Three leaders soon entered the room through the darkness. These leaders weren't from the other parts of the world, though; they were from Canada, Mexico, and Brazil. The leaders of the Western Hemisphere.

The first who entered was the president of Brazil, Senhora Relampago. She was not just a leader but a gracious one, who provided her people with free food. It was all too kind, but then the graciousness became demanding. She raised their taxes sky high, and her people had to pay every bill, or they would be forced to work and live in her coal mines. She absolutely detested bums living in her streets.

Then there came the president of Mexico, Senor Maestro Paz. He kept his country free of crime longer than the other leaders. He increased the number of police forces at his noble fingertips, but in truth, the streets were filled with crooked cops who would do anything to get anyone behind bars. The lawyers and bail money were all unfair and unjust, and Paz certainly made sure of that. His country may have been full of barren ghost towns, but at least there was no crime.

Then there was Marin, who was the most decent of all of them. His tendency to lie to his people was a way to protect them and to cover up his cluelessness about everything around him. Running his country became too stressful for him, so he played video games and drank alcohol to ease the tension, even if it meant ignoring his family. Then one day, he hit his wife in the head with a controller for interrupting his game. From that day, he knew he had to stop and change his ways. Without games, alcohol, and a happy family, he was slowly turning into a lonely man who couldn't stop thinking about collecting virtual coins from floating blocks.

To run a country and gain supreme authority in this world, one must be among the ruthless and the powerful, and he was the one who sat across from the three. He was a careful and low-profile man whose face was rarely seen on television screens or in public, for his face was always in the shadows. He was a man who maintained eighteen years of presidency, and he made sure that not a single soul could take his rightful seat. He was a true president of a controlled world, and he was called "President X."

Once all were seated, the shady president urged the leaders to try the pretzels. Each took a piece and ate the salty treats. Needless to say, the taste was salty, but the pretzels were dry and terrible. When they asked if there were any glasses of water present, the shady president said that there were none, and he kept it that way. He was crueler than they had thought. With that being said, the meeting began.

The president placed his elbows on the table, exposing his red suit and white gloves. He spoke to them in a deep voice, "Welcome. I'm very pleased that all of you made it on time on such short notice. For the record, I'd like to keep this meeting brief, so for the sake of time everyone should provide a short answer. So, Mrs. Relampago, how are things?"

"Very fair, can't complain," she said with a half smile.

"Good," said President X. "Mr. Paz, did you ever get that birthday card I sent you?"

"Yes, it was very poetic!" he said with a fake smile.

"Excellent. Mr. Marin, how are things with the family?"

"I'm unsure," Marin said with a frown. "Things have been terrible, we—"

"Nice to hear that," the president interrupted. "Now, enough of the chitchat and on to the business at hand. As many of you suspect, Marin is having a situation most serious and curious. In the past month, monsters have been rampaging through the streets and destroying universities. There are children going insane and causing disturbances. Not only that, but Alaska was covered in magma, and Canada was shrouded in a cloudlike dome. Now, Marin, what is going on?"

"I might have some idea," Marin said. "*Mon Dieu*, I can't bring myself to say what's causing this. I mean, with so much going on, I can hardly—"

"I said *brief*."

The president instructed him to get to the point. Marin started to drip a bit of sweat. Through the watchful eyes of his security staff, Marin said everything that had happened was believed to be the work of squirrels. His words were very silly, but he had proof. He reached into his suit and pulled out some camera photos. He showed still shots of a squirrel stealing equipment from science labs and hardware stores. Then he showed a picture of the same squirrel marching through a military base with undead soldiers. His nation was under attack by woodland creatures, and he did not know what to do. Laughter was to be expected from the others, but they only displayed silence.

Senhora had a thought and said to Marin, "I think I know how you can fix this little problem."

"Really? How?" Marin asked.

Senhora shouted in a country accent, "Grow a pair, and BB gun them varmints! Ha-ha-ha-ha-ha!"

She and Paz laughed at the man's hilarious misfortune; it was all too hard for them to take seriously. Marin pleaded for them to believe him, but the sound of Paz hitting the floor made them laugh even more. President X just sat in silence. He did not find it funny at all.

"Silence!" he yelled, instantly putting everyone in a still state. "This is no laughing matter. Squirrels maybe flea-ridden vermin, but it's no secret that animals in this world are intelligent and civilized. They can do whatever we can do, but what they can't do is plot against us and expect to win. This is the work of dark forces beyond our comprehension. These unknown forces are plotting to take over our land, threatening everything we have worked so hard to achieve, and I want it stopped, Marin. Otherwise I'll replace you with a squirrel."

Some often wondered how President X was put in charge in the first place, and some wondered why the leaders were his cronies. No one knew the answer to the first question, but the answer to the second question was money. The three leaders made many gambles and left many debts unpaid to the president. Owing to these various circumstances, they had no choice but to be his subordinates.

President X told Marin to fix his monster problem within the year, or there would be consequences. With that said, the president stood from his chair and instructed the rest to leave, right before he slipped into the darkness like a weightless ghost.

Later that night, Marin arrived at his cozy mansion in Canada. He trotted the hallways and examined the portraits of his late ancestors, alone. His family had left him hours before, and he was by himself with no one to talk to. There was no one around to ease his worried mind. There was no video game or liquor strong enough to make him forget about squirrels trying to take over his country.

He stepped outside and walked through his courtyard in the dark. The calm and quiet of the yard did provide an ounce of peace. He sat on a picnic table and tried to think about what to do, but all he did was pound his head on the table, hoping the mild concussion would give him an idea. It did not help; it just made a red bruise on his forehead. Marin just sat there with his head on the table, wishing he knew what to do.

He closed eyes for a brief second. When he opened them, he saw two tiny blurs in his fuzzy vision. They trailed toward him on that table and stopped at a respectable distance. Marin wiped his eyes and saw two tiny squirrels: Aval & Evel.

"*Mon Dieu*! Squirrels!" Marin cried as he fell to the ground. When he stood up, he became a little frightened but a bit curious. He observed their clothing and their upright structures as well as their plate of freshly baked cookies.

Evel smiled at the man and said, "Mr. Marin! Such an honor it is to be in your presence. I am Evel, and this guy with the cookies is Aval."

Aval said hi and immediately told him to try a cookie. Evel did not find his bluntness so polite. The least he could've done was give Marin a chance to respond. Marin just stood there and pointed his shaky hand at the squirrels. He feared that they were sent to execute him. For a final request, Marin pleaded to play one last video game. The two squirrels found him very silly. Aval almost made a sarcastic remark, seeing that their only weapons were cookies.

Evel tried to calm the man down by saying, "We are only here on the nicest mission to meet the most important man in Canada."

Then Marin said in a loud voice, "I'm not a fool! You want to take over the human race and create some kinda Zootropolis!"

"That's absurd," said Evel. "We'd pants the Queen of England before we'd even consider doing something so criminally foolish. We just wanted to meet our favorite man in our most favorite country and offer him sweet chocolate-chip cookies. Yet I see a man who takes us for evil and vile creatures just by looking at us! It's enough to make me want to cry…"

Evel started to cry while Aval hummed a sad tune, which made Marin feel really guilty. Maybe it was just a peaceful visit. Maybe it was a chance for him to sit down and actually chat with some squirrels.

Marin apologized to his guests and said that it was a pleasure to meet them. When all was forgiven and it was time for him to taste the cookies, they were already cold. Unfortunately, Marin did not want them. He explained to the squirrels that he did not enjoy the taste of chocolate—it was too rich and too fattening. Evel couldn't believe her own ears. She felt offended to hear anyone shun the good nature of chocolate.

Evel threw away her manners. She grabbed a cookie from the plate and flung it right into Marin's open mouth. It went down his throat, and he gagged for only a second. He feared that he would soon gain a few pounds or break out from the delicious toxin. He called her crazy for doing such a thing, but Evel disagreed. As soon as she knew the cookie was deep in his belly, she proceeded with her devious plan. With a snap of her finger, she commanded him to call her "Master."

Marin suddenly twitched and stood as still as a statue. His eyes stared into the distance with a lifeless gaze, and drool ran down his mouth as he said, "Master."

This was also one of the many tricks vampires could achieve. They were capable of controlling any living being by making them digest their remarkable and mesmerizing blood, fresh or otherwise cooked into food. They would have their own mind-controlled slaves. Evel chuckled, for she had total control over a country's leader.

14

TYE, THE TORTURED TARANTULA

Deep within a forest on a very late afternoon, a blinking fire granted the dark surroundings a shred of light. The light came from a secluded burrow behind tall trees, where traces of rotten flesh and broken bones were scattered. It was as if such savagery was done by monstrous hands—or should I say human hands. The secluded home was dug by the very confused creature that was Tye the Tarantula.

Very recently he started capturing victims from the loneliest of parks, to the darkest alleyways, and even from their own homes by using steady stealth. Tye would then carry them into his little burrow and use them as he pleased in many unusual ways. He muttered to himself in that hole with extreme concentration, since he had no one else to talk to. Regrettably his behavior seemed to be the worst that day.

"Size eight? No, it's a size three," he said. "Need to cut the cords, veins upon veins make 'em thick. Use the tongue? No, an actual tongue is too silly; liver skin is the substitute. Smooth out the shoulder blade to…yes, this makes a great sole! Glue…sew the rib tips…stitch the loose flesh…and behold! I made a perfectly crafted baby shoe! Body parts courtesy of a grievin' widow named Abby. Her child will never again go barefoot in public. But I need the other half to finish the set."

Tye found himself a new, unhealthy hobby of creating shoes from body parts. Being the insect monster that he was, his main goal was to hunt and kill in the shadows. Yet he could never get shoes off his mind. So he improvised by making mutilated shoes to fulfill all of his purposes. Again I say, very unhealthy.

In the middle of constructing the second baby shoe, he accidently cut the shoulder blade a bit too short. He made it an inch smaller than he intended. The simple mistake caused him to rip the footwear to shreds, leaving a sloppy mess on his dirty work desk. He needed a new shoulder blade, one that was from another widow to give it the same feel of sorrow. But where could he find a grieving widow at such a late hour, especially on a Friday?

Tye cleaned himself of the blood with an old bathrobe as he fetched his dusty top hat. He then leaped out of his hole like a trapped spring popping out of a can and into the woods to find a sad and lonely woman to finish the set. He leaped from tree to tree and swung from the branches in an aggressive rush. He was madly dead set on his desired target. He really wanted to find another human of the sort so the last baby shoe was complete. He wanted satisfaction!

Suddenly, he stopped on sturdy branch, standing still as a statue and silent as a mouse. He might have found a victim in the wild, but that wasn't the case. Tye only stood in that tree, and he only looked at his dirty hands. It seemed like he was starting to think for the first time in a long while. He thought about what he was doing. Looking for human parts to create more shoes was an odd mission. He then thought about a child wearing his own mother as shoes, and it suddenly felt so wrong to him.

Thinking of it all did not make the tarantula happy or laugh in a sick kind of way. Tye only felt guilt. He felt the harsh unnerving pain for the people he crafted into shoes, all fifty-seven of them. Tye possessed a horrible mind he did not want anymore. He did not want to be involved with the evil vampires' plans or make shoes anymore. He just wanted to be a simple spider again.

Before he could grieve in that tree, he heard little voices coming from below. It sounded like innocent young voices. On the grassy path below lay the two squirrels, Bell & Bill, resting after long travel. They were still determined to head up north and find the legendary wolves.

For the moment, the two relaxed near the tree and ate more PB&J sandwiches, unaware that they were being watched by a curious creature from above. Tye wanted to get a closer look at the two—mostly at their shoes. He crept down the tree, slowly making his way without a sound and carefully eyeing their movements.

One of his hands then broke a weak branch. He hid behind the tree, out of sight from the squirrels' wondering eyes. Fortunately, they were not worried about the small noise. They figured it was only the natural ambience of nature.

While they ate, Bell brought up the conversation that some people think that PB&J is a racist sandwich. They believed it was created for a single race to enjoy and not by others. Bill became puzzled as to why anyone would even think of that. It did not make any sense.

Then a sudden voice came from behind their ears and said, "Ya don't say. Next thing ya know, they'll be callin' shoes racist."

The squirrels turned around and discovered a humongous talking spider in a top hat. They screamed at the top of their lungs and ran away from the abomination. They came across a hill, where both tripped and fell down the bumpy path. They rolled down until they hit a very large boulder, where they quickly took refuge in the small hole under it.

Bell & Bill stood still and remained quiet, hoping the terrifying creature would not find them. They were safe, unless Tye could push the boulder out of the way with no trouble, which was exactly what he did. He moved the boulder and examined the shocked squirrels. The two were terrified, but not defenseless.

Instead of the old cricket bat, the two armed themselves with sharp knives and warned the spider to stay away. Even when threatened by squirrels holding knives, Tye couldn't resist taking a closer look at their shoes.

"I must take a gander at your shoes," he said. "Wait, these are boots! Are they handmade or manufactured? The craftsmanship is nice, but it has an avant-garde feel to it."

"Back off!" Bell yelled as she warded off his curious hands. "Don't think we won't kill you!"

Tye blinked his many eyes, scratched his head, cleared his congested throat, and said, "Really? Ya seem awfully scared to even harm me. I doubt y'two ever killed a monster in your whole lives."

"Oh, we have," Bell said with courage. "We killed a powerful witch, so don't think we won't do the same to you!"

Hearing the statement, Tye had to think for a moment. The death of a witch, the disappearance of the short-lived darkness, and two blond squirrels. He pieced everything together and knew that they were, in fact, the famous Bell & Bill! Personally, he thought they'd look a bit more dangerous. What he saw were just two regular squirrels with an appetite for snacks.

Nevertheless, Tye thanked them for removing such a terrible evil, which made Bell & Bill awfully confused. Why did he thank them for killing a fellow monster? Tye had to explain that his fellow monsters were not the ones he knew. They'd become something worse. Aval & Evel's rule was driving them all mad.

"Mad? You monsters are beings of cantankerous evil!" said Bell. "You're all mad from the start."

Bill finally spoke. "Trust us, we know, and we're the ones who are going to stop all of you."

After hearing that, Tye shook his head and said, "Try as ya like, but it's far too late. My friends and I were harmless before. There we monsters were, calm as day, sharin' our woes to one another without a care. Then those vampires arrived, commanding us to do as they say or die where we stood. Intimidation is their method of gettin' their way. They pushed us to do unspeakable things to win their approval. As a result, this land is turnin' into a nightmare for everyone."

Tye assured Bell & Bill that it would only get worse. Soon no one would be able to stop an army of undead soldiers, packs of hungry werewolves, and of course two bloodthirsty godlike beings ruling over it all. Bell's and Bill's stomachs turned queasy after hearing the story. The land was in more danger than they had thought. Stopping such evil would be like putting a Band-Aid over an oozing heart. It would continue to flow until there was nothing left.

"There must be a way to stop this," Bill said. "I mean, the vampires are the real problem. Without Aval & Evel around, the monsters would have no reason to continue. All we have to do is go to the wolves up north and—"

Bell quickly pressed his mouth shut and said, "Bill! Don't tell this thing our…vacation spot."

"Hmph, doesn't matter if I 'ear y'plans or not," said Tye. "You think we care whether those bloodsuckers live or die? The others are takin' joy in what they do—and so was I, but no more. As for your 'wolves' up north, they don't exist. It's merely a false story, a no-luck hunt to steer adventurers like you off the tracks. Mainly it's a runnin' joke 'round 'ere, if you get the meanin'."

"N-no, you got it all wrong!" Bell said nervously. "That place is really our getaway home to relax this time of year."

Tye saw past her lies, and he urged Bill to have a voice in the team. If what Tye said was true about the wolves, why tell them? Why should they believe him? Well, because if Tye was heading down the same road, he would've wanted someone to stop him. The ones who told Bell & Bill to go there were only trying to protect them, because facing Aval & Evel was a death sentence.

There were many thoughts going through Bell & Bill's minds. In the midst of silence, they wanted to know the tarantula's name. He wanted to give his name to the curious squirrels, but then a murderous urge started to grow.

Tye hadn't made a shoe for minutes, and he looked at Bell & Bill like untouched equipment. He reached his hands toward the squirrels, and he wanted to make tap-dancing shoes out of them. But he pulled away. The thought of killing became pointless to him, like their journey.

The poor thing silently left them and climbed up a nearby tree. He concealed himself within the leaves, hiding his hideous face from the world once more. Bell & Bill did not know what to think of it. Maybe, just maybe, he was different from the other monsters.

Tying laces and crafting a shoe,
everyone should learn how to do,
except for a sad tarantula.
Tye seeks a real purpose,
but it does his soul no service.

Simple days of eating bugs were gone;
remedial hunger for humans last so long.
It all goes away in the mirror;
please let it simmer.

A beastly beast of human and spider,

or tarantula to the acclaimed wiser.

He has very little to lose and little to gain,

when nothing but shoes keep him sane.

Once alone, Bell decided it was time to go back to gather their things and leave. To where, they didn't know. Before they went, Bill looked up at the tree and saw the tarantula hiding in the shadows. It was strange at first, but Bill felt really sorry for the creature. Sure, he was terrified by the very sight of the monster, but he had a rather strange feeling about him. He thought that maybe not all monsters were heartless beings but troubled creatures in need of guidance and acceptance. Maybe Tye was one of the few monsters that just wanted a place in this world.

Tye needed help, and it would've been poor manners to abandon a tortured soul, creature or not. Bill told Bell about his theory, and she called him crazy. They had no time to help a depressed spider. She wanted no part of it, but when Bill presented the idea of befriending a monster to get them closer to Aval & Evel, she was quickly persuaded to come along and help Tye.

The two squirrels climbed up the tree and saw the tarantula deep within the shade of black shadows, making a shoe out of twigs. The white shine in his eyes peered through the darkness, giving off an eerie atmosphere. The scary scene made the squirrels think twice about confronting him, but the two gulped and proceeded regardless.

Tye asked about their business, but again, they wanted his name. It was odd for Tye, because no one in their right minds would bother with him or ask his name. Those squirrels were definitely different, and their heads seemed to be in the right place, so he told them his name was Tye.

He then asked them about their business again. The squirrels came closer to the creature with cold feet, and they told him they were there to help him. They wanted to help him find happiness in his troubling life and, in return, he'd help them fight Aval & Evel.

Tye knew they wanted something, and the longer they troubled him, the more he wanted to rip them apart. He rejected their offer and told them to leave. There was no happiness in his life or a way to obtain it. All he could do and would ever do was make shoes, shoes, and more shoes. He was a freak of nature, and that's all he would ever be. Bill told him not to say such things. He was a special kind of creature with an extra set of hands that could be used for many different kinds of things, like playing various instruments at the same time and being a one-man band. Tye could run a speedy restaurant by being a chef, server, and busboy. He could teach a nation to read again by making dozens of books in one year. The tarantula still wasn't convinced; he couldn't possibly do all that if he had shoes on the brain. All he could think about was making more shoes out of anything he could find. From near to far, from far to near, all he ever saw was footgear.

By the time he said that, he'd already made four sets of shoes out of twigs, and then he threw them away to make room for more. It was clear to the squirrels that he had a shoe problem. It made Bill come up with a helpful but stupid solution. Bill told Tye if he ever got the urge to make shoes, just think about mangoes. That's what people did when they wanted to hold back a sneeze.

And if that wasn't enough, Bell told him of a way he could be seen not as a freak but as a hero. He just had to help them defeat Aval & Evel. It was a chance for redemption, a way for everyone to accept a creature like him. All he had to do was take Bell's hand and become friends.

She reached out to him, hoping he would accept, but there was slight hesitation on his part. There was no way he could do such a treacherous thing as side with mortals. He could have made them into fur boots right then and there and ended their journey. It certainly would've gotten him on Aval & Evel's good side. However, how could he kill these small creatures who wanted to save the land and be his friend? With hearts so pure as to offer a monster like him friendship, perhaps it was time for a better change.

He dropped the twiggy shoes and slowly lent his index finger to Bell's tiny palm. Both touched, and at that moment, Tye wanted to make shoestrings from her flesh—until he took Bill's advice and thought about mangoes. As he thought about the fruit, he noticed that he did not desire to make shoes from her flesh. He didn't have a murderous urge at all. All he did was experience a meaningful connection with a creature for the first time in his life.

Later, in a nearby town, the two squirrels introduced Tye to the other woodland creatures to show him how it felt to be on the good side. The little creatures were obviously scared of him, but the heroes told them that Tye was not like all the other monsters. He was not at all heartless or cruel, but he was a gentle shoemaker looking for acceptance. They urged one of the townsfolk to come up and greet the tarantula.

None bothered to come near the monster, but a tiny skunk child surprisingly walked toward the tarantula and gave him a broken shoe to fix. Tye grabbed the tiny footwear, and with the little equipment he had stashed in his suit pockets, he fixed it in the blink of an eye. The child was amazed, and the others were as well.

Soon more came and observed him and talked to him. Tye felt so important. It felt special to have others admire him. Later, believe it or not, the townsfolk were in his hands, and he was spinning them around like a fuzzy merry-go-round. Everyone laughed, and everyone smiled at the sight of goodness that had just entered their little town. The tortured tarantula never felt so happy to experience the joys of acceptance.

15

VISION OF LOVE

Elise and Barbosa sat together near a small lake on a quiet afternoon, watching yet another radiant sunset over the horizon. They grew to enjoy each other's company and their freedom of being murderous monsters.

Elise liked having her father around. He was funnier than usual, and he was the only one she trusted to pass the time with. She felt so safe and so content that she had no need for another companion. But all of that changed when a certain squirrel arrived that evening. It was a gray squirrel dressed in a white southern dress, and her smile was as bright as the sun. Her name was Abigail, and she was calling for Barbosa as if he were a pet.

Barbosa took one look at the lady and sprang from the ground with excitement. He rushed over and gave the lady a great big hug, as if it had been years since they had last met. Elise watched her father hugging the peculiar woman, and she was rather confused. She didn't know who she was or why she dressed like a southern belle. Elise even witnessed them jumping around like idiots and swinging around in circles like morons.

The sight made her sicker than she already was. Elise rose from her spot and asked what was going on. The two happy squirrels blushed, for they wished for a better time to surprise her. It was revealed that this Abigail was a fellow werewolf, and she was dating Barbosa.

It was a wonder how a sophisticated lady like Abigail fell for, shall I say, a slob like Barbosa. Well, there was a sensible reason why she was attracted to him. She was deemed insane, and she showed it by dressing as different characters every day. The two first met a month before at a human bachelor party, coincidentally stealing cans of beer. They saw each other trying to get the same can, and they immediately fell for each other. A complicated lady and a simple-minded man made the perfect couple.

Elise said in a disgusted tone, "This can't be happening."

Barbosa held Abigail's hands and replied, "Well, it's true. We've been going out for like a month. We have long walks through meadows, and we just love skipping out on checks together."

"Oh gosh, running out on checks!" Abigail laughed. "I declare, I could never find a good dress for those."

"But we do those things, sorta," Elise said. "Why do we need a third wheel like her?"

"Look, Elise, my nights are sad and lonely," said Barbosa. "I longed for companionship and a little something more. Then I met Abigail, the snookie to my wookie, and someday, she'll be a lovely mother to you."

"That's right, sweet pea," Abigail said to Elise, "I'll be the best mother you've ever had. I'll raise you like you were my young'un and make you blueberry pies till the cows come home. Then we can make burgers!"

What a surprise it was. The two squirrels were already thinking about marriage, and Elise would soon have a new mother. She was expected to jump for joy, but she did no such thing, never in a million years. The idea of some stranger, let alone a walking stereotype, taking the place of her dear mother made her stomach turn. There would never be another mother for her.

Elise looked at the lady with a mean look and said, "You will never ever be a part of this family. As far as I'm concerned, you're just some screwball floozy."

Both gasped at the amount of disrespect. Why, Abigail was likely to faint. Elise was serious, and she planned to keep the father-daughter bond tight and unbreakable. Barbosa had to say something. He explained to Elise that he knew it was difficult for her to accept another as her mother. It was hard for him too, but he did have certain needs. Needs that did not involve a father and a daughter but between two passionate adults. He decided it was time to give Elise the Talk.

Elise felt more disgusted, and she decided to neglect the Talk. With that attitude, he told her to venture out and find a love companion of her own to feel that same sickening feeling she would soon understand.

Experiencing a better part of life was a nice way to pass the time after all. Personally, Elise didn't want to go, and she didn't want to leave. Then she saw how awfully happy the two were together, for they had found their special spark in their sad lives. Elise felt like a child trying to take away their happiness, and that was surely unfair.

Barbosa looked so happy when he was with Abigail, so much more than he was with his daughter. Elise would never call that lady her mother, but she would let Barbosa keep his joy. Elise took a deep breath, and she went away to search for a lover of her own, right after she spat on Abigail's shoes.

Out into the world Elise went, searching for the obscene and pretentious feelings that inhabit all teens. Love. She sought to find a mate for friendship or a suitor for passion. Along the dusty road of solitude, she tried to piece together the connection between companionship and happiness, where physical contact was involved. She had to ask herself if the simple pleasure of accepting oneself was good enough. Perhaps love was more than just self-fulfillment.

Before the late sun dimmed her view, she felt the need to visit a nearby town of humans to see if they too had companions of their own. She wanted to know if they too held hands while making silly puppy-dog faces, skipping and dancing like it was a calm summer's day. She observed the humans from the branches of a cozy pine tree and found that everyone was doing the expected, only more.

The couples clung to each other's chests, mimicked each other's movements, and whistled like songbirds. Their smiles were brighter than the streetlamps themselves; their chatter made more noise than loud jazz or a runaway train whizzing on by in a circle with no end whatsoever. They were all infected by a contagious disease spread by the infamous lovebug.

Raindrops started to shower down on the town, soaking the lovers and dampening the ever-so-lonely squirrel, Elise. She ignored the weather change, for she was amazed that many still sought love in a world full of evil and misfortune. Maybe the concept of not regular love, but true love, has the effect of easing one's pain, making everything seem so simple. Elise never understood that particular kind of love, because such things only existed in fairy tales on discount shelves in bookstores.

Her vision of love was a bleeding heart being punctured with an iron spike, caged within a barbed-wire prison and hanging over an open flame fueled by lust and fiery obsession to spread one's seed to the lucky few who would one day raise putrid criminals and sickly whores who were the spawns of Satan himself.

It was merely an idea of how she saw love today, but oh my, what a vivid imagination she had.

However, she had a mere liking for a particular red squirrel boy not too long ago. It was no longer relevant, like her journey. Accepting her curse as a werewolf made seeking companionship disappear into the forgotten winds. Seeking affection was gone, all thanks to the thrill of killing and the joy of being bad. She looted whomever, fought whomever, and knocked down crutches for no reason whatsoever. Being bad satisfied her in a way no other emotion could or would ever do. She had grown so used to it that she needed no such thing as love.

Let the needy play their song; the fulfilled will always block out the noise.

Dear Elise left the town and proceeded back home. Staying in the rain, stalking couples, took somewhat of a toll on her body. She began to sniff, and she began to sneeze. It was cold and dark; she needed shelter.

In just a few minutes, she came across a small campfire just right on top of a cliff. The fire was protected from the rain by an oversize black umbrella with red stripes. It was stuck in the ground and was strangely crooked, but it was curved to suitable position.

The spot was empty, and there wasn't a single soul in sight to guard the property, so she took it upon herself to take refuge under the umbrella. The grass was unbelievably dry, and the flames felt comfortably warm. It felt nice, and it made her so calm and so relaxed that she could've slept there.

But she wouldn't allow herself to sleep in a suspicious place—not again. There were plenty of creeps lurking in the shadows, waiting for the opportunity to pounce on a sleeping girl such as her. Elise became smarter. She started carrying a handy switchblade knife in her right pocket to slit any throat.

It might have been the right time to use it, because she could sense a strange presence around her. She turned left, right, back, and front, and then she finally got up and looked around. There was nothing in sight, just the surrounding trees showering under the rain.

Perhaps she was being paranoid, though she had every right to be. When she came back to her quiet little spot, it was already occupied by something much stranger than a stranger.

In the midst of her shock, the stranger slowly turned to her with a menacing grin and politely said, "Salutations…"

That strange stranger was none other than Boogeyman Barney, gazing at Elise with a delightful grin. He welcomed the squirrel and invited her to sit down. She refused. She pulled out her switchblade knife and was prepared for anything the creature had in store.

Barney looked at the small knife and just chuckled. If she was going to do any damage at all, she would need something bigger than that. Barney was there because she needed a friend, someone just as bad to relate to.

"Come now, Elise," he said. "Put the toy away and have a seat. I don't bite…much."

"How do you know my name? What are you?"

"I'm not a what. I'm a who," he answered in a confusing way. "My name is Boogeyman Barney, the lost 'who' on the side of you monsters. It is a pleasure to meet a squirrel with a mind such as yours...you should really stay. You'll catch your death in the rain."

The campfire's light showed the sadistic face of the man. The stitch that ran down to his mouth, the nails that pierced his head, and the shady eyes could tell a twisted tale of a deranged killer.

Elise couldn't trust that face; however, she was curious about how a boogeyman existed. She escaped the rain and sat across from the man, holding her knife, wanting the fire to keep them separate.

She observed the strange fellow. "So you're a boogeyman named Barney. I never knew one existed, but I can guess why you're here. You're here because I've been very bad, and you lured me in with this cozy spot. What are you going to do next? Scare me? I'd like to see you try."

"You presume too much," Barney said. "I don't own this property at all. We're merely trespassers here. As for scaring...that's really not my forte when dealing with kids like you. The process I do is tweaking the mind. It's a special skill I do that gives my victims a special kind of high, one where they can never come back down again."

As pleasant as that sounded, Elise felt that it was disappointing. She said to him, "So instead of scaring naughty kids or killing them, you just mess with their heads?"

"More or less," he said.

"That's just lame. How can you even call yourself a monster?"

"Well, I try to scare, and I try to kill, but I cause nothing but happiness. I bring them the joy of eliminating their fears. No children I come across are ever scared, and they kill me with such wonderful imaginative deaths. I must confess: it gets tiresome. I thought it might be comforting to sit down and chat with a fellow monster for a change, but I can see you'd much rather slit my throat."

"It's called 'self-defense.' I don't trust anyone these days. People are nothing but liars and deceivers who would do anything to get what they want. I can never trust, never love, and never care."

"Never compare, and never bear."

Then the two uttered at the same time, "Never share," instantly causing a connection. Elise's eyes widened as she experienced a shock in her chest, as if he completely understood her. It was weird at first, but Elise felt like she had found someone she could truly relate to.

The two began to speak about their likes and dislikes in a weird manner. They enjoyed the comparisons and interesting facts they never expected the other to like or hate. They even spoke about their many ideas of life and worlds beyond. The conversation lasted for an hour, and eventually Elise was caught rambling on about everything being so pointless.

Whatever life, country, or planet Elise would live in, there would always be a swarm of annoyance just around the corner. Barney agreed and said that the key to make it all go away was a good metal spike through their skulls. Elise giggled at the funny suggestion, but then she stopped.

She started to realize she was discussing philosophies of life with a boogeyman, quite possibly even flirting with him. He was up to something, and she wanted no part of it.

Elise stood up in a flash and wanted him to drop the lonely monster act. She wanted to know the real reason why he was so nice to her in the first place. Barney's eyes remained frozen. They were glued to the spot where she once sat. Soon they moved to her face.

Barney chuckled and said, "You're certainly cleverer than the rest, but not by much. You think you're safe with that toy? It won't help at all. I'm already inside your head. But don't fear, I like you, and I want to forever make you happy. Imagine, a life where you never have to look at everything in disgust and enjoy a daily meal of pancakes."

He stuck out his right hand and offered to complete the lonely palm with hers. All of her troubles and all of her hate would all vanish from her mind. All that was required was to take his hand and smile.

Elise easily turned down the offer. She knew the world was cruel, and she wanted to seclude herself from it, but happiness had its cost. If his vision of happiness involved going blind from the truth, she would rather live depressed to keep her sanity. Barney gave out a gentle sigh, pulling his hand to his chest, and wished that there were other ways to avoid the alternative manner. He really liked her, but they could never be friends.

Barney was lying to Elise the whole time; he was doing more than just running around and scaring children; he was destroying their minds. Every victim he destroyed gave him marvelous strength. He eventually gained the power to control their very actions, to make them perform the most devilish and horrifying things, like puppets.

He found it most amusing to experience life through a victim's eyes and hear the bloody cries from their poor families. The experience felt enriching to say the least, but those were ordinary children. He felt the need for a challenge.

Barney wanted to wreak a special kind of havoc by unlocking the potential of a special kind of monster—a very specific monster that could transform into a werewolf during slumber—and create other creatures tainted with the DNA that could possibly do the same. Elise's mind was the answer, and he wanted it.

If he broke her mind and unleashed the werewolf within, he could use that ability on the next cursed creature and the next and the next as well. Soon he would have total control over an army of insane werewolves. It would certainly be the perfect way to kick off an age of fear.

Elise pointed her knife at the creature with extreme bravery and said that she was not afraid of him. There was no shred of fear within her, and there was no way she could be broken by the likes of him.

Barney believed that everyone had their fears. They could lock it away with glee, but Barney would always have the key. No matter what weapon they yield, when they saw Barney, their fate was already sealed.

The whole world around Elise suddenly faded to pure darkness. A flash of light came, and she found herself on narrow dirt road that had a straight alignment of trees. The trees were larger than normal and more shriveled than usual. The leaves constantly changed color from white to black, and then they fell down like raindrops. Elise became very, very worried.

The world faded to darkness again; then light cleared it in the blink of an eye. The sudden transition turned everything into a neon subspace that showed all of her lost dreams as the area started to rain deadly green acid. Every drop that hit her made her experience pain like never before. Her body burned, and her very fur had melted to steam. Agonizing sores appeared everywhere, and they felt like sparks of fire peeling her skin.

It became dark. Another flash of light appeared, and she was in a land of smoldering red flesh, seeing the visions of her failures as the acid rain turned into a shower of lemon juice! Every ounce that blew her way stung her open sores on extremely painful levels. She screamed and hollered for it all to stop, but it continued to blow, and the visions continued to remind her of her own worthlessness.

It all faded to darkness, and calmness occurred. Elise lay there on the ground, unable to move. Her flesh sizzled red-hot steam, and her fur fell like dead leaves. Just when she couldn't take any more, another flash came. That time it was a vision of a very dark past. It showed her an event that took place in her own home, the night her mother was about to be eaten alive by her own family.

Elise and Barbosa both stood in their werewolf forms. The mother's pleas were unheard and ignored. That horrible vision showed the most shocking truth: Elise was the first who struck down her mother. Then there came the mauling, the tearing of limbs, and the sounds of breaking bones. The mother's screams were the most unbearable to hear. Poor Elise closed her ears and looked away from the terror. She couldn't take anymore. She screamed from the top of her very soul to make it all stop.

Suddenly, there was a sound of broken glass, and before she knew it, she awoke on the floor in her own bedroom. She looked around and saw that it was a calm bright morning. She was tangled in her bedsheets, and once she freed herself, she found no wounds on her body. Her body was perfectly fine, and she was wearing her favorite green pajamas. In front of her was her broken vase of twigs, which was possibly the thing that woke her from the nightmare.

She did not know if it was a bad dream or not. It was confusing to say the least, but she was glad that the pain had ceased. Without a second thought, she rushed out of her room to explore the house. Everything seemed normal but suspiciously cleaner than the usual messy scene. There were no clothes or leftover food on the floor, and the air smelled like peaches and breakfast being cooked.

She made her way into the kitchen and found Abigail cooking on their little stove, wearing a colorful conga outfit, no less. Elise slowly walked in and called her name, hoping to get a response. Abigail turned around in surprise and greeted her with delight. She walked over with a smile and tried to give her the biggest hug.

Elise quickly stepped away from the strange lady and asked what was she doing in her house. Dear Abigail explained that Barbosa brought her home last night, and he was letting her stay for as long as she wished. Then while he was gone to work that morning, she was left to babysit Elise. So Abigail occupied her time by tidying the place up and putting some scented candles here and there. She even prepared breakfast just for Elise.

Abigail grabbed the hot plate from the counter and offered Elise some eggs and bacon, with a special helping of pancakes. A strange feeling brewed within Elise's belly, the simple sight of that breakfast made her insides curl. She knew that none of it was real and that Barney was still toying with her mind.

Elise grabbed the fork on the side of the dish, and she struck it right into Abigail's left eye! She jammed the fork in the lady's eye so deep that she could feel it scraping the skull! She knew it was all a lie; she was way too smart to fall for such tricks.

What really proved it was when the fork entered Abigail's eye, she did not scream, curse, or faint. She simply stood there and bled from the wound, smiling. The strange lady dropped the plate of food to the floor, and she grabbed Elise's hand, wanting her to keep a grip on the fork, not letting her escape.

All of a sudden, she transformed into Barney himself, as Elise expected. He wanted to give her a world of joy, yet she violently refused. He gladly went with option number two. Her very psyche that kept her mind and body in check had to go, and it was holding a fork in his eye. It was time to conjure a nightmare that would demolish it beyond repair.

The morning light turned to blood red, and the house itself began to be ripped apart by very strong winds, hoisting everything into the red sky. Soon they were hovering above a field of fire on what little floor was left.

Barney made her ease the fork from his bleeding eye, and then he broke her arm with a firm twist, forcing her to drop the fork to the floor. With a slight struggle, he grabbed her by the tail and held her over the edge. There she saw that within the flames stood an endless number of angry and devilish demon squirrels. They were looking up at the girl, clawing at the air, hoping they could reach her. Elise couldn't hide it anymore. She was scared out of her mind!

"What is this?" she yelled to the boogeyman. "Is this hell?"

"In a sense," Barney said. "I seem to recall how your vision of love involved spawns of Satan himself. Along with lust and fiery obsessions to spread seeds to the lucky few who would one day raise criminals and whores…well, Elise, consider this an eternity of love and regret."

He released her tail and watched the poor squirrel scream into the cruel pits below.

Back in the real world, it was still a rainy night, and Barbosa had just arrived home. He wanted to tell Abigail that their picnic on the cliff had to be put off because of the weather. To his surprise, his house was completely destroyed, like it was hit by a wrecking ball. From the wreckage rose a devilish werewolf chewing on some mushy meat.

The savage beast he saw was his daughter, Elise. She had glowing eyes of white and a bloody mouth that possessed a menacing grin. In her right hand, she held Abigail's punctured head. Elise swallowed the remaining grub and then tossed the head away like trash. Abigail did not satisfy her hunger; she wanted more. She then turned to her father, who was frozen with absolute fear.

"Oh no," said Barbosa. "I knew we should've stuck with church!"

16

A NEW KIND OF RULE

It started out like any other day. Morning chirps from birds, yawns from the tired, and the crackling sounds of awakened bones, though these mornings in the land of Canada slowly turned into stressful ordeals, if not eerie. The humans witnessed something more than creatures stalking the streets at night, for their own children became more deranged than ever.

Kids all around were committing random violence and yelling out cryptic nonsense, and they were absolutely obsessed with pancakes. Many tried special medicines and brain-tinkering methods that asylums used to control their behavior. No matter what treatment they underwent, they still showed no signs of wellness, just the pitter-patter of madness.

Families everywhere shared the same problem, and no one could figure out what the cause of the disease was. Leading experts were also baffled, calling it an evolved stage of mental illness. Some schoolteachers believed that their minds were either trapped in another world or were being controlled by an unseen force. However, those were public-school teachers, and they were easily ignored. Whichever the case, it was beyond modern studies. With so much strangeness happening and with so few questions answered, the media had to address it in a way to ease the troubled populace. With impeccable timing, Monsieur Marin called for a special press conference at Parliament Hill in Ottawa.

It was a highly respectable landmark in Canada, the perfect spot for such an occasion. He invited loads of paparazzi, news writers, and international reporters, and he promised corn dogs for all. It was going to be an event of change, and it would be held in the open courtyard, at sundown. Some wondered why, but most just complied. Hopefully they would get some real answers or perhaps something more.

On that eventful evening, the setting sun cast a beautiful silhouette behind the historic Peace Tower. The humans were all gathered in that cozy courtyard, waiting for Marin to make an appearance. In the meantime, they chattered and stuffed their faces with free corn dogs. The streetlamps flickered, and the cameras were immediately turned on when Marin's name was announced from the speakers. The sun disappeared, the air felt a bit chilly, and all fell silent as the nation eagerly waited to see their prime minister.

Through the main doors of the Peace Tower came a small squad of men cloaked in hoods as if they were ministers of a dark cult. Their hands were hidden within their sleeves, and their heads faced to the ground as they made their way down the steps. After a pause, they spread out and quietly stood near the main podium, which stood on a large stage. It was an odd presence, and the crowd sensed it. It all felt so weird when they first arrived at the hill, especially when they saw a bit of fog covering the ground on a dry day. It was very odd if not troubling, and not even the tasty goodness of corn dogs seemed to ease their worries.

With an explosive yell, the prime minister jumped through the doors and presented himself in an eccentric manner. He arrived in a dark-red leather coat with torn sleeves that had little chains hooked around the shoulders. He wore a long white sleeved shirt with black leather gloves and had three black belt buckles around the waist. He had black leather boots and white pants that had multiple zippers and chains. As for his makeup, well, picture Marilyn Manson with a devilock hairdo. He was absolutely fabulous in the eyes of gothic lore.

He was overjoyed to see a large turnout, but his people could tell he wasn't quite himself. Marin was never overjoyed and would never wear ridiculous attire. They could have mistaken him for a clown. Nevertheless, he did a little dance and a twirl as he made his way to the podium. He leaned close to the many microphones that were placed before him. He grasped the podium with his finely manicured hands and shouted, "Hello, world!"

The crowd stood in shock, for they did not know how to react to that type of face. Marin thumped a few microphones; he wanted to make sure they were on because he was feeling slightly embarrassed by the silence. Marin decided to break the ice and begin the conference.

"So, nice weather to have at a conference, right?" He did not receive an answer. "Yeah, not too cold, not too hot, perfect time for the little monsters to come out and play, right? Anyway, I understand that there are a lot of questions going through your little heads and itching in the back of your skulls, correct? Like an irritating itch only a doctor can scratch, and I'm the kind of doctor who can scratch it with an enlightening claw! I would call myself Dr. Claw, but I think that name's already taken."

Marin spoke very oddly too. He moved like a wiggly swan and had the exaggerated voice of certain actors, although the voice had a more feminine touch. It prompted a random reporter to stand out from the crowd and speak his mind.

"Is this some kind of joke?" yelled the reporter. "I came here to get answers from our leader, not some Tim Burton reject!"

Oh! What a nasty snap. Marin inhaled and exhaled hard as he tried to calm his violent side. He moved the conference along, surely remembering the reporter's face afterward.

Marin ground his teeth. "OK, right to the point. We are gathered here on this glorious evening to answer your many questions. But to sum up everything, we are experiencing change for a better future. We are embarking on a new page in history, nay, a new chapter in the book of existence! That chapter is named Nevermore."

The crowd began to grumble to one another, asking about his meaning and whether or not electing him was a good idea in the first place.

Marin continued, "All of you are probably thinking that it means an end to all things, especially after that dome of darkness deal. Wrong, it is a new beginning. You see, I came across actual vampires some-odd nights ago. That's right, actual vampires with pale faces and sharp fangs. I personally thought they were disturbing freaks—like you presume about me, but you could not be even wronger. Those monsters were real, but they're the same as you and me, no matter what shape or form. Their culture and their way of life don't discriminate or trivialize."

The crowd became worried about where the conference was heading. In another part of the country, the televised event caught the attention of the three heroes, Bell, Bill, and Tye. They silently spied through the windows of a human family viewing the conference, and they were worried as well.

Marin went on, "Those vampires explained to me that we should not fear monsters; rather we should embrace them and welcome them into the world so peace may appear above the horizon! Otherwise none of us will survive…Not. In. The. Least. Which is why I converted myself to the beautiful dark side. I shall be the leader of that future, and let my brothers and sisters be what they truly are, monsters!"

Everyone gasped. The whole viewing world was dumbstruck by Marin's words! Bell & Bill knew that Aval & Evel were somehow controlling the prime minister, and it was all hard to take in. Soon everyone on Parliament Hill started to overreact in a threatening way—they wanted to overthrow their leader because of the dark path he took.

They began to boo. They threw thrash and half-eaten corn dogs at him. Marin just stood there and took it all in, smiling as he did. Somehow the idea of food being thrown in his face came to him as a thoughtful gesture. He was a bit famished from not eating anything in days. The angry reporter from before rushed up the steps and came toward Marin with violence in his eyes. In a split second, the hooded bodyguards ripped off their robes and revealed themselves as Frankenstein soldiers! They were armed with AK-47s that showed no warning of use. They fired at the reporter, reducing him to a pile of swiss steak.

There was screaming and panic, though no escape was possible, because all around them came more Frankenstein soldiers. From the very dirt below them, from the high rooftops, and even from the corn-dog machines. Their weapons were loaded and ready to shoot everyone on sight. Marin then raised his right hand and ordered them to cease fire, for the moment. In order to prevent any more bloodshed, he urged his people to not move, scratch, or even sneeze. Any sort of funny business would've been unwise. The frightened crowd whined and quivered, and their bodies crouched down. It made Marin so pleased. The simple press conference had become a massive hostage situation.

Marin signaled one of the cameramen to come closer to the podium. That cameraman nervously made his way up the steps and slowly focused his camera on the menacing prime minister. Marin snatched a microphone for himself, stepped away from the podium, and made a comment about that angry reporter.

"I'm glad that douche pickle died," he said, "because now I can tell all of you the future in peace. These monsters here are our proud Canadian soldiers, undead and fully upgraded. They are stronger, immune to pain, and committed to their job of protecting and destroying. You might be thinking, 'Golly, these are the same soldiers that attacked the University of Toronto!' So I can't stress enough that they are dead serious. Ha! I made a funny!"

No one laughed.

"But don't take it the wrong way," he said. "These wild soldiers had to be contained, and they're now more obedient. I can promise that after today you will no longer live in fear. In order to do that, there must come change. Soldiers and cops across this country will immediately be frankenized for your better protection. These tireless and obedient creatures will watch and clean these mean streets while you sleep soundly in your beds. Then there are these werewolves. They are our allies too, but they will no longer hunt the innocents. They will instead feed on the hateful criminals in our prisons."

He continued. "The death penalty will indeed be brought back better than ever. Next comes the part where we adjust. I want everyone to bring out their dark and artistic sides, so you may feel happily free, like me. I want to hear pipe organs in the air, possibly some death-metal tunes here and there. I want to see settings of haunting decorations and expressive clothing, like goth or steampunk. The streets will be paved with darkness galore, not as a scene of doom but as an expression of our pain toward life. Our nation will be the most peaceful and radical country ever to have spawned. The land of the disturbed and the home of the arts, Nevermore!"

There was no joyous reaction from anyone. They felt as though they were being taken over by a new form of Nazis: Gothzis. Marin saw their worried faces, and even though it made him happy, he wanted them to be happy as well. He signaled the soldiers to lower their weapons so that the crowd could relax and hear his ultimatum.

Marin said to his people, "In kind spirit of your cooperation through these changes, I promise that your taxes will be lowered by eighty-five percent! Now, what do you think of that?"

The crowd, well, who could say what ran through their minds that day. The idea of taxes being practically nonexistent brought about a sea of surprising emotions. Soon all cried out to Marin, "Long live Nevermore!"

Everyone cheered, and all danced in delight! They praised their leader with the sound of applause! Bell, Bill, and Tye couldn't believe that people would be so fickle, so quick to change attitudes when money was involved. And just when they thought it couldn't get any crazier, Marin presented the world a quick opportunity. He pulled out a drawn picture and held it close to the camera. It was poorly drawn but easily identifiable. It was a picture of two blond squirrels and one giant spider with human hands.

Marin stated that those three creatures were responsible for the uprising of insanity in their children. He claimed they were cancerous monsters, agents of trickery, followers of douchebaggery who were sent to drive kids absolutely insane. It was all for their twisted pleasure of tearing families apart and strengthening the stereotype that all Canadians ate nothing but pancakes. He wanted to purge those three creatures from life.

He motivated vigilantes and bounty hunters by putting a price on their heads. The lucky one or ones who brought their heads on a silver platter would be rewarded C$1 million! Surely, Bell knew that no one would be foolish enough to believe such a tale and greedy enough to hunt down two squirrels and an insect. But unannounced to her, Bill and Tye were stricken with fear as they noticed a large group of hillbillies aiming their shotguns in their general direction.

Meanwhile, at the top of the Peace Tower, Aval & Evel were enjoying the sweet victory of ruling over a country. Aval had to give Evel credit for an astounding plan. She smiled and held him close, saying that it was all too simple. It was all a matter of greed making morality and good judgment seem clear, nevermore.

17

OLD SAINT YETI

Did it happen? Did it finally come to be? I am very happy to say that it did. Aval & Evel transformed Canada into their own horrific paradise, named Nevermore. Everything was reconstructed to a traditional time where dark cathedrals, demonic statues, stone spikes, and cobwebs were as normal as dirt. The streets had less traffic, for the humans walked the streets in their unique styles of expression. As anyone could tell, the populace was a sea of black. Everyone had dark umbrellas during the day and shrouded cloaks at night. They wore sleeveless coats in the evening and striped pajamas in the morning. Traditional stylers and poseurs were all welcome, for everyone had the opportunity to express their dark and artistic side.

Music was often played through the days, from soft violins to gentle piano keys and sometimes loud strums from electric guitars. The marvelous sounds gave the air its fair share of dread, and it made the humans feel more relaxed. The nation was at peace, and all were content. They were safe from any harm by the criminally crooked, all thanks to the monsters who watched every corner on every street. The guilty, however, were shown no mercy, and traces of unnecessary evil were punished.

Silence, maturity, and deathly justice made the country of Nevermore peaceful. It even made major news coverage around the globe. Channels all over began to speak of Nevermore's weirdness and strangeness, especially from its neighbor, the United States. On a typical Monday afternoon, an American TV news channel told the nation about Nevermore.

"Good evening, fellow Americans!" said the old-fashioned anchorman, Chris Galley. "Turn off the lights, and bring out the jack-o'-lanterns, because we have news so haunting that it'll make your Christian neighbors scream in terror! The country of Canada underwent a drastic change one can only see as becoming a Halloween nation. It is now called Nevermore! Monsters that we thought had vanished have indeed turned the nation into a controlled hot spot for all things wicked. You heard it here first! The streets are filled with vicious creatures and gothic fashion! Their stock markets are plummeting, and no one seems to care! They don't care indeed, because the nation's people seem to be taking the change very well, and here's what they had to say."

The on-screen monitor then showed a reporter interviewing a man in a black suit and top hat, casually walking through a park full of poets and magic performers. The man said to the reporter, "At first I was kinda terrified that monsters were allowed to walk the streets. It also didn't help that my wife was forced to be frankenized, with her being a cop and all…but crime has gone down wondrously since then, and that's a good thing."

They cut to an overdressed woman in a green miniskirt, holding and petting a gray pigeon on a street corner. She said to the reporter, "The whole gothic scene really isn't my type of fashion. Then again, I do look cute in leather boots and waist buckles, and don't even get me started on these hair highlights. And these new lines of makeup? Hmph! Watch out, Lady Gaga."

Then they cut to a shirtless man covered in tattoos, who said, "I was like, whoa! This is totally Halloween Town, man! Hallows' Eve all year round! WOOO!" The interviews ended, and Chris Galley returned to the screen.

"As you can see, these strange locals found some light in the darkness," he said. "Speaking of Halloween, it is just a few short days away! In celebration of that devilish holiday, the prime minister, Monsieur Marin, has announced a special party that will be held in Nevermore's Mount Royal Park. He's inviting everyone around the globe to witness the premiere of Nevermore's first metal band, '¡GothFro!' A colorful band composed of talented and frankenized musicians! Am I as terrified as you are right now? You bet your bottom dollar! So stay home and lock your doors before sundown! For all we know this could be the beginning of all things wicked and an end to our modern civilization! Pray for your lives, stay safe, and remember to stay tuned for an update on the American eagle who loves to eat American apple pie. It's patriotic goodness!"

As America watched, so did President X. He watched the news cross the many screens in his office and pondered what Marin was up to. He was very concerned about the changes Marin carelessly bestowed upon his country. President X clenched his fists as he heard the distant laughter from other countries.

Many times he attempted to bring Marin back to his senses, yet the gothic prime minister just sat in his medieval throne, painting his nails black and mocking the president in their short conversations. It became clear that Marin did not care about the economy or the ramifications of his actions; he wanted to act like every day was Halloween. President X, at that time, could only sit near his doomsday button and wait for an opportunity to erase the dark country from the map.

Later, in the snowy plains of Greenland, a crashed cargo plane exhausted its last flame before the frost doused it into smoke. Inside there was pounding and a clank, a push and shove, and then a quick punch from a disfigured fist that opened the door to the outside.

From the plane came Bell, Bill, and Tye, surviving yet another heated encounter with bounty hunters. From town to town, the three kept running into people who wanted to collect their heads. The heroes were still framed, and no one bothered to hear their words; they only cared about the money. They would've been killed from the start if it weren't for that strong tarantula by their side.

The recent group of bounty hunters led them on a flight misadventure. They were trapped in an airborne plane surrounded by heartless cutthroats and ruthless killers. The heroes were able to take them out, thanks to Tye's unhealthy urge to make shoes out of live human bodies. They were freed from their greedy clutches, but since none of them knew how to fly the complicated machine or use parachutes, they ultimately crashed to the frozen snow below. They were stranded in the middle of nowhere.

There were no manageable supplies left from the plane, only the clothes on their backs and Bell's cricket bat. There was no reason to stay, so the two squirrels climbed on Tye's back and planned to head back to civilization. They needed to take down the vampires through rain, sleet, or snow.

An hour had passed since Tye carried the squirrels through the snow, and he started to feel his hands turn into frost. He started to wonder if being a good guy was worth all that trouble. Just when he thought it couldn't get any worse, a chilling blizzard began to storm down on their heads. He sarcastically laughed at such timing.

The heroes became cold, hungry, and weak. All they could do was rough it and keep on going, no matter how harsh it was. Despite blizzard, sickness, or the frostbite on Tye's hands, they were determined to stay on their quest.

Then with a sigh, the tired tarantula collapsed from cold. The freezing squirrels fell off into the snow and were covered in frost. They wobbled up from the crash, slowly heading over toward the tarantula and pleaded for him to wake up. It was hopeless, and soon Bill collapsed from the cold as well. Bell desperately nudged the two to get up, but nothing worked. She took her trusty bat to try and poke them awake or possibly smack them awake. Before she could, she too fainted in the snow.

They rested soundly and had a feel of eternal peace. Bill witnessed his life going by in seconds. He relived a time where he and Bell spent a night at their grandmother's house. She offered the two some hot cocoa, and it sure felt nice to have some right then. Bill held out his cup and wanted to try it first, but instead of a regular pitcher, the old lady carried the hot cocoa in a gigantic pot. Before the boy knew it, she poured it all over his body and watched him scream in pain!

The scalding heat woke him up. He leaped up in a panic and immediately hit a wooden wall, and then he fell back to the wooden floor. He looked around and wondered where he was. It was a toasty wooden cabin with a pleasant fireplace, and in the middle of the room were nine suspicious reindeer playing a game of poker.

To his left he saw his sister and Tye covered in blankets and drinking cocoa. To his right he saw a big, fuzzy, apelike creature in red-and-white fur, creeping toward him with its oversize hands. It inched closer with its sharp yellow teeth, its scraggly white beard stained with brown liquid, and its soulless black eyes that seemed like the windows of an abyss. Bill screamed at the top of his lungs and ran, but then he hit the same wall again.

The fuzzy creature shook his head and said with a low voice, "Smart boy you are. The others tried to go through the door. I was just trying to heat you up with a cup of hot cocoa, and then you knocked it over yourself like a loon."

Bill was wet yet warm, but he was still however terrified by the monster. He turned to Bell and asked her what was going on. She shook her head as well and said that they weren't in any danger. They were rescued from the blizzard by this red yeti that went by the name of Santa Claus.

Was he hearing her right? Was it truly old Saint Nick himself? The jolly bringer of goodwill whom all knew and loved was a yeti? No, the true Santa was a jolly fat man in a red suit with cherry cheeks. What Bill saw in front of him was a bare-naked yeti with red-and-white fur. As for cherry cheeks, his pale blue skin could hardly show red at all.

He did have a beard, a big belly, and reindeer, but what creepy overweight man wouldn't? Bill and the rest could have seen the creature as an impostor, but no matter how hard they denied it, it was the truth. All of it was. Jolly old Saint Nick was an abominable snowman all along! Bill still denied the truth; he didn't want to believe Santa Claus was a yeti at all.

The yeti sighed and dropped a blanket on Bill, and then he sat down in his brown easy chair. The yeti looked so sad, so depressed that even squirrels wouldn't accept the truth. They wanted to believe what has been fed into their heads since childhood.

"I'm so tired," the yeti said. "I've been on this earth for over eight hundred years. I presented myself so many times, and everybody still prefers a human with cherry cheeks. I tell myself that it's only about keeping the spirit of Christmas alive in today's youth. In hovels, apartments, or cardboard boxes, I find a way to make their day and let them feel grateful to be alive. All the presents and all the treats are nothing compared to a child's smile on Christmas morning. That's what I work for every year. If it means being portrayed as something nice that they find scary, then who am I to argue?"

After hearing such a tender speech, there was no doubt that he was the real Santa Claus. Though he looked sadder than a bum on a street corner. To make him feel better, one of his reindeer, Rudolph, handed him a bottle of scotch. Santa thanked his booze buddy and chugged down the alcohol. After drinking half the bottle, it gave him some energy to say "Ho-ho-ho," minus the cheery spirit.

Bell & Bill had to ask him why he wasn't full of cheer, especially close to the Christmas season. The yeti belched a bit and told them that there was no Christmas that year or ever. The yeti decided to give up on the business, because it wasn't making the world a nicer place. It used to be nice, and he used to be a regular yeti.

There was no need for questions, for he felt to be in a talking mood. He decided to tell his guests his tale. In the beginning, he was an ordinary yeti named Salamear, young, free, and full of happiness, but all around him were others who were sad and suicidal. He wanted to bring them joy, but he had no way of approaching them without having weapons pointed at his face.

All his attempts failed, and just when he was at his lowest, along came a raven. Raven, the wishing raven, as a matter of fact. Not knowing the consequences of wishes, Salamear wished to have the power to bring joy to the sad world, where everyone could wake with smiles instead of moans and farts. She granted his wish and made him the phenomenal bringer of joy.

All seemed well, but the downside was that he could only use his holiday power once a year, on the night before the humans' holy messiah was born. It was her evil intention to make them forget what that day was really about. She was tricky that way.

When it came to bringing joy, Salamear hardly minded the trickery, but a bit of sadness always seemed to come his way. Most of the humans couldn't stand to see his monstrous face, so they later portrayed him as a friendly-looking man with a friendly name, Santa Claus. The day he hoped would bring happiness eventually became a day of greed. Everyone exploited the image of Santa Claus and sold it for marketing purposes. Some even made him look like a perverted creature and drove his good name through the mud. All of the shameless acts soon drove him to the point of depression.

He hasn't delivered presents in nearly three decades, for reasons he couldn't explain to his company. Salamear stopped spreading the joy and retired to the outskirts of Greenland with his reindeer. Finding happiness the best way he knew involved alcohol and the occasional female companionship. Other than those, nothing could keep him jolly like he used to be.

Tye walked over to the sad yeti and told him how they were very much alike. They were tortured beings who were once proud creatures. He also commented on his bare blue feet and how shoeless they were. His feet were cold, and they needed shoes. He wondered if one of the reindeer could provide a warm suitable wear from their skin. Noticing no reaction, the tarantula became embarrassed and eased his urges by thinking about more mangoes. Salamear suddenly forgot about everything else and wondered why there was a seven-foot-tall, multihanded, talking spider in a top hat offering to make him shoes out of his own reindeer.

Salamear left that question for later; he wanted to know why two squirrels and a giant spider were out in the blizzard. Once Bell finished her cocoa, she told him about their mission to take down the evil tyrants of Nevermore. The three had to get back to the mainland as quickly as possible or who knows what could happen next. The tyrants might turn Alaska into one big Hot Topic store, inciting a full-scale war with America.

That sounded awfully serious to Salamear's ears, and he was curious who those evil tyrants were. Tye said their names clear as day: "Aval & Evel."

Before he could continue, Salamear made him stop for one brief second and told him to repeat those names once again. With a pause, Tye said their names once more: "Aval & Evel."

Their very names caused Salamear to rise from his chair with a hostile look. The yeti breathed deeply with escalating rage as the reindeer slowly moved into a corner with caution. That big creature huffed and puffed and went completely psycho! He threw his chair across the room, flipped the poker table up to the ceiling, threw the shelves full of toys to the ground, tossed his jar of cookies through the window, and tossed a log through another window. Finally he flipped over a sofa and smashed it in half with his bare hands!

His rampaged ceased, and his living room was completely trashed. The two squirrels hid in terror behind a pile of logs, while Tye sipped some of his cocoa and called it delicious. Bell & Bill were worried that the mention of those vampires might have upset the yeti in some kind of way. Salamear found joy out of all things in life, but he had a deep-seated hatred for Aval & Evel. The reason for that, surprisingly enough, was those two heartless bloodsuckers canceled Christmas.

Thirty years ago on Christmas Eve, Salamear was in his workshop at the North Pole. He went through the naughty and nice lists for the second time before his departure. He hoped that Aval & Evel were nice that year, but they had been naughty for too long.

They despised Christmas because it made others happy, and he figured it was time for a change. Using his mystical and whimsical holiday magic, he summoned the ghosts of Christmas past, present, and future to give those vampires a healthier attitude for the season. The ghosts arrived at their gloomy home and followed the procedure of loss, regret, and revelation to make them change their ways for a better future. It went well at first, but before Salamear knew it, they vanquished the three ghosts.

They destroyed them, and he couldn't believe it—his spiritual friends vanquished at the hands of squirrels. It was very devastating. He needed to sit down, and he needed a moment to himself. Later, when he could stomach the courage to hop into his sled, the vampires came out of nowhere and unleashed a torrent of rage and violence. They destroyed his workshop and set it ablaze. Even Salamear's holiday magic was no match against their vampiric dread. Aval & Evel overwhelmed him and beat him until his bruises had bruises.

His workshop, his home, all were burned to the ground, but he and his reindeer were spared. It was a warning for the yeti to leave the vampires and their past alone. They demanded that he give up Christmas and his life as a jolly intruder so no one would believe in him again, and no home would be his dumping ground for junk. Where the only joy anyone should feel was another day spared by Death himself.

Sadly, he agreed without question. Otherwise they would have ended his life where he lay. But if the vampires should ever see him again, there would be no more warnings. With a deadly stare and a shot of spit near his feet, the vampires flew off into the night sky and left the poor yeti to wallow in shame.

And that's how Aval & Evel canceled Christmas. I love that story, but why those vampires didn't bother to sink their teeth into that yeti and gain his powers was brought into question. Maybe the thought of gaining holiday cheer wouldn't have sat well with their stomachs. Salamear lived in silence ever since, wishing for the day that Aval & Evel would get what they deserved. He believed that time had come. He decided to help Bell, Bill, and Tye bring the tyrants down once and for all!

But he did not have his powers yet, and they did not have tools to fight them. How would they stand a chance, especially with deadly soldiers and half the world looking for them? The yeti said not to worry, for he already formed a master plan of taking them down, personally. As for sneaking in and finding them, let's just say Rudolph knew a guy who knew a really smart guy, who knew an even smarter guy, who knew an ex-baker who worked in machinery.

That evening the four motivated creatures set off on their journey through the treacherous blizzard in a nine-reindeer open sleigh. The secret contact lay beyond the land, and they made it there in a flash. There they found a small military base along Greenland's borders, where they met the ex-baker whose name remained secret. So they just called him "Ex-Baker." Rudolph explained the whole situation to the man. He told him that everything and every second were crucial to stopping the vampires' reign.

It was rather strange at first, but the ex-baker agreed to help them win the fight. He couldn't see any harm in it, as long as he didn't have to fight. If the great Santa Claus had a huge vendetta with two squirrels, he would hate seeing them in person. The ex-baker then led the team into his base and offered them weapons while he made some preparations.

Tye was armed to the teeth with razor-sharp hunting knives; Bill was given an explosive crossbow with shotgun bolts, and Bell finally traded in her worn-out cricket bat for a powerful broadsword. Excellent armor plates were even strapped to their bodies and were soaked in garlic juice for better protection. Salamear had no need for any of that; his fists and vengeful wrath worked just fine.

At the stroke of midnight, they traveled back to Canada completely undetected. Though it was not by air, land, or sea but underground. All thanks to the ex-baker's high-speed tunneling machine, Sir Hole Plower. With its sturdiness and excessive amount of juice, they could ride it all the way until they hit the mark they desired that sounded weird when the ex-baker said it. Rudolph sure knew some strange people.

18
WISHING RAVEN

Have you ever wished for something you never had before? Something you have wanted for so long that you relied on starlight, abandoned wells, even prayers to bring it to you? I did, and trust me, they're as reliable as a deaf sloth in the dark.

If we always wish, and it seldom comes to be, why bother at all? Fortunately, there was a creature that could answer our calls, and her name was Raven, the wishing raven. She was a mischievous bird born from the pits of darkness, whose only purpose was to cause tragedy in life. But don't be afraid of her intentions; her deepest desire was fulfilling humankind's greatest desires. No longer did you have to wait for a miracle to happen; all you had to do was wish upon a raven.

Let's start off with a very messy street urchin, hanging out in a dark alleyway in New York City. It was a little girl in ragged clothing with the dream of being famous, complete with everlasting fame so she'd be free from the homeless life. It was something she hoped would happen in a split second, but one should know it could never happen in a million years. Yet lo and behold stood a wishing raven on her lap. The raven said that a pretty girl like her should not have to cry or worry at such a young age.

The raven arrived to answer her call, to end her suffering once and for all. She was gracious, that bird; she would do anything to see the smile of a child so small. No need to dream or hope; the child just needed to wish upon that raven, and that would be all.

The child wished that she was famous, where she would live in a fancy house with rich parents! The raven saw that hopeful smile and was happy to give her a nice life of fame and riches. She waved her wings about and emitted a black mist that engulfed the two in a vanishing shroud.

It took a second for the child to see again, and she found herself wearing fancy clean clothes, sparkly clothes that smelled like flowers, but where she ended up was not her vision of a home. She was locked in a windowless room along with other children with the same sparkly clothes, while their ankles were chained and shackled to the walls.

She did say she wanted a fancy home, so she lived in millionaire's mansion, but she resided underground. As for riches, her new parents made their profits introducing children to adults who loved them in a...special...kind of way. That new life was not what she wanted. Then in a split second, two men in tuxedoes opened the door and took the child to an unknown location.

She was scared by it all, and she pleaded for the raven to answer her call. The raven smirked from a high ledge and said that it was what she had wished for. She was removed from that alley and should be grateful for her new life forevermore.

There was then another human with a wish. It was a cubicle man suffering from depression and hopelessness in the same city. He worked for a disrespectful corporation that paid him less than a regular programmer, practically making him a code monkey. He needed a miracle, or else he had no choice but to kill himself, but there was no need for that. Through the open window flew in the raven, greeting the code monkey with grace. She said a hardworking man like him shouldn't throw his life away so easily.

The raven arrived to answer his call, to end his torture once and for all. She was thoughtful, that bird; she would do anything to see the body of a man crawl. No need to beg or pray; the code monkey just needed to wish upon that raven, and that would be all.

The man wished that he was set for life, where he had a pretty wife and a nice home of his own. Where he would never have to work a day in his life again. The raven saw that desperate smile and was happy to give him a wife and a home. She waved her wings about and emitted a cloud of vanishing black mist. When the darkness cleared, the man found himself in a white suit, in a comfy white chair in a huge living room of pure white.

He was happy. He finally had it all. But where was his wife? He realized that a chain was present in his right hand. At the end of that chain was a scared little child with a spiked collar around her neck. The man discarded the chain and rose from his chair in terror. What was going on?

The scared child explained that she was his wife. Not only that, but he also owned many other children, and he locked them away in his dungeon for personal clients. That's how he achieved his fortune—by running an underground pedophile ring!

He never wanted to do that. He wasn't a pedophile. The man became scared; it was not what he had wished for at all! He called for the raven, but then he suddenly heard loud sirens outside his mansion doors. Through the windows he saw dozens of police cars and officers occupying the front yard, demanding that the sick monster come out and accept his fate. The scared man ran to the back doors, away from the police, until they smashed through all the windows and busted through all the doors. They surrounded him, and he begged them to stop so he could plead his case.

They did not want him to be heard, so they chose to ignore him. The officers opened fire, and the code monkey was depressed nevermore.

The raven often connected wishes to one another. Combining misfortunes into one big train wreck amused her. Whether others survived or not, the important thing was that they all had a taste of instant fortune.

Why wish upon a star with such ambition,
when you can simply wish upon a raven?

Raven, the wishing raven, is not picky;
she grants wishes to any kind of dummy.
Wish all you like as much as you want;
she shall deliver onto you with a taunt.

Why work yourself to death for no reason,
when you can simply wish upon a raven?

No task or payment is required to have your wishes come true.
She's a fascinating bird that takes joy in how your wish affects you.
If you wish for a better life,
she'll introduce your neck to an iron spike.

Why think of others like a boring old virgin,
when you can really wish upon a raven?

Giving the poor large amounts of wealth would be awfully kind;
she'll replace your blood with cash and she knows they won't mind.
Like to wish what it'd be like if you were never actually born?
Your spirit will be stuck in limbo and forever you are torn.

She will grant what you most adore,

but do be careful what you wish for.

If you care to wish upon a raven,

then you dare to wish upon Satan.

On the night of Halloween, which was lit with a marvelous red moon, loads of tricks or treaters flocked to the streets in delight. All the human children in Nevermore dressed like their favorite characters and carried around bags for sweets as always. The goths and rockers, however, hung around cemeteries, making pentagrams to summon ghostly spirits from hell. You know, the normal things that happen on All Hallows' Eve.

The woodland creatures were, however, locked away in their homes. They were ever so afraid even to go outside anymore. No venturing out, trick-or-treating, and no pentagrams they would dare make. So sad that they missed out on all the fun.

The raven absolutely loved that time of year, though there weren't any wishes that needed granting. In fact, she hadn't granted a single wish in over seven months. Most became wiser and began to catch on to the danger of her powers. They decided to make their own wishes come true by making them happen for a change. The raven did not mind; she knew some were too weak to carry out such independence. In the meantime, she took some time for herself. She even decided to go to the premiere of ¡GothFro! in Mount Royal Park.

The raven arrived, and she was amazed by the turnout. There was a dreadfully bright stage of wicked splendor, surrounded by hundreds of attendants. All the humans were finely dressed in cloaks and gowns, metal chains, and leather pants. They were patiently eager to see the world's first Frankenstein band. How exciting it would've been to see monsters having a band of their own.

The stage lit up in glorious green flames, and intoxicating mist showered down to the ground. The lights then went dark, until one light from the upper rails shone on a special guest making his way to the center stage.

Monsieur Marin appeared in the spotlight and welcomed all of his people. He wore his usual Marilyn Manson attire, but this time he added a long black line across his mouth with crooked marks to give the illusion of a stitched mouth. He thanked them all for coming and wished them all a hellish Halloween. All cheered as he stuck out his arms to the sky and hyped them up for the main event. The spotlight went away as he moved to the far left of the stage and prepared to introduce the band. One by one, the lights revealed the band members with their personal colors that were the same as their ink-splattered skin.

There appeared Ghostly-T, the white keyboardist, who started off with some soothing key notes from his keyboard. Crypt-C, the blue guitarist, strummed a few electric riffs on her frightening guitar. Blood-E, the red bassist, made things a little deeper with his booming bass strums. Poison-P, the purple drummer, created a hard rhythm on the drums that made the band speed up intensely. Finally, there was the tall vocalist with a torn afro, Toxic-Z the green voice, who let out a hard scream!

The band played their first song with intensity. They jammed out and rocked the crowd out of their boots! It was amazing! The band was talented, connected with the fearsome music, and in tune with their spooky instruments! It was enough to make the raven bob her head up and down. She seemed to enjoy herself.

Now, it has come to some attention that we know less about the raven and more about her abilities. What was there to tell, though? She was a creature that didn't eat, sleep, or have any personal interests in anything other than evil. There were hardly any blunders in her life, other than the supreme penalty for not granting enough wishes. Humankind's wishes were her life's work; granting their foolish hopes and dreams was her means of staying alive.

If she didn't grant at least one within seven months, she would perish from existence forevermore. That Halloween night at the stroke of midnight, the raven would die, and her purpose would end evermore.

She did not mind death at all; she was made to serve her creator and fulfill her purpose of spreading misery through hopeful desires. Without purpose, there was no need for anyone to exist, which hardly made for a sad backstory. The raven was simply a heartless spirit, a sadist that naturally loved to ruin lives and catch a metal concert afterward.

She was like a subtler version of Nutilda. Like a true definition of a witch without a heart. Her likes, dislikes, and the way she acted were no different from the humans in attendance who couldn't help but bob their heads to such excellent music.

The band finished their long intro song, and loud applause came from their audience. The band stood emotionless with no feelings whatsoever, only the urge to move on to the next song. They began to play their next number, but a loud rumble shook the stage. Everyone felt it under their feet; it was as if an earthquake had come to mess up all the fun.

Out of the earth came an iron drill that wrecked the front barricades. All screamed and backed away, not knowing what came from below. What emerged was the drill machine, Sir Hole Plower. It rose from the dirt and parked on the surface for all to see. The machine stopped, and the drill ceased to spin. From the sliding door came two blond squirrels, a black-and-orange tarantula, a red-and-white yeti, and a portly ex-baker in pink overalls.

The team looked at the big sea of dark followers and figured that the ex-baker clearly miscalculated his readings. The crowd quickly identified the squirrels and spider as the scoundrels from the wanted signs, the ones responsible for the spread of madness. The crowd was enraged at the very sight of the evildoers. They booed, yelled, and started throwing trash at them. Before the squirrels could explain themselves, Marin hopped in front of the machine with a microphone and asked if everyone was ready to destroy the monstrosities of Nevermore.

Everyone agreed without hesitation and immediately rushed toward the machine. With a quick gasp, the heroes went back inside the drill and locked the door tight. As the band played their next song, the ex-baker quickly reversed into the open hole, escaping certain doom. The heroes thought they were safe and out of harm's way. Unfortunately for them their presence caught the attention of the raven. The time was precisely eleven o'clock, and if she was to die in one hour, she wanted to go out watching an exhilarating conflict come to an end.

A dark cloud appeared inside their little machine and swallowed them whole. It engulfed them in mystical shroud that took their bodies away, leaving the ex-baker alone to ponder what had just happened. The group dropped down on a stone surface, confused as to where they were and how they got there. They appeared to have been brought to a castle rooftop near the park. That grim rooftop was covered with weeping statues of angels holding spears, and the edges were planted with spiked gates bigger than a grown human.

The squirrels and the spider felt a chilling presence as clear fog swallowed their feet and as the bloodred moon hovered over that castle. It was like a classic horror setting that was sure to have an ending most grim. It was indeed the raven's intention, for across the heroes stood the king and queen of Nevermore, Aval & Evel.

All characters were brought together, thanks to the raven. All faced each other with much anger and hate. The raven smiled with joy, observing it all from a nearby weeping statue. The very sight of the heroes put the vampires in a foul and despicable mood. The intruding yeti, the traitorous tarantula, and the two blond squirrels that dared challenge them. Oh, how long Aval & Evel waited to come face-to-face with their poisonous cures.

Bell & Bill saw their silent anger but was astounded to see that they looked like darker images of themselves. Tye pulled out his knives and showed no regrets for siding with the good. Salamear stood there with his arms folded, figuring out which skull he wanted to crack first. They were all set and ready for anything. One thing was for certain: someone was going to die.

Tye spoke first and taunted the vampires, saying they couldn't possibly touch them with garlic surrounding their bodies. It looked like surefire protection. Unfortunately, what the group should have known was that garlic itself did not completely ward off vampires; they just couldn't stand the smell of it. Which was why Aval & Evel took out two clothespins and stuck them to their noses, now unable to smell a thing. Tye had goofed big-time.

Without stretching, cracking, or even talking, the vampires slowly walked toward the group with death in their eyes. Bill began to shake, and Bell began to guard herself with her sword. The two asked Salamear how they were going to fight them. The yeti blew out some air through his nose and told them there was no way to fight them. Those vampire squirrels were as wicked as they were powerful and would surely kill them in seconds. It immediately made everyone lose their faith.

Salamear did however have a plan, much more a secret weapon. It was a surefire way to take out the vampires with ease, and it was perched on a weeping statue. His secret weapon was Raven, the wishing raven. One wish was all that it took to kill anything in the world.

The three heroes already knew about her and warned the yeti not to wish upon a raven. He paid them no mind at all; he wanted to see Aval & Evel die at his feet. The yeti began to call out his wish, but Aval leaped through the air at incredible speed and kicked the yeti square in the jaw!

It was a hard hit that made a harsh cracking sound, enabling saliva to escape from the mouth and shoot in the air. The fierce blow launched the yeti into a statue that impaled his chest with a stone spear. He was unable to escape. He gagged on his own blood and let out his last breath before drifting away.

The vampires killed Santa Claus, and that was the last straw! Tye screamed a foul roar and an unceasing rage at Aval. He used every arm and every swipe to cut that squirrel to bits. The strikes were a breeze for Aval to dodge, for every swipe that came his way cut nothing but air. Aval vanished into a cloud of darkness, escaping the tarantula's thrashing.

In a split second, he reappeared and kicked a knife out of a hand. It flew toward Evel, and she grabbed it with great timing. She vanished as well and reappeared next to Tye, only to slice off one of his arms! The limb fell to the stone pavement and twitched for a few seconds before it became motionless. The tarantula cursed her name before she called him a traitor.

Bell did not wait around. She took her sword and tried to slice Aval with his back turned. He saw her coming, and he punched her square in the face! He sent her flying into Bill and into a wall, where Bill accidentally fired his crossbow in a wild direction. Luckily the explosive arrow hit the spear that held Salamear, and it made his body crash to the ground.

Tye then came after Evel with every force in his body, but even with her, he could hardly cut a string of fur. She was more slick and graceful than Aval. With him distracted, Aval grabbed one of the tarantula's hands and cracked it beyond repair. He took the dropped knife, and with another failed swipe from Tye, Aval sliced off an arm. Tye cursed his name before Aval called him a betrayer.

Bell regained herself and saw a surprise before her eyes. Salamear's body managed to rise from the ground. He was somehow still alive. The bloody yeti pulled out the spear from his chest and threw it to the ground. With a cough, he called out to the raven again. The raven waited patiently with a smile. Bell yelled at him and warned him not to wish upon that raven.

Salamear still didn't listen. Before he could say his wish, Evel dashed toward the spear and flung it right through his belly! The yeti gagged and coughed in deadly pain as he fell, lifeless. Bell covered her mouth in complete shock!

They'd killed Santa Claus again! It was two times too many! Bill summoned the courage to stand up. He reloaded his crossbow. He aimed his weapon at those vampires. He had a clean shot at Evel and immediately took that chance, but that clever vampire practically predicted his plan.

Evel vanished and reappeared behind the boy. She quickly turned his aim toward Bell and made him fire at her chest, sending her flying into a statue. The armor she wore was enough to protect her, but it left her insides in a mess. Bill then took on Evel, but his weak fighting skills gave her no rush of adrenaline. It was most pitiable. She caught an incoming fist with her palm and immediately cracked his entire arm in one twist.

It wasn't the only thing she wanted to break. Once he was down on one knee, crying in pain, she stepped behind the boy and planted his head to the ground with her boot. While his face was rubbed against the hard floor, she eyed his short fluffy tail sailing in the breeze, untampered with by any hand throughout his life. She grabbed it with both hands and ripped it clean from his body!

A burst of rushing of blood sprayed down his legs, and he yelled at excruciating heights. Evel played with the tail as she watched the boy roll around in pain, and then she tossed it away. Out of nowhere, Bell came at Evel with her sword in hopes of performing a swift kill.

She missed as Evel vanished away. Her blade hit the ground, but unfortunately it cut through Bill's left hand! He cried even harder from the agonizing pain. Bill was covered in his own blood and tears, and Bell abjectly apologized, but there was no time for forgiveness. Evel suddenly appeared behind her, but Bell swung her sword around to slice off her head, only to cut yet another cloud of dark vapor. It was getting extremely annoying.

Another reappearance, and the vampire tossed Bell over to Aval. With such quick reaction, he kicked her square in the jaw, which sent her rocketing into the sky, dropping her own sword. Once she was many yards away from the castle, Aval grabbed her sword, opened his wings, and flew up at incredible speed. The wounded Tye was momentarily distracted, giving Evel the opportunity to pick up a knife and fight him head on.

In the air, Bell tried desperately to move herself away from the incoming squirrel but was met with another forceful kick by Aval. The blow sent her rocketing down toward Bill, crashing on top of him with devastating sounds of shattered bones. Both were weak and hurt, but the pain did not end just yet. Aval flew down like a speeding bullet. He struck the sword not only through their weak armor but also straight through their fragile bodies to the stone floor!

It looked very painful, but Bell & Bill did learn a valuable lesson that night. If they did not strategize or properly train their bodies to take on these ruthless killing machines, they could surely bet they'd get their asses kicked.

The squirrels were stuck in a bloody shish kebab, while Aval aided Evel in the fight with Tye. The poor tarantula was covered in his own gooey green blood, and he was down to his last two arms. He couldn't fight anymore, and he'd let everyone down. He wept as he made a final attempt to cut Aval, but the vampire leaned to his left and avoided the attack, where he cut off a hand and listened to Tye cry.

Evel then eyed Bill's crossbow and bolts lying on the ground. She couldn't help but give such fancy equipment a try. She discarded her knife and picked up the crossbow. She loaded it with a heavy bolt and pointed it at Tye's head. It was time to put him out of his misery.

Aval spoke no words to the one-handed creature but gave off a scornful look of disappointment. He turned to his wife and told her to end his life. Still alive but barely moving, Bell & Bill cried for the vampires to stop and to spare their friend's life. Calling him their friend did not sit well with the vampires, because monsters and mortals could never be friends. They were dying enemies, and thus it should remain forevermore.

Bell & Bill looked at Tye, wanting him to live, letting him know he was their friend. The tarantula was very truly touched that they called him their friend. Friendship was all that he'd ever wanted and a cure for his shoemaking urges. Tye used his remaining hand to doff his hat to the squirrels and thank them. They were the kind of mortals that made a monster feel not so monstrous.

Tye closed his eyes, Evel pulled the trigger, and the creature's head exploded from the blast. Tye, the tortured tarantula, was no more!

The two blond squirrels started to break out in tears, but they couldn't. They were only able to cough blood. They could not remove the sword; it was stuck in the ground. They were on the brink of death, and the vampires sought to finish them off personally. Aval walked toward them with deadly intentions as Evel discarded the crossbow and stretched out her arms. It was over. Bell & Bill's journey was coming to an end. The scared squirrels whimpered as they held each other's hands, hoping for a painless death, hoping they would be together in the afterlife.

The raven looked at the bloody mess and was quite disappointed that the fight was so one-sided. She wanted excitement, and she wanted a fight to remember in her final hour, not a massacre. What might one expect when powerful vampires were involved? Either way, it did not satisfy her.

A fair fight and change of tides was the answer. To make things more interesting, Raven decided to aid the half-dead squirrels and give them the same powers and skills as Aval & Evel but with a little more kick. She lifted her wings and concentrated her energy to copy their abilities to the ones who needed it the most.

A powerful shock wave came from the squirrels, flinging the vampires across the roof. A darker atmosphere arose from the castle grounds, and before the vampires stood their true mirror images. Bell & Bill rose from the ground and felt an exhilarating rush of rage course through their veins. Their fur was turned to silky black, their teeth consisted of sharp fangs, and their faces were paler than ever. Aval & Evel couldn't believe their eyes: their blond enemies had become powerful vampires!

There was just the matter of removing the sword and the garlic-drenched armor from their bodies. They pulled the bloody sword from their stomachs and threw it to the ground as their insides began to heal at an alarming rate, yet Bill's lost limbs did not grow back. Bell & Bill ripped off everything to their undershirts, while Aval & Evel dusted themselves off and threw away their clothespins. Those four squirrels stared at each other. They circled at a steady pace and thought of the many ways to kill one another. The raven smiled with excitement and knew that it would certainly be a grand battle.

Aval & Evel vanished and reappeared behind the two to lay in a quick strike, but Bell & Bill quickly caught their fists. The evil squirrels were positively shocked. Bell & Bill's eyes glowed red and stared directly into theirs, giving the impression that they had finally met their match.

The four struggled in the test of strength, and the heroes were making the vampires sweat. Aval & Evel decided they weren't going to play any more games. They used their shadow abilities to subdue them. Their shadows connected, and shockingly enough, Bell & Bill did the same and struggled with the shadows as well. They knew how to use their powers and knew every move they made, thanks to the gracious powers of the raven.

Aval & Evel growled in frustration and vanished again to attack from every possible position. Bell & Bill's minds reacted the same as theirs and blocked everything that came their way. All four angry squirrels vanished at the same time and reappeared time after time, throwing blow after blow hoping to score a hit. All over the rooftop, they battled at incredible speed until their wings opened simultaneously, and they took the fight to the skies.

There I stood in amazement and saw powerful furry creatures fight in the bloodred moon. Each hit was caught, each grab was countered, and each maneuver was met with unshakable encounters. They were too evenly matched. No one stopped for a second, and no one cared how low he or she had to go to put the other one down. It was so exciting. I'd be spilling my popcorn if I had some.

The four squirrels eventually bit one another deep in the flesh and forced one another to crash back down to the castle's roof. They fumbled along the hard surface, and every squirrel had their face down to the concrete.

Just when Evel had one knee up, there came Bell with a smashing blow to the head that slammed her face to the stone floor. Bell turned the weakened vampire over and began to pound away on her pretty face. As Aval began to rise, Bill came out of nowhere and delivered a punishing kick to the crotch that made him squeal like a pig. As Aval fell to the ground in pain, Bill turned him over and began to stomp away on his highly sensitive testes.

Bell & Bill finally laid one earth-shattering punch to their faces that cracked the concrete floor. Aval & Evel were motionless. They'd done it. Aval & Evel were finally defeated. I did not imagine that I would say those words, but there was no denying it. Oh, those unbearable words.

The raven praised their marvelous performance. She was delighted to see such excitement in her dying hour. The only thing that would've made it complete was to see the victors kill the fallen tyrants once and for all. Bell & Bill couldn't have agreed more. With Aval & Evel still down, Bell retrieved her sword and ordered Bill to stack them facing upward. Even though he had no left hand or a tail for that matter, his strength enabled him to toss Aval on top of Evel with ease.

Bell rose her sword and was prepared to behead them with one swift blow. Before she ended their lives, she paused to fantasize a brand-new future. She would display their heads to the world and then use their new powers to kill the rest of the monsters and become the true saviors of Canada! Bell & Bill would become an unstoppable force no one would dare cross or they would meet the same fate as Aval & Evel. The forces of hell would then be nothing compared to them.

After she yelled such a statement, she suddenly gasped and lowered her weapon. Bill wondered what was wrong; he told her to finish them right at that moment. She grunted as she raised her sword once more. She desperately wanted to kill them; it was the whole reason they traveled across the land in the first place. Bell had the opportunity to kill the evilest creatures in existence, but deep in her heart, she knew she couldn't. Something didn't feel right with her.

Bell took the weapon to her face and looked at the mirrorlike shine from the sword. She saw no reflection at all. Then she turned to the fierce creature with hellish red eyes that was her brother, who commanded her to kill squirrels that were already down. She didn't like what she was seeing. She told Bill they needed to look at themselves and what they had turned into because of their vengeful rage. They had become monsters themselves. Bill took in her words, and he didn't like what he saw either.

They'd turned into soulless vessels of evil they wanted to cleanse from the land. If they killed Aval & Evel, they would've been no better than them. They would've taken their place and become the same bloodsuckers everyone hated. Bell & Bill did not want that; they wanted to be fair and just, like real heroes. They decided to keep them alive, for the moment, to let them be judged for their sinister actions and be forced to call off the rise of monsters and restore Canada from Nevermore. The raven was awfully disappointed.

Just then, the wounded yeti coughed up a loud hunk of blood as he began to move once again. Salamear slowly stood from his knees and pulled the spear out of his body for the second time. The jolly old yeti proved harder to kill. With his weak breath, he commended Bell & Bill's decision to let them live, but the vampire power could not be free in the world. Salamear called out to the raven and wished that the four squirrels were no longer vampires.

The raven smirked, lifted her wings, and drew their vampire essence into the sky. The vile cloud of red evil was expelled through their mouths, and the fog that plagued their feet ascended. Their pale complexions and even their fur reverted to their original colors. Surprisingly, Aval & Evel's original fur tone was revealed to be brown and black. Fangs, wings, and thirst for blood were all gone in an instant, making the vampire name exist nevermore.

Back at the concert, the prime minister they had under their control was released from the spell. Once Marin came to, he questioned what he was seeing, hearing, and wearing. It all came as a nightmarish image to him—although seeing how his people were so happy around him and seeing the number of pretty women around him, he couldn't have cared less!

With all things settled, Salamear still had some unfinished business. He built up the strength to walk again, and he made his way toward Aval & Evel. The dazed squirrels looked up at the bloody yeti and chuckled a bit.

Salamear cracked his knuckles as he ho-ho-ho'd with glee, and then he beat the holy bejeezus out of those squirrels times three!

The world was safe from vampires, and the raven could live another seven months. Dear Tye did not die in vain, and Santa Claus had his revenge. It seemed that everything had worked out, but Bell & Bill wondered how the yeti's wish would affect the world. That of course would be known in time. Without saying a word, the raven flew back to the concert to hear ¡GothFro! once more. She enjoyed her Halloween night and continued to rock evermore.

19

SEE, HEAR, SPEAK WITH EVIL

The warm November sun came as the joyous night of Halloween had ended. All of the demon lovers remained in their beds all through the day, while some lay intoxicated in the messy streets. They were snoring away to refresh their bodies and to ignore the postholiday blues. Never opening their eyes or window curtains to the harsh sun, they preferred the misty grayness of yesterday's clouds and the bloodred moon that peered through them. Not only that, but they also felt the new day was a peculiar day. Something was amiss, and they could sense in their hearts that the land suddenly was empty. Like the only candle being snuffed out during a bedtime story or a saved video game file that had suddenly been erased, it was depressing.

The answer lay deep underground in a large room surrounded by steel-plated walls. In the middle of the room lay two glass prison cubes that contained the fallen, injured, and former monsters, Aval & Evel.

They were locked in separate cells, promptly strapped to medical beds due to their brutal defeat and painful beating. Their faces were swollen and patched; their limbs were in casts and were hung by hooks and strings. The two were so fragile that even a light cough made their ribs shatter. There was no way to escape or even move in their condition, as if they were vegetables glued to the floor of a glass safe.

They could, however, see and hear the mockery outside of their cubes. They were surrounded by happy critters partying in celebration. They laughed, they danced, and they toasted the guests of honor: Bell & Bill. They'd finally become real heroes, and they celebrated without a care. Bell drank and ate herself silly. Bill felt a bit self-conscious from the bandages that replaced his hand and tail. It was time for joy, and some of the guards even spun him around the room to lift his spirits; too bad none of the women touched him.

The party ended when the prison announced its regular lockdown. The guests departed, leaving the place in a mess. Salamear did not make his appearance in that small prison, but he promised to show his face when Aval & Evel were put on trial. In one week, the former vampires would be brought to a woodland court to be judged by creatures of the highest degree.

Aval & Evel would be forced to call off the monster invasion and then be executed by being tossed into a blazing furnace. Nothing else was good enough for those evildoers. Their deaths would be a glorious event that would bring an end to the monster era, and Salamear was sure to have a front-row seat. There would be no tears or mourning afterward, just another party.

In the meantime, Bell thought it would be a great opportunity for her to write a biography of the villainous squirrels before their execution. She dreamed about being an excellent author and felt their life story would be a great start. What harm could it do? Surely Aval & Evel wouldn't mind, as studious as they were. She went over to their cubes and told them her idea in a mocking kind of way. She teased them about telling their horrible history to the world and how all the money would never reach their broken palms.

The eyes of the evil squirrels were full of anger, as they began to breathe harshly through their nostrils. If they had the strength, they would have grabbed her neck through the glass. Instead, Evel spat in her direction, leaving a wad of loogie on the clean glass wall. They did not like Bell's idea, but she would undertake it regardless. Tomorrow, Bell & Bill would sit alongside Aval & Evel and have interesting chats. For the sake of history, the world had to know what the vampire squirrels were really like when they were still around.

The heroes left the room, and the guards locked the doors. Aval & Evel were alone in that quiet room of party garbage. The torture of being laughed at on their deathbeds, powerless to do anything but wait for their own execution, was quite a tragic humiliation. After everything that had happened, one would think those two would blame each other for their misfortune, but it was pointless. What happened had happened, and they had to sit through the torment in silence.

It couldn't have been the end for them, no way. I was confident that those squirrels would find a way out of that mess. I watched them for a while, yet I only saw them lying still like kindergarten paintings.

Aval felt an itch on his right arm, but he was unable to scratch it through the casts. He wiggled his arm in hopes of settling the itch. It was no use; the itch was protected too well. He became enraged. He moved the arm up and down, back and forth. He even moved it diagonally in a swift movement until his arm became a shadow that went through the cast.

It was rather sudden. It went through the cast like a ghost passing through a wall. His arm was free. He couldn't believe it. Neither did Evel. When Aval moved his arm, the broken bones snapped back into place and operated like normal. Not only that, but the bruises on his face also began to subside at his will. It was becoming eerie. Evel wanted to try something: she took all her strength in her arms to smash the casts together. When she did, they shattered into pieces.

Their status as vampires were gone, yet their supernatural and dark abilities still remained. What an astounding discovery and what sheer luck! Aval & Evel were unhinged from the weaknesses that had plagued vampires for centuries and became a force most superior. Salamear's wish to the raven did nothing but make them stronger. Aval & Evel looked at each other and planned to spend the rest of the day a little differently.

The next day arrived, and what a sunny afternoon it was. Clear blue skies and cheery faces were displayed through the woods. Life felt great, and the woodland creatures lived free without the worry of vampires stalking the streets.

Bell couldn't have agreed more. She and her tailless brother were traveling back to the holding cells with backpacks full of snacks, pencils, notebooks, and a pair of blue reading glasses for the special interview. Along the way, they traveled a lively road filled with happy children and smiling adults that greeted them with marvelous praise. The creatures cheered and gave them plenty hoorays, constantly calling them their heroes.

The two squirrels enjoyed the feeling of being the saviors of their homeland, despite their ace in the hole being the will of a raven. They soaked up every bit of appreciation, filling their souls with more understanding of their accomplishments. They smiled all the way to the prison, but as soon as they made it to the elevator that led to the underground cells, Bill became nervous, if not worried.

He saw the look of the suspicious-looking squirrel guard inside the elevator. It was as if he saw a ghost or something far worse. Bill immediately sensed danger in his queasy belly and figured it was best to forget about the interview.

Bell dragged him into the elevator and assured him that nothing would happen during their stay. The evil squirrels were injured, strapped to beds, and caged in hard glass. Unless the elevator exploded on the way down, there was absolutely nothing to be afraid of. Once inside, the squirrel guard slowly pushed the button, the doors closed, and they took a quiet ride deep underground. No one said a word until Bell asked the squirrel guard to tell Bill everything would be all right. The guard hesitated for a second and then quickly nodded his head with a half smile.

In less than ten seconds, they made it to Aval & Evel's holding cells. Once Bell & Bill walked inside the room, they noticed it was unnaturally dim, and they heard the sounds of classical violins swimming through the air from an old record player. The room was clean of trash. It was spotless, but the floor smelled like scented death. The steel walls were covered with purple-and-green drapes with black patterns that looked like splattered inkblots.

The glass cubes were covered in drapes as well, but more interesting was on top of them were illuminating candles near two empty chairs. Bell & Bill had the strangest feeling that something wasn't right. That feeling went from bad to worse when they spotted two creatures who had reappeared in those chairs. Those two creatures were eating hot cheese pizza and looking down at the squirrels that were filled with fear.

Aval & Evel were out of their cells.

As soon as Bell & Bill could comprehend the discovery, the guard squirrel went back to the elevator and closed the door, locking them inside. He apologized and told them it was for the safety of his family to do what Aval & Evel said.

Bell & Bill rushed over and pounded on that door and yelled for the guard to let them back in. Sadly, he ignored their cries and rode the elevator back to the surface. Bell & Bill had never been so hopelessly doomed in their lives. Without warning, Aval & Evel extended their shadows and pulled them toward the cubes.

They yanked them to front and froze their bodies in place. The evil squirrels hopped down with the chairs and sat before them like king and queen. Bell & Bill still couldn't believe Aval & Evel's powers had returned, but then they thought theirs remained as well. Quickly reacting, the two blond squirrels immediately used their powers to escape from their hold—well, I should rather say they tried. Bell & Bill did not retain their powers and still remained as mere mortals. They were afraid and confused out of their minds.

Aval explained to them that it was all because of Santa's wish. He wished that they were no longer vampires and nothing more. They would no longer fly like bats or have a thirst for blood or have skin as white as snow. They could then live in sunlight and eat garlic-drenched food forevermore. As for Bell & Bill, the gift was only temporary, and it was immediately taken away because the raven was cruel that way.

Aval spoke the truth, though those were the first words he had said to them since they first met. Come to think of it, they hardly spoke a single word in the previous chapter. I must say, it was an excellent narrating experience.

"Yeah, bravo on that silent chapter, Mr. Allen Poe," Evel mocked me. "I had so many one-liners that would've made that fight more amusing. Like, 'Check this twice, Ice-Hole.' Or '*Hasta la vista, Spidey.*' Those were gold."

Bill looked at Evel with a lost expression and wondered whom was she talking to. He wondered if she had a case of schizophrenia, so he nervously asked her, "Whom are you talking to?"

"I'm talking to the narrator, duh. He's over there in the corner." Evel pointed at me, and I greeted the confused squirrels with a little wave. "Don't pay him any mind. You'll forget he's even there."

Bell & Bill looked back at Aval & Evel, ignoring me as they came to realize their inevitable fate. All hope was lost; they were going to meet their grisly end. The evil squirrels were about to introduce the blond squirrels to their maker up close and personal on a first-class ticket, with no hope of a round trip.

"A nice choice of words," Evel said to me, "but we don't plan to kill these blonds just yet. Aval and I discussed this whole biography deal, and I am happy to say that we accept. We've always wanted our own book made, especially with us as the stars. So to make sure we have your utmost attention, we'll keep you two down here for the duration of our stay."

As I plainly saw it, they were making the classic and dumb villain mistake of letting them live. Surely there were other more talented authors in the world to write their biography, as opposed to the ones in front of them who clearly wanted them dead. Besides, only one of them was a writer; the other was clearly deadweight. I asked Aval & Evel why not end the squirrels right there and leave the underground prison? When they heard my good question, Bill quickly begged Aval & Evel to ignore me.

"No, no, no!" he said. "I-I can write too, and I'm the editor. We'll be more than happy to write your book; j-just please don't kill us! We'll do whatever you say, and we'll do whatever you want! Just have mercy!"

As the boy sniveled like a spineless worm, Evel found herself enjoying it well. She leaned closer and rubbed his cheek, feeling the wet tears run down the side of his face. She was starting to like him, and she urged him to grovel some more. Bell told that insane squirrel to leave her brother alone, or else Evel would be in so much trouble that she'd have to beg the reaper for mercy. That sparked a bit of hostility between the ladies. Aval was starting to like that feisty girl.

Moving on, Aval told everyone to behave. Otherwise the situation would escalate to a hellish level of dynamic proportions. It may have looked like imprisonment for Bell & Bill, but at least there were buckets in corners that acted as bathrooms. Daily meals were to be discussed later on, but first they had to get some pages out of the way. The evil squirrels released the heroes, sat down in their chairs, and told them to proceed with the interview, much to the heroes' dismay.

After a short preparation, Bell & Bill wore their blue glasses, sat on the cold floor, and started to interview Aval & Evel. Bell asked them questions while Bill jotted the notes as they spoke. Bell started with simple questions: where did the two originally come from, when were they born, and when did they move to Dew Leaf.

Aval answered first and said that they grew up in the wondrous and serene land of Paris, technically making them French squirrels. Both were raised in a sophisticated woodland community, where creatures began to wear clothing composed of black-and-white-stripe patterns. It was a nice time and a decent place to live, compared to today's fast-paced society. They'd been through wars such as the French Revolution, but their town was pretty much untouched. He ended his answer and asked for the next question. Bell then asked how old they were. If they lived during wars, their age had to be brought into question.

Evel answered the question by saying, "How old are you two?"

Bell sighed and said, "Please, don't answer a question with another question."

"But you two are so interesting to us," Evel said. "Sure, Aval and I are elegantly entwined squirrels who are also cannibalistic vessels of evil, but you two—I don't know, and I don't get. What made you come all this way to kill us in the first place?"

"We came here to stop you two," Bell answered, "because your very presence is causing the uprising of monsters. Your deaths would've caused it all to end, and no one would ever fear monsters again."

Evel scratched her head and said, "That's a bit contrived and unrealistic, but…nah, that's just contrived and unrealistic. I could understand it if we destroyed your town or took a whiz in your cereal on Christmas morning, but you want us dead because we exist? That's messed up."

Aval then said, "Even if we do die, the monster name will still live on, and our followers will avenge our deaths by bringing an end to the mortal era. So be a good girl, and tell us your ages."

Bell sighed. "Fine. We're both sixteen."

Aval couldn't stand the number six, but Evel found it quite cute. She eyed Bill sitting so innocently and so scared. If his eyes made contact with hers, he had to look away until she brought him back with a little smooching sound. He felt very afraid, knowing the same lady that detailed him started making kissing noises at him. With a smack upside the head from her husband, Evel stopped, but she was just having a little fun.

So, Evel finally answered how old they were. Before they were transformed into vampires, the two lived to the healthy age of 19 or 17. It was hard for them to keep track of their specific age after two centuries. With the best of her knowledge, Evel said, they were 217 years old, born in the year of 1797. Bill wrote it down and decided to add their loss of memory of their exact age, for extra information.

After just two questions, Bell was already fed up with the idea of writing their biography. It felt too common and too boring to be a real page-turner. Where was the enthusiasm if they were being held against their will? What was the point of even trying to sell such a book if the two evil squirrels continued to live on and be feared and hated by the world? She had to move on regardless; there had to be something interesting about them that was worth writing about. She asked for more details on their hometown, why they came to Canada, and how were they bitten in the beginning.

Before Aval had a chance, Evel cut in and answered. She said that their hometown was a village called Retick Creek. It was a woodland community with a majestic riverbank where some would go just to swim and relax at night. They'd even lived with the richest family ever seen. So rich that they never understood the definition of expensive. Their home was the envy of the neighborhood, as were their lives. They were practically the most popular squirrels in all the land. The local critters would visit every Wednesday evening and offer gifts upon gifts at their doorstep for a chance of entering their home just to get a glimpse of what it was like to be wealthy.

Evel assured Bell that they weren't rich snobs; they were highly paid and loyal agents to the French human leader, Napoleon. Whenever he needed information gathered or enemies poisoned, the whole family of squirrels was there to carry out the tasks. In return, they were paid handsomely with gold and succulent food.

That made Bell somewhat interested, but a sudden question came to mind. From the way the tale was told, they were practically living in the same house. Bell asked if they were orphans raised in a rich foster home, sticking together when they left. Evel did not want to answer it. Neither did Aval. They told Bell to ask them another question. Bell was persistent and wanted an answer, but they still refused. There was something about it that made them feel very uncomfortable, like it was a dark secret.

She said it was important for the book, and she did not want any kind of runaround. If they wanted the readers to know everything about them, they had to give them every little detail. Evel sighed and said that it was not a foster home. They were living in a regular fancy home, with the same biological parents that others dreamed they would have. If it weren't for their dear mom and dad, Aval & Evel would have never existed. Bell thought about what she had said, and the words worried her. She connected the pieces by observing their identical faces, and she had the most awful of thoughts.

Bell slowly stood from her spot and said to the two squirrels, "Hold on one second. You mean to tell me that you two creatures, a married couple of pure evil, are actually brother and sister?"

Aval looked at the girl and said, "It took you this long to figure out we're actually twins?"

Bell & Bill jumped back in shock and disgust! The very thought of siblings being married to each other caused them to question everything they were raised to believe in and abruptly blow chunks all over the floor! I would have lost my lunch too, if I didn't shield my eyes from the spew fest.

Now to me, I didn't see it as a big shocker when I first discovered they were married siblings. Others in this world would marry the same gender, some would marry transvestites, and some would marry inanimate objects. Incest, however, takes some time to get used to, but I was still rather fond of those squirrels. The only thing they could do that would really tear my inner soul apart was if they stole my inner soul and trapped it in a snow globe or physically killed me. Either one would be just as tragic.

Knowing the awful truth made Bell sick to her stomach, but she also saw it as a subject of great interest. It was something most curious, most taboo, and one of the most interesting things to write about. The ideal story came to her in a flash: a tale of two strange siblings falling in love! Forget the boring old biography. Bell's readers would surely love the immoral love story better!

Aval & Evel did not want that. They did not want their biography thrown out the window for some sappy love story. They wanted to be remembered as highly respected beings and supreme rulers, not miserable soft hearts. Bell ignored them and told Bill to start writing fast, for they'd struck gold. She asked the evil squirrels how they became so romantic with each other. Was it during the lonely years of high school, or was it a quiet night in a cemetery where they had each other's company to bask in the moonlight?

Aval & Evel started to become annoyed, and when a personal subject came about, like if they ever had children, Aval grabbed that pestering squirrel by the shirt and warned her to stop. She was stepping across a border even they did not dare approach. Bell chuckled nervously and complied, and he released her. Evel then snatched the notebook away from Bill, shredding all the pages to pieces.

They were angry, and after a harsh growl, the evil squirrels vanished from the room in a cloud of dark vapor. There was no telling where they went or if they would return, but the blond squirrels were not at all peeved. They had some snacks and more notebooks tucked in Bill's backpack. With a few bites out of some oatmeal cookies, the two immediately started to plan the perfect love story.

But not all was perfect back on the surface. I feared that everything turned for the worse, because it only took one wish of the raven to mark the end of all things. Whether a recent wish or one made long ago, I worried for the future.

That evening near the dark borders of Nevermore, Roger Hazelnut walked through yet another forest in search of a theater. He was lost again, because he could never get good directions. Before he could curse nature itself, he sealed his mouth out of fear of what he saw up ahead. He saw a long line of Frankenstein soldiers marching into an empty parking lot of a little store.

Feeling curious and rather bored to death, Roger decided to investigate the gathering. He quietly snuck behind trees with extreme stealth and rolled behind rocks with caution. He stopped behind a boulder and discovered that there was a whole army of soldiers surrounding a meat shack.

Surely they weren't there for lunch. It was a fierce confrontation between Vince and Weegee himself. Vince was perched on the roof, facing down at the long-lost swamp creature, questioning his existence. Vince wanted to talk to the lazy and absent monster and ask why he did not do his part of killing his share of mortals. Weegee could only look around and feel sorry for the frankenized humans. Vince was absolutely appalled. How could Weegee feel sorry for them after the many times they harmed him in the past? The swamp creature could not answer a thing; he felt the same anger toward them as Vince did. They performed many harsh acts, but that did not mean a young squirrel had to do the same.

Weegee wanted to save Vince. He told him about Aval & Evel's defeat, and there was no reason to impress them anymore. They would soon die for their crimes, and unless all monsters wanted the same fate, they had to submit. He was surprised the child didn't know about it sooner, though the look on Vince's face was shocking. Weegee knew about their defeat. He knew they were captured, and instead of looking for them and saving them, he told Vince to stop and submit.

That little squirrel became enraged, so very enraged. He refused to stop, and he refused to listen to another word from that waste of scales and fins. He abandoned his hope for Weegee, and without a second thought, he ordered his soldiers with rocket launchers to blow him to smithereens.

In the blink of an eye, the soldiers aimed their rockets and fired at the creature, leaving him only a millisecond to reason with the child one last time. But it was over. Weegee was blown away by the surrounding assault and was reduced to splattered jelly on the pavement. The child challenged the monster to come back from that. Roger was surprised and horrified to see monsters do such a thing to one another. Needless to say, it was very naughty.

Howls were heard throughout the area as a horde of werewolves came through the forest. They were crazed and hungry, and they smiled sadistically as their eyes glowed pure white. Roger was frightened that one of them would spot him and eat his flesh, but the strangest thing happened: they saw him but walked right past him. It was clear they came for the Frankenstein monsters themselves. Maybe it was best for Roger to lie low for a bit.

The werewolves stopped when their beastly leader leaped from the trees and landed on top of Weegee's remains. It was Elise, slobbering and twitching like an escaped patient from an asylum. She smiled and growled at the child in a shaky motion. Vince was overwhelmed by the intrusion but slightly confused as to how the creatures were able to transform in the middle of the day.

Elise spoke in an odd tone and in a rather hesitant voice, like she barely had any control over what she was saying. She told the child that his time was truly over. His poor soldiers were taking orders from a squawky squirrel that used them for revenge. She wanted them to join the side of true monsters, to take part in wiping the land clean of all living things and turn the world into a true living nightmare, just for fun.

There was no way his loyal soldiers would turn sides so easily, for they were under his control and would never abandon him. Vince knew she lost her mind and immediately told the werewolves to leave or he'll make them leave in pieces. Elise steadily grinned and made it clear they would never leave until the soldiers joined them to see the green squirrel die. Vince heard enough and told his soldiers to fire at the werewolves.

As they readied their weapons to fire, something happened. The undead soldiers began to feel a torturing sensation in their brains—a pulsing, view-changing experience that ended with them standing still as their eyes glowed from yellow to white. They started to smile and moan for pancakes. Vince was outraged that they did not fire or speak without permission. He pulled out his mind-control device and set it to the highest setting and ordered them to attack. The soldiers heard the ringing in their minds and immediately ripped out the chips from the side of their heads, throwing them to the ground. Things were not looking too good.

He didn't think it was possible, but he had lost control over his creations. Just when it couldn't get any worse, a slender, grinning creature appeared in the corner of the child's eye. It told the child who he was and spoke of his terrible folly. Everything the creature said became clear to the squirrel. The long-awaited sin that Vince made from the very beginning had finally showed its ugly face and aimed to take everything away from him. The soldiers raised their guns at the awestruck squirrel and sprayed him with a barrage of bullets! Vince fell from the roof and down to the cold ground, where he lay motionless.

His fall from grace brought maniacal laughter to the many insane monsters. The crowd paused and hushed, and then they immediately ran out into the world to create loads of chaos. The parking lot was still and quiet, but not empty. The curious comedian walked over to the squirrel to see if he was actually dead. He knelt down next to the squirrel and turned him face up.

He saw that the little squirrel was very much alive, despite being filled with bullet holes. He did, however, find it very hard to breathe with punctured lungs, which made him talk in a wheezing voice. He acted calm and no longer felt anger, just shock and sorrow. Everything he thought would make his life better led him on a path of being turned into swiss cheese.

Vince did not know who that bug-eyed chipmunk next to him was, but he needed the stranger to do him a slight favor. There was no time to waste, and it would take Vince some time to repair himself, so he asked the chipmunk to go and free Aval & Evel from their prison. Of course, Roger had to ask why he should even think about freeing them. They were the reason Canada became a depressing hellhole. To Vince, it certainly wasn't the case, but they were the only ones who could save it from a much greater evil.

Roger was more confused than usual, so he made the little green squirrel explain the whole situation, as much as it pained Vince to do so. He pulled himself from the ground and began his story by saying that it all started on a dark and stormy night.

He'd tried to reanimate an army of dead soldiers for the first time that night. Everything was set in place, and all he needed was one lightning strike. A miraculous bolt of light soon struck, and a massive surge of energy coursed through his devices and soon through the bodies. Vince was filled with excitement. He couldn't wait to control his own army of monsters, but lo and behold, the procedure did not work.

The dead bodies merely twitched for a brief moment, right after the energy roasted their skin, and nothing more. It was a failure; he had failed so miserably that he couldn't call himself a creator or a monster. It was enough to make anybody give up and end their pointless lives so that they might fail nevermore. Until Raven, the wishing raven, came to him in his time of sadness and told him that not all was lost. There was still another way to complete his goal, and it was the simplest thing to do. She offered him a wish to bring back the magic and the fear monsters had longed for. Not only would the resurrection of the dead be possible, but anything supernatural could infest the world with its sinister presence.

Vince refused still. He claimed that if Paulie could bring bodies back from the dead, so could he. Raven laughed at the silly squirrel and told him a very awful truth. Paulie did not bring a tireless and bloodless corpse to life with just lightning and stitches; he made it possible by wishing upon you-know-who…

Vince then knew the dark truth behind his existence, so what else could he possibly do? He gave in and made that wish, and his army came to life on the second try. Because of that one wish, the monsters finally made a true comeback, and a true Nevermore was born. Now they were all paying for it, because the magical fear that came to the world took on a grotesque form of pure evil: Boogeyman Barney. He was a creature of psychological horror hell-bent on driving the world into a wasteland of madness. Aval & Evel were the only ones who could stop him. They were the most powerful beings Vince ever knew; they could destroy mythical spirits in their sleep. If they died, the world would be plunged into a never-ending nightmare.

The child asked Roger if he understood everything he had just said. It was all so much to take in and very hard to believe. So Roger nodded his head and confessed to Vince that he did not understand a thing.

A chuckle came from afar. It was a grinning soldier holding a live grenade in his hand. He stood there laughing at their conversation and told them that the worst was yet to come. He tossed it to a nearby tank full of gasoline, knowing that it would certainly cause a massive explosion. Roger grabbed Vince by the arms and ran out of harm's way.

Roger realized that only torn arms were in his hands, not the rest of the body. Vince told him to leave as he just sat there on the ground. He knew it was too late to be saved from anything anymore. Before the explosion, the Frankenstein squirrel closed his eyes peacefully, knowing that he would soon meet his real parents.

Kaaabbllaammm!

A bright burst of flames blasted through the building and reduced everything in its wake to piles of burning cinder. Roger was caught in the explosion, and Vince experienced the same feeling Weegee felt when the chaotic fire shattered his limbs and bones. After briefly admiring his handiwork, the soldier set off to rejoin the others on their barbaric killing spree. Just yards away from the fire lay the burning chipmunk, desperately trying to put himself out by rolling on the ground. Roger eventually ripped away his clothes and his pants and left himself only in his tighty-whities. He was safe nonetheless.

He stood and gazed at the horrible scene, holding Vince's lifeless arms deep in his clutches. He felt terrible that he couldn't save the green squirrel, and if what he said was true about the boogeyman, then he knew he had to fulfill his last request. Roger never thought he would do it in a thousand years, but he had to find and rescue Aval & Evel.

The next morning, back in their holding cells, Bell & Bill had just emerged from a long night of writing and brainstorming. Over thirteen pages of ideas were written in one notebook in a specific order from good to bad. They were really dedicated to their newfound story. They stretched their stiff muscles and yawned. Aval & Evel had yet to return. Maybe they really did abandon them underground. Suddenly a puff of smoke appeared before them, and through it stood Aval & Evel. Bill quickly hid the special notebook in his backpack.

The dark vapor vanished. The evil squirrels were carrying bags that smelled of something foul. They were feasting on oozing, disgusting, bacteria-infested, double-bacon cheeseburgers. Ever since their curse was lifted, they enjoyed gorging themselves with fast food.

Without blood needed as their main source of nutrition, they were free to eat anything their hearts desired. They first wanted to try burgers, and they instantly fell in love in one bite. Aval & Evel were certainly more relaxed, and they looked rather cheerful that morning.

"Afternoon, kiddies," Evel said as she sat in her chair and presented the blond squirrels with a bag of twigs. "Here's a little snack for you two. You're going to need all your strength for the dozens of tales we have in store for you."

"Twigs? You brought us twigs to eat?" Bill moaned as he wiped his eyes. "How come you didn't bring us real food?"

Aval sat in his chair, finished off his burger, and answered, "Because we're evil, basically. Hmm…I wish we had more of these delectable treats back in the old country. All we ate were leaves and twigs, all day and all—"

Before he could finish his sentence, Evel slapped his shoulder and told him shut up. Bell & Bill sensed something was up.

"Leaves and twigs? That's interesting," said Bell. "Since when do rich families eat twigs and leaves?"

Evel said to her, "Last time I checked, we were squirrels living in a different time." Evel began to munch on her cheese-covered fries. "We did not have burgers or fried chicken or these heavenly potato slices covered in melted cheese. Though we did eat exquisite blueberry pies and cheese quiche from the village while maintaining our high status as dignified and healthy squirrels."

"This still doesn't make sense," Bell said. "To my understanding, vampires maintain their present figures forever, and you two look way too skinny to be pie eaters. Now you're scarfing down junk food like you never ate a day in your lives."

"We are celebrating," Evel said with a stare. "We're celebrating our new life while you're stuck down here writing our book."

"You're celebrating by eating garbage."

"Rusty cans and broken bottles are garbage," said Aval. "Junk food is like a happy clown tearing out my sad little heart and filling it with gallons of satisfaction. Every time I sink my teeth into something greasy and foul, I flow down a deathly river of ecstasy as I bid my troubles farewell."

"Wow, you two must really like junk food."

"We don't like it—we love it!"

20
JOY OF JUNK FOOD

Aval & Evel sprang from their seats like springs and sang a pleasant love song about junk food.

Cheeseburgers with lots of cheese,
bacon burgers with lots of sauce,
would you kindly supersize me, please?

Pizza we share all day and nachos all night;
thinking about dessert feels so right...
Baby,
Baby, pass the ketchup...

Unhealthy? Yes,
as most may see,
but it's a joy,
to me...

As soon as they finished the song, Aval held Evel in a romantic dance pose, and they sipped on some ice-cold slushies.

21
MOONLIGHT TEARS

"What the heck was that?" Bell asked the squirrels why they were singing about food.

Regrettably, Aval & Evel tended to get a little dramatic from the slightest sense of joy, but never had I known them to sing at all. It was most peculiar; it was as if they found the key to true happiness by feasting on heart-clogging morsels. Personally, I saw it as the first state of losing their minds due to all the freedom. It also began to frighten Bell & Bill. So trying to avoid any future sing-alongs, they continued with the interview.

There began a barrage of questions and answers that made up their days. Most answers they got told how high-class Aval & Evel were as children, but some were a bit weird and quirky, and those they didn't seem to mind answering. It provided new material for Bell & Bill's love story.

At one point, Bell said to the squirrels, "One thing that I can't figure out are your eyebrows that seem to point upward. What are they? Are they part of some Chinese makeup?"

"Very perceptive, but wrong," said Aval. "It is a Japanese style where some paint dots on their foreheads that act like eyebrows. It's called *hikimayu*."

"So you two use that style because…?"

"We use them as permanent marks to show how confused we are with this world. Plus, we thought it looked cool."

Bill wrote it all down but thought of a different way to use the concept. Their dots on their foreheads would be a way to show how identical they were, as opposed to dressing the same way. He turned the name hikimayu to head hickeys, since they looked like dark leech sores.

As Bell watched them eat some chili dogs, she had to say, "You two are obviously cannibals. You love to eat meat, but you won't eat vegetables unless they're fried like onion rings. Why is that?"

"Well, for starters, we weren't born cannibals or meat freaks," said Evel. "When we were turned into vampires, the taste for flesh caught our taste buds when we bit down on our first victims. We liked how the tenderness of fleshy skin and squishy flab felt in our mouths, and it filled our stomachs with such satisfaction. The diet grew on us, but we had to avoid eating the midsection of the bodies, for it is full of fudge we dare not eat."

Bill nearly threw up again, but he controlled himself. As he wrote down the gory notes, he thought of how this information could be used in a sensitive kind of way. They ate to survive like most animals do, and they shared a feast on every Valentine's Day. They would give each other the bleeding hearts of a suffering couple, to show that their love would be stronger than others. Well, he had to make the story dark somehow.

Bell continued her questions, asking, "If you two could live in one place that wasn't a graveyard, where would you go?"

Aval thought about it for a moment and answered, "We would live in a huge mansion, on a cliffside overlooking a bloodred sea."

"Of course," Bell said in disappointment. "Don't you two like anything that isn't filled with dread? Something that makes you laugh or smile in a nice kind of way, like movies? Do you two like movies?"

"We're not too fond of movies today," said Aval. "They are too predictable and too caught up in money-grubbing methods to catch the attention of the masses. Like sex, superheroes, reboots, gun-crazy maniacs in deserts, and explosions every five seconds. We can't help but frown on such lackluster productions."

"OK, so you two hate movies. No surprise there, I hardly took you for—"

"Wait! It's not that we hate movies," said Evel. "We are just particular about what we see. There is an exceptional movie that we see and will always see. It is a treasured and wondrous masterpiece that we never knew existed."

"Let me guess. *The Nightmare Before Christmas*?"

"Oh-ho-ho, don't get stereotypical with us. The movie I'm talking about is a spectacular motion picture that made us laugh for the first time in many years. It is called *The Emperor's New Groove*. It was a sight to behold, and it became a joyful experience for us. The cartoonish animation was astounding; the facial expressions captured every exaggeration imaginable, and the jokes left us in pieces! We never felt so entertained! Why, we watched it all day and all night until our eyes bled! It is our single favorite film of all time…but don't write that down. People might not take us seriously."

Interesting! The evil vampires of Nevermore adored an animated film that wasn't completely filled with gore. A movie about a heartless ruler being turned into a creature, more specifically a llama, going on an adventure with an ordinary villager to help him turn back to normal. The villager later finds out he's not at all heartless but really a good person deep down inside. Bell & Bill knew they were getting somewhere.

Two days passed, and Bell & Bill learned a lot about those weird squirrels. Their likes and dislikes were unworldly; their taste in cultural morals and standards were informative to say the least, and surprisingly, their constant bickering with each other made them laugh. Eventually they felt rather comfortable talking to them; they even told some of their favorite things. Like PB&Js were their perfect food of choice.

There were no torturous screams or violent conflicts, just pleasant conversations. It was almost as if they were becoming friends. It was as if no longer being vampires made Aval & Evel more relaxed and carefree in many ways. It was like they were reverting to their old silly selves but worse. The squirrels I used to know changed into friendly junk-food-loving slobs I couldn't stomach looking at!

I was afraid they were losing themselves, or perhaps it was some kind of ruse. Gaining Bell & Bill's trust had to be part of a devious plan. Aval & Evel were setting them up for something foul and horrible. That had to be it. They were leading the blond squirrels to a gory end or something far more worse.

On the third night, Bell & Bill were safely snuggled near the cell cubes, using the drapes as sheets and their backpacks for pillows. Sound asleep they were in that room, having pleasant dreams while snoring like bears. All seemed peaceful until Bill felt a sudden chill in the air. He woke from his slumber and found that he was placed in the middle of a dark and mysterious graveyard. He looked around in confusion and wondering if it was just a bad dream. But it was not, because near a tombstone leaned the mischievous Evel, telling him it was as real as it could be.

She snatched him away from Bell and took him to an eerie location to have him all to herself. The boy jumped up in a fright! He pulled out a sharp pencil from his pocket and told her to back off. Evel did not feel threatened at all.

She extended her shadow and froze Bill with no hope of escape. With a slight turn of her hand, she made him drop the pencil to ground with little resistance. She then skipped along the dead grass and stopped to stare at the boy with curiosity in her eyes. His nervous sweat ran down his face, and his bones shook in terror. Such timid nature intrigued her. She could do anything she pleased, and no one would be able to hear his screams.

Evel put her arm around his waist, and she used the other to hold his only hand. Before Bill knew it, she made him dance in a graceful manner as if they were at a ballroom party. The boy was absolutely scared for his life. Evel told him not to worry; there was nothing to be afraid of yet. She just wanted to dance, for she and Aval had not danced in a graveyard in many months. She had to find someone to share her idea of fun with.

Meanwhile, in the underground cells, Bell slept soundly as if there was nothing amiss. But then she felt a finger poking her shoulder and waking her up. The peculiar Aval was sitting in Bill's spot. Her brother was nowhere in sight, and she asked him where he was. Aval said he was most likely with Evel, which caused her to panic. She knew Evel would torture her poor brother in unspeakable ways, but she had another problem to worry about. She was alone in a dark room with a man staring at her with cold and unfeeling eyes.

Bell reached for her backpack to find a weapon, but Aval quickly caught her hand. He paused, leaned closer to the scared girl, and softly whispered in her ear, "I will not harm you…yet."

Bell could feel his breath against her cheek, and his eyes never once strayed from hers. She was afraid for dear life. She feared he was going to torture her in many terrible ways. But instead he pulled away in an abrupt manner. He stared off into the distance, like there was something troubling him. Bell did not care what he had on his mind; she had to arm herself with something to ward off the creepy squirrel. Before she could, Aval confessed something to her.

"Everything you heard from us was a lie," he said. "This was all Evel's idea."

Bell paused, sensing that Aval had become vulnerable and was finally telling her the truth. The answers they gave were all lies to make them look good, except for the dots painted on their foreheads and their likes and dislikes. How they were really raised and how they behaved were things they did not feel the need to speak about. It would've brought them nothing but depression.

Bell asked why he was telling her all that, but Aval needed an answer first. He wanted to know the real reason why she wanted to write about them in the first place. It had to be something more than just a career starter, because no one in their right mind wanted to sit down and get to know Aval or Evel. Bell had no other reason really, but she soon became curious about Aval's behavior.

"You seem more troubled than usual," she said.

"I'm not," said Aval. "I'm just tangled with questions. You two came all this way to kill us, and you had that opportunity, but you spared us. I cannot understand it."

"Well, that's what good people do," she said. "You two wanted us dead, but you kept us alive. There has to be some other reason besides the book. Maybe you're playing some sick game with us."

"We are not sick; we're just…confused."

"Maybe I can help you understand, but first you have to tell me the truth."

As the two talked, Bill and Evel continued to dance the night away in that graveyard. For a nice finish, Evel leaned over and bent his body to the ground, slowly moving her head close to his. She aimed to land a smooch that would suck the air from his lungs. Instead, she dropped the boy to the ground just to mess with him. She chuckled, but Bill was not at all amused. He got up from the ground and dusted himself off. He asked Evel why she brought him to a graveyard in the first place.

"I just wanted some fun," she answered. "You act so scared of me all the time, so I took it upon myself to show you that I'm more merciful than Aval."

"You ripped off my tail!" he said as he showed her the bandages. "I have to go through life without a tail!"

"True, but I was mad at the time," she said as she rolled her eyes. "I'm actually a comfortable individual one could grow to love."

"You ripped off my *tail*!" he stated again. "You're crazy!"

"Crazy? Is it crazy to express one's feelings? Is it crazy to show gratitude for releasing a dreadful handicap from my life? Then, sir, call me deranged."

"Gratitude? You mean you're being thankful?"

"Well, I'm not being despicable, for once. Aval and I just feel so liberated after that wish. We feel changed! We feel so free! We feel like nothing can stop us from taking our rightful place as squirrelly rulers of the world. This special night is a way of thanking you and your sister."

"But Salamear is the one you should be thanking, not us."

"True, but dancing with a fat vengeful yeti really doesn't do it for me."

"So, you show your thanks by dancing? Well, that's not so bad."

Evel snickered a bit. She looked at Bill and said, "Oh, that was just act one. We have a whole night ahead of us, and by the time we're finished, you'll never look at girls the same way again."

It was clear what Aval & Evel's intentions were. As part of their revenge, they were going to defile the young squirrels and scar them for life. It was twisted, if not sickening. Then after all was said and done, they would take their notes and leave them to rot in that underground prison. I thought that had to be Aval & Evel's dastardly plan. It was horrible, if not evil. Evel told me not to be so odious. She assured me that my theory was only one-quarter accurate. Her words truly puzzled me.

That purple-dressed squirrel inched closer to the terrified boy, but before she could do anything, Bill quickly asked her a question of great interest. He asked her how merciful she would be as queen of the entire world, and it indeed caught her attention. She said that her subjects would gather around, and they would lend her their hands in mercy; she would touch those palms as a sign of forgiveness.

Evel felt so excited about those words that she went over to his backpack and tossed him a notebook and a pencil. She told him to write everything she would say. Unknown to her, she gave him the notes of the love story they were planning. He silently gulped and began to write on a blank page.

Back underground, Aval began to tell Bell where they were really from. They were indeed from France and were raised in a sophisticated community, but they did not live in Paris. They mainly resided on the outskirts of the city. The hometown they actually lived in was named Devilla Lane.

They wanted to forget that name because of the bad memories. Retick Creek was just a small creek that passed through the town, where kids would go and frolic in the water. It seemed to be the only peaceful place at the time. It was untouched by war, and no blood was ever spilled there. There was only laughter, sparkling water, and large numbers of butterflies some critters happily ate.

It was a true sight of beauty, but Aval & Evel could never venture out and experience the joys of that creek. They were among the strictest of families that lived on the highest cliffside. Their folks were very shrewd and saw no point in having fun that didn't make them richer.

Their family was rich, but not at all happy. Their home was surrounded with iron gates, where green life never bloomed from the amount of dread within them. Nobody smiled; no one even chuckled. Everything was governed by rules, serious and strict. Aval & Evel had to stay and obey every command without question, in order to be as dignified and well mannered as their parents.

Aval & Evel were strictly educated every week; they were dressed with dusty makeup every day, and they worked as entertainers for their parents' monthly parties. It was more like a correctional facility than a real home. Aval & Evel often looked outside their bedroom windows and fantasized about what it was like to play in that creek. They wondered what it was like to have friends and to frolic like naked songbirds without a care, rather than being turned into uptight zombies. Bell began to feel sorry for them.

Aval carried on and said that their parents were only dedicated into aiding Napoleon. Whenever they left on their daily missions, they would leave the highest-paid guard squirrels to make sure Aval & Evel stayed confined in that house. As determined as those siblings were, they managed to escape the yard a number of times, but they were always captured by the highest-paid guard dogs their parents could afford.

Whenever they would do something that angered their parents, no physical contact was ever made. They were instead locked away in a cold windowless dungeon with no food or water. There were no dates specified for their release, just whenever they thought it was necessary to let them out.

Every time they were released from their captivity, Aval & Evel grew quieter and colder. It was easy to see where their dark attitudes came from; it was the one thing they were used to. Their parents had to make them more mature and disciplined than the other kids. Their idea of punishment came from the grandparents. If one wanted a better life, one must suffer first.

It bothered Aval to relive those memories, but it was necessary for their book. Bell slowly and cautiously patted his shoulder to comfort him. Remarkably, her gentle touch did not bother him, or her, at all. It drove him to place his hand on hers and gently squeeze it. Both of them smiled slightly right after their eyes met.

Back at the graveyard, Evel constantly raved about her and Aval's supposed years of providing past dictators with helpful information. When some tried to cross them out of sheer fear, which was all the time, the vampires killed their loved ones in the most horrific ways.

Speaking of horrific deaths, Bill felt the need to ask, "How did you two defeat the three spirits of Christmas?"

"Oh!" she said with a smile. "How nice of you to wonder about our triumph over those broken records. Those spirits were crafty as well as untouchable. So how could one kill haunting spirits that were created to teach us lessons? Simple, you destroy their purpose. We did not give them the satisfaction of being emotional.

We annoyed them to the breaking point, and eventually they perished by exploding into clouds of sparkly dust. It's really funny how fragile apparitions can be. When that ghostly dream was over, we woke up that Christmas morning feeling rejuvenated as ever. Then I think we had swine for breakfast."

"Right before destroying Santa's home?"

"Exactly. He was lucky we didn't stuff his stocking with a Christmas tree, deck his halls with deer antlers, and jingle his bells with barbed-wire baseball bats. Wait, that sounds too extreme. Don't write that. No, wait. Do it! No! I'm not sure if it fits with the other exaggerations I said before. Can I see that notebook for a moment?"

"No! I mean, I think they're horrifically fine as they are. No one on Earth makes exaggerations darker than you."

"Aww, you're so sweet. Aval hardly compliments me in my time of questionable doubt, but you, you tell me what I like to hear. So honest, so sweet."

Bill thanked her, but he quickly became nervous once she moved closer to him. He started to step away, but he tripped. She crawled near his level and moved her fingers through his chest, instantly freezing him in fear.

Before he could speak, she placed a finger on his mouth and told him to be silent. She told him to relax and close his eyes. She grabbed his notebook in a swift movement. Realizing what had happened, Bill tried to get his book back, but he was restrained by her shadow again. He was grounded, giving her a chance to read it.

She looked through the pages and noticed many unfamiliar notes, mainly passages that were not part of their sayings. They were altered and changed into a mushy mess of sorrow and pain, like a love story. Evel looked through more pages, until she saw a passage that suddenly caught her eye. It was a page titled "The Beginning."

Aval made his way to a peaceful resting ground on that cold November night, and he couldn't help but notice the sounds of sorrow coming from the lake. To his surprise, he found his dear sister, Evel, wallowing in the shallow mist of her own sadness and grief. It had been so long, too long since he had seen her or heard her voice. It was a painful sight to behold, for her shadow depicted nothing but shaky shoulders and the lifeless tail of a suffering squirrel.

He moved next to her and did not bother to alarm her; he simply wanted to know what was wrong. Evel pulled her head from her hands and was surprised to see her brother. His presence did not stop her frown, but her tears ceased for a brief moment. She said she so felt alone, so distant from the world. No matter who she thought was her friend or spiritual partner who could open a door to a new life, they only saw a vampire. She did not belong anywhere in such a cold and unfeeling world.

She pulled out a clean razor and wanted to slit her own throat right then and there. Aval stopped her and tossed the razor into the lake. He stared at her with a worried look that tried to hold back tears. He confessed that he went through the same pain, and he wanted to die as well. He could not bother to end it, because he thought she would miss him ever so much. That's why he stopped her, because there was no Aval without Evel. Without her there was no earth, heaven, or hell, just a hopeless void of eternal darkness in his life.

Aval's words were so honest and so sincere that all her pain suddenly went away. Her tears were wiped, and the two took that moment to admire their sad eyes, and how the moonlight seemed to make them sparkle more than the waters beyond. They felt so comfortable together. Their faces began to blush bloodred, like a sudden warmth was pulsing through their lifeless veins and melting their ice-cold hearts.

Aval & Evel leaned closer than ever before and shared a loving kiss that seemed to last forever. The two vampires were lonely nevermore.

The End

After reading it, Evel experienced a stream of emotions going through her. There were hundreds of things she could have done, but the one thing she wanted to do most of all was to scream at the top of her lungs. And that's exactly what she did.

Meanwhile in the cold dark prison, Aval and Bell sat close to each other and were still deep in conversation. They were like magnets, unknowingly becoming closer. The only difference was that one of them knew what he was doing and silently waited for the prey to be entrapped by the spell.

Bell asked Aval, "Why does your wife take charge in these crazy ideas? Is she the dominant one?"

"No, she's not," he said. "I'd get my way on a good day. She gets her way because I like seeing her happy, but she's never happy, so I don't care anymore. What about you? Don't you take charge over Bill?"

"Of course, I mean I have to. He's not as brave as me. Someone has to take charge; otherwise, we wouldn't be a team."

"Do you love him?"

"Yes, I do, but not like you and Evel. He's all I've got left, and I strive to be strong so that both of us can live. You should probably do the same, Aval."

Aval nodded his head and said, "I guess you're right. You'd make a really cute adviser."

"Well, I try," Bell said as she turned away and blushed. "Anyway, onto this hate problem. There has to be more to it than a lost childhood. Why do you two hate the world so much?"

"What's there to explain? No matter how hard we try to fit in with you mortals, it's never enough. What could we possibly do to mask our indifference and our curse? Being nice did not help because we were pushed around, used, and abused. This world is a foul pit of heinous expectations. What kind of a god would allow all this to exist anyway? No god."

"Aval, there is a god. You just need to find the right path. There's still a chance for that."

"I've been down that path, and there is nothing but darkness. I'm lost and forever suffering."

"Aval, you don't have to suffer alone. There is always a way to find the light."

"Maybe I've already found it."

In the midst of silence, Aval placed his hand on Bell's knee. She froze a bit, but she did not scream or move away. His touch was so gentle and so alluring; she had to place her hand on top of his. Bell looked into his eyes with wonder and curiosity. She forgot about everything else and was drawn in by his dark gaze. They inched closer to each other and were about to give in to the moment, but Evel and Bill appeared in the room. The sudden appearance immediately caused the special night to end.

I tell you, if I had to sit through one more love scene, I was sure to shoot myself. Now that I thought about it, Aval & Evel weren't that seductive with anyone else, because they hated everyone. So trying to have their way with their enemies seemed a bit out of character, and it worried me even more.

Evel told Aval her discovery of the love story being written behind their backs. It even pained her to admit that Bell & Bill were better writers who understood love more than they did. Aval soon threw away his sad-face persona and became outraged as well. Bell & Bill were told not to write a mushy love story, but indeed they had. As a result, Aval & Evel saw them as enemies once more and decided to dispose of them once and for all.

About time, I say.

Bell walked over to her terrified brother, defending them while trying to calm the evil squirrels down as much as she could.

"Don't do this," she said. "This is the Aval & Evel people want to read about, not some bloodthirsty brutes. We made you two relatable and cute. We made you look good. Isn't that what you wanted?"

"Enough of this nonsense," Aval said in a serious tone. "We show an ounce of mercy and let you write our book, yet you mortals still try to screw us over. As far as I'm concerned, there is no book."

"So that's how it's going to be?" Bell said. "You'd kill us because we wrote something positive about you two? Fine, but if you're going to kill us, then that wasn't my last question. My last question is this: Did you two ever have children?"

Evel warned the girl, "Don't you dare go down that path."

"Oh, we are double-dog daring, princess!" Bill bravely spoke behind Bell's back.

Aval & Evel warned the two to shut up, but Bell was not afraid at all. They had nothing left to lose. The evil squirrels were going to send them to the grave anyway, so they might as well get an answer. Aval & Evel sighed once more as they confessed the horrible truth.

They had children, but they were adopted. Two young teens actually, but not as old as Bell & Bill. The children were not squirrels. They were a cub and a snake. Bob and Susie were their names. Sure, it sounded crazy, but they were treated as outcasts, and no one wanted them; they were just like Aval & Evel.

They took them in, and the first week of parenting was very difficult. Susie kept wearing trashy and bright-colored clothes, while Evel just wanted her to wear suitable clothes in black. Bob wanted to play sports all day, but Aval wanted to teach the illiterate jockey how to read. It was very difficult to connect with them and very hard to parent such a pair. Aval & Evel eventually accepted the children for what they were, and they later made them official vampires.

Then one night, Aval & Evel wanted to show Bob and Susie their favorite film, *The Emperor's New Groove*. By having their children experience the same joy from that movie, their souls would have known true happiness, but there was nothing happy about that night. When the teens were asked to watch the movie, they said they'd already seen it, and they hated it. Aval & Evel could've understood if they didn't like it, but hate it? It was absolutely shocking that living breathing things could hate such a joyful movie.

Evel did not have the heart to tell the rest; it was too awful to even think about. With a deep breath, Aval took it upon himself to tell. After hearing how much they called the movie stupid, boring, and forgettable, the two squirrels snapped in an unforgiving rage. By the end of the night, Aval & Evel skinned them alive and burned their bodies. They believed that if people hated something that brought nothing but joy and laughter did not deserve to see anything ever again.

Bell gasped at such gore and was very much convinced that they were evil. With that being said, Bell & Bill thought those vile squirrels would decide to skin them alive as well, but then something happened. Aval & Evel started to cry. They wanted to skin the poor squirrels, but they couldn't ignore the strange feeling in their bellies. The thought of harming their children tore them up so much that they could not express their hatred. They couldn't tell them how much they wanted to rip out their throats, because it was hard just to speak the words anymore.

It was then that Bell realized Aval & Evel were becoming soft in front of her eyes. They were feeling, and they were caring, because their evilness had vanished with that wish. The more she thought about it, the more it made sense.

Aval & Evel didn't bother to torture them or make an example by ripping off Bell's tail. They didn't harm one piece of fur off their heads the entire time they trapped them in that same room. The once soulless squirrels fed them, talked to them, danced with them, and even tried to kiss them. The answer was clear without a question. Bell spoke her mind and claimed that they could not harm them or anyone else, because their hearts were soft as milk.

Aval wiped away his tears and moved closer to Bell. He stared her in the eyes with a menacing look and said, "What makes you so sure of that?"

Suddenly, a new voice was heard inside the room. From atop a cube cell, Raven, the wishing raven, appeared to interrupt their little conversation.

That sneaky raven said to Aval & Evel, "Bell is right. I stripped away the evil and made you lovable forevermore. Where you shall kill a soul, nevermore."

22

GLOOMY SUNDAY

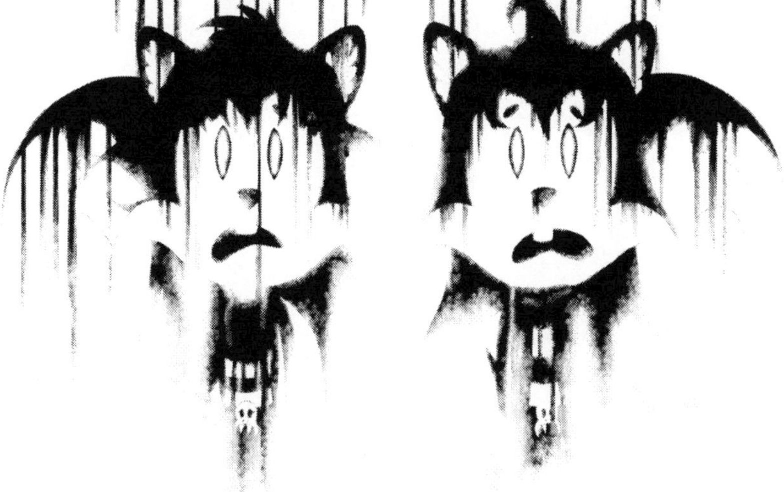

It was a gloomy Sunday and an even more bloody day, when Aval & Evel's violent nature was taken away. The words of the raven were true. She stripped them of their wicked tendencies and turned them into softies. They could've threatened and scared whomever they wished, but they couldn't kill a single butterfly even in their dreams. Aval & Evel did not believe the raven at all; the two still had the will to kill.

To prove that theory, Aval took his right hand and aimed to puncture Bell's heart. He shaped his arm in the form of a spear and launched himself toward the girl. Once the hand was close to her chest, his whole body froze. Aval could not kill the girl, but that stubborn squirrel did not give up so easily. He shook his body to break the hesitation, and step by step he moved in closer. Sadly, he only possessed the will to squeeze Bell's chest like it was a tomato.

Both blushed, and all were appalled by the shocking display. Aval pulled away; he was shaken and overwhelmed. He thought he would never see the day when he couldn't rip out a heart. There was no denying the awful truth: they were harmless, and they could not do a thing about it. The traitorous raven was pleased to see their sad faces, but she wanted to break their spirits even more. She revealed the truth behind the rise of monsters and the return of fear. All that had prospered from the beginning were not by their hand but by the wish of the little dead squirrel, Vince.

She smirked as she told them her devious ploy. "The very idea of a child creating Frankenstein soldiers is beyond unrealistic. The idea of werewolves spreading their disease with clumps of fur is too silly. The idea of a fat witch casting opposite and limitless spells is terribly stupid. And the idea of two miserable squirrels ruling over anything is just a pipe dream. Now all your comrades are dead, and you vampires are to blame."

Everything in Aval & Evel's conquest was truly and emphatically a road of ruin. Because of them, their monster companions and their only fan were gone forever. Their hearts suddenly became guilt ridden and oh so fragile. It weighed down on them from such high levels that it made them see how terrible they truly were.

Making the squirrels feel that way was merely one part of her visit. The raven did not stop at just Aval & Evel; no, she felt the need to rip away the spirits of Bell & Bill. She flew down beside them and spooked them, making them fall to the floor. She told them that they were a grand part in her scheme.

"I had to find a way to make you squirrels fight Aval & Evel, so I brought a mummified crocodile with a cursed music box to you. It was all a trial organized by me. It was made to drive you on a mission to make these vampires live nevermore."

Bill thought about her words for a second and came to a sudden realization. He said to her, "You were that shady squirrel on our boat!"

After hearing that statement, the raven chuckled at Bill's cleverness. "My, you are smart," she said. "I wanted to see them fall and hopefully have you two take their place, but that plan failed miserably on many levels. Now I guess this world is defenseless against my greatest creation, the boogeyman."

The raven was no doubt the reason Barney came alive. That creature was never meant to exist outside of a child's imagination. He was a forgotten imaginary friend gone bad, so she decided to put that fearsome creature to use. She gave him the powers that enabled him to spread through the minds of every single creature on the planet and make them go mad. Very soon the monster would destroy everything, and the only ones who had the power to stop him were huddled in a corner in a shroud of self-pity.

Aval & Evel sat in that dark corner, blankly staring at the ground in deep depression. It was all very sad, although Bell & Bill saw it as deplorable. Their simple lives were ruined, their family had perished, and the population was descending into chaos for no reason at all. They saw it as pure madness!

"Why?" Bell asked the raven. "Why would you do all of this?"

The raven bluntly answered, "I was created to cause pain and misery. What do you expect? Monsters or mortals, good or bad, I don't choose sides. I'd watch any living thing suffer and make them face their own emotional hell, where they are powerless to change their fate in a life-altering puppet show I purposely designed for my own amusement. That, my furry friends, is what being evil is all about."

"Raven, this is crazy!" said Bill. "You need to stop this!"

"It's defiantly too late for that," she said. "My work here is done. This world will soon be destroyed, and I'll be moved to another planet my master chooses. There's not much hope for this crumbling rock unless one of you squirrels care to make a lifesaving wish."

Bell & Bill became silent, as the raven had thought. She flew up and perched herself on a cell cube and told the four squirrels to not be so sad. A world full of deranged psychos wasn't as bad as it seemed. They just had to pray that the boogeyman would bring them to a world of pancakes before they met a painful demise. The raven then covered herself in black mist and bade the squirrels farewell as she vanished, leaving them to weep in defeat evermore.

I hate Sundays. I truly do.

Meanwhile, on the surface above, relentless death and destruction spread through every waking corner of humanity. Madness ravaged through Nevermore, and it quickly spread to America, Mexico, and Brazil and soon to the entire world. It was the boogeyman's playground, and he laughed and laughed over the chaotic calamity he had created.

President X seemed to be one of the last few left untouched by the twisted creature. He was safe in his dark office, but he couldn't ignore the fiery explosions coming from his city. He realized it was too late to destroy Canada, and there was no way to contain such a thing.

The only solution was to contact Marin and tell him to control his monsters. He reached him via satellite, and as his large TV screen came down from the ceiling, he saw Marin in his trashy, bloodstained office. He was smiling more than usual, and he was about to enjoy a plate of pancakes. He was very happy to see the president. He greeted him with a pleasant salutation, but the president was in no mood for formalities.

Every country was in chaos, and he immediately ordered him to call it off; otherwise, they had to result in nuclear strikes. Marin laughed a deep and sinister laugh as he took a beating heart and gently squeezed what little blood it had onto the pancakes like it was syrup. After there was nothing left to squeeze, he tossed the organ away and ate the sloppy pancakes with his bare hands. The sickly display deeply disturbed the president. It made him feel like he wasn't talking to a human at all.

President X pounded on his desk and told him to listen, for it was not a joking matter. Unless they did something, everyone would die within weeks. Marin laughed again and continued to chew away on the bloody pancakes. He assured the president that no one would die within weeks. They would die by sunrise. Before the president could question what that strange man meant, the connection was cut off. There was only a blank screen. President X was furious, but he couldn't reach Marin again after that. He was gone.

The president fell silent for a minute or so, trying to figure out how everything had gone downhill into this sadistic ditch. Maybe it was the fault of squirrels after all. He rose, and in the large windows behind him, he watched his country being set ablaze in the blackness of night. All the hard work and the soul-crushing decisions he had to make were being destroyed by something he couldn't stop. It was enough to conjure a tear on his mysterious face.

Then to his surprise, the TV screen came to life on its own, and it showed a live recording of ¡GothFro! in a clear white room. The broadcast was shown in all countries regardless of language. The band felt the need to perform a very special song worldwide. Instead of playing a song full of hard rock and loud metal, they decided to play a sentimental piece that seemed appropriate in that time of crisis. The group began to play the last song the world would hear in its final hours: "The End of the World" by Skeeter Davis.

The band played the somber song, and it sounded quite pleasant to the ears. In every home people were instantly glued to a television screen. No one could look away, and no one figured out why. They did not stare in awe or confusion; they were lured in by a hypnotic trance.

The boogeyman drew them in. That creature appeared on screen, and he was seen in everyone's personal vision. He just stood there in front of the band and smiled directly at the camera. Halfway through the song, he made his move. He coursed through everyone's mind, instantly driving the remaining populace mad with little effort. Then it happened. Everybody fought one another in hysteria; cars drove into anything in their paths; trains rammed into one other, and airplanes crashed down from the skies. Law and order were nonexistent; women and children cried, and the air was filled with smoldering red death.

To make matters worse, President X had also fallen victim to the boogeyman's control. He was stricken, motionless, and frightened. His greatest fear of a doomed world was magnified by visions of demons defiling the once-green and beautiful land. In truth, the president really cared about the beautiful planet earth and all the things he adored when he was young.

The chirping of birds was replaced with screams. The ocean was tainted with blood and fire, and corpses dirtied the ground. Most pitiable of all was that no life-forms would evolve to their most purified states. All of it was taken away, and all because he couldn't destroy Canada earlier. He could not stand to see life suffer anymore.

What he did next was an honorable solution to fix the doomed land. He walked toward his desk and unlocked a secret compartment by flipping a few switches in a specific order, revealing a big red button that rose from the middle of the room. He did not bother with the doomsday button, for this particular button had the power to launch every nuclear missile in the world and wipe the whole slate clean. It was the Game Over button. Without a second thought, the terrified president pressed the button, and then it was all gone.

The only way to survive the annihilation of Earth was to be underground, like squirrels concealed within a prison beneath the surface. Aval, Evel, Bell, and Bill sat silently in that cold room, having no idea what to do in their hopeless state. They sat apart from the others, thinking back on their decisions and daydreaming about being back in their homes, eating nice snacks. Bell & Bill liked the idea of PB&Js and cookies, and Aval & Evel favored nachos and cotton candy.

However, the very thought of more junk food made Evel sick to her stomach. She rubbed her aching belly and felt a slight lump. She hiked up her striped corset and saw the big flab of fat that was her tummy. She started to whimper. She could not stand being fat, especially because of the very things that excited her taste buds more than blood. Bell & Bill covered their ears to block out the noise, yet her ceaseless whining was too loud.

Slight vibrations shook the room, and they heard soft booms. They ignored those noises, because the squirrels already knew the world was coming to an end. Nothing really mattered anymore. Knowing this, Aval felt the need to come out and say his piece, which would hopefully ease Evel's whines. He laid his hand on her belly, and she slowly grew quiet. Aval gave out a long sigh and said what he'd never said in a thousand years.

"Bell, Bill, Evel, I'm sorry," he said. "This was all my fault. Everything that led to this point was from my pride in my curse. I thought I was defending it, but it ended up controlling me. I lost myself, because I could not stand being mocked for a fool. I was just trying to stand up for myself."

Evel wiped her eyes, and she felt the need to say something as well. She laid her hands on his and said, "No, I'm the one who's sorry, Aval. I'm the one who dragged you to that snobby restaurant in the first place. I should have known that evening would end in blood, because that place was full of jerks we've despised since childhood. I was just trying to save our relationship."

It was all so sad and so true, but then I confessed to the squirrels that I played a larger role in that age of horror. I hinted to Aval & Evel to go to a restaurant I knew they would hate, and I got them so worked up that they had no choice but to kill every living thing in sight. Did that make me a bad guy? Maybe so, but all I wanted was to see Aval, Evel, and an era long forgotten come alive once again. Perhaps that made me a nostalgic good guy.

Once I had finished, Bell looked at me with a hard face and said, "No, Mr. Narrator, that makes you a gore hound. All three of you are to blame, and now we're all going to die. But what's the point in pointing fingers? We're all doomed... How did you two become vampires anyway?"

"I thought we were done with questions," said Aval.

"Nothing matters anymore," she said. "You may as well tell us the truth about your origin."

Aval & Evel really didn't feel like talking, but since nothing truly mattered, they humored them. Stories about how others become vampires are sometimes filled with excitement and drama, but it was not that kind of story. It was more of a journey through hell. It all began with them being locked away in their dungeon back in Devilla Lane after another failed attempt to escape their home. Their parents had to leave to meet up with Napoleon, so they decided to keep them locked away until whenever they returned. It was a special occasion and a gathering in Waterloo, Belgium.

Many days passed, and the two squirrels adapted to the darkness, the hunger, and the sounds of solitude. The vision of death coming to take them away seemed to be the only thing they ever thought of. Then it came time to decide which one was going to eat the other to survive. Aval offered himself to Evel, but she refused to resort to cannibalism. She told him to eat her instead. Before she finished talking, he was already gnawing on her leg. Evel changed her mind. She kicked him away and began to strangle him while he was down. She was depriving him of air so that he wouldn't suffer being eaten alive.

Aval wanted to fight for his life. He grabbed a nearby rock, and he was about to knock her brains out, but the dungeon door opened, and cast a ray of light upon the squirrels. Through the light they saw their faithful squirrel butler, coming to free them of their captivity. He couldn't stand to see them suffer any more, much less kill each other.

The butler freed them and told them to leave for Retick Creek. He wanted them to enjoy themselves, to go out and be the playful kids they should've been. That butler was the only kind squirrel Aval & Evel ever met. He even brought them some pie and water that day. The two teared up with joy and wasted no time in gobbling down their meal.

Later that night Aval & Evel ran through the yard in their swimsuits, passing the peaceful guards with their heads held high. The butler hoped to high heaven the two would forget about their parents. Little did Aval & Evel know that their parents didn't survive Waterloo. Aval & Evel technically had the power to do as they wished, and the butler saw to it to set them on a new beginning. What a nice squirrel he was.

Aval & Evel finally frolicked in that creek. They were happily splashing about, throwing water at each other, and laughing together like never before. They finally found true happiness. But it was short lived. A tall shadow fell on the two squirrels, and they were frightened to discover that it was a human with white and shiny fangs. It was none other than the vampire lord, Dracula, who had come in search for a midnight snack, and he knew just what he wanted: squirrels. He sank his teeth into their small bodies, and he drained them of their blood as well as their future.

Aval & Evel fell into pure darkness. They could not see where they were or what they were doing. They did, however, feel an extreme rush of thirst, and somehow the craving was satisfied with spots of red filling the darkness vigorously and spontaneously. It was a peculiar experience, and they couldn't control it; they just wanted more.

Just when the rush had ceased, their senses came back. They could see again, but they did not like the scene of bloody corpses that covered their front yard. Together, in their hands, they held the dead body of their faithful butler. His blood, as well as everyone else's, was all over them. The vampire squirrels had killed them all.

Aval & Evel hated what they had become, and they wanted to change all of that by hunting down Dracula. They had to slay the alpha vampire as a means for revenge and a chance to end their curse. So on one horrible night in the highest tower of Dracula's castle, the two squirrels confronted the monster, face to face. The conversation wasn't long nor was the fight, because within two minutes, they had already carved the monster like a bloody pumpkin.

The lifeless dark lord lay on the floor with his blood splattered across the room, and the squirrels waited for the curse to be lifted. They waited patiently in that dark lair, still seeing each other's pale faces, still possessing razor-sharp fangs, and still feeling cold from the inside. There was no denying it that Aval & Evel were forever cursed to roam the earth as vampires, lost and out of place.

Eventually, they wound up staying together. They did not care for others, and neither one could go through life without the other. Soon they learned to control their cravings, and they even became lighthearted in order to make friends, which was why they moved to Dew Leaf. They wanted to get away from the growing wars in their country and live in peace and experience the serenity of Western civilization.

During their time of coexistence with the mortals, they still found no happiness. Some were still scared of their evil presence, while the rest simply disrespected them. Soon enough the townsfolk called Dew Leaf "Nevermore" because dark and brooding monsters were living among them. It was very insulting.

Through the tireless years of pain and mistreatment, Aval & Evel's hearts began to wither and turn cold as ice. They began to like the idea of Nevermore and decided to become the legendary monsters they were meant to be, by killing to satisfy their hunger.

They decided to make peace, and then they broke that peace, and they ended up in an underground prison. When it came right down to it, Aval & Evel were two confused squirrels trying to live in a cruel world. The absolute reason why they never wanted to drain all life and become gods was because they wanted to live like normal squirrels again. Aval & Evel hated their curse.

Their bodies could never survive in the sun, they could never look in a mirror, they could never eat regular food that wasn't filled with blood, and they could never have true friends since everyone in the world wanted them gone. They were pitiful creatures doomed to live in eternal suffering, and the only thing that made it less painful was sharing that pain, forever together. That was the origin of Aval & Evel, and what a sad one it was.

Talking about the pain and hatred of their curse reminded Aval of something he completely overlooked. He was reminded of a way they could become vampires once again. Inside the eyes of their trophy snake lay syringes full of their vampire blood.

Aval stored them as a backup in case the two ever lost their powers and needed to restore them. One injection from those would turn anything into a blood-craving monster. Their ferocious will to fight would return and give them a chance to stop the boogeyman! Evel used to laugh at Aval for using their own blood as emergency backup, but looking at the current situation, she knew he was always the smarter one.

They would have expected Bell & Bill to have some interest, but unfortunately the blond squirrels fell asleep during their story. Aval & Evel saw them as the other mortals in their lives. No one cared about their pain, except for their childhood butler. What was more tragic, dare I say, was that Aval & Evel couldn't remember his name.

Aval & Evel decided it was best to accept their punishment and let everything go in peace.

23

SAVE OR DESTROY LIFE

Bell & Bill continued to sleep soundly against the drape-covered cells, and Aval & Evel sat in their corner steadily dozing off. Their eyes closed, and they slowly drifted away, spending their time in dreamland. If you're still wondering why those squirrels stayed in that prison, it was more than obvious that the land above was completely swept away by the nukes. It seemed like the safest place to be was underground. It possibly could've been their final resting place, lying in a dark room of colorful drapery, empty pizza boxes, and bone-dry slush bottles.

When Aval & Evel started to snore, a slight rumble came from the outside walls. It was not enough to wake the squirrels, but it soon got louder and began to shake the room all around.

Their eyes opened, which turned into a wide gaze. They saw a giant drill ripping through a wall, and it soon made its way into the room. It was the ex-baker's drill machine, and from the sliding doors came Salamear and Roger Hazelnut, who was disguised as an apple. They had survived the bombs, and they'd come to free the squirrels. Bell & Bill were very surprised and relieved to see their friends again. There were many questions that ran through their minds, especially what led Roger to be dressed as an apple, but there was no time to answer all of them.

Roger did, however, explain his reason for being there. He said that a little green squirrel told him to rescue Aval & Evel, for they were the only ones who could stop a boogeyman named Barney. He was glad to see all squirrels in one piece, so without haste, he told them all to get in the drill.

Roger's effort was most honorable, but it was no use. Bell told him that Aval & Evel were in a deep state of depression and were cursed with the inability to kill anything. They were as useful as firewood in the middle of a heat wave. Then again, there was a mention of vampire syringes.

If Bell & Bill had listened to Aval & Evel, they would have known about them. It was an opportunity to retell their tale, but Salamear already knew of their many secrets. He knew about their stash being tucked away in the head of their trophy snake. He was Santa Claus, after all. It was part of his job to know everything about a person, and it intrigued the ex-baker. Yet when he asked Santa if O. J. Simpson was really innocent from all of his crimes, the yeti quickly claimed irrelevance.

There was still a chance to defeat the boogeyman and save the world from complete extinction. All they had to do was head back to Nevermore and retrieve the syringes from their house. The yeti grabbed all the squirrels in a flash and took them into the drill. The doors closed with everyone inside, and off they went to Luminous Acres.

Many hours had passed since they dug through miles of heavy dirt and the densest rubble, and what a quiet ride it was. Everyone couldn't help but stare at Aval & Evel's still bodies, as if they were sad puppets looking at the floor. They were still sad over the events that had happened because of them. The ride was indeed very quiet.

Eventually the mighty drill emerged from the underground and onto the lawn of Aval & Evel's home. The look and feel of that place did not feel like a home at all.

Everyone stepped out of the machine and observed the wretched and apocalyptic aftermath created by the nukes. There was no sign of green life for miles; it was nothing more than a desertlike wasteland full of crumbled tombstones. The ground was a wave of crumbling dry dirt, and the air was shrouded with green mists of radiation that covered the sky above. Even the tallest mountain couldn't be seen.

The only good fortune was that their home still stood, but it was tilted to the left with roots pulled from the ground. It was seen as the last beacon of hope, although Aval & Evel saw it as their poetic resting ground. Aval & Evel stood there and reflected on how their lives had grown into a vast wasteland of hopelessness. It was where the story had started and where it would end.

Bell & Bill had to make them move; there was no time to dawdle and absolutely no time to be emo. They had to find the syringes even if it meant dragging them up the stairs. Aval & Evel heard them well and advised them not to use the word "emo" again. They saw no need to be dragged; they knew where the syringes were hidden and could easily find them on their own.

They slowly climbed up the dirty and shredded stairs, too depressed to even vanish to their balcony. Worried that they would stray from their goal, Bell & Bill felt the need to accompany them, while the others stayed inside the drill to avoid the toxic fallout.

Inside the house in the middle of the wildly trashed living room, Aval & Evel took a moment to observe the tragedy of their undoing. Every corner had downed furniture, and the books covered the floor along with pieces of glass from the completely shattered balcony window. After that moment of reflection, Aval & Evel proceeded toward their stuffed trophy snake that lay in the far-left corner. They ripped out the eye buttons and dug deep within its sockets to pull out not two but four shiny syringes filled with their vampire blood.

Bell & Bill were oh so relieved to see those nifty devices. The world would be saved from an even greater danger. Aval & Evel would then be looked upon as heroes, and there would be a chance for them to start a new beginning! Those thoughts were immediately swept away when Aval, deliberately and intentionally, crushed a syringe with his bare hand.

As the blood flowed from his hand and onto the floor, Bell asked the crazed squirrel, "What the heck are you *doing*?"

Aval shook his hand clean and answered, "We are accepting our punishment. We are horrible beings that deserve to die."

"Aval is right," Evel said as she crushed a syringe with her hand. "Our lives have been nothing but one disaster after another. We can never make anything right. There's no redemption for us."

"Stop it!" yelled Bell. "You two need to stop! There is still a chance to save the world! Just stop breaking those syringes!"

There were only two left, and if Aval & Evel broke them, the vampire name would die along with the world. Those squirrels did not care anymore; they just wanted it all to end. To ensure that, Aval & Evel used their shadows to immobilize Bell & Bill. Those blond squirrels wanted to kill the monster name, and so they would have their wish.

There Aval & Evel stood in the middle of the room holding the last remaining blood that had cursed them for centuries. They planned to crush them both at once. Both raised the syringes in the air with their heads held down and eyes closed. Bell & Bill began to feel the rush of desperation and cried their lungs out to make them stop, but their words went unheeded. There was no stopping them.

It certainly felt like the end for all life, so Bell & Bill took drastic measures and looked to the one person who had the power to talk the squirrels out of it: me. Those squirrels begged and pressured me to set things right. It was silly for me to get involved, and it was futile to try to make them change their minds, but then I was reminded of how all of it started. It was all because I wanted to see monsters rampage again, and the thought of it weighed heavy on my heart. I would've never forgiven myself if I let this world die because of my actions.

It was time to redeem myself and save that doomed world. Within a split second, before Aval & Evel could crush the syringes, I cried out two words that grabbed their attention and opened their eyes.

"*The Munsters!*" I said with a shout.

The squirrels stopped and looked at me. They wondered what I was talking about, so I made it clear.

"*The Munsters* is an old TV show I remembered long ago. The main cast were famous monsters like you, Aval & Evel. They had powers and personas so frightening, that they could scare people without even trying. You'd think they would be as dark hearted as you, but they were good-natured and brought laughter to everyone who watched the show."

"Why are you comparing us to them?" Aval said with a moan. "Those jokes are the reason we are forever mocked. They are media puppets to this torture."

"That may be true," I said, "but they were loved. They showed a better and funnier side of monsters. They showed that they weren't all just pure evil. Come to think of it, you two are jokes yourselves. Your relationship and names are a parody of Adam and Eve. Your bickering is full of silly comebacks. Most of all, you're squirrels; you're silly-looking squirrels!"

"What's your point?" Evel moaned.

"My point is that I was wrong," I said. "You two don't have to be like the gory and hate-filled monsters the world assumes about you. You two used to enjoy messing with others rather than killing them in cold blood. It pains me to say it, but those were the true Aval & Evel I knew. As long as you two stood together, nothing ever bothered you; just like in *The Munsters*. But that Aval & Evel are far gone now. I can't recognize my favorite squirrels anymore. I only see sad creatures, giving up on everything just because they can't stand themselves. You two can still change. There is still a shred of good in you, and I implore you to never be the ones who ruined your lives. Be the ones that saved your lives. Be like your butler."

After that, Aval began to feel a deep unknown emotion he couldn't describe. He was sad and yet felt lifted, dumbfounded but no longer confused. It was an indescribable mixture of many emotions blended into one. He looked over at Evel and saw her tearing up, easily guessing she felt the same way.

She looked at Aval and confessed that I was right. Their actions and choices through the years were never really them; none of them were. She did not want to be some cruel creature living by the rules of horrible monsters. They could never be like their butler either; she wanted to be something more.

Before she could say anything, a huge explosion flared through the window and forced all the squirrels to hit the back wall. No damage was done, nor did it destroy the house. The squirrels wondered what was happening. Once the smoked cleared, the squirrels rushed to the balcony window and saw a horrific blaze of fire emanating from where the drill once stood.

It was destroyed, obliterated by the heavy shells that were fired from several tanks surrounding the yard by an army of deranged monsters. Seven tanks, 633 undead soldiers, and 6,026 werewolves stood outside Aval & Evel's home. It was a legion of insanity. To make it worse, adding them up was a total of 6,666 terrible things, and that number did not sit well with Aval.

From the crowd of monsters came the possessed Elise, showing Aval & Evel the very world they had wanted: a world of fear. That werewolf told the squirrels it was all over and to destroy the syringes, or else they would be met with an unrelenting rage of terror. The threat was made, but then the four squirrels turned their attention to a bloody body that crawled from the fires of the drill.

He was the only one to survive the horrific explosion. Roger Hazelnut, with his weak breath, called out to the squirrels to never give in, never surrender, and put an end to the boogeyman once and for all.

Roger looked around at the horde of drooling monsters holding guns, and he could tell that something was about to head his way, so he decided to tell one last joke. It was when he traveled through the terrible trenches of Nevermore and experienced its great splendor of darkness and tragedy. He said that all of it was better than sharing a bed with his humongous wife. Roger had to tell them how big she was. He said that every time they fell asleep together, they had to send a—

Bang!

Just like that, before he could finish his joke, a sniper's bullet whizzed through his skull and ended the poor chipmunk's life. Bell & Bill yelled in tears, calling out his name once more. It was too much. Santa Claus, Roger Hazelnut, and everything else they held so dear were taken away from them. It was too much for Bell & Bill to take.

Elise called for the squirrels to destroy the syringes again or they would soon join their friends in the afterlife. Aval & Evel, hardly feeling a shred of sorrow, saw how hard the crying squirrels grieved. They saw how the insane soldiers stood there and laughed at the tragedy. They saw a true scene of monstrous heartlessness.

Those were real monsters. That's how cold and foul Aval & Evel were from the day they decided to turn against the world. They did not like it at all; it was not what they had wanted to be. They then knew what they wanted to become. They no longer wanted to be monsters, nor did they want to be soft hearts. They wanted to be themselves again.

Aval & Evel took the syringes and pointed them toward their necks. It caused the boogeyman to incite all tanks to fire at the squirrels.

Boom! Ba-Boom-boom! Booommm!

Shots were fired, and the shells smashed the tree and blew it all away, but it was not the end just yet. When the tanks had fired, Bell & Bill held each other tight one last time. Instead of experiencing the fiery demise, they felt a cold shiver around them.

The two opened their eyes and looked around the dim room that was Aval & Evel's dungeon. Bell & Bill were the only ones there, and right beside their feet were clumps of white fog and two empty syringes. They heard howls and screams from above, and the two quietly moved toward the cellar doors to quench their curiosity. Bell slowly opened one side of the door and saw the clear surface of fire where the house once stood, but up in the sky was something greater.

From the wicked shadows of the night sky flew down the blazing mad duo, the king and queen of Nevermore, the renowned vampire squirrels: Aval & Evel!

Those vampires touched down on the ashes of their home and retracted their huge wings. Their nefarious pale faces intimidated all who watched as the ground flowed with their immense fog once more. They stood tall and brave, and vengeful death gleamed in their murderous eyes.

Aval carried his battle-ax while Evel wielded two dual swords, which they quickly snatched from their dungeon after they dropped Bell & Bill off. It reminded them to stomp the open door shut in their faces, to make sure they got the message to stay out of the way. Bell & Bill fell down the stairs and were hurt from the fall, so they surely knew Aval & Evel were back.

It was the hour of judgment for those who came into Nevermore and destroyed the vampires' sanctuary. There were no questions asked as to why the boogeyman, of all creatures, bothered to come and declare war on the vampire squirrels. There was only a loud intro to an epic song played by ¡GothFro! on the other side of the cemetery. The song made Aval & Evel bob their heads a little with the desire to see some heads roll.

As they gazed upon the surrounding army, Aval held his ax on his shoulder and gave Evel her chance to say her famous battle line: "I hope you kept the receipt, 'cause all of you just bought a first-class ticket to hell!"

With a slight and disturbing chuckle from Elise, shells upon shells and bullets upon bullets flew in the vampires' direction at incredible velocity. In a split second, the two vanished before anything could touch their fur. The impact of the explosions was enough to break through the dungeon doors, which nearly charred Bell & Bill to a crisp. In another split second, Aval & Evel reappeared to share a beheading of a Frankenstein soldier and a werewolf.

The majestic sight of blood spraying through the air like loose fountains filled their hearts with a sense of joy and pleasure. They wanted to feel it all through the night. Aval & Evel's killing spree began, and one monster after another fell to the ground without a fighting chance and without heads.

Those vampires went through those creatures like speeding bullets. They surely and surprisingly mowed down half the army within minutes! The werewolves couldn't scratch them; their hands were always the first to go. The soldiers inside the tanks were introduced to live grenades stolen from other dead soldiers. It was like seeing two razor blades soar through a field of grasslike metal tornadoes, destroying everything in their wake.

It was amazing! I mean, you should have been there to experience such awesomeness! It was an exhilarating fight and a beautiful massacre that was literally raining blood! Limbs flew, bones shattered, and painful screams added excellent harmony to the loud songs.

In roughly twenty minutes, the whole army was in a mass of bloody piles, reeking of unpleasant smells. The only ones left standing were the vampires covered in blood and the band, ¡GothFro! who had just finished their last song, which ended with a high-pitched scream from the lead singer. To make it an even a grander finale, Evel used the last tank to blast the band into oblivion.

Ka-booommm!

What an excellent way to end a fight. The way that explosion came about would have made me jump up and spill my popcorn, if I had some still. Nevertheless, I was proud of Aval & Evel, but it was not over just yet.

In the moment of silence, Elise stood among the flames of ruin and held Bell & Bill in her hands. She used them as hostages and ordered the vampires to surrender or else their only friends would die. Evel rolled her eyes and told the insane creature that they were not their friends. Evel pointed at the creature and said the only friend they had in the world was a llama holding a silver ax behind her.

Elise quickly turned around and saw nothing. It was but a mere distraction for Evel to use their shadow powers to freeze her and release Bell & Bill from her clutches. Once freed, Evel gave Aval the opportunity to deliver the final blow. He twirled his ax as he carefully aimed at the target, and then he threw the weapon at the frozen creature. With incredible speed, the mighty ax plunged its way into her skull.

Blood was spilled, a low cry was heard, and Elise was finished. The glow from her eyes diminished, and the twisted smile finally went away. With her last breath, she told the vampire squirrels, "Thank you."

Evel released her body and let her fall to the dirty ground, where the werewolf finally drifted away to the great beyond. As Aval retrieved his ax, the two burned mortals looked at the two bloodstained vampires and did not know what to say. A simple thank-you for saving them would have been nice, but Aval & Evel knew that they were beyond being thanked.

Bell told them not to say that, for the vampires redeemed themselves by saving their lives. Aval thought it wasn't a big deal; he just didn't want them to die. He couldn't believe the words that came out of his mouth. He had to cover it with his hand. Evel couldn't help but feel the same way; she did not want them to die either.

Bell then realized something; Aval & Evel did not crave their blood or insult them or hit on them during the whole conversation. The vampires remembered how to care and have a heart. Bell & Bill smiled and thanked Aval & Evel for showing that even the most wicked creatures could still have a shred of good inside them.

Aval & Evel then jerked their mouths and muttered that they generally appreciated Bell & Bill for talking to them. It was enough thanks for Bell & Bill, bringing to a close a tender moment between enemies who became friends. It surely would've been a nice way to end the story, but it was still not over just yet.

Aval turned to me and groaned, "Ugh, don't say it's not over. We killed an army of asylum rejects. Can't it just be over? Unless you're going into detail on how to get rid of this radiation and rebuild our house, there's nothing else to do."

Evel said to Aval, "He's right. This was too easy to be the end of our adventure. There is an anomaly of some nature that we completely overlooked, but what?"

Before I could provide the answer, a strange and vile creature appeared in the corner of their eyes. That tall and slender creature sarcastically clapped for their momentary victory. He chuckled through his teeth and greeted them with a polite salutation.

Aval told Bell & Bill to go back into the dungeon while they took care of one last monster. The mortal squirrels could not see what they saw, but they fled without question, for they knew what monster still remained. The vampires finally stood face-to-face with the boogeyman.

Evel opened her mouth and bopped her head for forgetting that there ever was a boogeyman. Apparently, he was mentioned so many times that she mentally blocked him from her memory. Because really, she got sick of hearing his name.

Although, his appearance could have fooled them. They always saw a boogeyman as a creature shrouded in darkness and mystery. What they saw was a decolorized ice-cream man with a candy cane sticking out of his butt. It became clear that they weren't scared of him; they were making fun of him.

They even mocked his childlike name by saying to each other, "Oooh, watch out for Barney! Oooh, fear has a new name, and it's Barney!"

They shared a little laugh with that. The boogeyman still chuckled, even after being insulted, but it was time to get serious. He had to confess that he intentionally left Aval & Evel for last, because their peculiar minds would be his greatest challenge. He told the vampires to be afraid and brace their spines for the upcoming chill.

The boogeyman spread his arms and turned their entire world pitch black, as if he'd flipped the switch to their eyes and made them completely blind. With a gentle whisper, he welcomed them into his world, and the final battle began.

24

FEAR ITSELF

The boogeyman is without a doubt the definition of fear. Scaring is a challenge when it comes to the brave and the otherwise emotionally numb. That was no obstacle for him. The best way was to break their minds and make them cause pain to others around them to show how terrible they truly were.

When the day finally came when he destroyed the world with a nuclear holocaust of horrific annihilation, he had one last challenge. He had to break the minds of Aval & Evel. Those ruthless vampire squirrels were the naughtiest of the naughty as well as the most fearless of the fearful. They were dragged into his world, and they were his to torment as long as they were sane.

He took the squirrels and placed them in separate worlds of their deepest fears. Aval's eyes were cleared from the darkness and showed him a room most terrifying. He was brought to a playhouse full of dancing dolls, singing sunflowers, and pink walls covered with painted rainbows. Now, to the average person, it didn't seem terrifying at all, but Aval was very much disturbed by all the colorful and childish antics in that room.

What was more disturbing was that each doll had the number six painted on its belly with glitter. A pair of happy dolls then focused his attention to the middle of the room, where they unveiled a familiar object. It was a white piano, and he remembered it well—too well. His parents made him practice for days on end on that horrible instrument. He detested it for being so complicated, so essential, and so pressuring to bring a perfect performance to a crowd. That was the whole idea.

All the dolls and all the sunflowers wanted him to play it. Their party wouldn't be complete without some real music to dance to. Aval shuddered. He could never handle being judged while playing such an instrument. He told those prissy creatures to gather in a circle and play with their own little instruments, for he was not their entertainment.

The little creatures, slightly angry, frowned. That remark sent out a wave of violent throbbing veins through the dolls and flowers, but then they felt happy again. They knew he would play for them; he had no choice.

Just then, a skinless skunk appeared next to the squirrel, clapping her bloody hands and chanting, "Play some tunes…play some tunes…"

It was the same skunk that was skinned alive so many years ago, haunting every shred of his being. Out of the blue, a long stream of barbwires burst through his legs, making him bleed and yell in pain. The sharp wires entangled his muscles and bones, taking control of his movements, and forced him to walk to the piano.

Evel opened her eyes and discovered she was in a dark void full of bloodstained mirrors. She walked around in a wonder, observing the mirrors, which showed absolutely nothing, not even herself. It was kind of boring. What was there to fear? All she could do was walk through the black space, alone. Perhaps that was the whole point, for she could not stand being alone. Evel did not snap, and she did not lose her cool; she merely mocked the boogeyman's attempt to break her or scare her. She said that he should look in a mirror and fix that oozing sore he called a face. There was no response.

Evel shrugged and walked in a different direction until she heard a distant voice say, "You are fat and ugly."

She had been insulted and had no idea who said it or where it came from. Then another voice called her a worthless basket case. Evel began to get annoyed, and she demanded the voices to show themselves. There was nobody around, nor did they exist; the voices were there to drive her mad with insults. The disturbing part was that all of them sounded just like her voice.

"You unattractive featherweight," a voice said, "no one loves you but your brother, and even he wants you dead. Your name is dumb, and you will die alone…I hate you. I hate you with every bone in my body. You deserve to be here. You're an unforgivable piece of nothing."

It continued to insult her, and Evel began to rage. She searched the whole area to find the source of that terrible and hurtful voice. What kind of heartless being would say such things about a lady like her? She had to know who, but she did not have to wonder too long. She finally saw an image in one of the mirrors, which revealed the awful culprit. It was the image of herself as a child.

Meanwhile, Aval was tortured by the agony of wires going through his body, moving him ever closer to the piano he so hated. Every step he made caused the dolls, flowers, and more images of dead bodies to clap and chant for him to play. Like the disfigured diners from Chez Snobby, the wretched bodies of Bob and Susie, the rancid body of Ivil, and the rotting corpses of Tye, Elise, Santa, and Roger.

What shook him the most was the appearance of bullet-ridden corpses that were his parents, dusting his seat with ghastly smiles. He had no choice but to sit down on that bench and appease the horrible creatures in attendance.

Meanwhile, Evel stood in shock and covered her mouth at the idea of being insulted by herself. The words she had spoken—those exact same words—had run through her mind all her life. She couldn't bear to hear them from her child self. Evel turned away from the mirror, but the little girl appeared in the other mirrors. That little girl wasn't going away; she was there to haunt her. It continued to mutter hurtful remarks and awful truths that would make even the strongest being break down in tears. Evel had no choice but to endure the attack on her very soul and well-being.

The two vampires were in an inescapable mess with absolutely no hope of mercy. What could those poor squirrels do to get themselves out of that situation? Well, it was doing the one thing they were best at: being defiant little rascals.

Abruptly, Evel found joy in seeing her lovely self once again and decided to mock the ghost by saying how adorably ugly she was back then. The little girl was very insulted, but then she became confused when Evel wanted to play some patty-cake to pass the time away.

The girl didn't know how to respond to that. Evel was curious whether the kid was in another world beyond the mirrors, so she took two fingers and poked a mirror over and over again, which annoyed the child. And just to really mess with her, whenever the girl started to speak, the vampire cut her off by making silly fart noises with her mouth. Apparently when it came to being playful with possible apparitions, Evel was no stranger.

Meanwhile, Aval did what most forced piano players would do in times of pressure. He pressed one single key over and over again, annoying the snot out of the guests. The enraged creatures began to yell as their faces turned into twisted demons. They wanted to rip his insides out and put his head on a platter.

What an impatient crowd they were, calling for blood when he was just warming himself up for the real performance. With the power of imagination, Aval made some dark shades appear over his eyes and conjured a spotlight setting for himself. He cracked his knuckles and began to play a slick, clean, and soulful musical piece. The creatures were very confused; they thought he couldn't stomach playing the instrument with an audience. Apparently when it came to winging it, Aval did not disappoint.

He summoned a microphone for him to sing into, and he sounded like a real angel accompanied by drums, horns, and many xylophones in the background. Aval gave the creatures their party music, starting to feel a bit impressed with his talents. The music became louder and louder, so much louder that it could be heard in Evel's world.

As the little creatures became worried, Evel started to sing along with Aval's distant voice in her head. The minds of those siblings connected strongly with each other. Then in a glass-shattering display, Evel broke that dark world of mirrors and took the girl to a real party. They flew down to Aval's world in a flash. The little girl landed inside the open piano, and there came Evel to shut the lid on her past. She landed firmly on the piano, and she danced and sang along with her talented brother. The two vampires played along in their little nightmarish world, enjoying themselves and happily keeping their spirits unbroken. They turned the party up so much that all the creepy creatures danced along in delight.

The boogeyman saw them perform, and he stroked his chin with intrigue. He did not see it as a problem, for he had something else in store for the two. In a flash, he ripped Aval & Evel away from their party and put them in a very unsettling location. They were back home in Devilla Lane in their old front yard. Instead of grass or trees, it was a land of black ooze, lifting from the cold dirt and into the bright-orange skies of gigantic tornadoes and chaotic lightning.

There they sat, holding a familiar body in their arms. Aval & Evel held the dying body of their kind butler, with his blood dripping from their mouths and clothes. Their hearts jumped, and their eyes stood frozen. The weak butler desperately looked up at the squirrels and asked why they had to kill him. He'd showed them nothing but kindness; he freed them from their captivity, and they showed their thanks by taking his life.

He called them heartless murderers who did not deserve to live at all. He should have left them in that dungeon where they belonged, and the world could have been at peace once more. Aval & Evel were heartbroken. The one life that truly mattered to them talked harshly to them, so very harshly. They wanted to apologize, but they had to know his name.

When they asked for his name, the butler said in a weak voice, "You don't deserve to know my name if you can't remember it."

Evel looked down at the dying squirrel with her eyes so sad and said, "You know, I always thought of you as Mr. Pengy Pants…"

"W-what?"

Evel then continued with a different tone. "Yeah, Mr. Pengy Pants! You know, like a penguin. All you butlers dress like funny-looking penguins for some reason. Oh! I bet your name is Alfred!"

Aval sampled some of the flowing blood and said, "No, he couldn't possibly be an Alfred. He tastes much too young to be some crusty old butler from an overhauled comic book series. Maybe he's a Geoffrey."

Evel sampled the blood too and said, "I disagree. He tastes way too stable to be some anger-repressed butler from a drastically syndicated sitcom. It's clear he's a Betty Von Quarius the Second."

"Evel, what kind of name is that for a French squirrel butler?"

"Hey, who knows? Maybe he's a British squirrel maid that was once a lady now turned male. I can picture it so well. Her sex change outraged her hometown, and she was exiled for her morally confused actions. She was doomed to travel the lonely roads until she found our fancy home. She pleaded to stay because she was driven by her love of serving, cleaning, and gracing us with her cute furry cheeks. Yes, she did—"

"Evel, that makes the least bit of sense. Sex changes were never around at that time."

"Aval, you don't know what goes on in England. Anything could've happened there. Isn't that right, Betty Von Quarius the Second?"

"What's wrong with y-you two?" The butler groaned. "I'm dying, and my name is not Betty."

"I don't know," said Aval. "That name really suits you, and it rolls easily off the tongue."

"Then it's settled!" Evel grinned as she pinched the butler's cheeks. "When you pass over to the afterlife, you will be remembered as our cutie-wootie transvesty Betty!"

As the two giggled through the horrific scene, the butler evaporated through their arms in dark specks of ash. From those specks formed the boogeyman, who appeared before the two snickering squirrels to join in their little laughter. He stopped and asked why they were acting so disturbingly funny.

Evel then threw a pebble at the creature's face and asked why he took away their transvestite butler. The boogeyman giggled some more until Aval threw a big rock in the creature's direction. He easily dodged it with a lean as Aval told him good and well to respect the dead, no matter what gender they were.

The boogeyman had no choice but to destroy their inner psyches. With a loud snap of his fingers, the destructive storm was cleared from the skies and the ooze was sunk back into the ground. From above he conjured the bright sun that shone white light with immense heat and powerful glare.

The vampires felt the scorching heat and screeched in pure agony! The two fell to the ground while their bodies steamed and roasted like bacon. Their screams sounded so wonderful to the boogeyman's nonexistent ears that he laughed in joy and satisfaction. Soon their psyches would fry, and their minds would become shriveled shells of what they once were.

After a while of watching the vampires burn on the ground until they were charred to a crisp, he could sense something was wrong. He observed both closely and found that the pain was gone and was replaced by a state of relaxation. The two found it to be a nice experience, and it was a great way to bring back color to their skin.

The boogeyman began to twitch his right eye, and the nails in his head began to loosen and ooze black blood. He knew a better way to kill them. He conjured two flaming wooden stakes and plunged them straight into the vampires' hearts. Both lit up in flames!

Oh no! It was too much to watch—the great Aval & Evel were done for. Those unfortunate souls would have surely called it quits, thrown in the towel, and cashed their final paychecks—if they did not find the time to chat about it.

Evel was whistling about and noticed how calm Aval was. She said to him in a relaxed voice, "You look awfully comfy. How does it feel?"

Aval yawned hugely and said, "It is surprisingly painful, but I'm really not feeling the full effect here. I mean, my body is already roasted from the sun, so what's the point of setting me on fire with a burning stake? I can hardly feel it. It's kinda like toasting toasted toast before puncturing it with a flaming toothpick."

"Wait, it's like toasting toasted toast?" Evel said as she steadily turned her head toward him, crunching her burned neck. "You can't toast a toast."

"Yes, you can; all toasters do that. Just put a piece of toast back in the toaster as many times as you want. It becomes crispier with every session."

"Oh, well, answer me this: Can you pop popped popcorn?"

"Indeed you can. You just need the right kind of firecrackers."

"Ah, insightful." Evel turned to the boogeyman and said to him, "Hey ice-cream man, can you conjure up some iced ice cream? 'Cause those would taste really good right now, along with some watered-down water. He-he!"

The boogeyman was getting annoyed. I mean really, extraordinarily annoyed. He scratched his arms clean of skin, his eyes bled black blood like a fountain, and his everlasting grin began to twitch into a frown. He tried his best to bring it to a still, but he could no longer take it. The grinning boogeyman finally frowned.

His body shook nervously as he said to them, "Aval & Evel, you loathsome bags of annoyance, what is *wrong* with you?"

The loud devilish voice he used made them snicker. The two squirrels vanished from their crusty shells and reappeared on his shoulders, looking unburned and unharmed. The two gently explained to the nervous man that they learned how to deal with horrific nightmares, sad deaths, and psychological pain by finding a bit of humor in them. That was the true and disturbing power of screwiness.

The boogeyman fell to his knees and stared blankly at the ground, trying to remember how to smile again. Just then, the squirrels disappeared, and he was left alone. The world around him turned pitch black.

He stood and wondered what was going on until the dark void opened like the hands of a giant. The new void he stood in was a huge space full of dark-purple-and-green energy waves heading toward the skies. He stood deep within massive palms that were owned by two giant floating heads.

It was a nightmarish image of Aval & Evel's floating hands and heads that looked like they were horrifically ripped from their bodies and were altered like victims in a science experiment. Aval's eyes were incredibly bloodshot, and his mouth was mechanically stretched to the sides of his face. Evel's eyes were bandaged yet bleeding. Her head was punctured with a glass tube filled with A-positive blood while her lower jaw was completely stripped away. Their hands were furless, veiny, and covered with coursing tubes and punctured glass.

The floating heads told him they too could be as twisted as he was. The boogeyman may have been fear itself, but they'd suffered through greater nightmares in their long life. So much so that they were able to eliminate anything that could plague their minds.

The boogeyman would be their next challenge—or I should say next victim. Their mighty hand of judgment rose to the sky and was prepared to deliver a devastating blow. Barney could have escaped; he could have fled from his impending doom, but he was too awestruck by the idea of two little squirrels passing judgment on him. The boogeyman was in his own nightmare. Then a thunderous and earth-shattering pound from the fist obliterated the creature into dust. A flash of light soon came into their vision, and Aval & Evel were brought back to reality. It was over. Aval & Evel destroyed the boogeyman.

It was a glorious achievement and a stupendous victory for the two vampires. The two grabbed each other in a sweet embrace, knowing that they were more powerful than fear itself.

Just when Aval called for Bell & Bill to come out, a deadly cough came from behind him. He turned around and, to his surprise, saw Boogeyman Barney standing on his knees. He looked smaller than usual, shrunken to about their size, and his body began to drip away like a melting candle. Obviously, Aval & Evel groaned and cursed the creature's existence. He just wouldn't die.

Barney suffered and ached, but he had the strength to laugh and call the vampires traitors. He was everything they had asked for, yet in the end they turned to the side of good. He expected Evel to do such a thing, but Aval? Barney may have been a foul creature, but at least he was more of a man than Aval could ever be.

Barney claimed to be a true monster of horror, but Aval himself was just a mentally confused poseur that couldn't decide if he loved men or women. He called Aval a useless creation, a failed ruler, and the worst vampire he had the misfortune of laying eyes upon. The insults struck a huge nerve in Aval. He was very tired of hearing that voice and intended to end the boogeyman once and for all.

He walked toward the menacing creature, watching him smile away, daring the vampire to kill him. Aval granted his wish. He drove his bare hand through the creature's chest and pulled out his black heart. Barney cried out in pain and fell to the ground, bleeding in an oozing puddle of death and defeat.

With no regret, Aval crushed the heart like a rotten fruit and said to the pathetic creature, "It's over, Barney. You lose."

It was apparent that it was, but just then, Barney stopped his aching sounds and slowly turned to Aval with a big smile on his face. Something was very off. Barney began to chuckle, which turned into a maniacal laugh, and Evel soon laughed along with him.
Something was terribly off and wrong. Aval wanted to know what was so funny. Then out of something that could be seen in a horrible dream, Evel vanished away like a fading mirage. Aval's face turned still with shock; he could not comprehend what was going on.

Barney soon ceased the laughter and said with a deceptive smile, "On the contrary, Aval. It is you who has lost…everything."

He laughed again, and as he vanished away, he showed Aval whose heart he'd truly torn out. On the ground, lying in a pool of red blood, was his dying sister, Evel.

Aval was absolutely terrified; it was all a trick. Through a series of trials, the boogeyman figured out Aval's weakness and made him kill it in order to be eternally broken. He made him kill his own sister. The boogeyman had truly won.

Evel was dying, choking on her own blood. Aval had to do something! He got down to the ground and tried to put the heart back into her body while trying to patch the hole with his own hands. The wounds weren't healing; she wasn't going to make it. Aval wouldn't allow it to happen. He told her to hold on, and he told her to stay with him.

He held her close and he desperately continued to put the heart back in place, but it was no use. It was far too late. Aval started to cry. He didn't want her to go. Evel looked at her crying brother, and she desperately used her left arm to feel his face one last time.

With her last breath, she only said his name. Her arm fell to the ground, and she became motionless, while her eyes slowly closed themselves from the world forever. Aval shook her and told her to wake up.

"Evel, please Evel," he whimpered. "Evel, wake up, come back! Don't leave me! Wake up! Don't go...don't go..."

She was gone, and Aval was severely broken. He held her close and let out a stream of tears, apologizing for everything he had done and wishing that she were still alive. It was the saddest thing I've ever had to describe. I couldn't help but cry.

Across the field stood Bell & Bill, witnessing the whole scene. They felt terrible for the poor vampire. Seeing him cry made them realize that monsters weren't all that different from mortals, for they could still shed tears for the ones they had lost. No matter how much Aval & Evel argued or resented each other, they loved each other, and their lives were nothing without each other.

Bell & Bill did not want to see any more death, though there was not much left to be seen. They wanted everything to be right again. Perhaps a wish was the answer, for beside them flew down the wishing raven. That bird smirked and remarked insultingly that the monsters got what they deserved. It didn't feel like the right moment to say such things. The squirrels wanted to curse her so bad but were too sad to do so.

Regardless, the raven felt generous and offered one last wish before she could leave that world. She gave Bell & Bill a chance to set everything right again, though there would be no guarantee that the outcome would be perfect or precise. The two squirrels had to think carefully. They looked back at the suffering vampire holding his sister close, never letting her go. They saw how much he cared and how much he regretted his actions. It gave Bell an idea. She knew exactly what to wish for.

Bell turned to the raven, took a pause, and told her wish, "I wish Aval could see everything that led to this tragedy, back to the moment when he snapped in that restaurant. I want him to know what would happen if he stuck to his monster pride. I want him to change for a better future."

The raven had to ask her, "Are you confident that Aval would change after seeing these events in his head? Imagine the alteration—he might use it as an advantage to make all of this worse."

Bell told that raven in strong confidence, "He'll make the right choice, for Evel."

With that, the raven slowly opened her wings and emitted a flash of bright-purple light that spread through the entire universe. She captured all space and time and sent it back to the past, in hopes that the dark future would exist nevermore.

25

LIFE IS BRIGHTER WITH YOU

A long time ago, on a dark and chilly night, two vampire squirrels were dining in a fancy restaurant on a nice mountainside. The food was horrid, and the drinks of blood were vile. Needless to say, it was a bad evening. Aval hated it the most; he couldn't stand it all. Then he saw a little squirrel with straws stuck in his mouth that looked like fangs. The child began waving his jacket like a cape, and he pretended to be a vampire, entertaining his family and others around as well.

The child shouted in a deep Dracula voice, "Hey, everyone, gaze upon me! I am Count Veggula, and I vant to suck your minerals and proteins!"

Every squirrel in the restaurant laughed. The whole restaurant enjoyed the joke about vampire vegetarians, which was pointed at Aval & Evel. Aval couldn't take it anymore; he finally snapped and smashed his own table with his own bare hands.

"Enough!" he yelled.

The restaurant grew silent as all eyes turned to him. Evel was shocked to see her husband act in such a way, and she told him to be calm. He would not be still, and he would not be calm. He was about to speak his mind until a bright-purplish light flashed in his eyes.

That spontaneous flash of light showed him a world of visions that began with him and Evel killing every squirrel in that restaurant. It showed him a land ruled by monsters, a country ruled by goths, and a world of madness, death, and destruction. It was so very strange, and it happened so very fast that he didn't know what to think of it. Then he saw a horrifying image. He saw himself losing someone very close to him: Evel.

The visions were then sucked away, and the flash of light diminished from his eyes. He was brought back to reality, frozen and filled with large amounts of emotions. He looked around the room and observed all the concerned faces on the squirrels, especially Evel's.

He stared at her in silence. He became scared, and he ran out of that restaurant like a bat out of hell. Evel did not know what came over him. She apologized to the squirrels around her and immediately chased after Aval, ignoring the fact that someone had to pay for that broken table.

Later, in the middle of Luminous Acres, Aval sat in the grass, gazed at the bright moon, and pondered what he had just seen. He was troubled and confused; he had no idea why he had to see such awful visions in his head. Then along came Evel, who was rather angry with him. She'd searched the mountains, lakes, their home, and even trendy clothing stores for him. She wanted to know why he had to scare those squirrels and run out like a lunatic.

Aval was amazed she would go through the trouble of finding him. He admired how much she cared. He told her to sit down, and he started to explain what had happened. He saw what appeared to be a psychic vision, but it felt more like a warning. They took part in a grand conquest and eventually ruled over Canada, but everything went downhill. They lost their fellow monsters, two blond squirrels beat them to a pulp, they had their house destroyed by maniacs, and it all ended with Evel dying.

He said it was a vision of things to come, and he did not want to relive it all by massacring the squirrels in Chez Snobby. That's why he ran away.

It was a lot for Evel to take in. Seeing a vision of things to come sounded a bit crazy, but it was not uncommon in the process of revelations. The part that interested her the most was that he had passed up a second chance to conquer the world because he wanted her to live. She found it so romantic! That was all she wanted from that night: a rekindled spark to show how much he loved her. She hugged Aval tight and wouldn't let go, knowing that he loved her more than the world itself. He enjoyed her warm embrace, but he couldn't hug her back. He loved her but as a sister and not a wife.

After some hard thinking, he suddenly admitted that their whole relationship was wrong. A brother and sister shouldn't be married to each other. It wasn't normal, and it wasn't right either. He suggested they would be better off not being together anymore.

Evel was absolutely shocked. She thought he was using an excuse to leave, because he had found another mate, possibly a male. She feared that he was turning gay. She refused to live her days helping her own brother pick out scarves and pink shorts.

Aval assured her that he wasn't turning that way, nor had he found another. The visions he saw were filled with much unpleasantness, and he didn't want to suffer through them again in any way. The marriage had to end.

Even if they did go their separate ways, he was still worried for monsterkind. Monsters would still be seen as jokes and abominations. Mortals would still treat Aval & Evel like oddities, and they would forever live in a cruel world. The mortals would never accept them, and eventually they'd want all monsters wiped off the planet. Nothing would change for the better.

After hearing those words come from his mouth, Evel reminded him to stop having such negative thoughts. She could've said a lot of things, but she said the most profound thing: "We don't have to be monsters; we can just be different."

Those words of wisdom never crossed his mind before. She also believed that if push came to shove, they could still stand up for themselves and fight, even if it did break the peace. She was getting tired of it anyway, especially being vegetarians, after eating some tofu. She didn't mind spilling some blood or eating some meat from time to time. It didn't have to lead to a monster revolution, though.

As for their marriage, she found it difficult to defend it, considering everything he said was true. It wasn't right, and it was pretty pathetic, but she did not care; she wanted to stay with him. Aval brought order to her life. She drove herself crazy over the littlest of things in her lonely days; she even talked to people who weren't even there. She was convinced that I was a figment of her imagination until Aval came by and saw me too. Evel needed Aval in her life.

They helped each other through the bad times and saw each other through the good times. They won many battles and made many memories. They even liked the same animated movie about an emperor llama. Sure, they drove each other crazy, but much like life itself, nothing is ever perfect.

What was perfect was being with someone to give order to their crazy life and excitement to their dull life, which formed a bond that was meant to be. No squirrel in the world made them more complete when they simply held hands, and it took them until now to realize it. As long as Aval & Evel were together, they could turn their tragic lives into a wonderful song.

I see clouds of gray, black roses too.
The rain comes and goes, that much is true.
As I bleed from my heart…life is brighter with you.

I see skies of gloom, no sun in sight.
The moon lights the sky for children of the night.
As I bleed from my heart…life is brighter with you.

The blood of the living that tastes like apple pie
does not compare to that sparkle in your eye.
When I'm with you, I can always be me.
When I'm with you, my soul feels free.

Our world is forbidden and frowned upon.
But they don't seem to mind when we sleep at dawn.
As I bleed from my heart…life is brighter with you.

I knew…

from my bleeding heart…life is brighter with you.

Aval & Evel were reborn.

The next morning, the world and all of its beautiful creatures were back to normal. The squirrels continued to live their happy lives, the birds chirped once more, humans dressed and acted the way they wanted, and the grass never looked greener. Everyone couldn't help but feel a bit of joy in their hearts, even the other characters who died a painful death in the dark story. It felt like they were all given a second chance to live.

Elise, that troubled squirrel, woke up early. She found that her room was clean, and she did not find blood on her hands. She did not transform into a werewolf in her sleep. She felt so amazed; she had been cured of her transformation disorder. She had to go tell her father the good news, and he was awfully surprised to see her happy behavior. She even wanted to go to her mother's grave to tell her the good news; that is until Barbosa told her to stop. He felt that her routine of talking to a tombstone all day was unhealthy. He also felt a sudden feeling to care where she went.

He said that her mother would always know when she's happy and if Elise ever wanted to talk to or hang out with someone, he would always be there for her. He even offered to take her out for breakfast and skip out on a check for fun. For Elise, it was very strange that Barbosa started to act like a real father; perhaps it was another sudden change. Without a second thought and for the first time in many years, Elise and Barbosa ventured into the world together.

Roger Hazelnut, that funny chipmunk, took a break from his travels. He was tired of getting lost and decided to vacation in the beautiful lake of Montreal, where he found a large number of humans and critters gathering to admire the sunrise.

He felt so relaxed and so free that he forgot he ever had a wife. He shared a spot on the lake with a drowsy human who shared his same thoughts. It was Prime Minister Marin, and he found the weird-talking chipmunk very entertaining.

Salamear—or should I say Santa Claus—woke up in his cabin at the fall of night and was about to start the day with some booze. Then he heard a knock on his door. He went outside and found no visitors, but there was a letter stuck to the door. He read it, and it was the most shocking thing he ever saw: a Christmas letter from Aval & Evel. They wanted him to bring large amounts of coal to feed their furnace for the winter. In other words, they wanted him to come back as jolly old Saint Nick.

The two vampires had indeed changed their ways, and they didn't stop there. On the windy shore side of Emplois, the vampires looked through the window of a very happy family sharing a nice dinner. They saw happy parents chatting with a jolly fish captain, who was lecturing the senses out of his two favorite grandchildren, Bell & Bill. The two vampires saw the good life they led, and they honestly did not know how to thank them for being who they were. So they decided to leave a bag of PB&Js and oatmeal cookies by their doorstep. With a knock at the door, the two blond squirrels discovered the bag and saw a note on it that said, "Thank you."

Aval & Evel did some good, but there was one last thing they had to do. They had to find that one missing piece in their lives. Later that night, the vampires went to Lesion Island to take part in the monster meeting. On that island sat Vince, Barbosa, Tye, Nutilda, Weegee, and even Elise herself, continually telling their pains and woes.

Then from a high hill came the two vampires, gracing the monsters with their fearful presence of fog and mystery. Hand in hand Aval & Evel slowly walked in, with a smile from Evel and another smile from Aval. The group gazed upon the vampires in shock, for they never knew they had the ability to smile.

Once the vampire squirrels made it to the circle of monsters, Aval said to them, "Fellow monsters, it's so nice to see you all again."

Barbosa suddenly became furious, and he snarled, "You lifeless pukes! You got some nerve calling us...wait, what did you say?" He was clearly expecting an insult.

"He said it's nice to see you guys," said Evel. "It's been many years since all of us were in one place. This is like a reunion of frights and fears. Come here, I want to hug each and every one of you!"

The group stared in great confusion. The once-miserable couple was happy and wanted to hug them. Those vampires were total strangers. The monsters refused to hug them, but one bothered to risk his own legs for that one chance. Vince ran over and hugged both Aval & Evel. The vampires held him close and didn't want to let him go. The child's day got better when Aval called him Vince. He was so astounded that his heroes knew his name and even abbreviated it that he thought he was in a dream.

"My, you two seem to be in a peculiar mood," said Tye. "Huggin' and smilin' without a care, I suspect you two have somethin' foul in mind."

"I certainly agree, it's hard not to see," rhymed Nutilda. "They're buttering us up to get on our good side; they couldn't hide it even if they tried."

"Yeah," said Elise, "they're probably here to make us go back to our murderous ways."

Vince looked at the vampires with a big smile on his face and asked if it was true. Were they going to make them go on a bloodthirsty rampage? Because he was hoping that they would. He had so many enemies he wanted to get rid of, especially one human who made him into a hideous creature. Revenge would've been sweet, and a revolution sounded really great to him.

Aval & Evel said no, they did not come to start such a thing. They were there for the simple pleasure of hanging out with their kind and actually getting to know one another. They wanted to be good friends so that they could be at peace with each other. After hearing that, Vince stepped away; he did not believe what he was hearing.

The two vampires started with themselves and said that they enjoyed cartoon movies and junk food, like regular people did. They then asked the monsters what their favorite things to do were, hoping to build some connections.

Evel asked Tye if he enjoyed a hobby other than making shoes. The giant tarantula did not know; all he ever had on his mind were shoes, boots, and sandals. He couldn't go a single second without them on his mind, and there was no changing it or his urges. That is, until Evel suggested that thinking about mangoes might help his unhealthy condition. It certainly helped her when she had to sneeze. Tye thought about it for a moment and figured that it might be the answer.

Aval asked Barbosa if he had a special talent. The werewolf looked at the ground and sighed. He confessed that sometimes at night, when he had the house to himself, he would go out into the yard and sing. Though he did not mean howl in the moonlight; he meant singing like he was performing at a high-stakes casino. He was pressured by the group to sing a short piece, and after some hesitation, he sang like a true professional, bellowing in the moonlight. By the end of the song, the monsters clapped as the howls of other wolves spread through the air.

Elise was however shocked to see her father sing. Her face was like a surprised child discovering that Santa Claus was actually a yeti. She was then asked by Evel if she had a talent of her own. Elise really had no specific talent, but she could say snarky yet funny comments. She told them that she could endure the most unbearable tortures, like living with a redneck version of Frank Sinatra. Everyone just laughed and laughed, but not Vince.

Evel asked Nutilda where she got her lovely ninety-nine-cent pendent. Nutilda was embarrassed to answer at first, but eventually she told her that she snagged it from a bargain bin. That led to an interesting conversation about how both of them acquired dresses and stolen accessories. The two ladies soon laughed together. The monsters were getting to know one another well.

Aval then came to the silent man-fish, Weegee, and asked him what he really did in his life. What did the creature do in his spare time he didn't bother to talk about? Weegee looked at the squirrels and surprisingly chuckled at the question. He told everyone that he was secretly Jack the Ripper, still cutting up prostitutes in his spare time. It was a joke, of course; he spent his days cutting wood in shapes of statues.

Everyone chuckled—all except Vince, who felt absolutely disgusted with them. The vampires then came to the child and asked him how he spent his days. Vince said that he spent his days waiting for his vampire heroes to return. He wanted them to lead all monsters on a quest to destroy the mortals, but all he saw were softhearted impostors.

The king and queen of Nevermore he knew had savagery in their blood. They lived to kill their enemies and strike terror into the hearts of innocents. They would never ever seek any kind of friendship. The vampires noticed his anger and urged the Frankenstein squirrel to cast aside his long-standing hatred, for it would only lead to a terrible future.

Vince couldn't look them in the eyes anymore, and he refused to hear their words. He did not care what the future held; he wanted to make his creator pay for what he did to him. He wanted Paulie to die, and he wanted the monster name to come alive again. He even asked the other monsters if they felt the same way, but sure enough, they saw him as the crazy one.

Aval & Evel stood beside the upset child and told him to let it go. They told him that they felt the same way every day. They secretly wanted to see the world burn and their enemies die at their feet. Even though they were monsters, the feeling of hate was never the best way to live any life.

Aval was grateful that some people showed him the way, and he intended to do the same with a particular lonely squirrel. Aval & Evel took the child's hands and offered him a chance at happiness, to give him the childhood they never had. They offered him a place in their lives, to be their little candle of light, their pride and joy, their son.

The group of monsters gasped loudly and were completely lost for words. Vampires adopting a Frankenstein monster for a son was certainly surprising. Everyone expected Vince to break down in tears, but he did not.

That squirrel pulled away from them and said, "Do you think I need a family? What I need is revenge! These mortals, these humans destroyed our lives, and you want to ignore that?"

"Watch your words," said Evel. "Our hands aren't clean either, but we intend to change that. We don't have to be the heartless freaks of nature everyone assumes we are. We can be a loving family like any other. We can live happily in peace together."

"Shut up!" Vince shouted. "There's no such thing as peace! We will always be killing machines, and nothing will change that! We are monsters, and they are mortals, and this world isn't big enough for both. I'm going to get my revenge with or without you saps."

Aval & Evel couldn't get through to the child. He was dead set on getting horrible revenge. He was going to continue the circle of violence unless someone said something about it. Aval gave it his try.

Before Vince stormed off into the woods, Aval grabbed him by the shoulders and said in a threatening voice, "Listen to me, you little mismatched brat. You can kill these mortals until the sun burns out, but no one calls us saps and lives to tell about it. Saps are fools like you who think the best way to deal with pain is to get revenge. That is never the cure. The best cure is to be with those who want you in their lives and will guide you to a better life. We offered you that chance, and you refused it with an attitude. I won't stop you, but if you leave, I'll show you how soft I am when I put you six feet underground. Right after I stick your limbs so far up your sorry butt that you'll spend the rest of your days coughing up bones!"

Vince was in shock; he was never threatened in such a way. Someone was willing to kill him to protect him from a dark path. It gave him the sense that maybe Aval & Evel did care like parents and would do anything to make his life better, even if it meant burying him. In Vince's strange mind, he saw it as pure love.

The child was so overwhelmed that he literally broke down in pieces. With his body parts piled on the ground, the vampires picked up the head and saw that Vince started to cry with a smile. The little Frankenstein squirrel looked at Aval & Evel and gratefully called them Mom and Dad.

The three squirrels finally became a strange but loving family. They were oh so overjoyed that they hugged the breath out of one another, and they soon felt a peculiar emotion in themselves. If I didn't know better, I'd say they were actually happy.

It was a cause for celebration on that glorious night, so they needed to go somewhere that was fun and not so dreary. Weegee suggested that they should all take part in a night of bowling. He knew an excellent bowling alley that would be thrilled to clear out for some real party animals. Who ever knew that a scaly man-fish had jokes?

Aval & Evel reattached their newfound bundle of joy and went off into the night to bowl with their newfound friends. Those monsters then lived a happy life forevermore.

It was truly a happy ending, and all in all, everything worked out swell in that world of furry creatures. I admit I was wrong for bringing about the uprising of monsters, but it did provide key thoughts. I could say a lot of cliché stuff about regret, misguided hate, and burying the past, but there was more to the story than that.

Monsters are considered freaks of nature and savage beasts with a thirst for blood. Despite the appearance, all of us can be monsters. There are times when we never see the bright side of things, because everything seems to be so dark and cruel. There are also times when we hate one another because of envy, beliefs, or, worst of all, just for being different. During those times, some of us kill and ruin lives just to please our dark nature. Those terrible few become blind to the point where they eventually hurt not only themselves but also the ones they love. Being a monster isn't about being born in a lab or being bitten by the diseased. It's how we choose to live that defines what we are.

Choose to plot evil schemes, or just stay up and watch your favorite cartoon shows. Go on a killing spree, or watch a nice sunset. Choose wisely, for being a monster is the result of losing yourself to the cruel world.

Don't ever lose your way, for we are all just as lost. But if we have someone or something to help us find our way, wandering will seem hopeless, nevermore.

THE END

The next evening in the White House in Washington, DC, the raven waited for President X to return to his office. There she stood on his desk, occupying her time by looking through classified documents about some silly nonsense like homeland security and equal rights among races. A speck of energy entered the room, and there came President X, teleporting into his chair.

As his particles completely aligned, the raven asked the mysterious president, "How was your little outing?"

"It was a different experience but refreshing nonetheless," he answered. He then reached under his desk, pulled out a small pearl necklace, and offered it to the raven. It was his way of showing her thanks for completing a very special task. She was flattered and graciously accepted his gift.

As the president placed it around her neck, he said to her, "I must say that the sun has never shone brighter. The economy is in the green, the citizens are sleeping better, and there's absolutely no war in sight. All thanks to my wish to set Aval & Evel straight and you for bringing a boogeyman to life. Where is it now?"

"That freak is locked away in a child's mind," she said.

"Good. He was quite useful but drastic at the same time," he said. "I did not have to be blown up by my own nukes."

"Hey, you're a guy who can't die. You get hit by one of those toys, and you'll be back in one week. However, there's one thing I can't understand. You knew what those vampires were doing from the start, and you could have stopped this whole ordeal from happening. But you didn't. Why?"

"Those vampires needed to be taught a lesson. As a result, a gothic wasteland ruled by monsters is certain to never see the light of day again."

"That's really strange, coming from you. You basically sold your soul to have your butt in that chair. My master wants you to keep your end of the bargain and cause some chaos, yet you use me to prevent it. That big wish you made was a huge nail in the coffin. 'I wish that events would play against Aval & Evel,' you said, 'so they would rewrite their mistakes!' You're lucky he has bigger fish to fry than you."

"I don't care about your master or the consequences of my actions."

"Then what do you care about?"

President X rose from his chair and walked over to his clear windows. He observed the splendor of the evening sun. His face was still consumed by dark shadows.

He answered the raven, "I care about Earth. It is a beautiful planet full of wondrous life and potential. The population, however, is the cause of its ills. It is full of ignorance, full of hate, and full of selfish pride. Those are the very reasons why creatures, races, and nations can't prosper as one. They need to be corrected, and that's why I took this job—to help them. In time, I will make peace a reality."

He then pushed a button on his wristwatch and without warning—

Kaboom!

Raven, the wishing raven, exploded on his desk, thanks to the new necklace that contained tiny explosives. After dusting himself of feathers, he returned to his chair. He sat down, propped his elbows on the bloody desk, and turned his fancy watch to the left. The simple turn deactivated his shadowy cloak, returning his appearance and voice to their regular states.

He looked at where the raven once had stood and said, "I will see to it that this world can flourish for that vision..."

...one
problem
at a time.

TO BE CONTINUED...?

Poems/Songs

<u>AVAL & EVEL</u>

In times of goodwill and life without grief
lived a town that was named Dew Leaf.
A place where many creatures lived in delight,
where they lived in harmony day and night.
Surely there were bad times in Dew Leaf,
but a better tomorrow came with great belief.

Though like in other towns with secrets so dark
lay a cemetery none should ever embark.
The dark side of Dew Leaf, oh so dreary,
lived two squirrels full of death and misery.

Husband and wife lived among the deceased;
night falls, and these terrible vampires shall wake.
So lock your doors and hide for goodness' sake,
for it's on the blood of innocents they're sure to feast.

Dew Leaf is no more;
it is their land,
forever named Nevermore.

SQUIRREL OF FRANKENSTIEN

Dreams crushed and hope lost,
finding purpose comes with a cost.
The dead will always feel pain,
as their family mourn in the rain.

Feelings for the undead are so bitter;
none have sympathy for bags of litter.
These creations were built so odd,
by others who wanted to play as God.

These creations of mad science can't help but cry;
their lives are pointless and they wonder why.
They are forced to live and never grow;
their simple lives are but misery and woe.

Somehow someday,
others will say,
we all end up that way.

A WEREWOLF'S DAUGHTER

A son for a mother,
a daughter for a father,
but for monsters of old,
very few stories are ever told.

Rare it can be,
to have a child of their own.
So uncommon do we see,
copies of a monster's blood and bone.

A monster to raise children,
teaching them to hunt, kill, and sing.
But children have no intentions to follow their fathers,
for nothing is more arrogant than an offspring.

BOOGEYMAN BARNEY

A vague memory or a haunting ghost?
He is a friend born from a nightmare.
Imaginary and never seen by most,
he is a shadow that lives to scare.

Like innocence in a child's mind,
it grows ever darker and less kind.
He is there when no one's around;
he creeps near you without a sound.

Boogeyman Barney is his name;
he thrives to drive children insane.
He detaches all truth from reality
and offers a life within insanity.

What would you do in a final stand,
if you should ever face this boogeyman?

FIVE DOOMED MONKEYS

Five little monkeys jumping on the bed,
one fell off and kaboomed his head.
Mama yelled a warning to quiet their whines,
no more monkeys jumping near land mines.

EVEL'S LAMENT

I stare out my window to see nothing.
A whisper in the wind and a parade of sand
but never the sounds of a classical band.

I become dreary and ever longing to commute.
I show my blissful and graceful marks as a dame,
though none will talk to a vampire of any name.

Hark!

Change is knocking at my skull as I cry;
I'm subjected to society's rules like a pet!
Chains for norms and shackles for fools!
Why so cruel not to accept?
And why so ignorant to deny?

THE CURSE OF THE MUSIC BOX

The music box of a broken king.
Attacking one's heart is its deal.
From what others made Kalazar feel,
now into a song the box will sing.

Three songs it will play,
the ones you love get taken away.
The pain of loss showers and pours;
death isn't funny when it happens to yours.

Let the box play its fourth song,
for the end is never wrong.
You'll be happy death is cruel that way,
when it steals your sorry life away.

NUTILDA BROUGHT SOME BUTTER

Nutilda brought some butter, some apples soaked in gin.
Mix it all up in a pot until aroma can
ascend into her nostrils, and sneeze right in the stew.
Makes an excellent preservative for sticky-icky
brew in several toenails, ripped strictly from a bear.
A little dab of bunny blood would give the scent some
snare right in a mirror, then collect the broken glass.
Scrape the skin off dirty bitter rats that said to kiss their
as a matter of fact, pour a bowl of spinach dip.
No need to add some salty chips; they make the bubbles
rip out all the cotton, from a kitchen oven mitt.
Pour a batch of smelly, nasty, yucky, chunky oily sh—
it's turning purple; onions make it green;
a pair of dirty underwear that makes a Mormon scream.
Oh good gracious! She forgot the leech and snail!
She'll make it up by adding a little dainty doggy
tell it's almost ready, a potion filled with doom.
Just add a little nitro to give the kick an extra boom!

NUTILDA'S NUTTY SONG

Nevermore is on the rise;
vampires lead to my surprise.
Everyone's doing well and going strong,
while I do everything completely wrong...

Tired of doubt,
I'll try one out!
I'll cast a dangerous spell so subtle
it'll turn this tree into a yellow puddle!

Twinkle binkle, sorry tree,
watch me turn you into pee!
No wait!
I turned it into chocolate cake...

I'm a witch, I think,
but my magic simply stink...

So I'll try out yet another one!
Hexing a human is always fun!
There's a man jogging up a hill so free.
Maybe I'll turn him into the smallest flea!

Hexus reckless, stupid man,
being a bug will shorten your life span!
Oh snap!
I sprouted angel wings on his back...

I'm a witch, I think,

but my magic simply stink...

My rut is turning into a ditch;

being this way makes me twitch.

I can't get my way without acting like a bitch...

There's nothing more I can do.

My days as a witch are through!

Boo-hoo!

But wait...

I then met a sweet girl,

who was as pretty as a pearl.

She showed me the light, and it was swell,

so I granted the sweet girl one free spell.

She wanted a rainbow tail only she could feel,

but instead she was eaten alive by a slimy eel...

Farewell, my friend,

indeed a sorry end.

You have shown me the right way.

I have found what I was doing wrong:

my magic works like opposite day!

Like a backward game of truth or dare!

Like a turtle outrunning a lazy hare!

Like a river flowing through the air!

Like an atheist sinner saying a prayer!

It all makes sense!

(It makes no sense.)

It's perfect sense!

(It's perfect nonsense.)

I see it now.

I'll try one nooowww!

Hocus-pocus, willow wake,

fill this land with delicious cake!

Oh dear!

I just made lava appear!

Krittle cradle, inky blot,

take me to a hellish spot!

Oh my!

I went to a heavenly place in the sky!

My opposite theory is certainly right,

but I need to get out of here.

I can't stand all this light.

Aaahh…

A simply gorgeous night,

yet it's not completely filled with fright.

Now is my chance to do this right!

Hello world!

Nutilda is no longer a tasteless hack.

I tell ya, it's good coming from heaven and back!

My naughty little spells have gotten well,

so gaze and gawk as I raise some hell!

I cast this moose with healthy legs;
now they're boneless if not dismayed!
I cast this bird family with hearts of gold;
now their hearts are frozen solid cold!
I cast these chipmunks with the size of dogs;
now their bodies are the size of frogs!
These trees over here could be much cleaner;
now they come alive looking so much meaner!

This is the happiest I've ever been.
I will never feel so down again!
So run and hide, my little pretties,
I have the power to crumble cities!

Until then,
my deepest wish
is to turn my body into an ugly fish.
Furrow turrow, shapeless bowl,
give me the body of a fat, ugly troll!
Oh joy!
I look good enough to be in Playboy!

I'm a witch, I think,
my magic no longer stink.
So I'll close this song
with a sexy wink.
Wink!

NEVERMORE FOG

Can you feel the void of this place?
Can you feel the bits of water on your face?

My fog is as wondrous as a star's gleam
and more inviting than boiling hot steam.
Huge and mysterious,
welcoming and curious.

It does more than lie around like residue;
it dampens the feelings held inside of you.

This fog is a gas in a playful way.
Searching your mind for equality,
begging to share your worst quality,
it wants to be friends, and it wants you to stay.

TYE, THE TORTURED TARANTULA

Tying laces and crafting a shoe,
everyone should learn how to do,
except for a sad tarantula.
Tye seeks a real purpose,
but it does his soul no service.

Simple days of eating bugs were gone;
remedial hunger for humans last so long.
It all goes away in the mirror;
please let it simmer.

A beastly beast of human and spider,
or tarantula to the acclaimed wiser.
He has very little to lose and little to gain,
when nothing but shoes keep him sane.

WISHING RAVEN

Why wish upon a star with such ambition,
when you can simply wish upon a raven?

Raven, the wishing raven, is not picky;
she grants wishes to any kind of dummy.
Wish all you like as much as you want;
she shall deliver onto you with a taunt.

Why work yourself to death for no reason,
when you can simply wish upon a raven?

No task or payment is required to have your wishes come true.
She's a fascinating bird that takes joy in how your wish affects you.
If you wish for a better life,
she'll introduce your neck to an iron spike.

Why think of others like a boring old virgin,
when you can really wish upon a raven?

Giving the poor large amounts of wealth would be awfully kind;
she'll replace your blood with cash and she knows they won't mind.
Like to wish what it'd be like if you were never actually born?
Your spirit will be stuck in limbo and forever you are torn.

She will grant what you most adore,
but do be careful what you wish for.
If you care to wish upon a raven,
then you dare to wish upon Satan.

JOY OF JUNK FOOD

Cheeseburgers with lots of cheese,
bacon burgers with lots of sauce,
would you kindly supersize me, please?

Pizza we share all day and nachos all night;
thinking about dessert feels so right...
Baby,
Baby, pass the ketchup...

Unhealthy? Yes,
as most may see,
but it's a joy,
to me...

LIFE IS BRIGHTER WITH YOU

I see clouds of gray, black roses too.
The rain comes and goes, that much is true.
As I bleed from my heart...life is brighter with you.

I see skies of gloom, no sun in sight.
The moon lights the sky for children of the night.
As I bleed from my heart...life is brighter with you.

The blood of the living that tastes like apple pie
does not compare to that sparkle in your eye.
When I'm with you, I can always be me.
When I'm with you, my soul feels free.

Our world is forbidden and frowned upon.
But they don't seem to mind when we sleep at dawn.
As I bleed from my heart...life is brighter with you.

I knew...
from my bleeding heart...life is brighter with you.

THANKS
A THOUSAND BERRIES
FOR READING

13188925R00234

Printed in Great Britain
by Amazon